**ANTANAS
SILEIKA**

BRONZE

A NOVEL

VINTAGE CANADA EDITION, 2005

Copyright © 2004 Antanas Sileika

Published in Canada by Vintage Canada, a division of Random House of Canada Limited,
Toronto. Originally published in hardcover in Canada by Random House Canada,
a division of Random House of Canada Limited, Toronto, in 2004.
Distributed by Random House of Canada Limited, Toronto.

Vintage Canada and colophon are registered trademarks of
Random House of Canada Limited.

www.randomhouse.ca

Library and Archives Canada Cataloguing in Publication

Sileika, Antanas, 1953–
Woman in bronze : a novel / Antanas Sileika.

ISBN 0-679-31298-6

I. Title.

PS8587.I2656W64 2005   C813'.54   C2004-906980-2

Book design by CS Richardson

Printed and bound in the United States of America

2 4 6 8 9 7 5 3 1

The Battle of art is very much like war. All fame goes to the leaders, while the rank and file share the reward of a few lines in the order of the day; and the soldiers who die in the field are buried where they lie—one epitaph must do duty for a score of thousands.

—HENRI MURGER, *The Latin Quarter*

For the score of thousands

WOMAN IN BRONZE

PART ONE

THE SEASONS

Busy old fool, unruly Sun,
Why dost thou thus,
Through windows, and through curtains, call on us?
Must to thy motions lovers' seasons run?

—JOHN DONNE, "The Sun Rising"

THE RAINY LAND

FOREIGNERS CALLED THE LAND BY MANY DIFFERENT NAMES, but in their own language, the local people called it the rainy land, as if they still remembered some sunnier country their ancestors had come from. Mists and showers were more common than clear days, and massive thunderheads rolled across the low green hills and valleys from spring until fall. The ancient gods were still very close to ordinary people in this part of Europe. Lightning strikes were so frequent that the old people placed prayer books or crucifixes on the windowsills to protect themselves, or fell to their knees to say the rosary if they were caught outside in a tempest. The rosary was no guarantee of safety. If you were struck by lightning and could still move, you were to heap earth over your chest so it could pull the electricity out of your body. The trick did not work if you were already dead.

This green and rainy country was one of the great forests of Europe. In the deep wild woods, the last aurochs lingered and wood bison snorted and huffed among the giant oaks and thorny undergrowth of the forest floor. The grand dukes and *grafs* and great landowners rode out from their *dvars,* hunting among the moss-covered fallen trunks and peat bogs for game that had disappeared from the rest of Europe hundreds of years before. Half-wild woodland people cultivated small clearings in the forests where they planted tiny fields of rye and flax and dried the skins of beaver, fox and marten. Somewhere in this forest lay a line beyond which the animals ruled, the wood bison and the bear, the wolf and the polecat, the boar and the stag, and if the hunter stumbled beyond this line, he might be ripped apart or trampled by the true citizens of the forest.

Time moved more slowly in the rainy land, whose people had been the last in Europe to accept Christianity. They had done so cleverly, with a sort of peasant cunning, to throw off the invading crusaders who were intent on building a Northern Jerusalem. The inhabitants took on Catholicism and clutched it to their breasts like stolen treasure. But the Christian saints and martyrs joined, rather than displaced, the old gods of sun and thunder. The woods and the fields remained full of demigods, and also full of devils.

For a time in the Middle Ages, the people of the rainy land had reared up like angry beasts to charge to the Black Sea in the East and to crush the Teutonic Knights in the West. Eventually they joined with Poland to form a great eastern union, the terror of Moscow. But over the centuries, the rainy land seemed to melt into Poland, and in time, Poland itself began to diminish, too, as it was nibbled by Prussia, Austria and Russia. Finally, Empress Catherine took one last bite, and Poland disappeared. The rainy land became a remote czarist province.

The rainy land slumbered, forgotten by everyone in the West except Baron Munchausen, whose adventures there nobody would believe, although the locals would have found nothing extraordinary in anything he said. The place stirred as Napoleon marched through twice, but his passage changed nothing. Then came brief flames of revolt in the nineteenth century, after which the countryside was covered with gibbets, reminders of the futility of resistance. The forests filled with fleeing rebels who died there or adapted to the woods to become new forest folk, feral after decades in the wilderness.

One such man, a rebel of 1831 named Stumbras, came out of the forest years later and bought the land for his farm with money of uncertain origin. He stank of the swamp, and may well have been part woodland monster. If he was a monster, he was a shrewd one. The thirty hectares he bought were fertile, and the ancient town of Merdine was conveniently close by if one needed to obtain some product of civilization, such as lamp oil or matches. Once Merdine had been a fortified city, a bulwark against the crusaders, then a provincial market, and finally, in Stumbras's time, a crumbling country town that was shrinking into a village.

While surges of momentum prevailed in the West, where railways and factories sprang up, the law of inertia endured in the East. The Stumbras sons and grandsons prospered modestly generation after generation, innovating slowly, adding a chimney to the house to replace the primitive hole in the thatched roof, and adopting the long-handled scythe to replace the short one.

By the beginning of the twentieth century, the village of Merdine gave little sign of its ancient prominence except for the church and the empty cellars of a ruined fortress on the hill. The village was made up of fewer than two hundred wooden houses of squared timbers, huddling close to the narrow sandy roads. It did not even have a proper main street, just a collection of twisting alleys. The heart of a very old town remained, but all of its outlying houses had been lost to the encroaching fields and orchards. The local manor house stood beyond the village, a fine building of yellow brick and fanciful turrets, inhabited by Graf Momburg, the descendant of a German who had done favours for a friend of the czar. The estate had seen better times. Most of its fields had been sold off to enterprising peasants, and the raging old *graf* was busy drinking up what remained.

The only vestige of glory in Merdine was the church just down from the remains of the old fortress. The town wags claimed Merdine was the safest place in the world to commit adultery because the couples could perform the sin in the castle ruins and then roll down the hill to say confession in the church below. Barring a lightning strike on the way down, they could have their earthly pleasures and their divine ones as well.

Napoleon himself may once have remarked on the beauty of the Renaissance church, but the place had been remodelled twice since he'd passed through. White plaster had been laid over the brickwork, but it never held very well, and came off in patches the size of a woman's palm. Green moss grew up the walls on the cemetery side, and smelled strongly of urine. No clerical interdiction seemed able to control the bladders of the town drunks, with the exception of the most prominent drunk among them, Graf Momburg, the German, who felt that as a Lutheran he shouldn't piss on a Catholic church.

The church and the village, the manor and the farms and all the inhabitants might have slumbered on forever if not for the latest war, the one to end them all. In August of 1914, the entire Russian Second Army was annihilated at Tannenberg in East Prussia. The defeat was so total that the Russian commander reeled away, breathless in a fit of asthma, and shot himself in despair. The First Army did not do much better. The Russian line along the border buckled and the czar's remaining soldiers evaporated. The fighting continued on other fronts.

The triumphant German general was determined to civilize the occupied territories that the czar had neglected. The Germans were good organizers, and maybe they would bring some order into the squalor. But all they organized were requisitions from the farmers, and spies to make sure the quotas were met. Sly old Chichins, a Stumbras neighbour, hid a piglet in his grain barn, but a German with big ears came and listened and heard it squeal, and then wrote out a fine. Another neighbour buried an urn of butter to hide it from the requisitioners, but a German with a long nose came to sniff it out.

New threats now lurked alongside the devils, magistrates, generals and fauns of the countryside. Patriots and adventurers of various stripes took up arms to act as midwives to the new world that was being born.

This new world was barely visible yet from the vantage of the Stumbras home, a broad, dark farmhouse of squared logs and a low, thatched roof with a stork's nest on top. It had not been visible at all to Tomas Stumbras, the third of four brothers and two sisters. At first, he gave no more thought to the homeland where he lived than a woodland animal reflects on the forest. As he grew older, this world of his grew a little larger, first to the yard with its quacking ducks and the farm fields beyond, and then along the treed lane to the road. From there, the river was a mile down the gently sloping hill. The village and church lay the other way, a mile up the road along the same gentle rise. He did not think a great deal about his home, only about those who shared it with him. Nevertheless, little by little the stories by the kitchen fire accumulated in him, tales of miracles, hauntings and marauding armies launched by politics that were practiced at a great distance from the place where he lived.

Tomas knew the history of Lithuania by the time he was fifteen, but the romance of ancient glory did not inflame him the way it did his brothers. No high school functioned during the war, and so Tomas was trapped in the seasonal labour of the farm. But even at fifteen, he was not content to live the way his ancestors had. The drudgery made him restless, and when he finally did awaken to the land in which he lived, with the self-assurance of his young man's eyes, he saw only its terrible backwardness, and he longed to escape from it to another, more luminous country.

DEVILS

FALL 1917

OLD KOTRYNA STOPPED WHEN SHE HEARD A NOISE. SHE looked down the long, dim hall of the Stumbras farmhouse and nervously fingered the knot of her head scarf where it was tied at her throat. It was midmorning, but the house was dim. The thatched roof hung low over the windows and cut off the daylight at the best of times, and by fall the inside of the farmhouse was dark most of the day.

Kotryna trembled and squinted, but it did not help her to see. Her eyes were bad, but her hearing was still good. Something was moving down there, near the massive ceramic-fronted bake-oven whose iron door opened into the hall. She heard a shuffle of cloth against tile, the kind of sound a devil might make. Her old enemy. What business did it have coming back now, when she was so close to death? She crossed herself and muttered a Hail Mary to ward off the imp in the oven, where the flames were burning, still too hot for the loaves to be baked later that day, but comfortable enough for a companion of Lucifer.

Decades before, when the house still smelled of newly sawn wood, she had been about to walk down the corridor when a tiny demon stuck his head out of the hot bake-oven. He pointed at her and laughed silently, covering his mouth, childlike, to hide his pointed teeth. He was no bigger than a newborn. This was not

Satan himself, but one of the many minor imps who populated the land. Their diminutive size made them seem harmless, even playful.

Kotryna had been tempted to smile along with him, as if he had just told some kind of joke, but she stopped herself in time. The imp was holding the bake-oven door open with one hand and making faces, his red-black visage split by a grin. The imp stuck his finger up his nose, and then sucked his thumb. He rolled his eyes until only the whites were visible. He smelled nothing of brimstone, as she might have expected, but more like a farmhand farting in the morning after a night spent drinking beer. The imp scowled at her unwillingness to smile and pulled the door shut behind him.

No one else was in the house except for her mother, who had a small room to herself where she muttered prayers all day long, clacking the beads of her rosary and crossing herself repeatedly until there was an unhealing sore on her forehead. Her husband did not like to keep the mad old woman in his house, but Kotryna had no place else to put her. Too bad her mother was too weak of body and mind to walk, for Kotryna could have called to her to bring out the protective statue of a saint. Instead, she ran outside to her husband in the fields, where he and the farmhands were planting potatoes. He and the two hands rose up from their crouch when they saw her coming, and stood waiting with their hands on their sides to support their tired backs. She took her husband aside and whispered into his ear. He laughed when she told him, in case the hands had overheard. Then he came back with her, plodding heavily across the damp fields. He crossed himself when he entered the house, and took two crosses made of Palm Sunday fronds off the wall. The bake-oven door was closed. With the greatest speed possible, he threw the door open, tossed the holy fronds inside and slammed the door behind them.

Then he went to the kitchen and sat down at the table, where Kotryna served him a glass of milk and a slice of her black bread spread with honey. He ate it slowly. It would have been bad luck to talk about the demon visitor, so they said little, but she was less frightened with him there. After he had finished the bread, he waited awhile, and then finally stood up and waited awhile more. He held his hands clasped in front of him so his wife would not see them shake. Finally, wiping his mouth with the back of his hand, he walked down the corridor, opened the bake-oven door and looked in.

"See," he said, "nothing." And he laughed.

Relieved, he stepped outside to spit in the yard and enjoy the sun on his face for a moment before drinking another glass of milk and returning to the planting. She watched him walk toward the fields. When he was far away, so far he must have thought she was no longer watching him, she saw him cross himself again.

Kotryna baked no bread in the oven that day. The room smelled of sourdough that had risen and then fallen back in on itself. A terrible waste. But she was not going to contaminate her bread with the smoke of a devil, even a small one. After the fire had cooled, she sifted through the ashes and found a bit of horn. The imp had escaped up through the chimney, but he had left behind a souvenir.

She buried the horn where the lane met the road, and for decades she crossed herself whenever she passed the spot.

That had been almost fifty years ago, but the devil was back. He knew about her sin, the greasy deck of cards she kept hidden in a drawer in her room. Demons knew as much as God, but unlike Him, they acted upon their knowledge. The devil was still as wicked as ever, as powerful as ever, and now Kotryna was old and he had caught her alone. Her husband was long dead, and her son had taken the family to church. Her rosary and prayer book were in the other room, in the corner beside the crucifix, the candle and all the carved saints. The devil never forgot. What were fifty years to an immortal?

The fall rains had started, turning the fields to muck, and the mist outside was so thick anyone wandering off the road could get lost in the fields or the forest. Kotryna was cold despite the many layers of linen and wool she wore, topped by an embroidered shawl and her best Turkish kerchief tied over her head. The worst part of old age was that the cold never left her once November arrived. The warmth of the bake-oven was unusually appealing, for all the danger of the imp.

The massive clay oven was as tall as a man and built into the centre of the house to distribute the heat evenly. In winter, the children slept right on top of it for the sake of the heat that it retained through the night. Now she had to get past the bake-oven to her sanctuary. There was no other safe place. Demons walked the countryside during Sunday mass, ready to snatch anyone impious enough to be far away from the communion rail. Her son, Leo, had left late for mass after roaring about the house as if he were going to eat his own son alive. The boy, Tomas, was soft and mild, qualities that drove Leo into fits of anger. But Tomas was good with his hands. He could carve a crucifix with vine leaves twisting around it, and even put tiny bunches of grapes on the vines. There were many other children, thank God, three other boys and two girls, yet none of the others excited Leo's rage. She had seen it before. Sometimes fathers could not stand the sight of their own sons, as if the difference they saw in them was an affront against paternity.

Another scratching sound from the bake-oven. The imp was mocking her, maybe looking at the pocket watch in his green waist-coat and waiting to see how much longer she would hesitate. Or the imp might not be wearing any clothes at all. Demons delighted in appearing naked to women, their male parts engorged, the better to shock the virgins and fill the married women with regret.

Kotryna remembered her scapular, the cloth picture of the virgin hanging around her neck on a string. That surely would protect her against the devil. She undid the top catches of her linen blouse and lifted the scapular from between her long, low breasts. Holding it out in front of her and whispering her Hail Mary, she walked down the corridor. She willed herself to keep watching the oven as she passed, and surely enough there was movement, but not from inside the oven as she had expected. The imp shot a hand toward her from the dimness atop the wide, flat surface of the stove.

Old Kotryna shrieked but she did not run. She would hold fast before the creature from hell. Her own hand flew out like that of a much younger woman, and she grasped a thin wrist.

"Look upon the Virgin Mary and turn to cinder!" she cried and, eyes shut tight to protect her soul, she pulled the devil forward so she could press the scapular against its forehead.

"Grandmother, it's me."

She recognized the voice. With a sharp jerk she hauled the boy down from his perch on the bake-oven. Taking hold of one ear, she slapped him across his cheek before he pulled away. Tomas was fifteen, but young for his age, though he stood a full head taller than she did. He let her slap him three times before he shielded his face.

"Enough!" he said.

"I thought you were the devil," said Old Kotryna, panting from the fear and exertion.

Tomas grinned. "Maybe I *am* the devil." He lifted his hands like the paws of a bear and showed his fangs. She slapped him again, knocking the joke right out of him, then reached forward to soothe the red, stinging cheek. The boy was too tender for his own good. She took him by the hand and led him into her sanctuary where the blessed candle was burning below the crucifix. She felt better as soon as she entered the room. In her old age, it was the one place where she could find peace. A high shelf ran around the four walls, and upon these shelves stood two dozen protective saints, all made by the boy. Tomas was a god-maker. It was more than a hobby, but less than a trade, this carving of saints. They were a foot or two high: Mary, the saints Francis, Isidore, Christopher and George, God the Father Himself, the Holy Spirit in the form of a dove and half a dozen worrying Christs seated with their chins held in their hands. When he could, Tomas sold his wooden icons to farmers, but there were never as many buyers as he would have liked.

Kotryna sat down heavily in the chair before her shrine.

"Now stop playing about," she said sharply, although the boy delighted her as much as he infuriated his father. "You shouldn't make jokes on the Sabbath. Satan is always looking for cracks to slip through, and a joke on Sunday gives him an opening. Why aren't you in church with your parents?"

She watched with dismay as Tomas's face fell. Why must he show the contents of his heart so unguardedly? She looked him over, for her grandchildren seemed to change between one glance and the next. He had a thick shock of blond hair combed to one side. He kept his hair a little too long, for otherwise it would stand up at the crown. His eyes were very bright, making him seem more innocent than he was. His skin was fair and sensitive, slightly pink at the wide cheeks from the constant exposure to wind and sun. He was thin, like all farm boys his age, but with nothing of a young man's awkwardness. There was something graceful about him, yet timid as well, as if he could turn suddenly, sniff the air and bound away into the distance at the least scent of danger. He was in his Sunday clothes, a navy blue suit of home-spun linen with a fine sash. His feet were bare because farm youths were taught to save their Sunday shoes for church. They walked through the fields with their shoes in their hands and put them on when the steeple came into sight.

She grew impatient with the traces of childishness in his demeanour. At his age, he could be either a child or a man, depending on the moment or what he wanted from her.

"Father destroyed my statues," he said.

The old woman sighed. Why did her son have to be such a hard man? She looked out the window to search for a way to respond, but all she could see was the thick mist. She shivered. It was dangerous out there, more dangerous than ever before. Armies were moving across the land, along with the more common thieves, murderers and devils. She wondered how to find the words for what she had to say to Tomas.

"He's only thinking of your own good," she finally said. "You need to be more practical. You're luckier than most. You have some skill with your hands and your father has enough to feed you. What more could a Christian want? Once the war is over, you'll have a good future in front of you."

"Tell me my future, then, if I have one. Take out the cards."

She clapped her hand over his mouth. "It's Sunday," she hissed.

But Tomas was persistent and she permitted herself to be seduced by her love for him. Perhaps she could distract him from his anger at his father. She turned the faces of the gods on her shelves to the wall, blew out the holy candles and draped a handkerchief over the small crucifix to shield the eyes of Christ from her actions. She reached deep into her drawer and took out the deck that was tied together with a piece of dirty string. The deck was very old. It had belonged to her husband, and he had given it to her when he became old himself and renounced the last of his vices.

She had the boy shuffle the cards, no easy task when the edges were so bent and frayed. Then he cut the deck twice, and the second time she took the top half and laid out three and a half rows of cards upon the bleached linen tablecloth. Unlike the charlatans who learned their tricks from books, Kotryna had no system of regular signs. One day the ace of spades might signal death and another the purchase of a good stud bull. For the story to come out, she had to give a little of herself to the cards. She waited until meaning rose out of the sequence before her. Kotryna could hear Tomas's breathing, hoarse and expectant.

"You are a lucky young man," she began.

"Will I be famous and wealthy?"

"Be quiet and let me speak." The boy understood nothing at all about the gravity of what she was doing. She gave him a stern look to silence him. "You will be attractive to women, a lady-killer." She could see him smile, but forced herself to stay in the cards. "Lucky for you, but not so lucky for the women. You must be very careful of everything you say and do, or you will cause a great deal of pain and suffer some yourself. Put aside your childish need for praise. You will travel, but never in comfort." She began to see other things, and she fell silent as she considered them. They were very bad. She did not want to see any more.

The effort of reading had tired her, and she wanted to rest, but Tomas still sat beside her, leaning on his elbows, eager for more of what the cards had to say. She could not look away or he would ply her with questions. Instead of telling him what she saw, she made up a story that might teach him a lesson.

"You have a great skill with your hands, but you must use this gift judiciously. You could make good money carving filigrees for windows, crosses for the churches. You're a first-class god-maker, and if there were still enough pious people in this land, you would make a living from that alone." She looked up from the cards, abandoning any pretense that she was reading from them. "Maybe we could apprentice you to a stonemason or a church decorator, but this playing with secular figures is the work of a child. You are too old to be making dolls."

His eyes darkened and he rose suddenly. In a moment, he was out the door with his shoes in his hands.

She did not want him out on the road while the countryside was empty of neighbours. She rose and went after him, calling from the door.

"Come back!"

But the mist had swallowed him.

Kotryna waited a moment. Then she closed the door and bolted it, and went to her shrine where the snuffed-out beeswax candles still scented the air. She would pray for him, and maybe her prayer would protect him until he reached the church. She took her rosary in her hands and looked intently for the picture of the Blessed Virgin up on the wall. But like the carvings of the saints, the picture had been turned to face the wall while she told Tomas's fortune with the cards. A sound came from the bake-oven in the hall, but she did not get up to take a look.

Tomas ran with his shoes in his hands until the house was far behind him.

Making dolls, indeed! She understood him no better than his father. Last month he had been to the Academy of Art in Vilnius and his eyes had been opened. The school was closed down because of the war, but he and his uncle Longin, his mother's brother, had peered through the tall, uncovered windows for a long time. A column of white statues stood along an immense, silent hall. These were not things made by children. They stood, or sat, or reclined as if they had no need of the world outside the locked academy. Tomas had stared and stared at them. They were like something from his dreams, friends he had known from his infancy but had never actually met. His fingers hungered to touch them. The only statues in Merdine were religious, but the academy figures were of secular men and women, some of them larger than life-size, all intensely white. Many of the statues were naked, and the exposed breasts were a delightful revelation to him. His uncle did not even make him look away.

They had walked through the city streets and parks and found other statues made of bronze not yet melted down for the war. There was a monumental Catherine the Great, which the Germans

had unaccountably left untouched. He stroked the bronze, aston-
ished by its coolness under his fingers. He had thought it would be
warm. He had knocked on it with his knuckles, and marvelled at
its hollowness. How could such big pieces be hollow? By what
process did someone make such things? His uncle did not know,
and art teachers had disappeared during the war.

Tomas's hands had been restless from birth, working at wood
with his knife, forming clay and chipping at stone. Now his hands
had found a proper object of attention.

When he returned home, the images of the statues seen
through the windows would not leave his head. While his
brothers snored at night in the room he shared with them and the
stink of Edvard's pipe on the table irritated his nose, he could
escape to the long, quiet hall of the Academy of Art. In his
dreams, he stepped through the window, and touched the cool figures. The images haunted him by day as well. A sharp cuff across
the shoulder from his father sometimes made him realize he had
slipped into a reverie while he should have been thinking of the
work at hand. But the work at hand now seemed petty and banal.

He needed to join the other world, the modern world, and the
only way to do that was to make statues of his own, even though
he would be stealing time from his chores. He went down to the
riverside where the Stumbras family dug clay to make bake-ovens,
rough bowls and whistles and toys to sell at market. He dug out as
much clay as he could fit into a sack, and hid it under the workbench where he did his carving. But making statues in clay proved
to be much harder than carving in wood. Building up was different from carving, which consisted of shaving things away.

The first problem he encountered was one of size. He dreamed
of life-size figures, but the volume of clay would have been too
great, and so he tried to build statues the same size as his carved
gods. But the clay did not co-operate with his fingers. When he
tried to build up a standing figure, the damp clay legs collapsed

under the weight of the torso. He began to understand how little he knew. He used sticks to support the clay, and the model no longer collapsed quite so readily. He wanted the figure to be a woman with breasts, such as he had seen in the city. She was to have an outstretched arm, and this needed to be supported from beneath, at least as long as the clay was wet.

The gods he carved from wood were merely symbolic representations of human forms, but he wanted this woman to look real. He quickly discovered that getting the proportions right was very hard. His first finished piece was all out of scale and his young woman grew older under his fingers, all bent and crooked and rough. He did not have the patience to let the figure dry out enough in the air, and so it exploded into fragments when he tried to fire it in an improvised brick kiln behind the barn.

After errors and disasters of all kinds, he managed to complete two statues of women, not very good, but recognizably human. One he modelled on their maid and another came from his imagination. They were entirely unsatisfactory in every way, right down to their colour, grey when wet and tan when fired. He painted them white to look like the statues he had seen in Vilnius. They were very bad, but they made him happy in a way he had never quite felt before.

Tomas knew his father would disapprove. First, he had stolen the time to make them. Second, carved saints could be sold for money, however small the sum, and a peasant never sneered at income. But he could not sell these statues. Finally, to carve the figure of a saint during the long, dark evenings of winter was acceptable, a pastime sanctified by devotion, but these women's breasts, though covered, were as prominent as those he'd seen in Vilnius.

It was hard to keep the statues concealed on a farm where eleven people lived, especially from his younger brother, Paul, who was the unearther of secrets, the one who could find a lost pocket knife, a whetstone dropped in a mown field, the tiny crack through which the mice came into the house. That Sunday morning, true to form, Paul had found the white statues in the granary, dug them out from deep in the rye bin and brought them triumphantly to their father.

Leo was standing in the yard, dressed for church in a suit that did nothing to conceal the great, bearlike bulk of the man. Leo's chest pushed at the buttons on his shirt and jacket as if his body was unnaturally constrained in clothing. He took the statues from Paul and stared at them, and then his face twisted in anger as he understood what he was looking at.

"Tomas," he barked, brandishing the statues in his hands. His son knew not to get within striking distance. "These are like prostitutes!" Leo shouted, and he smashed the two statues against one another, sending the white pieces flying in the yard.

"If you have so much free time, just tell me." His father was no longer shouting, but his face was all red and a drop of sweat hung from one of the tips of his waxed moustache. "I'll find something for you to do."

Tomas fled. There could be no escape in the long run, but in the short run he could distance himself from his father's wrath.

When Tomas did not return, Leo led his family column toward the church, embarrassed to be missing one member.

The mist was so thick it fell as fine rain on Tomas, and without an oilskin he was soon wet through. Homespun linen was a particularly Catholic form of clothing. It scratched even more when it was wet, a perpetual reminder of the discomforts of earthly existence. He could see nothing beyond a few yards into the fields on either side of him. For all he knew, devils really were keeping him company as he walked. But he did not fear them the way his grandmother did. He feared his father more, as much for the space the man took up as his wrath. No matter where Tomas found himself on the farm, his father's presence was there, squeezing the air out of him.

The soft earth of the country road seemed to weep from the way cartwheels had rutted its spine. Four horses would barely be able to pull a wagonload through this foul muck. Water covered the fields, the rain turning the farmland into an infinitely wide bog. The bare limbs of trees rattled in the wind, and Tomas could hear the cawing of ravens. He felt more than saw the gentle rise that signalled the approach to Merdine. He passed the shrine of the Virgin on the edge of town, and the mist finally thinned a little as he made his way among the Sabbath-empty houses toward the church.

The churchyard was quiet, except for the shuffle of an occasional horse in its harness. The Poles had their service three hours later, enough time for one group to have dispersed before the other arrived. Lithuanians had lived alongside Poles for centuries, but now that the Russian overseers were gone, the two nationalities were chafing against each other. Tomas made his way among the wagons to the front door, and pressed a kopeck into the hand of the beggar woman muttering the rosary there. He stepped inside. As always, the smell of the place hit him first, the stink of ancient mould that underlay the smell of every building in the rainy land. Then came traces of incense from thousands of funerals and Easter processions. The smell of beeswax had once been present too, but ever since the war, beeswax had become difficult to find, much to the irritation of the priest, who believed the villagers kept it themselves or sold it to the Germans for Ostmarks. As a result, the priest had to use sheep-tallow candles, and the whole building stank of wet wool, further enriched by the odours of the villagers and surrounding farmers who crowded into the church. In the midst of a prayer or a hymn, a hand might shoot out in frenzy to scratch at a devilish head louse that did not know enough to stay still in the presence of God.

Until Tomas had seen Vilnius, this Roman Catholic church was the most beautiful place he knew. For all the bad light and stench of assembled bodies, no finer place existed for miles around, unless one counted the houses of the gentry, which Tomas had never set foot in. The walls were covered in frescoes of saints, or emblems such as the eye in the triangle or the letter *P* overlying an *X*. The altar was robed in the whitest linen, and gold leaf covered the frames of the many paintings that had been donated by *grafs* in ancient times. Gold was the colour of God, the external manifestation of the divine. When he was five, Tomas had run away from the farm one sunny day and was found, hours later, sitting in the church. He had wanted to see the gold in all its glory. He had told his mother he wanted to sit in heaven for a while, and she had laughed nervously, afraid he had had a presentiment of his own death. She had taken him, over his childish protests, back to the world made of wood, straw and mud.

The priest was in a dark green stole, his back turned to the flock as he murmured in Latin. In the choir loft, the ancient organ began its asthmatic introduction to "Cast Thyself upon Thy Knees," wheezing through the holes in the leather bellows that no one was able to fix now that the war was on. The choirmaster feared the Germans might take the tin-clad pipes themselves to melt them down. Metal was as malleable as the souls of men. In peace, one made organ pipes of it, and the breath of God came through the tubes to sing His praises. In times of war, it was made into machines of death.

Tomas's father hated to be late for anything, so the family arrived at church so early that there was time to make confession and say a full rosary before the service began. Now he and his sons sat in near-identical homespun suits of navy blue, like conductors on a train. Leo had an orderly mind, so his sons sat according to age. Beside him came Edvard, as barrel-chested as his father, the one who would inherit the farm, the one who had to be reminded not to cross his arms in church. Next was Andrius, the family intellectual, his studiousness confirmed by a pair of wire-rimmed glasses that his father had hated to pay for but nevertheless enjoyed as a public mark of both his son's acumen and his own prosperity. Andrius bore none of the ill will of second sons. He did not want the farm. He was bound for greater things. Leo had left a gap for Tomas. Next sat Paul, angelic in his curls for all the trouble he had caused that day. Then came Jonas, the hand, who would prefer to stand with the other farmhands at the back of the church, but Leo Stumbras insisted. He treated his workers like members of the family, and it was important to him that the world see this. Jonas sat with the Stumbras men, even if his place was after the youngest boy.

Tomas's mother, Augustina, was across the aisle, a nervous woman too given to thought to make a good farmer's wife. Next to her came Janina, sulking as she always did. She frowned so much that no suitor had approached her, and her father was not yet willing to make any public declarations about a large dowry. He still had hope she could marry cheaply, for love. Vida, beside her, bowed her head in prayer, keeping her eyes averted as her sister told her to, for her eyes troubled older men and made the young ones act like fools. The serving girl, Maria, turned when Tomas came into the church, as if she sensed his presence.

Maria was wide cheeked and big breasted, pretty in the way of country girls, and at seventeen, almost two years older than Tomas. She often tried to protect Tomas, a weak pup in a robust litter, not only for his sake but her own. Tomas's tenderness appealed to her.

There was no future for poor girls in the families they served. If they did not marry, they were sent back to their own families by the time they reached their middle twenties. She needed to look out for her future, and this would be provided by the hand, Jonas. They were partners in adversity. To be sure, she loved him for himself, for his simple confidence and easy manner. But she loved him as well because together they might better their station in life.

Maria caught Tomas's eye. He smiled at her uncertainly and was about to look away, but she fluttered her hand toward the right of the church. He shook his head, not certain what she meant, so she looked pointedly at the candle burning over the confessional. He nodded, and made his way to stand in line there. Half her job was done. Now she needed Leo to take notice of his son's penitence. Maria dropped her prayer book so it fell to the flagstone floor with a loud slap. Leo glanced her way as she turned toward the confessional as if she had just noticed Tomas there. Stumbras followed her gaze, saw his son and was pleased.

Once inside the confessional, the boy could see the outline of the priest's head through the filigree in the wooden screen. The priest was nodding ever so slightly, listening with half an ear to what Tomas was confessing with less than half his heart.

"Ten rosaries and two days of fasting," the priest hissed through the screen when Tomas was done.

"I beg your pardon?" It was outrageous to give such a heavy penance. Had the priest seen into his heart?

"You heard me," the priest said.

Outside the confessional, Tomas waited by the damp side wall until the time came for communion, and when the Stumbras family walked up to kneel at the communion rail, he stepped into his place between Andrius and Paul. Like them, he held his hands under the white starched communion cloth, and stuck his tongue out far because the old priest had palsy and there was always a danger that he might drop the host.

When they got back to their chairs in the nave, Tomas sang the closing hymn to the accompaniment of the wheezing organ, and filed out of the church with his family. He looked behind him as he went, and Maria caught his eye again. First she looked at Leo, and then she mimicked a kiss. Tomas understood her sign, and the course of action it suggested revolted him.

Outside the church, the mist had finally broken and the sun was shining, but the light would not last in November. In the muddy churchyard, the horses were shifting in their harnesses, and in the street beyond stood the wagons of the Poles waiting for the next mass. Leo Stumbras stopped with his train of family and retainers at the exit of the church, surveyed the wagons and parishioners about him and removed his pipe from his vest. With no sign of haste, he stuffed the pipe. His family was accustomed to being put on show like this every Sunday.

His father looked up at Tomas suspiciously from the pipe he was lighting, scrutinizing his soft yet rebellious son. The sulphurous match burned and burned and refused to go out until it was shaken three times. But as soon as Leo's hands were free, Tomas took them in his own and brought them to his lips and kissed them.

In the deep country, in olden times, young people kissed the hands of their elders as a show of respect, but the tradition was waning. Elders who demanded it were frowned upon as being too strict, holding themselves up too high, like bishops with their rings. But young people who did it of their own volition made themselves dear by the act. What heart could not be softened by such a gesture of subservient love?

His father stood in shock for a moment. The young priest nodded at Tomas, as did some of the old women who hung about the front door of the church. Leo Stumbras felt the full force of the gesture with the eyes of the parishioners on him. He put his hand on the head of his son, ruffled his hair and pulled him forward to kiss him lightly on the head.

The crowd of parishioners spilled down the steps into the yard where the young men lingered in order to let the waiting Poles know that they were not quite ready to give up their right to the church. The grown men were happy to escape for a little while from their work on the farm. Their informal parliament was covered by clouds of smoke as they puffed on their pipes and stood around talking about harvests, the war and the prospects for the following year. The wives stood in their own throng nearby, and here the talk was lighter and laughter broke out from time to time.

Maria looked back over her shoulder at him as she left with Jonas and nodded, and Tomas was sorry to see her go without another word. There was no one else for him to talk to.

The young men and women walked a circuit in the town while they still had a chance to enjoy some of the rare autumn sun. Andrius and the village intellectuals gathered in the cemetery to talk about history and the progress of the war. Tomas flitted, always uneasy, overcome with boredom within minutes of standing with others.

Storm clouds blew in to cut short the hour of Sunday conversation. It was time to hurry home.

As the family walked along the road, they looked forward to their Sunday dinner. The food reserves were high—the harvest had been good and much had been hidden from the Germans. The seasonal slaughter had taken place, so the meat of the freshly killed pigs was sweet and tender. They would eat cold headcheese along with their potatoes and barley soup, or maybe their grandmother had made something rare for them. The rain was approaching fast, and the family moved quickly along the grass at the side of the rutted road. The younger ones carried their shoes in their hands although the earth beneath their feet was cold with autumn. Where the lane met the road, they caught the unmistakable smell of roasting meat, an unexpected pleasure. The rain began to fall when they were thirty yards down the lane from the house, and they ran together laughing.

Tomas was the fastest runner of them all, and as he was first through the door, he called out for his grandmother. There was no answer. The storm was upon them now, and Tomas's mother lit the oil lamps, for it had grown very dark inside. The Stumbras house was a sprawling single storey, with rooms that bled into rooms, sometimes with corridors between and sometimes without. The women went to take off their shawls before heading into the big kitchen, and the men stood by the door, wiping their feet and putting on wooden clogs. Sunday after church was one of the best times of the week, and the promise of an exceptional meal filled them all with gaiety.

"Go find Grandmother," Tomas told Paul.

The boy ran down to his grandmother's sanctuary, but she was not there. Her candle was out and the sanctuary was gloomy. The gods up on the shelf were turned toward the wall, and the table-top crucifix was covered with a handkerchief. Paul looked at the open prayer book. A playing card lay upon the page. He turned around and came down the hall to return to the big kitchen, where the others were talking and Janina was boiling water for tea.

In the corridor, the door to the bake-oven was slightly ajar, and when Paul went to swing it shut, he found it obstructed, as if fire logs had been put in there and not shoved far enough down. He yanked the door wide and saw the callused soles of his grand-mother's feet. A sickly smell of seared flesh came out of the bake-oven, and inside he could make out fingers curled into use-less fists and blackened by the flames. He bolted down the hall, screaming.

They pulled and pulled on the feet, but her arms seemed to have been seared to the sides of the bake-oven and she was very diffi-cult to extract. When they finally managed to get her out, they found her clothes had mostly burned away, as had her hair, but she still wore an expression of deep disgust, as if hell was more putrid than horrifying, a cesspool of infinite depth. Tomas noted that the skin on her shoulders had been torn away to reveal the thin muscles below, and stared, fascinated and revolted at the beauty of the muscle pattern.

How to explain the crucifix covered with a handkerchief? Above all, how to explain the playing card on the prayer book? Leo was looking at Tomas, waiting for some kind of clarification.

"I have no idea," Tomas said, and Leo Stumbras's moustache seemed to bristle at the ignorance of his son, the stupid one, the one who caused trouble and then walked about, oblivious.

"Think! We'll need to call the priest. What will we say?"

"She said she was afraid of devils."

His mother put her left hand to her mouth to keep from letting any words slip out, and then she crossed herself and signalled the others to do the same. Leo Stumbras considered what to do.

"Go for the priest," said Leo to Edvard, the steadiest of his sons. "Tell no one what you've seen."

But the only way to get the priest was to tear him away from his Sunday dinner, and the only way to do that was to tell his housekeeper about the gravity of the problem. The village telegraph set to work. By the time the curate was coming up the lane, half a dozen villagers were close on his heels, and soon after them two dozen more, as well as the commissioner of the *Oberbefehlshaber Ost*, the German administration for the occupied lands of Eastern Europe. Beside him came a drunkard and fool all rolled into one, Graf Ludwig Momburg.

Leo Stumbras saw his house turning into a spectacle, and he was furious. Once bad luck adhered to a home, it could never be cleaned away.

Janina and Vida had wrapped the body in linen to cover the ugly burns, and laid it out on the table in the sanctuary. They lit candles and turned the carved wooden saints so their faces could be clearly seen looking down upon Grandmother's body. They placed a linen towel over her face and a rosary on her chest, and then swept the ashes from the front of the bake-oven door. They also burned the incriminating evidence of the playing card. But there was to be no hushing up what had happened, at least not in general terms. The commissioner came right inside the sanctuary, and Graf Momburg forced his way in as well.

The commissioner, who had seen many ugly things in the war, nevertheless flinched when Kotryna's burned face was exposed. Such a terrible expression. Then he waited while the priest said some prayers and rubbed the blackened forehead with oil. He was a clean-shaven northern German, serious. He interrogated the family one by one in a thorough, scientific manner. He established that no one had seen any soldiers or bandits about. Then he rubbed his chin for a moment and ruled the death a suicide.

The roar that ensued made him realize he was the sole representative of the occupying force in a room with over a dozen Lithuanians and twice as many outside the farmhouse door. The outraged faces of the local peasants startled him, and made him more amenable to suggestion than he had intended. The priest insisted that the woman was old and pious and would never dream of suicide.

"The devil did it," muttered old Momburg finally, voicing what the others thought, but even then no one said anything more on the subject. To confirm it would bring more bad luck. To deny it would consign Kotryna's soul to hell. Drunkard or not, Momburg was a Lutheran, and if even a Lutheran recognized the work of the devil, then the work of the devil it was.

As for Momburg himself, he had been thinking of the devil a great deal lately. Satan kept coming to him in his troubled dreams, bidding Momburg to remove his boots before coming along to join him.

But the commissioner did not like the idea much. He was damned if he was going to write "death by demonic intervention" in his report and have his overseers laugh all the way to Berlin. He considered for a while, running his finger over his moustache.

Outside, the peasants were singing a hymn. He could almost hear the clack of rosary beads.

"Death by misadventure," he said. "She fell into the oven and only made matters worse by trying to get out."

"Death by misadventure," echoed the priest. Let her be buried in the churchyard. Word was passed outside. The relief was palpable.

The commissioner and Graf Momburg left; the priest stayed awhile to lead the family in prayers.

"What about the bake-oven?" Leo Stumbras asked after the prayers were over.

The priest considered telling them to destroy it, but why cause more trouble than he had to?

"Bring me some buckets of water," he said. When the women did so, he blessed the buckets, sanctifying the water. The women washed down the whole oven with it, inside and out, but there was one spot that seemed to stay hot a long time, and it took many applications of holy water before the oven stopped sizzling.

THE WARS
WINTER 1919

THE CZAR HAD DIED AND THE KAISER HAD RUN AWAY, LEAVING a vacuum in the East where nationalists, bandits and adventurers rushed in. The Germans were still nervously holding the lands they'd won so dearly from the czar, but they had been defeated and would not be able to occupy their eastern dominions for long. The French and English demanded withdrawal, and the issue would be forced at the forthcoming conference in Versailles. But if the Germans were wily enough, they might be able to install client regimes, so they permitted some of their former soldiers to keep their arms, and opened up the prisons and released criminals to flesh out an irregular army. As an added measure, they released the old Eastern European political prisoners, socialists and aging anarchists who might do Germany some good in the way that Lenin had done. The Germans were not the only interested party. The Reds had designs on the rainy land as well, and even the Poles were insistently offering a new union, but the Lithuanians decided they wanted the land for themselves. They would have to take the country and hold it, and for this they needed an army. Countries did not come cheap.

To a restless seventeen-year-old, all of the political and military turmoil seemed utterly remote, a fiction no more real than the stories of the uprisings of 1831 or 1863. At times, Tomas became excited when Andrius read in the newspapers of troops on the move, and he waited expectantly for the sound of hooves on the roads or the distant flash and thunder of artillery. At times, Tomas was sure that something was about to happen merely because he needed it to.

He sat in his outbuilding workshop, staring at the piece of maple on the bench before him. He turned it in his hands, studying the grain and considering what sort of saint he might cut out of the wood, but he felt too restless to settle on a subject. To distract himself, he often wandered the farm, studying the ducks as if they might turn into maidens, or watching his sisters, whose perpetual spinning, weaving and baking knew no seasons. Janina was the serious one, thoroughly determined to save the edible crusts of mouldy bread, fanatically driven to make her linen the whitest in the village. A parsimonious farmer could have done worse than to marry her, but suitors generally wanted some charm as well as thrift, and Janina had inherited too much of her father's nature to make her attractive to young men. Janina had enough peasant shrewdness for two, whereas Vida did not have enough for one. Just a year younger than Tomas, Vida was a dreamer, a starer into distances. Tomas had never determined what she was dreaming about. If he asked her what she was thinking when her weaving at the loom came to a long pause, she would look at him and smile, and say she was thinking of nothing at all. She, too, exasperated her father, although it was Janina who jerked on her sash to waken her from her daydreaming.

When Tomas needed someone to talk to, he went looking for Maria. He felt too old to speak intimately with his mother, whose attention was a mixed blessing. She was naturally nervous, frightened, a worrier who needed more consolation than she could ever give. Maria did not pretend to share Tomas's enthusiasm for carving, but she was always interested in what he did merely because he did it.

Tomas set the piece of maple down on the bench and stepped outside to look for her in the bare fields of early winter. He found her sitting on a wide tree stump alongside Jonas, near the gate guarded by Tomas's carving of the pasture god, Saint George. Every god had his particular responsibility, and nailed onto a high post that overlooked the field, Saint George had the job of keeping the foraging animals safe and their milk sweet. Tomas had painted his armour gold, but the paint did not hold well, and the saint looked as if he could use some home leave to patch himself up. The dragon at the end of his lance was similarly worn, more like the fossil of a dragon than one in its death throes.

Though Maria and Jonas were huddled together against the cold and talking intently, Tomas thought nothing of interrupting them. When Maria looked up at him, her eyes glistened more than was justified by the wind. Her head was covered by a woollen scarf, and her face seemed prominent and naked without its softening halo of hair. Jonas did not look at Tomas at all.

"The two of you are going to freeze out here," said Tomas. "Come on, join me for a walk down to the river. It'll warm you up."

"We're talking about something," said Maria.

"Well, go ahead," he said. "I'll wait." And he crossed his arms to keep himself warm.

"It's something private," said Maria, as kindly as she could.

As he walked back the way he had come, his shoulders hunched in hurt, Maria wondered why no one else in the family seemed to recognize that the boy needed a little attention. She looked back to Jonas. He was the very picture of a young peasant, ruddy faced and broad chested, with a mouth that smiled easily. He could have been a poster model for the Reds, had he been so inclined and if he'd had the habit of rolling up his sleeves to show his thick upper arms. But the people of the rainy land were modest, and men kept their sleeves rolled down.

Maria watched Jonas's gaze shift longingly to the fields, Stumbras land that he would have loved to own himself. The earth was grey and frozen, and the winter rye stood pitifully thin. A cold mist, which could not decide if it was to be water or ice, smudged the landscape, and the bare trees down by the river were just another shade of grey against the slate sky. This was the time that people travelled, while the roads were firm and the snow had not yet come, but there were not many civilians abroad that year. Any city dweller passing over the crusty road in a carriage would have shuddered at the monotony of the rural scene, and thanked God that he did not live in a place such as this. But farmers and hands like Jonas did not look upon the fields in the same way. To them, fertile black earth was as valuable as gold, maybe even more so because no one could easily steal it. Jonas felt himself a beggar sitting amid great wealth, for land provided income in good times and in bad. Slowly, very slowly, he had been saving his money, as had Maria, so that they could buy a few acres for themselves. But cash did not come easily to farmhands and maids, and they would need to save for at least another ten years before they could afford to marry and start a farm of their own. If the price of land did not rise. If their wages did not fall. But something else was on his mind.

"I didn't realize you were a patriot," said Maria.

"Even if I'm not, why should the Poles or the Russians or anybody else lord it over us?"

"Someone else will always be in charge of us," she said. "Priests, policemen, teachers, employers. If you go into the army, you'll have to follow orders. What freedom is there in that?"

"It's the prize I'm after when it's all over."

"Land."

"Yes." The provisional Lithuanian government had no money with which to pay volunteers, so they offered them promises instead: twenty-five acres or more to all volunteers.

"But who's to say you'll win? And who's to say the government will keep its promises if you do?"

"We have to believe in somebody."

"Each other. I believe in you and you believe in me," she pleaded.

He shifted and she could see the irritation building in him. He considered her words meaningless sentimentality. What good did words achieve? Jonas would put all thought of danger out of his mind because thinking about it would do him no good, and anyway, who could anticipate just what the danger would be? It was not clear who the volunteers would have to fight. Almost anyone could be an enemy: a neighbour, a former teacher or even a priest who had spoken Polish for so long that he had forgotten the language of his ancestors. The one Great War had broken up into many smaller wars with fronts that could appear anywhere. Jonas would let the leaders determine which battles to fight.

He had his hands thrust deep in his coat pockets, hiding them from the wind and the frost, and from her as well. He was afraid she might clasp his hands and beg him to stay. But he underestimated her. She understood that there were risks if he did not go. If they had to wait ten years to marry, she would be twenty-nine, and at that age first children often came with difficulty.

She wished they had enough money to book passage to America, but they did not and there was no one to borrow it from. Before the war, there had been agents who came and offered payment plans, but they had been too young then, and the agents stopped coming when the war started. For two decades before the war, men had gone to the coal mines of Pennsylvania, the slaughterhouses of Chicago and the weaving mills of Worcester. The ones who had loved farming fanned out across the United States or Canada. One of Leo Stumbras's brothers had been among them. He had gone to Canada and disappeared like a stone in deep water. Most of the ones who left kept in touch. They sent money back to their parents or brothers and sisters, or invited them to come over as well. One or two had even returned to visit, wearing ridiculous straw hats and endlessly looking at their expensive watches as if every moment they spent back home was a waste of time.

It was getting too cold to sit outside any longer. Maria could see that the choice was clear. She wanted to lean over and kiss Jonas to let him know that she understood, but someone might see them. She touched his shoulder instead, and he looked at her gratefully.

Leo Stumbras hated to lose a strong pair of arms, but he was not immune to the stirrings of nationalism. It felt good to offer someone up to the cause, and better a hand than one of his sons. Leo gave Jonas what he could: the money he owed him, an old bird gun more useful for bringing in partridge than taking down a man and a new suit of winter clothes. Augustina Stumbras sewed him a knapsack out of homespun linen and dyed it green. Inside the knapsack Maria put a jar of butter, four pounds of the dense, black bread the family baked each week, two pounds of smoked bacon and another of sausage. Jonas smelled of the smokehouse, and this smell was made stronger by two pounds of homegrown tobacco.

Now that Jonas was going to leave, he and Maria grew shy with each other, and desperate whenever they were apart. When they were together, she tried to keep a distance between their bodies, not daring even to brush against him. Better to wait until he came back. Better to wait until they were married. Think of the prize at the end of Jonas's military service.

The entire Stumbras clan came into the yard to see Jonas off. The two oldest brothers were a little envious, but their father insisted that he needed them to stay to protect the farm. The family waved and shouted farewells, but went no farther than the gate. Only Maria walked with Jonas down the lane and along the road so she could say goodbye to him alone.

Tomas watched them walk all the way down to the river and then past it, around the bend and in among the bare winter trees, whose branches, even at this distance, he could hear clacking in the wind.

Tomas would have liked to join the army, if only to escape the monotony of winter evenings, but he was just seventeen and looked even younger. At this time of year, the last light of day was gone by four in the afternoon. That meant he had five endless hours to spend with his family before his father sent them off to bed to save lamp oil. When he was a child, Tomas used to enjoy the long winter evenings because his grandmother or mother would tell stories as his sisters spun or sewed. But no one mentioned Old Kotryna now, and his enervated mother no longer told stories. His father and brothers twisted hemp for rope or repaired harnesses and tools and smoked their pipes, and the room smelled of the tobacco smoke that hung below the hand-squared beams. The ceiling and walls were whitewashed to reflect as much of the precious light as possible, but even so, the room was full of shadows.

Although visitors were few, some farmers appeared during the evenings, and the beaten-clay floor became slick by the door where they entered from the damp outdoors and shook off their coats. Every visitor was greeted enthusiastically, both because of the laws of hospitality, and because any visitor was a relief from the tight circle of family. Some families played cards, but since Kotryna's death cards were forbidden in the Stumbras household. The religious would spend an hour or two on their knees with the rosary, but Leo Stumbras was not an overly religious man. Sunday mass, feast days and a few Hail Marys before bedtime were enough for him. Other families played instruments and sang songs, but Stumbras did not waste his money on musical instruments. Andrius was the only hope of amusement because he read every evening, close to the lamp, and sometimes he would regale them with snippets from Hoffmann, Pushkin, Adam Mickiewicz or Mark Twain. Tomas dreaded the evenings, but as nine o'clock neared, he became filled with anxiety, knowing that he would not be able to fall asleep and would be condemned to listening to the snores and wheezes of his brothers.

More and more, Tomas found consolation in his small workshop attached to the granary, a retreat Leo grudgingly permitted him because he turned over half the money he earned to his father. He had built a workbench over which he hung his chisels and gouges. Hobbyist god-makers worked only with pocket knives, choosing the soft woods that were easy to carve, but Tomas was more successful than most. The chisels and gouges permitted him to work with tougher woods that withstood the elements better. Up on a shelf he had his own oil lamp, bought with his own money, and behind it a mirror to direct the light. In this room he kept all of the gods he was working on, but as soon as they were done, he moved them to the shelf in the main house, where the heavenly figures were always shifting about as he made new ones and sold the old. His mother tended to become fond of certain statues, and mourned them when they were sold, as one mourned a child gone off to make his way in the world. The workshop smelled strongly of the wood curing at one end, willow and basswood for ease of carving, cherry, pear and oak for work that was to stand out of doors.

Tomas spent some winter days in the workshop as well, and it was there his father found him one morning as he was sharpening his chisels. The air outside was cold, and his father was wearing his old wood-bison coat that stank of musk. The coat was so bulky he had to turn sideways to get in the door. Once inside, he took up a great deal of room.

He wanted Tomas go with his brothers to pick up a wagonload of hay that was owed him by their neighbour, Chichins. But he could read the look Tomas gave him readily enough. In a moment of paternal charity, Leo decided to let Tomas stay where he was, as the carving seemed to occupy him well enough. But now he had nothing to say to justify his presence in the workshop. He leaned over to the bench and picked up one of the unfinished gods that was beginning to come out of the wood, another Saint Francis who would likely have his hands stretched out to the birds.

"This piece may be the best you've ever done," he said, trying to convey his goodwill.

Tomas could not divine the generous thoughts running through his father's mind, so he looked up suspiciously at the unaccustomed praise and wondered why his father was choosing this piece. Leo read his ungrateful expression and felt the stirrings of familiar annoyance with his son, made all the worse by his own difficulty at finding words. He studied the piece in his hands and recognized that there was something unusual about it.

"Your gods don't look like the ones that other carvers make. Why is that?"

"I'm trying to make them more realistic."

To Leo, everything was real if it existed, and if it did not, it was not worth any thought. "The other ones I see look real enough to me."

"Well, they have heads and hands and bodies, but the proportions are distorted. Typically, the heads are very oversized. I want to make these new gods true to life."

"Where did you get such ideas?" Stumbras was perplexed, and he did not like the feeling.

Wondering how his father could have forgotten the smashing of his statues, Tomas said, "I studied the saints in the churches. Those are realistic, but most of the gods in the countryside are not."

Leo grunted. "Well, who made the statues in the church?"

"The deacon said they are cast in plaster and come from Vilnius."

Stumbras considered this and Tomas waited him out. His father breathed heavily in the winter and the wheezing went on for a while. Stumbras looked to the oil lamp, and Tomas could almost read his thoughts. Lamp oil cost money, but Tomas paid for it himself, so there was not much his father could say.

"Your customers have certain expectations. You shouldn't upset them."

"But I'm finding some interest in these new ones," said Tomas. "I have great hopes."

This was too much for his practical father. "Religious people know what they want, and you'll only confuse them if you try something different. You'll be lucky to sell a single one. And don't put any more wood into the stove today. It's stifling in here, and we've barely got enough put away for the winter as it is."

Leo went out the door.

Tomas returned to sharpening his chisel. He oiled the stone, turned the blade so the bevel was flat and then ran the edge in a figure-eight pattern in order to use the entire surface of the stone and not make a trough in the centre. He tried to concentrate on keeping the angle right in order not to deform the bevel. He calmly ran the blade over the stone a dozen times, then raised the chisel above his head and drove it deep into the wood of his workbench. He tried to pull it out in order to drive it in again, but it was stuck.

He took a canvas bag and went to the house. There he snatched some gods off the shelf and walked to Merdine.

On the outskirts of the village, in a copse by the road, stood a shrine much larger than most found in the rainy land. Merdine had the distinction of a rare half-life-size wooden Madonna in her own small house, perched on an ancient oak stump. The house was fronted by glass to protect her from the elements, and the fascia was lovingly ornamented with filigree. It was testament to the remoteness of Merdine that the local vandals were still religious enough not to have broken the glass.

She never failed to give Tomas a thrill of appreciation and envy, and he forced himself to study her in order to calm himself. The figure sat in the traditional posture of the Madonna, her hands crossed on her breast, a crown on her head and her eyes looking down at the earth. Her shoulders were hunched as if the pain was very great, and her face was grotesque and moving in its agony. She was not realistic, but Tomas admired her nevertheless. The light inside the glass-fronted box was poor, but he studied the statue intently, trying to determine for the hundredth time whether it had been carved from one incredibly large piece of wood or from smaller sections that were joined together. He did not have the courage to pry open the nailed door to have a better look.

When he felt more at peace, he continued on to Merdine. The odds of selling a god in town were small except on market days, yet he was determined to make a sale in order to spite his father. It would give him great pleasure to count out half the coins and place them on the kitchen table without a word. The cold had chased most people from the streets, except for two drunkards sitting out in front of the tavern and arguing garrulously. Out of desperation, Tomas went into the way-station tavern, a converted front room with a counter and bench and an underfed wood stove where prospective passengers met carters in order to arrange transportation among the villages and towns. Tomas did not have much hope in this place. Travellers were usually city people, and wooden carvings interested mostly country folk. A man was standing at the counter, drinking tea from a glass. He was short, solid, with thick black hair, unremarkable except for the sophisticated cut of his clothes.

"A statue of our Lord Jesus Christ?" Tomas asked, sticking one of his figures into the man's face. He was an awkward salesman and he knew it. Asking people to buy felt not that much different from begging.

The traveller set his tea down on the counter, but he did not let go of the glass.

"I'm a Jew. What would I do with this?"

"Maybe you'd convert," said Tomas. The Jew looked at him warily, trying to read his intent in his eyes.

"I have a Star of David for you. Maybe *you* could convert."

The shock on Tomas's face made the man laugh, and after a moment, Tomas laughed with him.

"Come on, buy my carving. You won't see another like it anywhere in the country."

"What's so special about it?"

"I'm experimenting with a new technique. Most country gods have irregular proportions. But I am an excellent craftsman, and you'll see the carving is realistic."

Tomas feared the man might be as perplexed as his father, but his words made some kind of impression. The man reached into his breast pocket and took out a pair of glasses. "Let me have a look at this wonder of yours," he said. He took the robed Christ figure and held it by the base, turning it around and around to look at all sides.

"You're right. It's pretty good, but you shouldn't have painted it."

"Why not?"

"Paint covers up the grain of the wood, making it look like plaster from a distance. This is a form of dishonesty. You should show the material you work in. Don't you love wood?"

"I'm a god-maker, aren't I?"

"Why cover up the wood as if it were naked flesh that needed clothes? Sometimes I think Lithuanians fear nakedness more than the devil himself. But the best gods are the ones that have been out in the countryside for a while and have lost their paint to the elements and time. They show real character."

"Doesn't this piece show character?"

"Some."

"Do you want to look at more?"

"I have time on my hands, but don't expect me to buy."

Tomas opened the bag and pulled out three Virgins with thin golden wire halos; two more Christs, one in full robes and the other half naked; a Saint Christopher with a tiny Jesus on his shoulder; a Saint Francis with a bird perched on the tip of his open hand.

"Not bad," said the man. "I can see you're trying to be different, and that is good. I was making sculptures when I was your age, too, although I can't say I made many gods."

"What do you do now?"

"I still make sculptures, but not here. Nobody in this country is interested."

"So where do you live?"

"In Paris."

"France?"

"The very same."

The man laughed good-naturedly. But Tomas was annoyed. He did not want this sculptor to think he was merely a country boy.

"So why would you ever come back to this place?" Tomas asked.

"I was visiting my parents in the south, in Druskeninkai. I haven't seen them since the beginning of the war."

"So you mean it's possible?"

"For what?"

"For a Lithuanian to be a sculptor."

"I'm a Jew. Maybe it's only possible for Jews. We are accustomed to travel, so we take to it easily, and as a rule, Catholics travel badly. You're rooted to the soil, and if you are uprooted, you pine for your homeland for the rest of your lives."

"I'm no peasant. I've been to Vilnius."

"If you want to be a sculptor, you need training."

"I'll find some training. And when I get to Paris, maybe I'll look you up. What's your name?"

"Jokub Lipchitz."

"Will you help me if I get there?"

"I don't even know you. Why should I do anything for you?"

"You'd be able to say you discovered me."

The man laughed for a long time and again Tomas laughed with him. When Lipchitz finished, he wiped the tears from his eyes. "By all means, look me up when you get to Paris," he said. Then he turned back to his glass of tea.

At the first deep frost, all the farmers had been happy to see the end of the mud. Instead of sinking up to their axles, the cart-wheels thundered over roads as loudly as if they were on kettle-drums. The furies of the winter were severe that year, blowing chill and violent. The icy winds turned lakes and rivers to glass, laying a thick, protective lid on the crayfish and frogs to give them respite from their hunters for the winter. Then the cold grew worse and all of God's creatures were driven inside to burrows and hollows and houses. Packs of wolves came out of the naked forest to sniff at the barn doors and leave their footprints beneath the windows at night. The storks were long gone to the south, and the empty nest on the Stumbras roof filled with snow.

One morning the family awoke to find the earth covered with a foot of fine crystals that caught the light of the sun. The big farm dogs leaped through the powder and the smaller ones disappeared into it, as did Andrius's glasses, which fell off as the whole family charged out into the yard to enjoy the pleasure of the transformed landscape. Vida and Janina laughed, and helped him look for the glasses. They frolicked outside until their neighbour Chichins plowed his way on foot up their lane to announce that a real army was rumoured to be nearby. Andrius and Edvard harnessed the sleigh and made their way with Chichins to town to discuss the defence of the village.

Later in the day, the air warmed, and the snow became heavy. The weather changed again, and in the early evening as the brothers returned from Merdine, the sky clouded over and it began to rain. But by midnight, the cold came back and the wet snow hardened. Twice more within the week, snowstorms hit the village and farms, and now no one was enchanted by the snow any longer except Paul, who asked Tomas to help him make snowmen.

"You're eleven years old," said Tomas. "you can make a snowman yourself."

"But not as well as you."

One snowman was not enough. Paul wanted an army of snowmen to guard the farmhouse, and Tomas accommodated him, rolling ball upon ball of snow to build up the figures, and then shaping them until some were sentries with stick rifles at arms, and others were sharpshooters whose outstretched guns would collapse at the next thaw. Leo would not have approved, but he was absent, trying to lay claim to an inheritance from a maternal uncle who had lived some distance away in Kuliai. In a mania of creation, the brothers filled the farmyard with two dozen defenders who looked comical by day, but whose protection felt real toward dusk, when the failing light made them seem human.

Soldiers were on everyone's mind. Jonas had not been heard from for weeks, and only God knew where the Lithuanian army was. Foreign soldiers were nearby, but their intentions were unclear. Isolated from the central government, such as it was, and vulnerable, the village committee made up its own defence plans, which included building a bunker down at the foot of the Stumbras lane where it met the road to Merdine. Leo would have objected if he had been home, but Edvard and Andrius wanted to play some role and so they manned their bunker, and others came when they were available. If attacked, the men were to hold this position until word could be sent to the village for reinforcements.

On a particularly bright morning in January, Tomas walked out among his snowmen. In one hand he carried a bucket of soup and a towel bag of boiled potatoes for the sentries, and in the other an axe, with which they could split more wood for their fire. The snowmen now looked like weathered veterans, some of whom had dropped their weapons at their feet. A crust of new snow lay upon the fields, unbroken except for the path down the lane where his brothers had passed back and forth during the night. Then Tomas noticed another set of footprints, leading to the pig barn. No set of footprints led away from it. He set down his bucket of soup and bag of potatoes and followed the trail.

He whistled loudly as he approached the pig barn, though his throat hurt from the cold at every intake of breath. He hoped to make as much noise as possible so as not to surprise the interloper. Frightened men with guns had already killed one of the villagers and wounded another. Maybe the man was a deserter from the renegade German Bermondt battalion, or a White Army soldier. On the other hand, he could be a Red, one of the advance guard, or a scout. The Reds held Švenčionys and Rokiškis, but the Lithuanian army, made up of ill-equipped farmhands like their own Jonas, was supposed to have stopped them there.

Outside the barn, Tomas stood for a minute with his eyes closed so he would not be utterly blind when he stepped into the dark enclosure. He felt the heft of the axe handle in his hand, and then he made a great deal of noise as he opened the door, banging his feet against the jamb and muttering to himself. He heard only pig snorts at first, and smelled the rank odour of the animals. Someone was there, all right. The pigs were uneasy, shuffling in the near dark.

"Are you the king of the pigs?" a voice shouted out of the gloom.

Startled, Tomas stepped back, clutching the axe.

"The pigs have no king," he said. "The pigs are democrats."

The voice roared with laughter. "A philosopher!" Out of the darkness rose Graf Momburg, visibly the last remnant of a rapidly disappearing class. His ancient black coat was now covered with bits of straw and smeared with pig shit. He wore a felt hat with a tired brim, thick woollen gloves and a scarf wrapped loosely around his neck. The eyes above the scarf were of a pink so intense they almost glowed, and the breath coming out of his mouth overpowered the stink of the pigs with the fumes of brandy.

"Ah, a young Stumbras," said Momburg, peering at him. "Which one are you?"

"Tomas."

"Embrace me, my son."

Tomas did as he was told. Both the Reds and the nationalists swore they'd get rid of the gentry, but the habit of obedience died hard. The old *graf* smelled worse than the pigs, and his embrace was so long that Tomas feared the man had fallen asleep on his shoulder. Finally Momburg pushed Tomas away to look at him more closely.

"An axe, I see," said Momburg. "Are you a Jacobin, come to cut off the heads of the ruling class, eh? A democrat willing to spill blood for the cause? Should I unwind my scarf and bare my neck to you?" The old man swayed in his place.

"You're safe with me, but you shouldn't be out on a day like this. You could freeze solid."

"I'm not so easy to kill. A lifetime of brandy has thinned my blood. I can withstand the cold better than any man for a hundred miles. I could walk barefoot to Warsaw. I am a remarkable specimen wasted in this boggy country. I am a pearl before swine, as the swine can attest."

Waiting for the *graf* to stop talking was like waiting for the second coming. It had to occur sometime in the future, but one could grow old anticipating it. Tomas interrupted the flow. "Come with me," he said. "I'll take you home."

"Take me home? Do I look like an old woman?" The *graf* shook himself, and bits of straw flew off his coat. The pig shit stayed where it was. Still, he allowed Tomas to take him by the arm, and together they went back outside. Tomas propped the axe by the pig-barn door, and went back toward the bucket of soup he had left in the snow. The *graf* continued to talk, always to talk, as if silence were made to be filled.

"Like a lamb to the slaughter," he muttered.

"Maybe I should send for your son," said Tomas.

"I embarrass my son."

"I'm sure that's not true."

"It certainly is. I was sitting at my own table when I turned to my wife. 'How will we live without a czar?' I asked. She had her face in her soup. She's a terrible glutton. She did not even look up. It had finally sunk in for me that the solid earth I stood on all my life was shifting under my feet. Whenever things change, it is for the worse.

"Did I give a damn that some German colonel was there at my table? So what if this colonel and his staff were eating my food and making polite conversation with my son and heir? So what if I praised the late czar? It's my food and my table. I can say what I damn well please.

"'The kaiser was far superior to the czar,' my son said, trying to show the soldiers that we remained pure Germans despite generations out here in the East. I grant he may be right. The czars couldn't clean up Russia in a thousand years. What business did they have trying to lord it over other nations? All they did was spread around the mess. But now we have no kaiser either. There are no rulers at all. The body has revolted against the head, and chopped it off. Insanity!"

"The German army is gone now," said Tomas.

"And we're even worse off!"

"I thought you didn't like them."

"At least they brought some kind of order. Today I took it upon myself to go and experience a little democracy. To make a study of it. I fortified myself for my researches with a little brandy. I intended to go down among the peasants, and I saw that your farm had soldiers around it. Snow soldiers! They made me laugh."

"I made them for Paul."

"The Lithuanian army will not be much better. I went down to your pig barn, and I lay down among the pigs. This, I said to myself, is what the world is going to be like as soon as the armies finish destroying one another. First the Bolsheviks will destroy everyone like me. Any man with education and breeding will be cut down. Shot. Or hacked apart with an axe."

"Who's to say the Reds will win?" Tomas asked.

"That's what my son says too. He thinks General Bermondt will save us yet. But who is Bermondt, after all? He's a renegade. A White Russian funded by Berlin with an army of fifty thousand adventurers. Bermondt does nothing but go up and down the countryside burning farms. You'd think he was the czar himself, with his scorched earth."

"Isn't there anyone whose side you are on?" Tomas asked.

"What kind of choice do I have? Then, on top of everything else we have the damn Poles, and the self-styled Marshal Pilsudski. But who is that man? He was nothing more than a socialist bandit before the war. Do you know I met him once? I was hunting some years before the war with several good men in the Augustav forest when I found Pilsudski sitting in a hut with no trousers. And you know why? His only pair was being washed. This is the man who is going to run Poland? I can even forgive him his poverty. Christ was poor once, too. But I cannot forgive him his eating habits. This Pilsudski eats no soup, no vegetables, no fruit. Nothing but meat and bread. This is a man in a hurry, I tell you. Anyone who skips the first and the last courses is a man who has no time."

Tomas retrieved the soup and potatoes he had left in the snow and led Graf Momburg down toward the bunker, which lay among a few trees where the lane met the road. The old man muttered to himself all the way there, and Tomas did not relish the long, cold walk to the manor house with the *graf* after he delivered the soup to the men. Tomas and his brothers had dug out the snow bunker and made embankments around their hollow, arguing endlessly about how much snow it would take to stop a bullet, and then arguing again after a brief thaw that turned the melted snow into ice. The bunker commanded a view over the road, and one could see for a mile down to the woods in the river valley. A small fire burned at the rear of the bunker, and Edvard lay there with his head on a pillow of snow. Andrius was smoking a cigarette and talking to two volunteers who had revolvers sticking out of the pockets of their overcoats. They said they were former soldiers who found themselves in Merdine and they had offered to help. A couple of rifles lay against the inside of the snow embankment.

"Mother sent something to eat," said Tomas, "but I'm afraid the potatoes are cold by now. I ran into the *graf* on the way here." Andrius and Edvard doffed their hats and shook Momburg's hand. Tomas introduced him to the strangers, who looked at the old man suspiciously. He returned the favour. Edvard reached inside his breast pocket for his wooden spoon. The men were stiff with the cold after almost two days of watching for movement of the renegade Bermondt army, or Poles, or Reds, all of whom were in the vicinity. The threat to Merdine lay everywhere and nowhere. The only news came in whenever a traveller brought a newspaper, days old, from Vilnius or Warsaw. They had no supply of arms except what they could provide on their own and what they had stolen from the retreating Germans.

Tomas had heard the rumour in the village that the two strangers in the bunker had been in the czar's army: Lithuanians trapped deep in Russia when the military collapsed. The lieutenant in charge of the defence of Merdine was glad to have them, and immediately assigned them to the Stumbras family bunker. The one named Liud was constantly troubled by a dry, racking cough, and he wore a scarf that he only pulled aside from his mouth to smoke cigarettes. He seemed to take orders from his companion, Byla, who amid all the privations of war managed to get enough moustache wax to keep his tips tightly rolled. Icicles hung from them, weighing the tips down and making him look like some sort of comic-opera villain. But his face did not invite laughter.

The potatoes had indeed gone cold. Tomas broke the half inch of fat that had hardened on the top of the soup, and used a cup to ladle it into bowls and pass them around. Liud pulled the scarf down from his mouth, stirred the broken bits of fat to remelt them and shoved half the big wooden spoon into his mouth.

"Damn," he said, and he spat a mouthful onto the snow at his feet. "It's hot! You said it would be cold."

The others laughed.

"The hardened fat on top insulated it," said Edvard.

"The boy should have told me it was hot."

"I'm not a boy."

"How old are you?"

"Seventeen."

"Damn right. Old enough to be down here with us instead of carrying soup around for your mother."

"Shut up, Liud," said the moustached soldier.

The others sipped at their soup more carefully, and Tomas told them his mother had suggested they come up to the house to warm themselves. They could go in pairs.

"Might as well," said Andrius. He took off his eyeglasses and rubbed them with his mittened hand. "At this rate, we'd be too cold to be much good if Bermondt himself showed up on the road. We can take turns. A little sleep wouldn't hurt, either."

"If Bermondt himself showed up," declared the *graf*, "every one of you would shit your pants. This is nothing better than a snow fort. Bermondt is a bad soldier, but he could wipe you out in a moment. And where are your reinforcements? Where is your strategic plan? Do you think a few guns around a village make you into a military force? An ape in a cassock does not make a priest, and a bevy of rustics with a couple of guns does not make an army."

"Who is this fool?" Byla asked, and he made a show of slurping his soup. The ice in his moustache melted and fell off in drops.

"I am Graf Momburg," said the old man, and he removed his hat and bowed deeply. "Who are you?"

Byla used the back of his hand to wipe his lips and moustache before speaking.

"Major Byla. Go home to bed before you get into trouble, old man."

"Major, indeed. More likely some upstart Bolshevik. You can not dismiss me like some peasant. As if the world were not already upside down, now we have Lithuanian patriots! This is not much better than animal patriots. Monkey patriots. Baboon patriots."

Byla stared at the *graf* and chewed a cold potato methodically.

"Graf Momburg," said Andrius, stressing the honorific and laying his hand on the man's arm, "let Tomas take you home. This is not your business here."

"Not my business? Am I not a citizen of this land? Am I not a member of the gentry? My family served the czar faithfully for three generations, and we are not ashamed of it."

"There is no more czar," said Byla.

"And the world is the worse for it."

Liud set down his bowl and rose. "Should I shoot him, Major?"

"Sit down," Byla replied.

"We'd be rid of his jabbering. I can't stand to listen to the jabbering of the landowners."

"He's an old man," said Andrius, trying to deflate the tension. "He drinks too much and thinks he's one of the old gentry. He amuses us and we indulge him. He is a fool and a drunkard, but if we ever lost him, it would be like losing the village idiot."

"Don't patronize me, young Stumbras," the *graf* roared.

"Why does he call himself a *graf*?" asked Byla.

"A pretension," said Andrius. "His ancestors were Germans."

"Do not speak of me as if I am not here," said Momburg. "I insist on being addressed directly."

"It's not a good time in history for a German to insist too much on his ancestry," Byla said. "He could be anything. He could be a spy for Bermondt," Byla said.

"For Bermondt? That son of a whore." Momburg was indignant.

"Why else would he be so interested in this bunker? Any *graf* should be hiding his ass in his cellar, hoping the Reds don't break through this way and gut him like a fish. Unless he is a spy."

"I am my own man," the *graf* insisted, but for the first time his voice quavered.

"After all," continued Byla, "what would a man in your position have to gain from the independence of Lithuania? The provisional government is calling for volunteers all the time and promising them land for risking their necks. Where do you think this land will come from? The new government will lop off a field or two from your *dvar* and give it to some peasant boy. Unless the Jacobins take over. Then they will lop off your head and take the whole estate."

"Come, come," said Andrius, "this is dangerous talk. Next we'll find enemies in our beds. The old man is a citizen of Merdine, and we are guarding the town. That means we have to guard him, too."

"But there *are* enemies in our beds," said Liud. "There were men I bunked with in Russia who turned out to be spies for the Whites. Men I had eaten with and shared a roof with were ready to betray us."

"Shut your mouth," said Byla. He set down his bowl.

"Aha!" said the *graf*. "You aren't patriots at all."

"I told you to be quiet once before," said Byla, rising. He reached into his pocket and pulled out a revolver, letting his arm hang at his side. "Go home, old man. Your time is over."

"Do you think I'm a child? Show me a revolver and I cower? You are one of the race of pigs that has risen up to rule us."

"Graf Momburg." Edvard spoke so rarely that everyone turned to look at him. "Go home now."

The *graf* opened his mouth, but for the first time in his life, he could say nothing.

"Not another word. Go home before you make trouble for yourself and for us. Andrius, give him a drink for the way."

Andrius reached inside his coat and removed a glass flask. He passed it to the *graf*, who looked at them all suspiciously, but then grasped the flask, turned it up to his lips, drank half of the liquor and then gasped.

"*Samagonas,*" he said derisively, "home distilled. The liquor of democrats. I'll be lucky if I don't go blind." He looked at them accusingly. "I'm going home." He turned from them, scrambled with difficulty over the lip of the bunker. He began to walk down the road toward the river. Puffs of condensed breath came up around his head.

"God preserve us from fools," said Andrius. "He's going the wrong way."

And indeed he was. The *graf* walked stiffly upright, but the crusty snow conspired against his dignified comportment. In places the crust broke and he went down halfway to his knees in the softer snow below. The men began to laugh, all except Liud, who had pulled the scarf back up around his mouth.

"Graf Momburg," shouted Tomas, "you're going the wrong way!" But the *graf* continued to struggle down the hill.

"You'll have to get him," said Andrius. "He'll freeze out on the fields if he keeps on the way he is going."

"Why should I chase after him?" Tomas asked. Instead, he climbed up to the lip of the bunker. "Graf Momburg," he yelled, "call the democrats pigs, but even pigs know the way back to their own sty."

"Tomas," said Andrius, "if you keep that up, he'll never come back."

The *graf* had gone not more than thirty feet when a foot became stuck under the crust of snow that he had broken through. He struggled briefly, and when he heard the others laugh, he twisted his head around to look back at them.

"Bastards! Pigs! You'll be lost without people like me. Monkeys don't know how to live without a ruler." He raised his fist at them.

"Is that a *spyga?*" asked Liud. The *spyga* consisted of the thumb sticking up from between the index and middle fingers of a closed fist. Across Eastern Europe, there was no greater sign of derision.

The bullet whizzed by so close to Tomas's ear that he thought an angry wasp had risen up from under the snow. Then the *graf* went straight down. Edvard and Andrius jumped on Liud, pushing his hand to the ground and prying the revolver out of it. He barely resisted, shouting, "Now he's nothing better than a bag of guts, a bag of shit. Good riddance to him and all his kind."

Andrius and Edvard were up over the embankment in a moment, and Tomas ran beside them to where the *graf* lay. Edvard turned him over and the smell of alcohol hit them. The old man's face was set in a pale grimace. He had not shaved that morning and the grey stubble was thick on his chin. He was not breathing.

Edvard slapped him lightly on the cheeks, but his drooping eyelids neither opened nor closed. Edvard felt Momburg's neck for a pulse. The others waited. "Nothing," he said.

"Open up his coat and listen to his chest."

Edvard did so. "Nothing."

The brothers stared at the old man's exposed, shrunken chest, which was unbroken. They removed his coat, lifted his shirt and jacket and looked at his bare back. There was a small bullet hole just to the right of his spine. The wound wasn't even bleeding.

"Where did the bullet go?" asked Tomas.

"I don't know," said Andrius. "It probably got lodged in there somewhere, maybe in his heart."

"Is he dead?"

"No breath, no pulse, no heartbeat."

It was not possible, thought Tomas. The old man had been holding on to him only half an hour ago. Could a man die as quickly as a pig? Although kaisers and czars fell and whole armies perished, he had never seen a man killed.

"Pick up his hat," said Edvard. Tomas did as he was told. Andrius buttoned up and tucked in the old *graf*'s clothes, as if propriety still mattered. The two older brothers each took the *graf* under his arms and dragged his body back toward the bunker. Tomas followed them with the *graf*'s hat in his hands.

Byla was scanning the countryside through binoculars. Liud was eating soup again.

"We're in luck," said Byla. "It looks like nobody heard the shot. Now all we have to do is get rid of the body."

"We'll take the body back in the sleigh," said Edvard. "His house is on the other side of the village."

"I didn't mean take the body home," said Byla. "I meant get rid of the body."

"We have to go to the authorities," said Edvard. "The village commandant will have to write up a report and someone will have to go to Violai for the Lutheran minister. The *graf* will need the last rites."

"I don't think Lutherans have last rites," said Liud.

"There will be no trip to the commandant. No report," said Byla. "Liud here is a fool, but I won't have him locked up for shooting that piece of trash. He would have talked himself into the grave sooner or later anyway."

"You can't just shoot a man and bury him," said Andrius. "If you get caught, they'll hang you for murder."

"We won't get caught. All we have to do is keep quiet and get rid of the body. Is your younger brother here capable of keeping his mouth shut?"

"That is irrelevant," said Andrius. "Your friend must pay whatever penalty the court decides. It's not for us to judge."

"*Irrelevant*," said Byla, mocking Andrius's tone. "You listen to me. Liud and I have seen many deaths over the last few years and one more means nothing to us."

"But why did you shoot him?" Tomas asked. "He was just an old man."

"Nobody shows a *spyga* to me and gets away with it," said Liud. He finished off the remains of his soup by tilting the bowl to his mouth.

"It's too cold to bury him," said Byla, half to himself. "We'll have to put his body in the river."

The river ice was very thick. The hole was already one and a half feet deep and it was hard for Tomas to reach the bottom with the axe blade. At the riverbank, the horses stamped uneasily, small clouds of breath shooting out from their nostrils and disappearing into the night air. No bells were attached to their harnesses. The pair stood tethered to the sleigh that held the *graf*'s naked body, buried under blankets. They had burned all of his clothes except his boots, and gathered the charred belt buckle and bone buttons to throw into the river. Liud and Edvard stood off to one side on the river ice, resting after their turns with the axe, as Tomas continued the job. Andrius and Byla had stayed back in the bunker.

"You should have made the hole wider," said Tomas, puffing between swings.

"Just make sure you get down as far as you can," said Liud.

The rhythm of chopping helped dull Tomas's thoughts. He was getting warmer through the work, and soon he would be sweating. He would feel cold when he stopped, but not as cold as the *graf*. He felt like laughing, anything to release the tension, but the others would think he had lost his mind.

"I wish you'd left his clothes on him," said Edvard.

"If the body washes up somewhere nearby in the spring, the clothes will give away his identity. No one can recognize a body after it's rotted for a time," said Liud.

"Then at least wrap it in something."

"Absolutely not. A naked body rotted beyond recognition is what we want." Liud had the *graf*'s boots on his feet, and he looked down to admire them. Liud had held out for the boots over Byla's objections. He took orders from Byla on most matters, but he categorically refused to give them up.

Water finally splashed up in the hole, and when drops of it struck Tomas's face and hands, they turned instantly to ice.

"Stand back," said Edvard. "I'll finish the job." He used an iron pole with a sharp point to punch out the bottom of the hole and Tomas scooped out the pieces of ice with a shovel. Liud stood back from them, rolling a cigarette. He was having difficulty. His hands were too cold to twist the paper together properly, and he kept losing the tobacco. Finally, he held the cigarette with his thumb and three fingers to keep it together, and lit the end. The match flared and died.

Even now, Edvard worked like a farmer, thoroughly, efficiently, without wasting any energy in unnecessary movements.

"Get the body," he finally said, breathless from his work with the pole. "The hole's big enough."

Liud drew on the rough cigarette two more times before throwing away the butt. Then he turned and walked up to the sleigh and uncovered the *graf*. He seized the body unceremoniously under the arms and dragged it back across the snow.

"At least a piece of cloth to cover his genitals," Edvard pleaded.

"Nothing at all," Liud said, puffing with exertion. "Who knows what piece of cloth the women in the parish might be able to identify?" Liud lifted the body as high as he could and tried to drop the feet into the hole, but the legs kept swinging apart. The body was a mannequin, made all the more grotesque by a flapping penis. Tomas felt sick.

"Help me get his legs into the hole," Liud ordered.

"It would be better to go headfirst. The shoulders are going to be a tight fit," said Edvard.

"Don't try to teach me how to get rid of a body." Liud's voice was rising.

"Then do it yourself."

"I will, but if I get my new boots wet, I'll thrash you for it when I'm done."

Liud dropped the body on its back beside the hole. Then he pulled the feet into the hole until the *graf*'s legs were in the water up to his knees, as if he were a bather wetting his feet in a stream.

"If he floats, I'll need the iron bar to push him farther along under the ice."

"Just get on with it," said Edvard.

Liud shifted the whole body forward, and then lifted from the underarms to get it down into the hole. The *graf* made it down to the hips, but then he got stuck. Liud leaned his whole weight on the shoulders, and pushed down, and slowly the upper half of the body began to slide into the hole. Liud held up the arms so the shoulders would not get stuck as the hips had.

Just as the *graf* was almost down to his chest, the old man seemed suddenly to come alive. He pulled his arms away from Liud, dropped his hands onto Liud's boots, and began to try to lift himself out of the hole.

"Jesus and Mary," shouted Liud, "he's trying to get his boots back!"

Edvard and Tomas stood fixed to the river ice as if they were frozen there. Liud dug madly in his pocket for his revolver as the *graf*'s grip tightened on his boots.

"If he's alive," Edvard shouted, "I won't have you killing him again!"

"I will kill him, I will!" Liud shrieked, and as the soldier had finally managed to pull his revolver from his pocket, Edvard raised the iron bar in his hands and struck him across the forehead. Liud dropped to the ice. Still the *graf*'s hands held on to the boots. Liud's feet began to shake wildly in a death spasm.

As if satisfied, the *graf*'s hands released their grip from the stolen boots, and the body slid smoothly under the ice.

"Quick, Tomas," Edvard shouted. "He might still be alive under there."

Tomas ran forward to do as he was told. He thrust his arm under the ice up to his shoulder and reached out. He felt something at his fingertips, but it was gone before he could get a grip on it. The slow, under-ice river current of winter had drawn the *graf*'s body away. Tomas pulled out his arm, and immediately the water began to freeze on the glove and the sleeve of his coat. His teeth were chattering as he looked to Edvard, who was bent over Liud, feeling for a pulse at his neck. He felt nothing.

The brothers squatted on the river ice, looking at each other. When Edvard realized Tomas was shaking, he made him take off his wet coat and put on Liud's. Edvard rolled a cigarette for Tomas and they smoked in silence, but both thought of Byla back at the bunker. When it became too cold to squat there, they began to walk around the sleigh to keep themselves warm. The coarse, homegrown tobacco stung Tomas's mouth and throat, but he was glad of it. After a while, Edvard knelt again to feel Liud's pulse, listen to his heart and watch for his breath. Nothing. They looked at the hole in the river ice. There was already a thin new sheet freezing over the top.

"Byla and Andrius will be waiting for us," said Tomas. "One of them might come down to check. What are we going to do?"

Edvard sighed and groped for words. "We're building a whole new world, and this is what it comes to," he finally said. "Come on. We'll strip down Liud's body and get it down the hole, too. Then we'll figure out a way to surprise Byla."

"He'll be suspicious if the two of us come back without Liud. There could be a lot more trouble. I could go back alone. I could do it for you," Tomas offered.

Edvard looked at his brother for a long time. "I'm the eldest," he finally said. "I'm the one who has to take the responsibility."

A light snow began to fall as the two of them walked toward the body.

It was blowing hard by the time the sleigh made its way back from the river. Through the snow, Byla saw Liud take the reins of the horses as Edvard jumped down from the sleigh and plodded toward the bunker. Byla stepped away from his place beside Andrius at the fire. He had not survived through two fronts and half a dozen skirmishes without developing a nose for trouble, and that nose was sniffing out something very bad. Where was the boy? Why was Edvard coming toward him when it should have been Liud? Just as Byla drew his revolver, he felt a strange pressure on his chest and a sharp pain. Only then did he hear the report of Edvard's gun.

Andrius watched in shock as his brother walked up to the fallen man and fired a second time into his chest. Edvard looked down at the body for a moment, and then up at Andrius.

As the brothers had no good plan, they had to make do with Andrius's improvisation. They would put Byla's body under the ice, too, burn all their clothes, spend the night in the house, tell their mother that the soldiers were manning the bunker and profess ignorance in the morning. Where the men had gone would be a mystery. Maybe they'd taken the *graf* with them.

"I've never told a lie in my life," said Edvard. "How am I supposed to start now?"

"I think we'll just have to get used to it," said Andrius. He turned to Tomas. "And as for you, I just wish you'd kept your mouth shut."

FIRE
SPRING 1919

UNCLE LONGIN'S SON, MAT, A BOY OF TEN, DIED OF INFLUENZA on the first day of spring in the city of Kaunas. The letter Longin sent to his sister, Augustina, arrived the following day thanks to a passing traveller, so the Stumbras family could have made it to the funeral on time if they chose. But Leo Stumbras forbade such a trip on the grounds that others in Longin's family were still sick and snow and ice still covered the countryside. Why go looking for trouble? Besides, Leo had the farmer's distrust of the city, where every shopkeeper seemed out to cheat him, and where clothes that looked just fine in Merdine marked him as a peasant.

Mat had been Uncle Longin's only son, and was spoiled terribly. Too much white bread had weakened him, or perhaps it was his habit of wearing shoes even in good weather, making his feet as soft as a baby's. But Leo was not heartless. Instead of going to Kaunas, the Stumbras family did its religious duty. They said an hour of prayers for the dead boy, and Leo even paid the priest to say a low mass for his soul, on a weekday morning, which cost less than Sunday.

The gods must have noted Leo's unusual expenditure, for within a week, a misery dividend arrived at the Stumbras home in the form of a package addressed to Paul. The parcel was an awkward assembly of heavy brown paper and string, and the entire family stood about admiring it as Vida went out to find Paul, who had been feeding the ducks in the barn. Paul returned with the feed bucket in his hand, the curls of his long hair matted. He looked at them warily.

"Uncle Longin sent you something," Vida said encouragingly.

"What?"

"We don't know. It's wrapped up in a package. Open it so we can see."

"Why would he send me something?" He knew that people were not in the habit of giving gifts, except the occasional handful of nuts or candies to a child. At a boy's confirmation, he might receive a coin, and sometimes fathers or brothers made wooden toys for the children. Paul had never before received a package, nor had he ever seen one received by anyone else. He stood uncertainly by the door.

"The rest of you stand back while he unties the strings," said Leo. "There might still be some infected air trapped in the package." He reflected for a moment. "Maybe he should open it outside."

"Influenza is not transmitted by objects," said Andrius. Leo sniffed but said nothing further. Tomas offered Paul his pocket knife to cut the string, but Janina did not want to waste it, and they had to stand around as she worked on the knots. When she was done, she stood back to let Paul unwrap the paper. Still hesitating, he put down the feed bucket, stepped forward, pulled back the paper as well as another layer of cloth wrapping inside and then looked up at the others, beaming.

"Skates!" he shouted, and the others were so surprised and delighted that they applauded his luck.

"Is there a note?" his mother asked.

There was. Augustina read it out. "'Every time I see these, I think of my poor departed Mat. Please use them in good health and say a prayer for your cousin each time you put them on.'"

The skates were wrapped in a cloth and coated with grease to keep them from rusting. As Paul started to rub off the grease, he checked the edges of the blades. They were sharp. His cousin must have used them no more than a few times before he died. Paul's good fortune was so great that the winter cold had dragged into spring, so there was still ice to skate on.

"Can I try them out now?" he asked.

"Yes," said his father indulgently, "but don't use these as an excuse for forgetting your chores."

Paul headed down to the river to try out his new gift, and the others dispersed to their tasks. Tomas went out to his workshop to test a new gouge he had bought in the market in Merdine. Good tools were very difficult to find, both because of the war and because not much fine decorative work was done in the vicinity. He had been lucky to find a quarter-inch gouge, and all the more so because it had a beech handle only slightly flattened at the end from the mallet blows its previous owner had applied. Inside the workshop, he sharpened the gouge with a rolling motion against the stone, and then used a very small piece of slip-stone to remove the tiny burrs. A good carver kept his tools very sharp and never turned them on a sharpening wheel if he could help it, because the heat made the metal lose its temper. Once the new gouge was very sharp, Tomas set it in its holder among the chisels, rasps, hand drills and rifflers and admired the wealth of instruments all lined up neatly in their holders above his bench. He was just about to begin carrying a fresh block when he heard a gentle tap on the door, and Andrius came in.

The workshop was warm enough to fog Andrius's glasses, and he took them off and wiped them on his scarf. He was carrying an old book in his hand, whose pages had come loose from the binding. Tomas could feel Andrius's hesitation. The secret they shared seemed to inform every word they spoke, and the three of them had become uncharacteristically gentle with one another.

"A new book?" Tomas asked.

"Yes. Dvarionis was visiting a cousin in Panevėžys, and he found this at the market. It was very cheap and he thought you might be interested."

"What is it?"

"A study of the wood carvings of Lithuanian churches, but it's written in German."

"I don't read German."

"I know that."

"And what's this about woodcarvings? Church statuary is plaster."

"It wasn't always so. In the old days there was a lot of wood, but the good pieces were carted off to Moscow. You know, Tomas, there used to be a civilization here, but it was swept away. Merdine was an important town in the Middle Ages. There used to be manor houses, but the owners were rebels, so they were burned down."

"What's that got to do with me?"

"I'm trying to make a point. We've been so pauperized here over the centuries that we have to take care of ourselves now. We have a responsibility to the country and to make ourselves safe from invaders."

"I'll happily look at the pictures, but you should try to get Edvard interested in saving the country. He used to care about that sort of thing."

"What are we going to do about him?" Andrius wondered.

Edvard was crumbling under the weight of his crime. The suspicions of the village were aroused by the simultaneous disappearance of Byla, Liud and the *graf*. Since Byla and Liud were last seen in the Stumbras family bunker, queries about all the disappearances hovered over them perpetually. The brothers' line was simple. They had never seen the *graf*. Byla and Liud had taken a night shift in the bunker, and had deserted by the following morning.

When Leo returned from a fruitless trip to get part of his uncle's inheritance, he marched into Merdine to declare that no committee had the right to deem his farm the front line. Let someone else offer up his land and his children. Leo commanded his sons destroy the bunker, and they did so without regret.

But while Leo kept the village at bay with his roar, he was also suspicious of his sons and kept asking them questions. Edvard grew more and more sullen, more silent than ever before. If he did break down and confess, Andrius and Tomas would be implicated as accessories.

Tomas could see that Andrius was disappointed in his lack of interest in the book, but Tomas was not inclined to feign emotions. After a little while, Andrius sat on a stool and began to read the book himself.

Paul forgot to say a prayer for his dead cousin as he tied on his new skates at the riverbank. The air was still so cold that his fingers hurt as he fumbled with the straps. At least the wind had blown away the snow from the river. Paul spread out his arms and hazarded a step onto the ice. Immediately his right skate twisted off and turned onto the side of his boot. There was nothing to do but return to the log on the riverbank, take off his mittens and get them right.

This time, his straps held, but his balance did not. Paul was down on his rump in a moment. He looked at the ice in reproach. Most of it was cloudy, but patches were as clear as crystal and he could see right through to the river bottom. This skating business was harder than he had thought. But just wait. Once he got good at it, he would skate all the way to the sea. In very cold winters, it was said, the Baltic froze solid. He could skate across the sea to Sweden then, or Ireland. He was not sure if Ireland was on the Baltic, but it could not be far off. He could take his skates off and walk if he had to.

Out in the middle of the river ice, he raised himself again, stood precariously for a moment and then he was back on his rump. His tailbone ached right through the two layers of pants and long winter coat he was wearing. He pushed himself up again and had a delicious moment when he glided forward a few inches. It was not really skating, but it gave him an idea of what skating might be like. Carefully, with his arms outstretched for balance and his eyes on the tips of the skates that protruded from his boots, he began to take tiny steps forward. It was no use. His feet slipped out from under him, but this time he went face down onto the ice, softening his fall with his hands. He laughed. It was just a beginning, but he knew he was going to be good at this. No one else in the village had skates. He would be a marvel to them all. Smiling to himself, Paul looked down through the ice. There was a ghostly pair of buttocks right below him.

Impossible.

He leaned closer. Yes, they were buttocks all right, under a foot of clear ice. The naked body and legs were stuck to the underside of the ice, but the top of the body seemed loose. He made out a man's back and a head of dark hair, arms drifting in the current as if the man were waving to someone at a great distance down-stream. Paul tried to stand up, but his feet slipped out from under him and he went down on the ice again. As he rolled over to push himself up and away from the spectre under the ice, his face came close to the man's back, and he could see a large black mole there. Any minute, the man would turn over and look at him and then plunge a fist through the ice, take him by the neck and pull him down under the water.

Paul scrabbled back to the snowy shore like a crab and ran all the way back to the farmhouse with his skates still on.

Through the window of his workshop, Tomas saw Paul running awkwardly into the farmyard. Even from a distance, he could tell that something was very wrong, and he pressed quickly past Andrius and out the door. Paul's face was covered with frozen tears, so Tomas took him into the workshop and settled him by the stove, where he and Andrius managed to get the story out of him through his gasps and cries.

"Keep him here," Andrius said, and he went out to find Edvard. Paul wanted nothing more than to run to his mother's arms, but Tomas insisted that he needed to remove the skates from his feet and to stay where he was to warm up better before going back out into the cold. Tomas petted his little brother's untidy curls and wiped his face, put a tin kettle on his wood stove and added some wood to the fire. Through the window he saw his brothers walking down the lane with axes over their shoulders. Edvard carried the iron bar. Tomas untied the blades of Paul's skates and made him sweet tea, but after a while he could not hold the boy any longer and he took him into the house, where the tears started yet again as he explained what he had seen.

"We'll have to go to the river," said Leo when he had heard the story.

"Edvard and Andrius have already gone down," said Tomas.

"If they found a body, they'll need the sleigh to bring it here."

"Wait," said Tomas.

"What for?"

"No use hitching the horses unless they find something."

Leo looked curiously at Tomas. He was unaccustomed to taking advice from this son, but he could see the sense in what Tomas said.

"Did it look like the *graf*?" Stumbras asked, turning back to Paul. "He just might have got himself drunk and fallen through the ice."

Paul sniffed. "He wasn't wearing any clothes."

"A suicide, then," said Stumbras. As he crossed himself, he thought that drowning was an odd method of suicide. Men more often did it by hanging themselves from a tree.

It would be hard to find out where the body was from. The river was long, starting back in Byelorussia and going on all the way to the sea. In the spring of 1915, after the fall defeat of the czarist Second Army, it had been filled with the bloated bodies of soldiers and the carcasses of horses that had floated downstream for hundreds of miles.

The door opened and Andrius and Edvard came in, covered with ice from the spray of water, but silent.

"Well," Leo said, "did you find anything?"

Edvard just grunted and shook his head.

"So you saw nothing?" Leo asked.

"Nothing at all."

"Put the boy to bed," said Leo. "It might be the beginning of brain fever."

Leo did not want word of Paul's vision to get around, but Janina and Vida let the story slip in the market in Merdine. Soon everyone was talking about it, and Paul was the focus of their conversations. Paul, it was decided by the village, had a talent for finding bodies. Maybe he was meant to be a priest, because even the dead confessed their presence to him. A woman whose husband had disappeared came to the house, asking Paul to walk the countryside like a bloodhound, for she suspected her husband had fallen down a well somewhere. Another had lost a gold coin and wanted Paul to help look for it. Leo discouraged them all. He wanted no more notoriety in his house, but he was fighting a losing battle.

Over the next two days, Edvard often sat beside Paul's bed and stroked his forehead. He pitied the child who was paying the price for his own crime. Again and again, Edvard turned over the events of that night in his mind. He should have overpowered Byla and Liud and tied them up before Liud shot the *graf*. He should not have hit Liud across the head so hard. Once he had killed both men, he should have told the local militia commandant what happened and risked imprisonment. But it was much too late for that. Andrius tried to persuade him that his actions were necessary, but no words could take away his crime. Edvard was a strong man, but he had never carried anything so heavy in his life.

It had been hard to get the body moving again in the slow, under-ice current, and he worried that it might get stuck at the next bend in the river. Then the whole town would know what happened. As for God, He already knew.

Three days after Paul had seen the body, Tomas looked up from the breakfast table at the sound of the dogs barking. Hoofbeats were coming up the lane from the road. It was unusual to have a visitor so early in the day, and any visitor might bring bad news. Before anyone had time to rise from the table, the door was thrown open. Herman Momburg had ridden hard, and there was sweat on him. Long and lean, he was as severe as his father had been dissolute.

"Look at you," Augustina Stumbras said to her unexpected and unwanted guest, "permitting yourself to sweat in this cold! You'll be down with the flu or the ague in a minute. Give me your coat. I'll make you some tea."

Herman Momburg did not reply. Nor did he remove his coat.

"Sit down," said Leo Stumbras, his tone halfway between hospitality and command. Stumbras was no lowly peasant. He would not be treated this way even by a member of the gentry.

Herman reluctantly did as he was told. "I've come to talk to your boy about what he saw," he said. Paul shrank back.

"Our guest here has lost his father," Leo said to Paul. "He needs to know what you saw. Stand up when you are speaking to an adult."

Paul complied.

"You knew my father," Herman said.

"Yes."

"Was it him?"

"I don't know. He was facing down."

"The colour of his hair?"

"I'm not sure. Dark, I think."

"Any grey?"

"I can't remember."

Herman Momburg reached into his waistcoat and pulled out a silver ruble.

"Do you know what this is?" he asked Paul.

"Yes."

"Tell me what I want to know and it is yours."

"All right."

"Was the shape of the body that of a young man or an old one?"

"I don't know."

"Was there nothing remarkable about this body?"

"He had a black mole high up on his back. On the right side and round, like a kopeck."

Momburg glared at Paul.

"That's enough," said Stumbras firmly. "Did the *graf* have such a mole?"

"How would I know?" Herman put the coin back in his pocket. "I hardly ever saw my father without a suit on his back, and never without a shirt. For all his failings, he was a gentleman. I know the old man was a fool, but he was my father, and if I find out who killed him, someone is going to be sorry."

"Killed him?" Leo Stumbras asked.

"Yes, of course. The people around here do not like Germans."

"No one hated the *graf*. Your family has lived here a long time."

"Not long enough, it seems, to earn the respect of you people."

"We respected him as much as he deserved."

"It galls me to think how uncivilized this place is, and how intractable."

"Your father was careless," said Stumbras.

"You mean he was a drunkard," said Herman. "Don't mince words. He drank up most of my patrimony. Still, it's all very strange." He looked around the table.

"What's very strange?"

"That three men disappeared off the face of the earth that night, and two of them were last seen here. There must be a connection. Whether my father was pulled into heaven by angels, or sucked down to hell by devils, it would stand to reason that there would be a witness. Well?" he asked when no one spoke. "Did no one see what happened to my father? You, the small one. What is your name?"

"Paul."

"Paul, did you see my father on the day he died?"

"No."

"You, the next one." Herman Momburg was speaking to Tomas. "Did you see what happened to my father?"

Tomas felt the burning eyes of Momburg, and the eyes of his father as well, and the heat rose in his cheeks. Momburg would work his way through all of them and God only knew what Edvard would say. Out of the corner of his eye, he could feel him tensing. Tomas turned to his father. "Do I have to answer him? We've been through all this before," said Tomas. "The *graf* wandered away. So did the others, the soldiers. Maybe they went together. Maybe they offered him a drink and they're in Warsaw as we speak, lying under the table in some tavern." Tomas gathered his courage and returned Momburg's stare.

"Yes, we've been through this enough, Herr Momburg," said Leo. "Leave us in peace."

"Peace?" Herman Momburg's hands flitted to his waist, as if he had some sort of weapon there, but either it was missing or he chose not to use it. "This whole country stinks, but your place stinks worse than any other. If you want to prove your innocence, find my father."

"We don't need to prove anything," said Leo.

Still, in an attempt to mollify Herman Momburg, Leo helped organize new search parties that fanned out across the ice over the next few days, but snow conspired against them, blowing in heavy and thick to cover the surface. The body was gone.

The last days of March passed slowly, colder than anyone deserved, and the first half of April wasn't much better. The days got longer and the nights shorter, but there was no smell of spring yet. Reluctantly, the snow came off the land and the heavy ice came off the water, revealing no secrets below, but the farm fields were still cold and black and shallow puddles were covered with thin ice in the mornings. Even the great forests and the copses seemed saddened that spring, with the cold wind blowing through their naked boughs. The winter rye had started to turn green in the fields soon after the snow was off, but the winds continued to blow throughout the days, and the nights were still subject to hard frost, and the green shoots began to turn brown. Even the field grass was afraid to raise its head—as soon as a single stalk arose, the wind cut it down again.

When the time came to begin work in the fields, the farmers could not wait for clement weather. They put on fur coats, hunched their shoulders and began plowing, although their noses were soon red with the cold. The plow horses seemed to hunch against the wind as well, bending their ears back. The shepherds huddled by hedgerows and lit fires to warm themselves, while their sheep licked at the bare earth. Those lucky enough to herd cows pulled their bare feet from their wooden clogs to warm them in the streams of urine for a few moments. The small children of the farmhouses could bear their confines no more, and they poured out onto the porches, but the winds bit at them and chased them back in. The yards of the farmhouses were as silent as if someone had swept them clean of people.

The vestiges of the bunker melted away at the end of the Stumbras lane. The armies of Reds and Whites were still fighting in the East, with the Lithuanians, Poles, Latvians and Germans mixed up in the fray. The provisional government was still calling in volunteers from across the country, and the Poles were upset about the provisional government's unwillingness to join them in a union. But in Merdine, the local militia no longer bothered to put up sentries, no matter how hard the local commandant raged at them. The men on guard duty had grown bored, and the planting had to be done. They had no time to play at war. Some of them felt the want of rope because they had been too busy over the winter months to twist hemp. As far as the farmers were concerned, now that the urgent needs of spring were upon them, the politicians and soldiers should play out their games in the cities.

Maria had heard nothing since Jonas had volunteered. Since the postal service had collapsed, letters depended on the whim of travellers who sometimes left notes for the locals at the rectory.

Maria began to go to early mass every morning so that she could go by the rectory door to ask the housekeeper if there were any letters. Usually, the old woman just shook her head, but twice she had looked again at the name on an envelope, while Maria's heart fluttered. Both times the witch had finally ended up shaking her head.

As the weeks passed, Maria's prayers became more fervent. On sunny mornings, the light shot in through the stained-glass window of the church, casting a rose pattern on the slate floor. Intense white spring sunshine streamed through the clear pane, illuminating the gold leaf on the picture frames, candlesticks and two mosaics, until the room glowed with the golden light of hope.

Where else could God be found, if not in such a room, where the smoke from hundreds of years of incense clung to the ceiling?

Maria was the youngest of the women who came regularly to the early mass. Sometimes there was a woman who was pregnant for the first time and afraid, and another who had had many miscarriages. The only regular men in the place were the organist and the priest, muttering in Latin and huddling over the altar and hugging himself, trying to keep warm in the drafty church. As for the organist, he preferred to make his presence felt through the wheezing, heavenly breath of the pipes.

On her way out, Maria dropped a kopeck into the hand of an old woman standing outside the church door. For luck. Then she made her way to the rectory, only to have the sour-faced housekeeper shake her head again. Maria gathered her scarf around her neck and huddled into the jacket she wore over her vest and walked through the village on her way back to the Stumbras farm, where she had begun to work again at Easter.

The ruts under her shoes were still frozen from the nightly frost. A black dog came running at her on the other side of the wattle fence, a mongrel noted for the fierceness of its bark and the cowardice in its heart. She picked up a stone and threw it at him, and the dog ran back up the yard to the house, yelping.

Most of the houses in Merdine had thatched roofs, but some of the more prosperous townspeople had put on wooden shingles before the war. Tomas had once told her that over the border in East Prussia, only the very poor lived in thatched houses. Andrius had a wealth of knowledge on all things German, and Tomas liked to pass on the information as if he'd discovered it himself. In Prussia, all the buildings were made of brick and had roofs of clay tile.

Maria greeted women out hanging clothes to dry or drawing water from their wells, but she did not stop to talk because the day's work had not even started. Yet she was happy just to see other people. They were a relief from the cloying closeness of her mother. Her brother, Feliks, was worse in his way, so slow of speech that he made Edvard seem eloquent by comparison. This long, cold season full of false hope was almost unbearable.

She turned up the treed lane to the Stumbras farm, looking first at the road beyond in case she should catch sight of Jonas walking toward her. And why not? Men came home on leave. But he was not on the road. Up at the house Tomas was sitting on the small porch, his feet resting on the higher of the two large stones they used as steps, his knees up, like a little boy. He was far too old to be waiting for her on the porch, but she was glad of it.

As he stood to greet her, she saw that his hat was in his hands—unusually diffident for Tomas. His thick blond hair was darkening as he grew older, but it still fell long across his forehead. His face did not show the usual flush of red on the cheeks, and his mouth was a straight line. She waved at him and smiled, but he did not wave back, just held his hat before him.

"Maria," he said when she approached, "I need to talk to you. Why don't we go for a walk through the fields?"

"I've come all the way from the church and my hands are freezing," she said. "Here, feel them." She put her hands on his and was surprised at the warmth that came out of him. "Is your father inside?"

"Yes."

"And you don't want to talk to me in front of him?"

"No."

"When are you going to learn to get along with him? Why do you provoke him all the time?" She could feel him stiffen even at this mild rebuke and she wanted to poke him gently in the side, to make him laugh, to pull his hair until he begged her to stop, anything to lighten his mood.

But then she looked down and saw the green bag beside him on the porch—the knapsack that Augustina Stumbras had sewn for Jonas before he went off to volunteer.

She looked quickly up at Tomas, but he would not look back at her.

Her eyes began to fill with tears even though she had not yet articulated in her mind what her heart already knew. The door creaked open behind Tomas, and briefly she still hoped to see Jonas step through it and come to take her in his arms.

But it was Leo Stumbras who came out onto the porch, his moustache as bristly as the hair on the back of a hedgehog. "Maria," he said sharply, "the will of God has been done. Resign yourself."

She steadied herself against Tomas. He put his arms around her and held her tightly.

"Compose yourself," Stumbras said. "Get your arms off the girl, Tomas! What will people think?"

Maria did not hear a word. Jonas was lost, and so was she, and she clung to Tomas to prevent herself from falling.

When the weather finally broke toward the end of April, Vida Stumbras gloried in spring, reading the Lithuanian poets to her dour sister. Janina gave little sign of her improved mood, but she did not snap the way she had done most of the winter whenever anyone spoke to her. Augustina Stumbras found herself frozen again and again in her daily tasks, overcome by sudden girlhood memories that were indescribably sweet and melancholy. The last snowbanks in the forests turned to foam and disappeared, and under the caress of the sun the hedges and the woods began to awaken and the grasses were called back from the dead. The rat reappeared to search out the last of the grain, and the polecat nosed around the chickens at night, frightened not at all by the barking of the dogs. The crow, the magpie and the owl made themselves known, and mice and moles began to burrow again through the earth. The fleas and the mosquitoes showed no respect for social standing, biting the poor and the rich alike. The bees buzzed among the early flowers, while spiders spun their hunting nets.

The pair of storks returned to their nest at the peak of the Stumbras roof, tapping and rubbing their bills together as husband and wife bid each other hello. The nest needed mending, and so they wove new twigs together, and then dined on frogs and toads grown fat at the rivers and ponds. The forest began to resound with the cuckoo, and swallows rose into the sky, turning swift arcs about the Merdine church steeple at each dawn and sunset. Last of all that spring came the nightingale, who sang alone when all the other birds were asleep.

One evening, when the women had already packed up their sewing and gone to bed, the Stumbras men lingered over their last pipes and cigarettes. Tomas leaned on the window ledge to breathe the fresh air of spring.

"Close the window," said his father. "Night air is bad for your health."

"I was listening to the nightingale," said Tomas.

"You talk like a woman," said Leo. "The fleas come in at night and bite you in your bed. Besides, someone could see you by the window and take you down with a single shot."

"Why would anyone do that?"

"Why not?" said Stumbras.

Tomas was sleepy and longed to be on his way to the barn where he slept on the hay in the spring and the summer, but he and Andrius had fallen into the habit of staying up until Edvard went to sleep.

The more firmly spring asserted itself, and the brighter nature grew, the more dejected Edvard became. The spring work should have distracted him from the winter murders, but they appeared to weigh more and more heavily on Edvard's mind. By now the bodies had been eaten by the river fishes and the bones had fallen to the riverbed for the crayfish to gnaw upon. But just when the brothers began to believe they would never be caught as killers, now that it seemed as if they were almost safe, Edvard was dangerously close to breaking.

Although she was full of grief, the season waited for no man or woman, so Maria turned to her work at the farm. It bothered her greatly that Jonas had died so far away from home. Who would take care of his grave now that the flowers were coming up? The man who had brought the pack on his way home for leave could tell her very little about Jonas, and he stayed for only an hour before going on his way. Only after he left did it occur to her that she did not know his name, nor the exact place where Jonas had fallen, nor where his body was buried. The grasses would grow in a tangle over the burial mound, and as time passed it would sink and become indistinguishable from the fields around it.

Her future had vanished along with Jonas. The miserable home where she grew up would be no refuge to her because it was going to Feliks, her sullen brother. The seven acres would be barely enough to support him and a family. He would always need to hire himself out to make ends meet, and how could she add another mouth for him to feed? She would be doomed to work as a serving girl forever, and in the country, serving girls aged fast. They worked outside almost as much as the men, and the wind and the sun brought lines to their faces. Then men stopped looking at them. What happened to the unmarried girls when they became old women? Maria had never thought of old age before. Maybe she would end up like the beggars at the church doors, hands always held out for kopecks.

In early May, Augustina Stumbras sent Maria out to the fields and woods to look for wild sorrel to make into sour soup. All of nature might have awakened, but for the farmers, spring was the worst time of the year because their stores were low and nothing much edible was growing yet, just mushrooms and wild greens.

Maria filled the basket, but on the way back to the farmhouse, she was overcome with grief at the sight of the carving of Saint George that guarded the gate near the stump where she and Jonas had talked before he volunteered. She dropped into grass just tall enough to make her invisible. Her basket tipped and the sorrel poured out onto the earth, but she did not care.

Tomas was out in the fields and woods as well, searching for good pieces of fallen wood to take back to his workshop for seasoning. He carried his mallet with him. Solid wood sang out when it was struck, while rotten wood made a sodden thump, a sound like the grunt of a drunkard. He felt restless, and could not put his mind to any task, including the carving, which ordinarily filled his time. But he needed to be doing something, or his father would assign him a job. The warm breeze upon his cheek filled him with a combination of fatigue and impatience. His knees and elbows wanted to stretch and his feet longed to walk, but as soon as he was up and about he felt drowsy. He was not thirsty, but he wanted to drink. He was not hungry, but he wanted to eat.

He wandered about, striking at wood harder than he needed to and picking up nothing, not even the branches that sang true. When he came upon Maria, she was sitting in the high grass, weeping with her face in her hands. It unnerved him to see her so, and he crouched beside her and touched her on the hand.

The field where they were sitting was sweet with the smell of grass and spring flowers. Grey bees flew among the small blossoms and a cloud of gnats circled not far off.

"What's wrong, Maria?" Tomas asked, a stupid question. Wordlessly, she began to strike him with her fists. The blows were not painful, but they surprised him. He seized her wrists before she could strike him any more.

"I'll never get out of here," she said.

"Why would you want to get out?" Tomas asked. "We'll take care of you."

"I want a life of my own, but there are not enough men for women like me. Half of the ones who went away to war will not come back. They're dead, or else they've found new lives for themselves. Those who have come back are either spoken for or taken by the drink."

"My mother loves you," said Tomas. "You can live your whole life with us. Edvard will keep you after they die."

She tried to pull her wrists away from him to strike him again, but he held fast. Her wrists were warm in his hands and he regretted the pain he had caused. He finally released her and sat down beside her in the tall grass.

"I'd keep you myself, if I planned to stay in Merdine," he said.

Maria wiped her face with her apron and straightened her hair with her hands.

"You'd keep me as your serving girl if you planned to stay?"

"I'd do better than that," he said, not really aware of what he meant, but wanting to promise her something to make her feel better.

"What does it matter, if you're not staying? And where are you going, anyway?"

"Away."

"Where away?"

The need to go had been building in him, like the pressure of rising water behind a dam, but he had barely been aware of it. Tomas did not have a clear destination in mind. He had spoken of Paris with Lipchitz in the tavern, but the city seemed as remote as a dream. To say he intended to go there would be ridiculous. Instead, Tomas seized on the first faraway place he could think of. He reclined on one elbow, and Maria mirrored his pose.

"To Vilnius," said Tomas. "It's a great city. I was there with my uncle Longin."

"The Reds hold Vilnius," said Maria, "or the Poles. Do you intend to go over to them?"

"I don't care about politics," said Tomas.

"Neither do I," said Maria, "and neither did Jonas."

The name of the dead man cast a pall over them.

"I'll be able to get to Vilnius," said Tomas. "There's an art school there where I could be a student."

"And who would pay for your studies—your father?"

"No. But I could work at night to make the money. I'd be a porter, loading wagons."

"I've never been to Vilnius."

"Oh, you'd love it. There are so many churches that when the bells ring for mass, the whole city chants in harmony. You could go to mass at a different church on Sunday every week of the year. The cathedral has three giant statues on it, a Saint Helen at the peak with a golden cross, and Saint Stanislav and Saint Kazimier on either side."

"Lucky woman, flanked by two men."

"There are alcoves across the front with more giant statues, Moses and Abraham, Matthew, Mark, Luke and John. The ceilings of the churches have fantastic detail worked into them, not like our miserable Merdine church."

"I thought you admired our church."

"I do, but once you've seen Vilnius, you can never look at your home the same way again. The ceiling of the Bernardine church has a solid pattern of six-sided stars that look like folded paper. Incredibly difficult stone tracery. Saint Mikalojus's ceiling is groined with carved wooden beams on the choir end, and Saint Michael's has stone rosettes and hearts above the altar."

"When did you visit Vilnius?"

"Two years ago."

"And you remember all this?"

"And even more."

"Tell me of something besides churches. I've had enough of them."

"Enough of churches?"

"I prayed for Jonas every day and it did me no good."

"The front of the city hall has nine different friezes, a sword, a patriarch with a shield, a ship, a griffin—"

"Stop!" Maria was laughing. "I didn't ask about Vilnius just to know about its buildings. What are the people like there?"

"It's very crowded. Sometimes the streets are so full of people you can barely pass."

"I don't like crowded places. I never feel as if there is enough air for everyone to breathe."

"But the streets are more colourful and varied than an Advent procession. Jews in rounded hats, Orthodox priests in tall ones, soldiers. Gentry in fine clothes with top hats on their heads and ivory-handled walking sticks, who ride around in carriages."

"But you're none of those. How would you fit in with them?"

"The city is full of ordinary people, too. That's the beauty of the place. At night Vilnius's windows shine like the Momburg house used to do on the evening of a ball, and the lights are so numerous that you feel you are among the stars. Uncle Longin and I were there for All Souls' Eve, and he took me out to the Rasu cemetery that covers two hills and a valley, and all the candles on the graves made it look like the dead had their very own city."

He stopped suddenly and looked at her, but she forgave him this reference to the dead.

"Tell me some more about the living," whispered Maria.

"The city is so big that you can't walk across all of it fast enough, so there are public trams drawn by four horses each. You stand on the corner until one arrives, and you will be taken across the city for three kopecks."

"It sounds wonderful."

"You could come and visit me when I'm a student at the art school."

"I'll never get to Vilnius."

"Why not?"

"How would I get there?"

"By cart as far as Kaunas, and then you'd take the train."

"Who has money for a train?"

"I'd send it to you."

Maria laughed "Will you be so rich in Vilnius?"

"Maybe not at first. But I'll do well in the long run."

"How long is the long run?"

"I don't know."

"By the time you have any money, you'll have a wife and children and then you won't even remember me."

"How could I ever forget you? I've loved you since I was a boy."

Tomas's face reddened. When the words came off his lips, he meant he had loved her like a sister. But that was not the meaning she seemed to take, and as Tomas looked into her brown eyes, he did not want to clarify what he meant. Reclining beside him in the fragrant hayfield, Maria no longer looked like the maid who had worked for their family for the last five years. His body sensed that she was what he had been looking for ever since the weather became fine.

Tomas reached forward and held her wrist again. She did not protest, but a sudden stillness came over her.

He leaned forward to kiss her, for a kiss was not so complicated. But a kiss was so short. He kissed her again and again, and then left his lips upon hers for so long that he ran out of breath and had to gasp for air. She laughed at him, but he was not angry at her for it. He wanted her very badly, in a way that was new to him.

And for Maria, Tomas had become many things all at once. He was the memory of Jonas. He was a future different from her mother's house or the Stumbras household. And he was also a young man.

At first, she only let him touch her through her clothes, cling-ing to modesty as best she could. They were inexperienced and clumsy. But many other lovers had stumbled over their first steps and found a way, and so Tomas and Maria, hidden by the high spring grass, found a way as well.

As the days passed, Maria had to tell Tomas to stop following her with his eyes when they were with his family—women were wise in these matters and they had to be careful.

But their new-found hunger was not easily appeased. Tomas sought Maria out, in stolen moments between the planting and the other heavy work. His father cursed him more often than usual, accusing him of being lazy, a layabout who disappeared at night to sleep beneath the trees. But the truth of the matter was that he was getting hardly any sleep at all. He would meet Maria in the night and they would talk and then make love until dawn.

Tomas's father would wake him at first light, and for the whole day he walked and worked as if in a dream. He would promise himself to go to sleep earlier that night. But when the evening came, he began to think of her again. He wanted all of her, to touch her, to eat her up. Over her laughing protests, he licked her face as they made love, and wrapped his arms tightly around her to hold her close to him.

They talked often of going away, yet they made no actual plans. Maria wanted to know everything about Vilnius. She asked him questions and he made up stories because he had so little to tell her, and then he forgot his lies and told different ones. She made him search the village for books about Vilnius, but all he could find were chapters in old geographies. They delayed their departure again and again because in each other's arms they were already far away.

—

In early June, the army of Bermondt descended on Merdine like a swarm of locusts. This particular freelance army had long since given up the offensive against the Reds, and although the Germans had no right to have armies in the old czarist lands, some said this one was being paid for by Berlin. In the Merdine market, talk turned to the army's plans. It might annex Lithuania and even Latvia to East Prussia and finish the job begun by the Teutonic Knights almost seven hundred years earlier. Perhaps they would just install a client regime friendly to Germany. Already, the princes of Germany were edging forward to propose themselves as monarchs for the new Lithuanian state. At the very least, the Bermondt army would form a defensive line to keep the Red Army from joining up with the remnants of the revolutionary fifth column of Reds within Germany itself, the Spartacists, who had been eager to take the government.

The soldiers were unfailingly drunk, planning to get drunk or hungover. They rode their horses straight through fields of grain, crushing it under the horses' hooves. The first hay was only just ready to be cut because of the late, cold spring. Bread was scarce for some of the farmers, and there would be no more rye until the harvest in August. The Bermondt men were a scabrous lot, dressed in uniforms made up of assembled rags from czarist and German outfits, with odd bits of exotica—English or French helmets or green American trousers. In order to recognize one another, soldiers wore white armbands with the Greek Orthodox cross painted upon them, although the soldiers were in no way doing God's work.

The villagers of Merdine did not know what this army wanted or how long it would stay, but it was clear that one family was benefiting from its presence.

The windows of the Momburg manor house blazed as Herman entertained Bermondt and his officers. They must have been paying him real gold, either marks or rubles, because the serving women said a wondrous amount of French champagne and brandy had appeared. Real gold always brought out the secrets.

Throughout the countryside, the peasants and farmers kept careful score of their insults and losses, debts to be paid if Bermondt ever pulled out. Herman Momburg was betting all he had on Bermondt. If the Reds came, they would kill him. If the Poles or the Lithuanians won, they would take his meagre holding. Only Bermondt offered him hope for the future.

Meanwhile, the provisional Lithuanian government was not standing still while loose armies wandered behind its lines. Already, partisans were harrying the Bermondt encampment at night. The only question was whether the general would stay and fight, or pull back to some other position.

Regardless of the politics, Leo Stumbras needed to bring in the hay. In a land of farms and pastures, grass meant wealth. Another few days of growth would have been better, but the weather was dry now. He needed to act fast, before any battles began, and he was short of labour because so many of the field hands had gone off to war. The Merdine farmers banded together, going from one farm to another, working in groups to speed the haymaking, deciding by lots whose fields would be done first and whose last. Come evening, one farm owner might sigh in relief to know that his own fields had been cut and his harvest was safe, while his neighbour, the next in line, spent a sleepless night.

Leo had spent just such a night, lying awake during the short hours of June darkness, praying for the sun to come up. Throughout the night he rose to study the sky for clouds. A rainy day would slow the drying and wet hay could not be heaped up for winter because it upset the stomachs of the cattle or turned black and rotted. By half-past two he was up, as were his wife, daughters and Maria, who prepared the morning meal for the men and women who were coming to mow and rake. They laid out beer and dug out two bottles of vodka from a hiding place, saving the same number for the end of the day. Then they set about making the barley-milk porridge and mashed potatoes that the mowers would eat before they went out into the fields. The few remaining potatoes were dark and purple, and some of the eyes were very long. The women had to light the oil lamp in order to see to cut out the bad parts.

The barking of the dogs announced the arrival of the mowers. Edvard, Andrius and Tomas went out to meet them—four men and three women coming up the lane from the road. Andrius called down to them in the darkness, and poured each of them a small glass of vodka before they came into the house for breakfast. Soon the room was filled with talk and laughter. They drank camomile tea sweetened with honey and ate the barley-milk porridge and the faintly purple mashed potatoes, hurrying to get down as much as they could before the first light of dawn broke over the fields. Augustina Stumbras poured more vodka judiciously, enough to keep the men happy, but not so much that they would get sleepy before they set out to work.

"First light," called out Paul, who had risen later than the others and came to the table in great fear that everything would be eaten before he had a chance to get something into his belly.

The men rose immediately from the tables and went out to the yard to get their scythes. The women and Paul stayed behind. They would rake later, after the men had cut their way through the field. Then they would shake the hay and turn it so it dried in the sun. The men had to hurry to complete the mowing before the sun burned off the dew and made the cutting more difficult. They followed Leo Stumbras out into the field, dressed in their long linen shirts and underclothing, for although the morning was cool, they would soon work up a sweat. The women would come out into the fields later, dressed in long shifts. This was the least amount of clothing women were ever permitted to wear in public, and when the sun was high and work hot, the men would take pleasure in looking at the figures of the women through the rough linen that clung to bodies, dampened with sweat.

The mowers formed themselves into a line, with Edvard at the head. He was the strongest mower, and so he had the honour of setting the pace. The men sharpened their scythes one last time with their whetstones, and waited for Edvard to start the first swath. A moment later, Leo began the second, and the rest did the same, each working a few yards behind the other in a step pattern across the field. Each man strove to cut his portion cleanly, leaving no upright grass between his swath and his neighbours.' The Stumbras men knew their field well, and so they worked barefoot, but some of the neighbours feared snakes or unfamiliar low stumps, and wore thick linen slippers to protect their feet. They also kept a sharp lookout for small, underground beehives, because the man who cut a swath over a beehive had the right to the honey he found, as well as the bee stings he would acquire digging it out. They were awkward at first, still stiff in the morning, but they soon found their rhythm, guided by Edvard's grunt at each swing. The swish and pull of the scythe against the grass filled the mind with a pleasant emptiness and brought a glow of sweat to the skin. Grasshoppers leaped from the grass and found themselves confused and vulnerable in the sunlight, their wings still wet and unable to take them far. Crickets and mice rushed into the unmown hay, and then had to flee again as another swath of cover disappeared.

A hare darted out of the grass, and old Gaidys, fourth man down the line, reached forward to slash at it with the blade of his scythe, but the creature leaped over the steel like an athlete, and the men laughed.

Tomas watched the hare bound swiftly along until it almost reached the fence, and wiped the sweat away from his eyes, grateful for the pause. He stood at the opposite end of the line from

Edvard, in the place where young men were put, those who could not be counted on yet.

Someone fired a shot.

The hare tumbled over itself as if it were continuing its imitation of an athlete, but it came down on the ground and did not move. A group of Bermondt soldiers was coming up the road. One of them, a hatless man with his hair shaved off against the lice, came running forward and lifted the hare up by the ears. A dozen men behind him cheered, and one of the two officers on horseback clapped his gloved hands ironically.

"The bastards," said Chichins. "They could smell the vodka in their sleep. If they turn up your lane, there'll be nothing left for us to eat or drink when we're done."

The mowers in the field waited and watched, and sure enough, half the band of soldiers turned up the Stumbras lane, led by their two officers, while the rest waited where the bunker had once stood.

"You go and protect our lunch as best you can," said Chichins to the Stumbras men. "We'll keep mowing."

The women had evaporated from the yard by the time Leo arrived at the house with Andrius and Tomas, who had followed along unasked. Reluctant to deal with soldiers and uneasy about any questions they might ask, Edvard stayed back in the field to lead the diminished band in its scything. Three soldiers stood about, smoking pipes and cigarettes. The two officers were already inside. Stumbras found them sitting at the breakfast table with cups of tea and glasses of vodka. The youngest one rose when Stumbras came in, saluted him and brought him over to the table where a map was set out. The older officer did not even bother to look up, and just kept sipping from his glass of tea.

"Please have a look at this map," the young officer said. He could not have been more than twenty-two, and carried himself with the exaggerated correctness of a young man trying to look older than he was.

He pointed out highlights of the surrounding countryside to Stumbras on the map as if the farmer were a traveller visiting the place for the first time. Stressing the height of land that the Stumbras farm covered, he asked if Leo understood the strategic importance of his farm. At first Leo merely nodded, biting his tongue at the way the soldier treated him like an unlettered serf. Then he began to run out of patience.

"I have a field of hay that needs to be mowed," said Stumbras. "You are welcome to stay for lunch. My wife will be happy to take food out to your men."

The young officer nervously ran his finger along the right side of his pencil moustache, as if straightening unruly hair. He looked to the older officer at the table, but the man said nothing. The young officer turned back to Stumbras.

"Don't you understand? We will need to begin our action in two hours."

"Action?"

"This height of land needs to be cleared for a proper defence. Our orders are to set fire to the fields, the woods and the house before noon."

Stumbras stood silently. The young officer watched him for a moment, and then began to roll up his map.

"Just a moment," said Stumbras.

"Yes?"

"The Poles and the Lithuanians are still chasing the Reds. You have no enemies here but a few partisans. Probably just some boys looking for excitement. There is no need for action."

"I have my orders," the young man said.

"You have orders to destroy my farm? What for? What harm have I done you?" Stumbras's voice was rising.

The young man kept looking to the older one. "This is nothing personal. It's an act of war. I will issue you with a note. When the peace has come, you will be compensated."

"If my family and I don't starve before then," Leo said. "It's coming up to midsummer. Destroy my crops now, and we'll starve by mid-winter. What kind of an army are you? Why do you need to make war on civilians?"

A fist came down on the kitchen table, and they all turned to look at the older officer.

"Be glad you're not being shot."

"What for?"

The officer drank again. "For disrespect to Germans. If it wasn't for us, the czar would still be lording it over you. You have two hours."

"I have no money, but there is still a little grain in the barn," said Stumbras, desperate now to keep them talking. "Six horses, too. You can have five of those. Just leave me one for the plow."

"I regret," said the young officer, "that there is nothing we want. I will leave two men in the yard. Please do not think of resisting."

"You'll be killing us!" Augustina Stumbras cried out. She had been silent in the corner by the cookstove. "It's too late to plant again. Where will my children lay their heads?"

The officers said nothing. The elder rose from the table and slipped the unopened bottle of vodka under his coat. The young officer turned back to face them one more time from the door.

"Please do not resist," he said. "My men have orders to shoot."

And then the two of them were gone.

"They can't mean it," said Augustina, and she went forward and took her husband's hands in her own.

"No time to cry now," he said, and he freed one of his hands from her grasp to brush her cheek gently. "Listen." He had to stop and compose himself. "Don't think now. Save what you can. Tomas, get the wagon ready in the yard. Maria, go out to the fields, quickly, and tell the other men to return to their homes."

Augustina reached for Leo's hands again, but he pushed her

away. Now was the time to act; there would be plenty of time to be sorry later on.

When he and Andrius stepped out into the yard, the women who had gathered to mow were keening. The men had stopped their mowing, and they watched Maria as she ran barefoot across the field toward them to bring the news.

Leo had seen droughts and floods, but to be told that his farm was to be burned was like being told that the atmosphere would soon catch fire.

"The animals first," he shouted, as he and Andrius ran to the barn and threw open the doors. "Leave the mare for Tomas to hitch to the wagon."

"Where'll we take the others?"

"Just free them."

Leo refused to consider the labour that had gone into making the pens and the troughs, and the very barn itself. There was no time.

One by one, Andrius led the horses to the door and slapped their rumps. Unaccustomed to freedom, the horses merely trotted a dozen yards and looked back at him, waiting.

"Away, away!" he shouted, charging them and waving with his hands. Edvard arrived from the field to stand breathless beside his brother.

"It's God's will," he said. "It's to pay for the deaths."

Leo saw them from the barn door and shouted, "Edvard, fill a barrel with rye seed and bury it beyond the yard. Deep. Tomas, harness the mare to the wagon and take it to your mother for the household goods. Find Paul and have him drive the ducks off the property as fast as he can. When you've harnessed the mare, leave it for your mother and come down the lane to the road, to the place where you built the bunker. We'll dig a fresh bunker there now."

The two soldiers sat on the edge of the well and smoked cigarettes as they watched the family's panicked preparations. Pigs refused to be rushed, and protested, squealing, while the ducks, hastened by Paul, waddled unhappily away, driven at a speed that wounded their dignity. Outside the door of the house, fine linen towels and tablecloths that had been carefully bleached and ironed lay in a heap, beside them hams and sausages that had been hanging in the chimney. Janina said nothing when one of the soldiers came over, broke off half a dozen smoked sausages from a string and returned to his place at the well. He cut slices with a bayonet to share with his friend.

Augustina wanted Tomas to stay to load the goods onto the wagon, but he ran across the yard to his workshop, intending to throw the seasoned wood out into the yard, where the earth was bare, so the blocks would not catch fire. He could scoop up his tools and then help the women fill the wagon. He had barely begun to throw the pieces of wood out the open door when his father appeared in the doorway.

"Don't be a fool. There are more important things."

"Not to me," said Tomas, barely looking up.

"We can't eat wood. Go back to the house."

Tomas intended to stop, but one more fine piece of seasoned oak tempted him. He was reaching for it with both hands when his father struck him across the shoulders. The wood block fell to the ground. As his father beat him across the back with his open hand, Tomas ran out into the yard.

"For once in your life, do as I say!" shouted Leo, and he stood there a moment longer to make sure Tomas returned to the house.

The wagon was already filled with domestic goods in chaotic disarray: iron pots and kettles, cups and bowls wrapped in towels, sacks of flour and urns of toasted flaxseed, lamp oil in a tin, a funeral dress, bowls of honey and pillows. His mother had taken all the household rosaries and looped them around her wrist, and the strings of beads kept getting in her way.

Suddenly the soldiers straightened themselves and looked into the distance, so Tomas stopped too and listened. Gunshots.

Maybe the provisional government had an army on the way. Maybe there was still hope. He stared into the distance where the shots had come from.

"No time, no time!"

His father was on him, forcing him up to the seat of the wagon. "Go down to the end of the lane. Your brothers are there already. Help with the digging."

Tomas's mother appeared at the doorway with another handful of linen, but his father pulled her away.

"No more time. Come down to the bunker now. "

"I haven't got everything."

"We have to save ourselves. Come." Not even allowing her a final look, he pulled her through the yard, Maria and the girls following.

Down at the end of the lane, Andrius and Edvard had felled one of the old oaks and were heaping earth onto the fallen trunk to raise an embankment.

The bunker was not finished by the time the Bermondt officers reappeared. The older one ignored them, but the younger nodded at them as he rode past.

The soldiers did as their officers had promised. Two dozen men spread out across the farm. One of them went inside the house, and when he came out, he held a torch lit from the stove on which Augustina had cooked breakfast that morning. The other men lit their torches as well. Two repeatedly touched flames to the thatched roof of the house. The flame gathered at the low corner where the thatch was not much higher than a man, and then a tendril of fire shot across the roof to the other side. Systematically, the soldiers worked their way from house to barn to granary to Tomas's workshop, and on to the other outbuildings.

The storks found no voice when the fire reached their nest of young, but they clicked their bills repeatedly. Mother and father stood and beat their wings, as if trying to push back the flames, but only fanned the fire. Soon mother and father rose up above the burning roof and circled over their nest as their babies screeched.

The fields were more difficult to light. The days had been dry and now that the dew was off the grass, it should have caught easily. Yet again and again, the flames blew out before taking hold. The soldiers tried lighting the grass where the wind would fan the flames. Even so, they had to work at it, flapping their coats in places to build the fire. The oats and the rye were harder still to light, but the men were accustomed to burning, and they and their officers eventually got the job done. A low wall of flame began to work its way through the rye and oats and hay. The heat built, so when the wall of fire came to the garden of potatoes and carrots, dill and beets, the vegetable tops burned as well.

The family watched from the bunker as the roofs of their buildings disappeared in smoke. Soon the nest and the young storks had been consumed and then the flames became visible through the windows and the glass popped out of the frames as if blown by a strong breath.

"Jesus, Mary and Joseph," Augustina intoned again and again, her hands clasped under her chin. She rocked back and forth as the home in which she had raised her children turned into a pillar of fire. The burning house gave off a strong odour of pine resin, making Leo remember his childhood when the new house still smelled of freshly squared logs.

Tears were flowing freely down Edvard's face. He was the one who would inherit the farm, and so he had a right to mourn more than his brothers. But it was not anger or sorrow that made him cry so freely. It was happiness. After the death of Graf Momburg and the murders of Byla and Liud, he had recognized that the rules of God were very clear. Edvard would burn in hell unless he confessed his sin to the priest; yet he could not because he would incriminate his brothers.

But now the fire had come to cleanse him. This was God's just punishment, and once he had suffered it, he would be free.

Tomas could not keep his eyes off the terrible beauty of the flames that ate up the house where he had been both sheltered and trapped. He had thought that he would never find the strength to tear himself away from his home, but now anything was possible.

He felt a hand slip into his.

Maria was weeping as if it were her own farm burning. She held his hand very tightly, and he briefly wanted to wrest it away.

Tomas's mother let out a wail and Maria dropped his hand.

"The gods!" she said. "I forgot to bring out the gods! They'll burn to cinders in there."

Saint Francis, with his hand stretched out and a miraculous small bird perched on his fingertips. Mary, Mother of God, with her crown and the seven swords piercing her heart. Saint Christopher, with the infant Jesus upon his shoulders. Half a dozen worrying Jesuses, and John the Baptist and Saint Kazimier. They had been sitting on their shelf in the parlour, waiting for buyers. The age of miracles was over. Now all the saints, and even Jesus himself, were being consumed by the blaze.

It seemed that Tomas could smell the burning flesh of his wooden gods in the air. Off in the distance, he saw Herman Momburg on horseback, watching the fire. The *graf*'s son took off his hat and waved.

SEASONS END

TOMAS STOOD BY THE GROTESQUE WOODEN MADONNA ON the outskirts of Merdine, but for once the sculpture held no interest for him. The sun beat down upon him, and he took off his hat and wiped his forehead. His mother had sent him to get a bottle of concentrated vinegar because a fishing expedition had proven wildly successful. The brothers had taken half a dozen large carp and two pike in one morning, almost forty pounds of fish. Augustina would dilute the vinegar with water and then submerge the cooked fish in the homemade vinegar to preserve it for a week or more.

Tomas watched the road, hoping that no one would pass and see him loitering. He was lucky to have been given the errand— his father tried to keep the family working every minute of the day on the burned farm. He felt his heart jump when he saw Maria coming as agreed across the fields, carrying a basket under her arm. He had not seen her since Sunday mass, when she had seemed to avoid him. When she got close, he wished he could throw his arms around her, but they might be seen.

After the fire, Maria had been sent home to her mother's since Leo could not spare the money to pay her. He told her she could come back the following spring if she did not find other work. No one had ever told Tomas about the sadness of lovers, who had always just seemed silly to him, smiling at one another or else coyly avoiding each other's looks. He had never imagined that he could join their ranks. Nor had he ever imagined the emptiness of days in which he would not catch even a glimpse of Maria.

She looked at him uncertainly as she approached, studying his clothes and his face as if he were a stranger. He beamed at her.

"I wish I could kiss you," he said. She did not return his smile.

"We can't. Not out here on the road."

"Let's go down to the woods," he said, taking her hand.

"No. Someone might see us."

"I want you."

"I know. But it's not possible now. If we begin kissing, we know where that will lead. Let's just walk into town."

The road was very dry and the sun was high in the sky. Their footsteps made the dust rise up and swirl around them. Several times, Tomas started to speak with her, but she answered his questions abruptly or not at all, and he gave up trying. They turned a bend in the road and came upon a boy who was using a rope halter to lead a foraging cow through the ditch beside them. The boy wore a ragged homespun smock that came to just below his knees. He was dirty and barefoot, with a switch in his hand. He looked at them dumbly as they drew alongside, and Maria gave him a kopeck before they passed on.

"Boys like that make me sad," said Maria.

Tomas said nothing. The fields and roadsides were full of child shepherds, both girls and boys, too young to do anything but care for the animals all day.

Tomas expected her to ask about the progress of the work on the farm, but she did not raise the subject, and he was grateful, for he was sick of thinking of the place. He put his hand on her arm for a moment and looked at her. She met his gaze, as if she were searching for something in him.

"Do you love me?" she asked.

The question irritated him slightly, but he nodded.

"And you want to be with me always?" she asked.

"Every second of the day and the night."

"I've been thinking of Vilnius," said Maria. "It's time we did something. There's no future for us here. If your father found out about us, he would beat us both and forbid us to see each other."

"I'm too old to be beaten, and you don't work for him any more."

"That's not the point. If you do love me, we have to make plans to get away soon."

"Yes, soon, but not quite yet. I don't want to desert them at a bad time. And besides, Vilnius isn't in Lithuanian hands."

"I thought you didn't care about politics."

"I don't, but I care about Vilnius and I see no way to get there without crossing the Polish lines. We could wait and see how things look after the harvest."

"I can't stay at home with my mother much longer. She is driving me mad. I'll have to look for another family to go to soon and I might end up somewhere far away." She pulled her arm from his and went on walking.

It was hard to think on such a hot day. Tomas would gladly have searched out some shady spot where they could cool themselves, and perhaps even make love. He could not concentrate on the future and he wished she would save the talk for another time.

"Do you have any money?" Maria suddenly asked.

"I did, but I gave it to my father to buy supplies for rebuilding. Do you?"

"I have a few silver rubles my father gave me before he died. It would be enough to get us to Vilnius."

"Aren't you listening? Vilnius is still at war."

"Vilnius, Kaunas, anywhere, as long as it's away from here."

"It would have to be someplace where I could study art."

Maria slapped her apron in frustration. "Which is most important to you, going away with me or studying art?"

"I don't see why you need to put it that way. I'm going to be an artist, a sculptor, and if you love me, you'll love what I want to do as well."

"But you have to think about how we will house and feed ourselves when we are away. Have you given any thought to that?"

"Of course I have. I'd go to school by day and work by night. You said you'd work, too."

"But *where* will we live?"

"We'd take a room."

"Together?"

"It's cheaper than living part."

"But no one will rent to us if we're unmarried."

"Then we'd get married. But can't we wait a little? I owe it to my family to help them rebuild first. Once I've paid off that debt, I'll be free. You planned to wait for Jonas and we can wait a little longer, too. It will be hard to be apart this winter, but maybe I could earn some money by then. Spring will be better."

"I'd like to go sooner."

"So would I, but there's nothing to be done about it."

He could barely get a word out of her the rest of the way into Merdine, and when they parted, she would not agree to meet him again.

Tomas lingered in Merdine as long as he dared, drinking in the sights of strangers on the streets and enjoying the brief conversations with those he and his family knew. The fate of the Momburg estate was still the cause of considerable talk. Shortly after the Bermondt troops withdrew to continue their marauding in another part of the country, the fine old Momburg house was gutted by fire. The unidentified arsonists were heroes in the town, all the more so as Herman Momburg and his mother had fled on the night of the fire and had never returned. The local council would hold their land until it could be redistributed, but the farm implements and other remaining goods melted into the countryside and village.

Here and there in Merdine a door sported a new knocker, a damaged wall was repaired with yellow brick, or a pair of candles stood high in a window, held by a new pair of candlesticks.

Maria walked to the far side of the village in search of a particular shop. The wattle fences along the street were unmended, and chickens sat upon the windowsills, wary of the sullen, emaciated dogs that panted in the shade cast by houses. Broken windows were patched with oiled paper, and men stood in the doorway of the tavern, and watched her as she walked by.

She made her way to the miserable shop whose only sign of commerce was a tin of lamp oil set behind the glass in a window. She stepped inside. The dark room smelled of the open barrel of herring, as well as smoked meat, sawdust, leather, lamp oil and camphor. But the place was not well stocked. The knobby end of a ham bone hung on a string from a hook in the ceiling, and by the dried look of the bone, the last meat had been stripped off some time ago. There was a small stack of caraway-flavoured hard white cheeses on the counter, but as these lasted practically forever, they might have been sitting there since before the abdication of the czar.

The severe woman who ran the store had not risen from her chair. She sat fixed in her place, watching Maria from under her kerchief with intense, bright eyes.

"Good morning," said Maria. The woman cleared her throat in reply. "I've come to buy amber," she said.

"I don't sell jewellery."

"That's not what I had in mind."

"What did you have in mind?"

The woman waited, but Maria would say no more. "I don't sell big pieces," the woman finally said. "Just dust and nuggets. Is that what you're after?"

Maria nodded.

"How much do you want?"

She had not expected this. "I don't know."

"It's sold by the measure. Usually one measure is all people want."

"Then that's what I want, too."

The woman crouched under the counter and came back up with a paper packet. She looked at Maria knowingly after she paid, and then told her if she wanted yew branches, she carried those too. Maria shook her head. She would try the amber first and come back for the yew branches if she needed them later.

Tomas ran into the wandering orchardman at the crossroads just beyond Merdine. The itinerant rustic was either a cunning tramp or a wise old man, depending on one's point of view. Leo Stumbras was of the latter opinion. The orchardman had stayed with them for a week or two every summer since Tomas was a baby, and he had not changed at all in that time. He wore the same brown hat and patched jacket and had the same knapsack on his back. In his hand he carried a heavy oak staff that he swung forward and struck on the ground on every third step, as if he were pulling himself along an endless ribbon of road. His white beard reached to his belt, and what could be seen of his face was covered in wrinkles. The twisted lump of his nose looked like a small, spoiled squash, and his eyes were grey-blue, washed out as only the eyes of old men could be.

He was one of the many merchant vagabonds who arrived at the doors of the farms: rag men who exchanged lumps of soap for worn clothing; tailors and cobblers who came to stay for a week as they did their work for the family; gypsies on their annual cycle of travel; tinkers and beggars who doubled as holy men to say prayers for the family. The orchardman made his living tending the fruit-bearing trees along his routes. His hands could work miracles, coaxing apple, cherry and mountain ash back to life even if they had not budded and blossomed in the spring. He knew how to make wine and spirits from the fruits of those trees. He knew bees so well they did not sting him. He could open a hive and plunge his hand inside without fear. He could read the future and past by the way the bees had stored their honey. If the comb was made in "tongues," it meant that someone in the neighbour-hood had been speaking ill of the owner, or the owner himself had sworn within the hearing of the bees. If the comb was made in longish "boxes," it meant that a coffin would soon be crossing the threshold of the house.

The old man was intensely religious, and upon entering a room he always bowed to the invisible gods in the four corners. He greeted everyone he met with "Glory to God in the highest." But he was not all mildness. If some boy did not answer him properly by saying, "And on earth, peace to men of goodwill," the child might receive a blow behind the ear from his wooden staff. Despite that danger, the children of the villages and farms loved the old man, as they loved all visitors who brought change to the dull, relentless rhythm of the country.

"Hail, young Stumbras!" said the orchardman. "Glory to God in the highest."

"And on earth, peace to men of goodwill."

"I am just on my way to your home. Have you been to town?"

"Buying vinegar for Mother. We've just caught forty pounds of fish."

"Oh, hail to this world, fresh from the rites of spring," said the old man. "God grant good summer cheer. You are an intelligent young man, Tomas Stumbras, but a strong body that works hard and long is the greatest gift from God. A simple peasant like you is superior to the rich men with paunches who toy with their food and complain of being ill all the time. Look at us, strong and healthy from sipping a little whey or buttermilk, and thanking God for any piece of sausage or bacon that comes our way! Oh, what a lucky man you are, young Tomas. Count your blessings.

Look up to the sun there, where it sits glittering in a cloudless sky. See how its hot flames dry up the flowers of spring and turn her garlands into feed for cows. Some of our plants already stand as wrinkled and bent as crones. Remember how recently the nightingale sang and the skylarks flew in pairs? The babies in the nests have grown and flown away to find their own food, making the world anew. Saint David says we are nothing more than grasses of the field. We blossom, and then we fade and turn to dust."

Tomas tried to tell the old man about the fire at the farm, but the old man listened little and talked much.

"Listen, young Stumbras, I have in my knapsack some magnificent seedlings, tucked carefully among the damp mosses. Apples, golden ones that I have cut for grafts from trees in the great houses. I have travelled all across the country this past year, and in that time I have seen manor houses emptied and the gentry fleeing. Some fear the Reds and others say the new government is no better. Who knows how much longer the orchards of the *grafs* will withstand fires? In some of those orchards I saw magnificent trees, many of them far older than me. And from each orchard I took a graft. We can't rely on the seeds, for the children of apples are no more predictable than the children of men and women.

"It is no good to shower too much love on children, just as it is no good to leave an apple tree to grow wild. Both need to be corrected. I have seen farmers who loved their trees so much they did not prune them, and then the branches grew tangled and the apples deformed and crowded. I have seen men permit mortally diseased trees to stand, when these need to be felled and their wood burned entirely to prevent the spread of scab and rot. Nature is a wonderful teacher, but many farmers are dullards, napping pupils, and even dunces whose actions bring on ruin."

The old man continued his sermon and he would have talked well past the lane to the Stumbras farm, had Tomas not touched his shoulder. He was so deep in his discourse on apples that he was almost at the site of the old house before he looked about him.

The remains of the log houses, outbuildings and barn had been pulled down and levelled, but the blackened fence posts and rails still stood, like a perimeter around a battlefield, although no battle had taken place. Tomas and the orchardman stood on a gentle rise of land as barren of buildings as if the devil himself had blasted them. The only structures were a series of lean-tos and crude tents and stacks of building materials.

The old man had stopped dead in amazement, so Tomas took him by the arm and led him up to the nearest lean-to. His mother and sisters were standing by a suspended pot that was boiling over an open fire. His father had triangulated three iron rods and tied them with a chain at the top. Into this pot went water and whatever food was at hand, usually barley or buckwheat for porridge, sometimes early potatoes and green onions in soup and, more recently, the fish that they had caught. The neighbours were generous, but some were afraid that the wars were far from over, and were husbanding their food carefully.

If the orchardman seemed stunned at the fate of the Stumbras farm, Tomas's mother was not much better. She stirred and stirred the pot, taking no notice of the old man.

"Did you bring the vinegar?" she asked her son.

"I did."

"I should drink it straight down. Then there would be one less mouth to feed. You'd be better off without me."

The old man fell to his knees in front of her.

"Glory to God in the highest," he said.

But Augustina did not respond. She looked down on the old orchardman, her face framed by the scarf she wore. One hand never ceased to turn the spoon in the pot, while the other constantly fingered the beads of a rosary.

"Didn't you have a Saint Florion statue in the house to protect you from the flames?" he asked on his knees.

"That traitor! He stood on the shelf looking down on the fire without even trying to perform a miracle. Our god-maker, Tomas here, had made him, for all the good it did us. Saint Florion burned up with the others."

They all turned at the sound of the wagon coming up the lane and the orchardman took the opportunity to raise himself and brush the soil off his knees. Leo Stumbras, with his sons, was bringing in another load of logs for the new house. While Edvard strode smartly alongside it with his axe on his shoulder and his sleeves rolled up, Leo sat slumped with his head turtled deeply into his shoulders.

"Glory to God in the highest!" the orchardman shouted to the men as the wagon pulled up, throwing himself on his knees again.

"And on earth, peace to men of good will!" said Edvard as he reached down for the orchardman and lifted him to his feet.

"You see what has come upon us," Leo said from his spot on the wagon. "We're buried in toil, and I'm afraid we'll have nothing for you. Stay for lunch, and then make your way to the next house. Come back to us next year."

"Wait, Father," said Edvard, and he turned to the orchardman. "Do you have seedlings?"

The old man nodded.

"Any grafts?"

The orchardman nodded again.

"Then stay with us for a while and help us plant the new orchard. What is one more plate, eh, Father? His experienced hands will bring God's blessing on the new trees."

Edvard had found God on the day of the fire, and it seemed to Tomas that the presence of God came with a certain amount of earnestness. Edvard happily shouldered the responsibility for rebuilding the farm, and doled out a monstrous load of work to his brothers, whom he exhorted to labour with the love of God in their hearts. He would have been unbearable to be around if they hadn't been so relieved that he wasn't melancholy any more.

Edvard was building a new world, one far better than the world of thatch they had left behind. He had to temper his enthusiasm before his parents, who had been diminished by the fire. His mother kept the rosary in her hand at all times, and thumbed the beads and muttered Hail Marys whenever she was not doing work that prevented her prayer. His father had started to shrink into old age. He told stories about his childhood, of olden days when men and women knew their place. He no longer bothered to wax his moustache tips, and after a time he found the soup-straining hairs around his mouth too much of a bother and shaved them off. To Leo and Augustina, no new buildings could make up for the loss of the old, no new fields make them forget the burning.

Edvard had determined that God wanted renewal, and so he was going to build a modern farm. Andrius wrote to Königsberg to get books on scientific farming. Science would increase crop yield. All their neighbours ever thought of were pigs for the table and an odd cow or two for milk, but Edvard had a good eye for the animals and the future did not lie there. The Prussians were fond of duck, so Edvard planned to make a much larger pond than the puddle they had had before, where he'd raise ducks by the hundreds. The new country that was being carved out of the ruined czarist empire would need sugar, so they would plant sugar beets. Even if there was no sugar refinery built nearby, there would always be a market for beets in East Prussia.

Edvard had taken to singing as the summer began to inch toward autumn. They were rebuilding; the foundation for the new house was ready, and the logs cut and stacked. There was already enough wood to build a granary and a rough barn for the animals. The hayfields had recovered, and by September there would be almost as much fodder as there would have been in June, though they had missed one harvest. The oats had been green, and so had not burned so badly despite all the best efforts of the Bermondt troops to destroy them. Against Leo's better judgment, Edvard had persuaded him to sign a loan from a new bank in Kaunas with interest at twenty-three percent so that they could buy materials for the rebuilding.

"The banks are worse than the Bermondt troops," Leo had said. "They'll own this place before the end of next summer."

"The trick is to borrow only a little," Edvard had argued, "and to pay it back as fast as possible."

In the weeks after the fire, they found a boar and a pregnant sow that had escaped the hungry marauding troops. They planned to slaughter the boar to feed the men who were coming to help them raise the new house, and to save the sow to replenish their pigsty.

Edvard threw his arm around the shoulders of the orchardman and began to take him around, starting at the foundation trench where the new house was going to stand.

"Look down there," said Edvard. "What do you see?"

"Stones," said the orchardman.

"How big?"

"Very big."

The orchardman, like a good guest, seemed to know when to seem impressed by the works of his host.

"That's right. We hauled them for miles. We're building a solid foundation here. No more sticks set in the mud. No more houses that sink over the years. This house is going to stand solid and strong and it will be up in a couple of weeks. We'll have painted wooden floors and a tile roof, too."

"Just give us back what we had," his mother said from the fire, wringing her hands as if talk of the future frightened her. "All of what you say is too much. Your pride will offend God."

"Your mother's right," said Leo. "You're expecting too much all at once. Nothing wrong with a thatched roof, or a wooden one if you have time to make the shingles. Nobody here has tile roofs."

"But they do in Prussia. Why should we be any worse than them?"

Edvard pointed out where the new outbuildings were going to stand. He was going to cover the logs with boards to make the house look civilized. Tomas would carve decorative fascia for the crossbeams of the roof, and the shutters would be ornamented as well.

"But how are you going to get all this done?" the orchardman asked. "Fall is near and winter will be on its heels."

"We have enough strong arms," said Edvard. "We'll lose Andrius in the autumn. He's going to teach high school in Šiauliai. But Paul can do some work, and Father is still strong. The women, too. We're counting on Tomas here as well. We'll broaden his shoulders and strengthen his back by the time winter comes around." Edvard slapped Tomas affectionately across the back. "We'll make a peasant out of you yet. Or a mule," he added with a laugh.

"I'm no mule. I'd rather go back to night school when it opens again."

"There will be time enough for school next year or the year after. What are a couple of years?"

Tomas planned to be gone long before that, but the knowledge gave him no pleasure. He turned and walked away.

"Don't be so sensitive!" Edvard called after him.

"I'm just going to look for more of my chisels," said Tomas. It was a poor excuse and they all knew it.

He went to the place where the old granary and workshop had stood and pulled out the pitchfork that was stuck into the blackened earth. The mystery of the chisels was ongoing. Only a few of them showed up after the fire, and Tomas sifted the ashes regularly to look for the others. The wooden handles had all burned away, but his files and rasps and gouges must still be there, some-where among the debris. But this time he found nothing after half an hour of sifting. It did not matter. Edvard gave him no time to carve, anyway.

Maria arrived at her mother's home, a hovel sunk so far into the ground that a trench had to be dug so the door could swing open. The thatch on the roof was covered with moss and the squared log walls were black with age. Her mother kept a gar-den and some apple trees, but there was barely enough grass for a cow. A goat was tethered to an iron ring set into one of the logs of the house. Maria scanned the yard for her mother or brother, and then called out their names when she opened the door. No one was home. She opened the cooking stove and blew on the embers to see if any were still alive. A few were. She heaped the live embers into a heavy iron skillet, and set it on the worn kitchen table.

She unfolded the package in her apron pocket and used the light of a low window to look at the contents, a palm full of amber fragments and dust. Some of the pieces were dark brown, like chips of wood, but others were a yellow so pale it was almost white. Maria lifted the amber to her nose and sniffed, but the smell was sealed inside.

She did not have much time, for her brother or mother might show up at any moment. She took a large pinch of amber and sprinkled it on a glowing ember. It caught fire and flamed up, and she quickly blew it out because she wanted only the smoke, the smell of ancient pine resin from the forests of the past. Maria inhaled deeply, held the smoke in her lungs as if she was starved for nicotine and then exhaled and did it again. She stayed still for a moment and tried to feel if the smoke was having any effect on her body. Her head swam a little, and she touched the tabletop with her fingers to steady herself.

Again and again, she sprinkled the amber dust on the embers and breathed in the smoke. When she had burned half of the dust, she took a towel and draped it over her head, the better to channel the smoke. After she had burned the whole packet, she sat back and waited. Though it was midday, it was dark inside the house. The windows were small and shaded by the overhang of the roof. When nothing seemed to happen, she added wood to the stove, chopped some onions and fried them in butter to cover the smell of pine resin. The odour of the onions was very strong and it made her eyes fill up with tears.

As the week passed, the house-building goods began to accumulate in stacks and mounds. Andrius took apart the wagon so it was only two sets of wheels upon axles. Andrius, Edvard and Tomas felled trees in the forest, lopped off the branches and tops and then set the logs upon the axles to make a wagon almost thirty feet long. Back at the farm, the logs needed to be squared on all sides because Edvard believed that only "barbarians" planed the logs on two sides. Day in and day out, in pairs, the men took turns pulling the long saw back and forth to cut boards to cover the squared logs and make the house look like the modern homes Edvard had read about in Andrius's books. One side of each board needed to be planed to make it smooth. Paint came in with a tradesman from Palemonas, a shade of deep green that had never been seen in the village or surrounding countryside. The glass merchant brought in ready-cut panes and the carpenter set up his workshop under a canvas roof in order to make the window frames. Edvard wanted the new home to be filled with as much light as a manor house. Boxes of nails from the blacksmith's lay under tarpaulins to keep them dry, and heaps of sand and flax chaff were secured against the wind so they could be poured between the ceiling and the roof for insulation.

Leo directed the brothers to dig up great heaps of clay from the riverside to fashion the oven. The clay needed to be washed clean of sand and grit, and then beaten and kneaded like dough. Augustina, Vida and Janina took willow branches and wove them into a dome inside the foundations of the new house. The elongated twig dome had a hole in the top at one end. Then Janina and Vida worked the wet clay into the willow branches and built it up to a thickness of almost three feet, closing off one end, but leaving the other open. The women made a flat place on top to rest food that needed to be kept warm during the day, and to provide a place to sleep on particularly cold winter nights. They had embedded a small iron cross deep within the clay for good luck, and to be doubly sure, had the priest sprinkle the bake-oven with holy water to prevent history from repeating itself. Leo kept a hot fire going inside the clay for three days, and by the time the fire cooled, the willow branches had all burned out and the clay of the new bake-oven was hard. Edvard was away for two days, and returned with a wagonload of blue ceramic tiles with which to cover the exterior, as well as new hinges and a bake-oven door with a copy of the holy image of the Virgin of the Dawn Gate cast in iron. The oven would span two rooms in the new house, the open end in the kitchen where the bread could be baked, and the other in the parents' bedroom to keep it warm.

Everything cost a great deal, and they mixed extravagance with parsimony, borrowing and calling in old debts for the building materials, but making do with poor food and clothing.

The plan called for doorways at either end of the house. One end would have six rooms for everyday use, and the other would have four more formal rooms, including a parlour big enough to hold forty guests, as Edvard intended to join the church committee and would need a room in which to entertain. He had wanted to make a two-storey house, but Leo drew the line. There was plenty of land, and if Edvard wanted a big house, he could extend it without going up a floor. Edvard did extend it, so much that Leo walked about muttering at the imprudence. The bake-oven could never heat such a monster, and they would need to buy two more expensive stoves and punch extra chimneys through the roof.

The clay roofing tiles arrived by wagon, and had to be handled with delicacy to keep them from breaking. No longer would the family need to worry about sparks from the chimney igniting thatch or wooden shingles. And although Leo was frightened by all the purchases and innovations, he was proud to have the wealthy landowners and townspeople coming to look at Edvard's building project.

The work was punishing, all the more so because of the great speed at which Edvard drove them. The fields and the animals needed to be tended as well, so there was no time for leisure beyond the smoking of a pipe after meals. Tomas barely had time to think of Maria, but he felt useful and content in the labour assigned to him. He worked first on the long fascia boards that would cross over one another at the peaks at each end of the house, creating tulip-leaf cut-outs with a small keyhole saw. The design was to be echoed in the shutters, decorative door frames, and verandah posts. He was finishing up the top curve of a fascia board when the orchardman came to watch him.

"You do good work, young Stumbras," he said.

"Each of us does what he can."

"But you devote yourself to woodcarving more than to other tasks. When you have to plow or dig or carry loads, you are the first to arrive at meals. But when you are doing this sort of work, you're the last."

"This kind of job is not really work to me. I can keep it up as long as there is enough light. I find it as satisfying as working on my gods."

"Will you make more when you have time again?"

"No. I'm through with gods."

He paused to wipe his forehead and to look up at the orchard-man. He expected the old man to be shocked, but he just tugged thoughtfully on his long white beard.

"Then what will you do?"

"I intend to go to art school in Vilnius once the fighting is over and the rebuilding is done here."

"I have been to many great houses in my time. I have seen private homes much bigger than most country churches, and these often have statues both outside and inside. As well as paintings so realistic that you want to shake the hand of the old *grafs* pictured in them."

"I would love to see what you've seen," said Tomas.

"I have been a student of nature, but I have been a student of men, too. Trees and men flourish best in certain environments. It is never easy to be uprooted, and no tree wants to have branches pruned and whole limbs cut off. But these are necessary measures."

Tomas did not know how to respond to the old man's words and went back to his work.

On the day of the house raising, half a dozen men came to build, their wives to cook and the children to watch the progress. The women congregated at the pot and the fire and set two tables with linen. The children ran about, ducking to stay out of the way of the men. The chief carpenter gave directions from his own table, but his real job would come when all the others had left and he stayed behind to put in the windows.

For that long day, even Augustina seemed less weighted with worries. She directed the women preparing food, encouraging girls to stir pots harder to prevent scorching and straightening tablecloths that had already been laid with great precision. The old orchardman had finished planting a scientific orchard for apples of seven types, both yellow and red, the different kinds suited to eating, cooking, preserving as fruit leather and fermenting into cider. He also laid out a gooseberry patch, sprouted plum and cherry pits and planted two pear saplings.

By early evening, the walls were set in place and the last of the rafters were tied together. Much still needed to be done, but the house stood ready for a proper roof, board siding, paint and windows. The women wove a wreath of oak leaves to raise up on the high point of the front rafters where the two fascia boards would cross, a custom that was said to bring good luck to the house. Edvard had climbed up to the crosspiece with Andrius, and the men and women below clapped as they nailed the wreath to the rafters. Then Edvard lowered a rope and his father tied a bottle of vodka to the end. He pulled up the bottle, and drank from it, then passed it to his brother. In a moment of foolishness that would have earned them their father's anger if the stunt had gone wrong, the brothers tossed the nearly full bottle of vodka down to the men below. Tomas caught it, and raised the bottle to the cheers of the others. He drank and passed it on. The brothers up on the roof rafters were about to come down to join the party below when Edvard spotted something on the road.

He looked hard, for the light was already beginning to fade and there was a moment of unease down below, as the Bermondt army had not been gone all that long and there was always a chance that some other army would show up to take its place. "It's two women!" he finally shouted down, and there was a collective sigh of relief. "And one of them is beating the other. Wait! They're coming up the lane."

The men and women below laughed, and turned to see. By then the first bottle of vodka was empty and they were passing a new bottle from one to another.

The two women were putting on a real show. An older woman pulled a younger one up the lane, all the while raining blows on her head. Tomas strained his neck to get a better view.

The young woman was Maria.

Her braids swung wildly around as she tried to escape her mother, and blood ran from her nose.

Her mother, Rima, dragged her into the yard and let go of her daughter. She was about to speak when Maria tried to run down the lane. Rima was fast for her years. She was upon her daughter in a second, hitting her across the head with a fist and knocking her to the ground. Then she turned to face the others, an old woman in a kerchief with her hands on her hips and her daughter lying at her feet.

"Leo Stumbras!" she called, and he stepped forward from among the others. "Look at the disgrace your family has brought on mine."

"What is it?"

"The poor young girl is pregnant, and the father is your son."

Edvard and Andrius looked at each other with incredulity, and then turned to Tomas, who would not meet their gaze.

"Which one do you claim is the father?" Leo roared.

"Tomas."

Leo looked at his son and knew the truth in a moment. Tomas was no good at hiding his thoughts. Leo Stumbras would have knocked his foolish son to the ground had it not been for the audience. Nevertheless, he needed to defend his family.

"You have no proof of that," he said. "She was throwing herself on all the men in the neighbourhood. Your daughter is no better than a *kurva*. Anyone could be the father."

"Are you saying your son did not sleep with her?"

"Maybe he did, but if so, he wasn't the only one." The men in the crowd laughed, but their women shushed them.

"My daughter came to work at your house and I understood she was in your care," Rima insisted. "Anything she learned about life, she learned here, for she was just a young girl when she came to this place. She told me she loved you like a father, and this is what you say. You should be ashamed of yourself."

He was, but the woman gave him no choice. "Come into the house and speak to me in private. You bring the girl and I'll bring the boy." He turned to the neighbours assembled in the yard. "The rest of you eat and drink. This is a small problem. We'll take care of it."

The others reluctantly moved away to the tables, since it would have been foolish of them not to eat the potatoes and pork that had been made for them, and not to drink the vodka. But those among them who knew how to play musical instruments did not rosin up their bows or open the cases of their accordions. To eat and drink in the face of a family's trial was one thing, but to draw music out of catgut under such conditions would have been insensitive.

The roofless house smelled strongly of sawn wood, and the floorboards and walls were pale yellow in the last light of day. Through the holes cut in the walls, they could see the fields around them and their neighbours sitting down to their meal. Stumbras did not even glance at Tomas, and he looked Maria up and down as if she were a horse he had been sold through deceit.

"Wipe the blood off your face," he said, and Maria spat on the edge of her apron and wiped away some of the stain around her mouth. Stumbras turned to Rima, who looked him in the eye and tried to keep the smirk of victory off her face.

"We have suffered many great calamities," Leo said. It was not clear to whom he was speaking, for he did not want to honour the mother by speaking to her directly, not until he had to. "And now you have brought another one on us. No good can come of this. Old woman, what do you want? Money?"

She raised the index finger of her right hand to underline her words.

"What kind of a question is that? What I want is for my daughter to be respectable, but it's too late for that, thanks to your son. What's done is done and there's no going back. Your boy disgraced her and almost made her a double sinner. She was trying to cast off the baby. What if she had succeeded? She would have gone to hell. What I want is simple. I want them to marry."

"You're sure she's pregnant?"

"Yes."

Stumbras turned the full weight of his gaze upon his son. "Tomas, is the child yours?"

"I think so."

"You're not sure?"

Tomas could see that his father was giving him a chance to deny it all. This was his opportunity to escape. He looked down at the new wooden floor.

"I am sure. I'm sorry."

His father nodded and thought for a moment before he spoke.

"You haven't even begun to be sorry yet. You'll have your whole life to be sorry. And Maria, as for you, you should be ashamed of yourself. You're two years older than my son. A woman's duty is to defend herself from young men. Did you think you would get a piece of this land? Never. Both of you will work for Edvard until your dying days. You'll eat heels of bread the others have left—the oldest potatoes and sheep's heads will be put aside especially for you. The parishioners will laugh at you behind your backs. You will have no money to send your children to school. This is what you have brought upon yourselves.

"As for you, old mother, take your daughter home. She'll get herself a husband, but she will live to regret it. I've seen marriages of this kind. The husband comes to hate the wife for the misery of their life and the squeal of his brats becomes unbearable to him. No matter. What's done is done. Now both of you women go out the other door and return to your home. I have guests. Tomas, don't show your face among them. And don't show it to me, either. The less I see of you tonight the better."

Leo stepped out onto the dark yard where the others were still eating.

"What is this, a funeral?" he shouted. "Edvard, light a bonfire. Gaidys! Are you so busy filling your stomach you can't play us a little tune? Augustina, pass me a glass of vodka and pour another for Gaidys to stir him to his duty. I want to hear music and singing. I want to see people dancing."

Rima beckoned to Tomas as she made her way toward the back door.

"Come walk your wife-to-be home, young man."

Tomas did not know what else to do. Out front, the family he had so recently belonged to was having a party. He could smell the food and hear the music starting up. But here he was, slinking out the back door with a poor woman and her daughter. He could barely absorb what had happened, and Rima gave him little time to do so. As they walked down the lane, an accordion joined the violin playing behind them, and two men began to sing.

When they reached the bottom of the lane, Rima said, "We're going to be related."

Tomas looked at Maria, who still had dried blood smeared on her face.

"My dear," said Rima, "it's not pleasant for a future mother-in-law to look at such a grimace as yours. Am I so much beneath you? You should be grateful to me. My son, Feliks, intended to come here and beat you when he found out. But I stopped him. I told him I would try to deal with things my way first, and now you see how well everything has turned out. You must have wanted Maria very badly to sleep with her, and now you can have her all you want."

They walked down the hill in the fading light of evening. Maria would not look at Tomas, and he was grateful she did not. He was very sorry for her, but not as sorry as he was for himself. No moon shone, but the sky was already filling with pinpoints of stars. They cast barely enough light for them to find their way along the ghostly road. Either the nightingale was gone for the season, or it knew to keep its peace. Behind them the fiddle and the accordion played gaily and the bonfire cast a tongue of flame and glowing cinders into the sky.

"Children never know how to arrange their own affairs," said Rima. "That's what parents are for. Your father squirmed there for a few minutes, but he's a fish on a hook and this barb is buried deep. Don't worry about him. When you have a brat to show him, his heart will melt and then we'll see if he can't be persuaded to become a little more generous."

The sky deepened to a rich purple in the west. Directly above them it was already black, except for the stars. Comets streaked across the sky that night, as if the heavens were giving a show of fireworks.

"I want to talk with Tomas," Maria said, her voice trembling but determined.

"So talk. I'm not stopping you."

"Mother, I need to talk to him alone."

"Ah well, an old woman is used to being thrown aside. I'll walk ahead, but not too far. There might be thieves on this road, and they could kill me in the wink of an eye."

Maria waited until her mother was out of earshot. Tomas thought he heard something behind them, but saw nothing when he looked. Slowly, they began to walk forward.

"Do you hate me?" Maria finally asked.

"I hate what's happened," said Tomas. They walked without touching. "Why didn't you tell me about the baby? I haven't seen you in weeks."

"I tried to once, when we met on this road."

"What stopped you?"

"I thought I could do something about it, but it didn't work."

"Do something?"

"There are ways of casting off a baby before it's a baby. I tried them all."

"How did your mother find out?"

"I tried one last remedy. Yew branches steeped in hot water. They made me sick, but the baby clung fast. I was too ill to remember to throw out the branches, and she found them."

"You did all those things without telling me?"

"Yes," she said. "What are we going to do now?" Her voice broke at the last word. "I can't imagine you staying here or giving up your carving."

Tomas took her hand. "We'll still have to go away," he said.

"Where will we go?"

"Maybe to Kaunas and then on to Vilnius when the fighting stops. I have an uncle in Kaunas who might help us. Maybe there is an art school in Kaunas, or someone I could apprentice myself to."

"It will be very hard without family to help us when the baby comes."

"Maybe you should stay behind while I go to Kaunas to find us a place to live. You would have your mother to look after you," he said. He waited. "Did you hear what I said?"

"Yes."

"What do you think?"

"I don't think I would trouble you in Kaunas. I think I would rather be with you than wait for you here."

"And I'd rather have you, too. But if I went ahead and found a job first, and a place to live, you and the baby would be more comfortable when you joined me. If I worked there for a while, I could send you money for a good midwife or even a nurse."

"But I would be alone."

"Your mother will be at your side."

"I want nothing more to do with her," Maria said, and then added, "what if I lost the baby? If the baby was gone, would you still take me away?"

"If it wasn't for the baby, I'd take you away with me this minute. But what chance is there of that?"

"I could try other remedies. But if I lost the baby now that everyone knows, I'd be ruined. Either way, we have to go away together."

"The joke would be on our parents, then, wouldn't it? My father and your mother wouldn't hold us in their clutches any more. We'd be free."

They heard a sound on the road behind them.

"Who's there?" Tomas called out.

"Just me, just me," an old man's voice said, and eventually the orchardman loomed out of the darkness.

"Have you been following us?" Tomas grabbed the old man by the shirt.

"I have," he answered, unperturbed.

"And have you been listening to what we said?"

"I have heard some things."

"What business did you have eavesdropping on us?" Maria asked.

The orchardman sighed, and he did not answer for a moment. He disengaged Tomas's hand from his shirt. When he finally spoke, his voice was soft. "Maybe we should keep moving so your mother does not come back."

The old man began to walk and the two followed. The air was warm and free of insects because it was so late in the season. But something, a slight ripening in the vegetation, or distant cold winds, changed the quality of the air a little and made the autumn feel very close.

"Nature is not as kind and gentle as many people like to think," the old man said. "Tell me, young Stumbras, what is the most aggressive bird of them all?"

"I have no patience right now for a nature lesson."

"It's a lesson with a point."

"The most aggressive bird is the crow," Tomas said abruptly.

"Yes. And also the most intelligent. Crows have been eating farmers' grain since it was first planted, and gobbling up barnyard chicks right in front of the henhouse. Crows are very hard to catch and very hard to kill. But have you ever been sent to climb trees to take their eggs?"

"Yes. When I was small, the neighbours paid me to throw crow eggs down from the nests so the birds would go away."

"And did the crows attack you?"

"No. They would land nearby and cry out and flap their wings, but they never attacked me."

"Yes. This is a sign of the bird's intelligence. It understands that it can always lay more eggs."

"What's your point?"

"To throw off a child is not a crime, especially not for those as young as you."

"But I've tried everything," said Maria.

"Not everything."

"Do you know another remedy?"

"It depends. Is the baby quick?"

"I haven't felt it move yet."

"And how long have you been pregnant?"

"I'm not sure. Three months, perhaps four."

"Maybe more?"

"Not much."

"So the problem is this. You have tried various remedies, but they were only good for the first month or two. Now you have a bigger problem, so you need stronger medicine."

"You have such a remedy?"

"I do. But you must be sure you want to go through with this. There is always some risk when one applies strong medicine. So Maria, answer me this, are you willing to take a risk in order to free yourself of this unmade child?"

"I am if Tomas promises to take me away from here."

"How much of a risk?" asked Tomas.

"Very great," said the orchardman.

"What should we do?" Maria asked.

Tomas thought hard. There was no question of staying where they were. They needed to get away. But if Maria gave birth, the child would hamper them in their new lives.

"Lose the child," said Tomas.

"And you promise you'll take me with you? You won't leave me behind?"

"We'll live in a new world. We'll get out of here. Kaunas, Vilnius, what does it matter where? Why stop there? Paris, or Canada."

Maria threw her arms around him. "Maybe America?" She asked.

"Why not? Maybe America."

"Young man, say your farewells and go back to your home. Maria and I will confer on this business."

"God bless you," said Maria.

"Let's not mention God's name," said the orchardman. "I am a religious man, but I believe God knows when to look away from time to time. Now say goodbye to each other." The orchardman turned away.

Maria came into Tomas's arms.

"I'm afraid," she said.

"You don't have to go through with it if you don't want to."

"But our lives will be better without a baby just now. Isn't that right?"

"Yes."

"And we'll get married the first chance we have?"

"At the first place where no one will ask after us. In Kaunas, or some other town along the way."

They kissed, and Tomas could feel her trembling. Or perhaps it was his own body shaking. When she pulled back from him, she put her hand on his lips so he would not speak, and then she turned and walked purposefully away with the orchardman.

No moon had risen, but perhaps Tomas's eyes had grown more accustomed to the night. Whatever the reason, he noticed for the first time that the orchardman was wearing his pack and carrying his walking stick, as if he was already on his way in his travels. But for all the improvement in his night vision, Tomas could not follow them forever, and eventually they disappeared into the darkness on the road.

Tomas kept his distance from the party back at the farm until the neighbours went home and his family went to sleep. Then he crept back to his place under the canvas lean-to. All night long, he flickered between hope and despair, and when he could no longer lie still, he got up and began to put aside a few things in case Maria was successful and sent word to him that they needed to fly. He rummaged in the dark to find an extra set of clothing. He located some of his carving tools, but was unable to put his hands on any coins—his father kept them by his bed. He searched among the food stores and took a half loaf of bread, some meat and cooked potatoes and then put everything in a pillow case. He walked all the way down to the trees by the river, and tied the bag on a branch, where it would not be visible from the road. By then he was very tired in spite of his nervousness, and he settled into his temporary bed in the lean-to for an uneasy hour's sleep.

He awoke under the outstretched canvas of his field bed when the sun began to warm his face. No one was stirring, even though it was well past dawn. City people thought farmers rose early through habit or duty, but flies were the real reason. All night long they fasted, but now they were beginning to bite. To sleep past dawn was a rare thing for a farmer's son, especially in the summer when there was so much to do. Tomas stretched out, still tired, and waved away the flies.

A man began shouting in front of the new house.

"Where is Tomas Stumbras? I must speak with him!"

Tomas came out from his lean-to and his brothers appeared from their sleeping places.

It was Feliks, Maria's brother. He was big and very wide across the shoulders.

"What is it?" Edvard asked.

"Maria is dying," Feliks said.

"What? Is she ill?" Edvard asked.

"She is dying of her own hand." Feliks looked at Tomas. "Mother had everything arranged for her. You did agree to marry her, didn't you?"

Tomas felt a pang of guilt but knew he must mask it. "Yes."

"Did you say anything to her last night, anything that would have made her despair?"

"Nothing," said Tomas. "We were going to be married."

"She took a bottle of concentrated vinegar and drank it some-time early this morning."

"That can kill her?" Edvard asked.

"It burns your guts, but you survive as long as you stay awake. My mother is trying to keep her awake to save her from dying. You must come with me."

Tomas followed him down the lane.

The August rye was heavy in the fields they passed, the ears bent over and waiting for harvest. Tomas wanted to ask Feliks questions to understand better what had happened, but Feliks was forbidding and silent, and Tomas was left to his own thoughts as they walked quickly along the road.

When they got there, two small girls were playing outside in the yard, likely children of the midwife inside. Tomas was afraid to go in, but Feliks bent to avoid the low lintel, and led the way in. The whole place smelled astringent, of vomit, vinegar and blood. Maria was moaning on the bed, and her mother knelt beside her with a bowl in her hands.

"I made her drink water and then vomit, but she doesn't take any-thing in her mouth any more. I'm not sure she recognizes me. Tomas, for the love of God, look into her eyes. Make her drink more water."

Blood and vinegar covered the bedclothes. Maria's face was white, her eyes wide and terrified. There was a web of bloody lines on her throat where she'd torn at the painful burning.

Tomas leaned in close. "Maria, listen to me. You need to drink water. Water will save you."

He saw no sign of recognition. She tried to tear at her throat again, but he held her wrists. Her head lolled and her eyes turned and she let out a miserable groan.

She could not be dying. All spring long, when he had held her, he'd felt alive for the first time himself. She was the one who awakened his need to get away, and how could he do so without her? He did not like to think of the words they had exchanged at the end. Only the orchardman knew what they had said, and now he was gone. He had done his job of pruning, but cut off a little more than he had promised.

"Mary, Mother of God, have mercy on us," her mother cried.

"If you hold her, I'll try to pour water down her throat," Feliks said.

But all they succeeded in doing was wetting the bed. She would take nothing down her throat, could take nothing. She gagged at the water, and vomited blood and vinegar.

Tomas was barely aware of movement on the other side of the room. There were women there, the midwife and two other village crones who had come with their knowledge of medicines and cures. They had no cure for Maria.

"Why isn't the priest here?" Tomas asked Maria's mother.

"We were afraid to call him. He won't come for a suicide."

"She needs a priest. I'm going to go to him," Tomas said, rising.

"He will smell the vinegar as soon as he comes in and know it was a suicide. Besides, you might not be back in time for her death if you go away now," the midwife whispered.

"It's not a suicide. She was trying to find a remedy."

"Then he certainly won't come. That makes her a murderer.

Besides, any midwife knows what concentrated vinegar does. It kills the baby, all right, and it usually kills the mother, too."

No one sent for the priest. Tomas walked about the room whenever Maria fell still and went back to her whenever she began to thrash about. After a time, they stopped trying to force water down her throat. Feliks went out to smoke, and then came back again.

Maria was getting quieter. Tomas thought that perhaps her condition was something like a fever. Maybe the crisis had passed.

"She's falling asleep," the midwife said abruptly. "You must keep her awake if you want her to live."

Tomas shook her and Maria opened her eyes for a moment. He looked into her eyes, demanding that she recognize him.

"Maria, do this for me. I love you. Stay alive for my sake," he said. But as if on a signal, as if his assurance of love had doomed her, she closed her eyes again.

After that, they could not wake her. She lay still for six hours, and early in the evening, she died. The women began their keening, and her mother collapsed into tears on the floor.

Tomas stumbled outside through the low door into the mean yard full of trampled cigarette butts. The sun was still bright, and it hurt his eyes. He could not stay here.

When he was a hundred yards from the house, Feliks came out to roar at him from the doorway.

"I'll kill you for this!" he shouted. Then he shouted it again, but he did not follow Tomas.

On the way home, Paul appeared and walked by his side. The boy had grown quickly lately, and would soon be as tall as Tomas.

"I'm very sorry for Maria," he said.

"The orchardman is going to be sorry, too." Tomas explained what had happened.

"I don't think you should blame him," Paul replied.

"But he told her to drink the vinegar."

"Maybe he did, but he didn't make her drink it. She did that herself. Anyway, you need to talk to Edvard and Andrius. They are going to meet you on the road."

"What for?"

"I don't know. They just told me to get you."

The road on the far side of the river from the Stumbras farm ran through a copse. Andrius and Edvard were there, sitting at the roadside, waiting for him.

"Well?" Andrius asked when Tomas and Paul came near.

"She's dead."

He nodded. Edvard stood with his arms crossed across his chest. "God rest her soul," he said.

"I'm sorry, Tomas, but there was never much chance she would live," said Andrius. "The peasants think people who swallow vinegar die if they fall asleep, but that's not what happens. The acetic acid throws them into a coma. There was nothing you could do."

"I was going to marry her."

Andrius nodded at this, but not convincingly.

"Andrius and I have been considering what to do with you," Edvard said.

"Do?"

"You can't go home. Father's talking to the priest, trying to buy a mass for Maria, but the priest is stern about suicides. The whole neighbourhood will be talking, and Father is furious. To say nothing of Feliks. It's better to go away for a while. You could go to Uncle Petras's down south in Seinai, by the Polish border."

"But for how long?"

"Maybe a year or two. Maybe longer. I copied down the address for Father's other brother, Nikodemus, in Canada. When we were boys, and you were hardly out of swaddling, he used to send us dollars sometimes."

"The family won't be able to send you to school," said Edvard finally. "And let's face it, no matter how hard I drive you, you'll never be any good as a farmer." He smiled. "There'll be no life for you around here now. I brought your bag along with some of your tools."

"And I have a purse with some money for you," said Andrius. "How much?"

"Twenty silver rubles. That will get you some distance, even if it's not across the Atlantic."

He looked at his brothers. In fairy tales, the older brothers were always trying to cheat the younger out of his birthright. But Tomas had no birthright. Maria was dead. He could mourn for her all he wanted, but that would not change anything.

"Maybe this is your chance," said Paul. "Maybe this is what you've been waiting for." Tomas stared at him hard, but the boy did not look away.

AUGUSTAV FOREST
POLAND, 1921

TOMAS STEPPED GINGERLY ONTO THE BED OF MOSS BEFORE him, feeling for solid ground. He had already sunk up to his knees in puddles of rank swamp water that moments before had looked firm enough to hold him. This forest was full of giant oaks, both standing and fallen, and small clumps of pale birches, thin ghosts in the twilight. Moss hung from the trees and grew on the forest floor, and streams coursed in hidden paths under cover of grass and lichen. The forest paths were misleading, especially at night. In the past, locals had built underwater bridges, *kulgrindos*— secret passages through the rivers and swamps. A knowledgeable man might wade across the shallows while an interloper would fall into the mud and sink to his death under the weight of his military kit. But those who had built the bridges were long since dead and the pathways forgotten. Tomas took every footstep with care.

The leaves began to rustle as the nocturnal animals stirred, but Tomas told himself he had nothing to fear. His ancestors had hidden in forests like these, carving out free lives away from the dictates of czar and *dvar*, far from the estates of the gentry where a man's life was worth less than a beast's. Tomas would have been wise to set up a camp for the night while he could still see, but he had found no place dry enough.

Suddenly his footing gave way and he pitched forward into a deep pool. The stink of the standing water rose up to meet his nostrils, and then he was under water from toe to crown. He resurfaced with difficulty because of the pack on his back, and dragged himself to solid land through the muck of the pool, pulling himself forward by gripping the roots of trees along the bank. When he was out, gasping and wiping the scum from his face, he felt inside his breast pocket. Damn. The oilskin had come unwrapped and his matches were wet. There would be no fire tonight.

Over the past two years, his shoulders had broadened through farm work with his uncle Petras. His face had lost its childishness and a few premature worry lines showed around his eyes. No one would call him a boy any longer. At his uncle's farm, he had had to work as hard as back at his father's place, but his uncle was a kind man and Tomas felt a little freer. He kept hoping to get to Vilnius, but the way was always blocked. Poles and Reds and Lithuanians all fought one another in the south. When the latest fighting had ended, Petras's farm found itself just inside the Lithuanian border. Tomas stayed there longer than he had planned, right through the harvest of 1921, and Petras would have kept him longer if he had wanted.

His uncle was a lover of books, a country intellectual who encouraged Tomas to school himself. During the days, physical labour kept Tomas's mind blessedly empty. And in the evenings, he enjoyed the concentration study required of him. But sometimes when he sat down with a book on his lap, thoughts of home prevented him from seeing the words on the page. He had never been happy in the house where he grew up, but he had been comfortable, with the easy familiarity of his brothers and whatever warmth his mother could spare for him. He did not miss his father, but he longed for Maria.

Sometimes, in spite of the proximity of his uncle, he would feel his throat clench and his eyes begin to fill at the thought of her. Once his uncle sensed that something was wrong, and he leaned forward to tap Tomas on the knee with his pipe, the warmest gesture the bookish farmer knew. Tomas could not bear the kindness. It opened the floodgates, and he put down his book to flee outside.

Night after night, he sat with Petras's books and immersed himself in words, which opened up the world to him. As the months passed, he began to consider the choices in front of him. There was no question of going back to his harsh father, the disapproving parish and the threat of Feliks looming up somewhere along a dusty road. Tomas was going to go to art school, as he had planned, even if Vilnius was in Poland now. But why draw the limit there? If he was going to go to art school and be a sculptor, he might try Krakow, or even Paris itself, if he dared. He was good at languages, and already spoke Polish and Russian freely. At his uncle's he began to study other languages, especially French and English, which seemed exotic to him.

As time passed, he thought often of Maria, but slowly the pain eased. She would have wanted him to do the best he could with his talent. Tomas began to see her death as only the last in a series of unlucky events that had dogged him as long as he stayed in Lithuania. When he reflected upon his part in the death of the *graf*, which foreordained the burning of the farm, and even his role in the death of his grandmother, he saw that he had been locked into a cycle of events that he could not control. But no more. Tomas decided to seize fate rather than be a victim of it.

Since Poland was technically still at war with Lithuania he needed to cross the porous border at an obscure place and hope he made it past the lines of the border police. Uncle Petras paid him his modest wages, and supplied him with a couple of hard cheeses and a loaf of black bread, as heavy as a headstone and not much smaller, to fill his knapsack. It was tough, heavy bread, and Tomas was lucky that the weight of it had not drowned him when he fell into the pool.

He took off his clothes and wrung them out. He had no others, so he put them back on. The nights were getting cool in September, but not cool enough to kill off the mosquitoes, which seemed as big as bees.

Tomas took out his knife and hacked off a piece of the dark bread. It had not softened at all from its immersion in the stagnant pool. He broke off a piece of the equally hard cheese, and chewed slowly until the bread and cheese softened enough in his mouth that he could swallow them. He had no desire to drink from the pool that he had fallen into. An owl began to hoot and the mosquitoes tormented him mercilessly, especially eager for the bare spots behind his ears and at his ankles. As soon as he finished eating, he would cover himself in his damp blanket and sleep until dawn. Then he would head west, toward Krakow, a dream much bigger than Vilnius.

After he wrapped himself in the blanket, covering himself as best he could against the mosquitoes, he became more aware of the night sounds of the forest. Small creatures made a great deal of noise among the leaves and branches, and bigger ones might follow. No one had seen bears for a long time, but if there were any at all, they had to be here. A pack of wolves might find him where he lay in his blanket like a sausage in a roll. A bison might crush him under its hooves. He tried to laugh off these thoughts, but the forest at night did not promote levity. He dozed for a few minutes, and then jerked awake when a particularly vicious mosquito bit his exposed wrist.

Tomas swore. As he settled down to sleep again, he thought he heard singing. He listened carefully. Bullfrogs croaking at night sometimes sounded like drunkards singing, but this noise was not that of bullfrogs. These were the voices of men.

He sat up. Did ghosts sing? Armies had been dying in this forest for centuries. A curious man with a spade could dig up the brass buttons of Napoleonic, German, Polish, Lithuanian, czarist and Red army uniforms. Did the ancient corpses sit up at night and sing together, comrades in death? Or were these new green men, living in the forest, new wild creatures who had given up civilization? Though he was frightened, curiosity gained the upper hand. Tomas packed his blanket into the knapsack. He was still damp from his immersion, and he was cold in the night mists.

He had to move forward carefully, slowly, to avoid the pools and to preserve the quiet. He felt his way through brambles that scratched at his hands and face, and exposed roots that were hard and uncomfortable beneath him. At times the singing would stop, and he stopped, too, in order to listen. The direction of the sound seemed to be so clear, but several times he turned in the dark, and soon he had no idea where he had begun from, and only a hazy idea of where he was headed. He reasoned that since he had been lost in the first place, he could not be any worse off.

As he drew nearer, he actually recognized one of the tunes, "Two Brothers," though the words were not in Lithuanian but Polish. These were the voices of the enemy, unless they really were ghosts, in which case they were the ghosts of the dead Poles. Did ghosts care about the nationality of the living? What identity papers did one show to the dead? Eventually he could see a glow coming from deep among the trees. He should have taken off his knapsack to be more quiet, but all he owned was in the bag and he did not want to lose it in the dark. On elbows and knees, he crept forward like a soldier crawling under barbed wire, until he could see into the arbour where the singing was coming from.

A great fire roared at one end of a clearing, and in front of it a spit had been set up. Two men were turning the headless carcass of a stag. The stag's head had been tied to a tree nearby, and it left a trail of blood on the tree trunk below it. Long wooden tables were set some distance from the fire, and at these tables sat about twenty men in military coats, some with pistols in front of them.

Rifles were stacked nearby, and bags of gear lay all about. Some men sat on stumps or upended logs. At one end of a table a man was playing a harmonium, and the others laughed and talked or sang along with the music, drinking foaming beer from pitchers, bowls and glasses, or drinking directly from bottles of vodka. Only one man sat in a proper chair, a great, carved chair with a high back. He had a heavy, square face, and a thick, black moustache that hung low over his lips. His eyebrows were thick, too, and his forehead high and imposing. His slightly receding black hair was combed up and back to exaggerate the effect. He wore a military greatcoat against the cool of the night mists, and a cigarette burned between the fingers of his right hand. Sometimes he sang a few words with the other men, but mostly he just watched them. On a small table by his chair stood a horn cup with foamy beer poured right to the lip, but the man did not drink. He stayed as sober as his sentries.

Tomas had eaten only bread and cheese for two days, and the smell of meat undid him. As well, the arbour looked like a merry place, like a country wedding. His desire for the camaraderie of the fireside drew him forward, and the pack on his back snapped a low-hanging dry branch. If he thought the music and the drunkenness would protect him, he was mistaken. These were soldiers, who always kept a portion of their brains ready to respond to ambush. They were on him in a moment, their merriment gone. With the rough hands they grasped him under the arms and dragged him forward, giving him a couple of sharp cuffs in case he was thinking of doing anything unwise.

"Bring him over here," the man in the wooden throne said. He did not shout. The men followed his orders swiftly, efficiently, like palace guards who understood upon whose good graces their careers depended.

"Empty out the knapsack and see if he has any weapons." They tipped over the sack and out came the bread and the cheese,

Tomas's carving tools and a spare pair of soft country leather shoes. "Now search his pockets." All they found were a few coins and a homemade pocket knife.

"Where are you from?" the moustachioed man asked him in Polish.

"A farm near Merdine."

"That's a long way. What are you doing here, slinking through the forest at night?"

"I'm seeking my fortune."

All the men laughed.

"He's a spy, Marshal, or an assassin. I'll have him buried before supper."

The moustachioed man laughed. "Maybe, but I've never seen an assassin carrying around so much good country bread." The marshal bent down and tried to break off a piece. Two of his men reached quickly for the massive loaf, and one cut a thick slice with his bayonet. The marshal sniffed the bread first, and then bit off a corner of it and chewed thoughtfully.

"There's nothing like Lithuanian bread, men. It's half the reason why I wanted Lithuania in the union. I can see you are ready to argue. Like good Polish nationalists, you all think that our own bread is as good or better. But I tell you, there is something about Lithuanian bread, the smell of old glory, maybe. The Lithuanians want no part of our union. So much the worse for them. But I miss their bread terribly."

Some of the soldiers nodded, but a couple of the older ones turned away, bored. Clearly this was a favourite theme of the marshal's.

"We taught your Lithuanian army a little lesson in this forest," explained the man, "one that they'll soon not forget. What do you think of that?"

"I don't know anything about it. It's not my concern."

The marshal studied him.

"What exactly is this fortune you seek?" he asked.

"I want to be a sculptor."

The soldiers laughed again. The marshal shushed them, although he smiled as well.

"Why not? Who's to say what will become of this young man? Years ago I had to hide in this very forest while my only trousers were being washed. This is a good place to retreat in order to gather up strength to try again, to lick wounds. I came back out of this forest myself once upon a time, and since then glory has come to me. Maybe glory will come to him, too."

"I still say he's a spy," said one of the marshal's men. "It would be more prudent to kill him."

"Maybe. What's your name, young man?"

"Tomas Stumbras."

"Stumbras? Did you make that up?"

"Why would I? It's my name."

"Can you prove it?"

"My name is carved into the handle of my pocket knife."

The marshal had one of his men check what Tomas had said. He looked at it carefully, and then looked back at Tomas.

"You must be a sign. Either that, or fate is dealing me a curious hand. I'm not just here to play at being the gentry, going into the forest for a little hunting. I am here with a purpose. I am looking for the wood bison, *żubr* in Polish, *stumbras* in Lithuanian. I want to see if there are any left after the war. *You* are the *żubr*, so I suppose I was meant to find you. But how can I be sure?" The marshal held his chin in his hand and looked carefully at Tomas. "You claim to be a sculptor?"

"Yes."

The man lit a fresh cigarette off the end of the first one and threw away the butt. One of the soldiers reflexively crushed it with his boot. "Here is our agreement, young man. We'll feed you some meat and give you a glass of beer, and you'll carve me a *žubr* tonight, a wood bison. If you're any good, we'll see what to do with you. If you're a liar, we'll shoot you."

He clapped Tomas on the shoulder as if he had made a very good joke and his men cheered.

They sat him near the fire, close enough that he was warm in his wet clothes. Steam started to rise off his jacket and trousers. A soldier about his age sat on the earth nearby, drinking and singing with the others, but keeping an eye on Tomas.

A wood bison. How hard could that be? He had never seen one, but he'd seen pictures enough when he had been in school. He took his tools and began to tap to test the soundness of the block of wood that a soldier tossed to him. The thing was to get the strength of the creature, the massiveness of it, a ton of flesh that could be thrown behind the points of the two horns. Tomas turned the block of wood around and around in his hands until he could see how the force could best come out, the grain of the wood along the length of the body and a slight curve from a branch that could be fashioned into the shoulders.

The light was bad, and he had to move as close as he could to the fire, until it was so hot that he broke out in a sweat and popping cinders went zinging past his face. But he knew what to do. An hour later, the creature was taking form, the bison beginning to paw its way out of the wood. Someone set down a glass of beer near him, and he drank from that. He stopped for a bit when he was handed a hunk of stag's shoulder on a wooden plate along with a piece of his own hard bread. He ate because he was hungry and the meat smelled good, but he was interested in the work now. He barely noticed as one by one the men put their heads on the table and fell into drunken sleep, and only the sentries pinched themselves and slapped their own faces to keep awake.

He had decided, at the end, to give the creature curls around the horns, as if it were wearing a golden fleece like the one he had read about in one of Uncle Petras's books. He began to carve fine, swirling lines into the mass of wood. It was late, just before dawn, when he felt a presence beside him.

"Have you sent your bison to the hairdresser's?"

The marshal was standing over him, peering down at the work. He had a bottle of liquor in his hand.

"I wanted to cut in some curling hair to make it look Greek," said Tomas.

"What business do you have doing that? The *żubr* is a northern creature. Simple and rough, but powerful and stubborn. Here, taste this."

He pushed the bottle in front of Tomas, who knew the drink by the spear of grass in the bottle. He drank a mouthful of the fragrant stuff, swallowed and coughed as it burned his throat. The marshal laughed.

"That's the taste of the wild, bison grass in the vodka, *hierochloë odorata*. That grass only grows where a bison has chosen to shit. The country is covered with patches of the grass, but where are the bison? Gone. They say the Germans shot them all with machine guns when they had nothing else to eat. The fools. Now tell me about that taste. What's the vodka taste of?"

"Not shit."

"No, they wouldn't use it if it did. It tastes of the earth, my young friend. It tastes of the muck and the swamps and the peat bogs of this nation, the mists out of which we come. I came into this forest looking for wood bison and instead I find you, Stumbras, my *żubr*. Tell me what you're a sign of."

"I'm not a sign of anything. I'm just a sculptor on his way to Krakow, or maybe Paris."

"Bah, Paris. You won't find anything there. Stay in Poland. You have a propitious name. What business does a Stumbras have going to Paris, eh? A bison in a china shop. You'll go extinct there, believe me. I know Paris."

"You've been there?"

"Of course. Nothing to see. Dandies drinking coffee and cognac on the Champs-Élysées. The West is decadent and Paris is the most decadent of all the Western cities. If you go there, you will get caught in a spider's web of desire. Loose women, drugs, the illusions of fame. All of these things will tempt you and eventually they will destroy everything that is good in you. Forget about all that. History moves in cycles, and the time of the West is over. We need new men to build a new world, rough country men who act boldly to seize the day. Men like that will come from places like this. This is the geographical heart of Europe. You belong here."

The marshal picked up the wood carving and studied it.

"It's not finished," said Tomas.

The marshal laughed a phlegmy laugh, spat and lit up a fresh cigarette. "Yes, it is. If I left it with you, you'd worry it until it looked like some Greek creature altogether. You'd make it into a minotaur. I like it just the way it is."

"So can I leave?"

"No. You're coming back to Warsaw with me. I came looking for wood bison, and now that I've found one, I'm not letting it go."

The entourage made its way to a forest road where two cars, a number of horses and half a dozen wagons waited along with carters and assembled servants. The marshal was briefed by two soldiers and one civilian at a table set on the grass where cups of coffee steamed in the chilly morning air. The stag's head and other game were piled into a cart. Not knowing what else to do, Tomas waited along with the others, stamping his feet to keep warm. Finally, the marshal rose from the table, shook hands with the men and walked to the car door that was being held open by an orderly.

"Please," Tomas shouted out in Polish, "what about me?"

A soldier standing by Tomas shoved him for his insolence, but the marshal beckoned Tomas to him.

"You will be taken care of, young man. You have had a stroke of luck, the kind of thing that only happens once in a lifetime. I'm counting on you to bring me good fortune. Now roar like a bison for me."

Tomas looked at him, confused.

"Never mind, I was only joking. Get into the cart. Everything has been arranged."

The marshal turned and stepped into the car and the orderly slammed the door shut. The car drove away. One of the soldiers beckoned toward a cart, and Tomas stepped over the hares and stags that were heaped unceremoniously in the back. The entourage moved off—first the cars and then the horses, and finally the carts, the last of which was Tomas's.

For four days, they made their way toward Warsaw, and then through it. Tomas had been a lover of Vilnius, but that city was not much more than a town compared with Warsaw. The peasant carter was taciturn, but he seemed amused by Tomas's wide-eyed reaction to the city. They travelled south until the city began to dwindle to wooden houses from stone and brick ones, and then empty lots began to appear among the wooden houses. Finally, when the first farms were visible just up the road, the carter turned into a complex of wooden buildings and under a wooden sign above the gate: Spetkowski Church Factory.

They were expected. The foreman, who introduced himself as Tadeusz Swanek, was standing in front of a large wooden workshop in a black-billed cap and leather apron. He looked as broad and strong as any farmhand. Tomas climbed stiffly out of the cart and Swanek put out his hand.

"You must be the new apprentice," he said. "Welcome to your new home."

Tomas looked around at the complex of wooden buildings. It was not exactly what he'd had in mind, but maybe it was a place to start.

PART TWO

THE SCHOOL OF PARIS
1926

Men are born, it seems, with an emptiness of soul,
and must take their qualities wholly from things without.
To be born thus empty into this modern age, this mixture of
good and ill, and yet steer through life on an honest course to
the splendors of success—this is a feat reserved for paragons
of our kind, a task beyond the nature of the normal man.

—IHARA SAIKAKU

We will begin with Bohemia unknown to fame, by far
the largest section of it. The ways of art, crowded and perilous as
they are, grow more crowded every day.

—HENRI MURGER

ONE

TOMAS STOOD WITH HIS SKETCHBOOK BALANCED ON THE railing of the Pont des Arts, the iron bridge that spanned the Seine. He drew the chaotic cityscape with its roofs, balconies, chimney pots and spires, his eyes flicking between the Île de la Cité and the page. On the quays to either side of him, fast cars sped, reflecting the sun on their windshields, making irregular bursts of light flicker on the periphery of his vision. He was still fresh enough in the city that at moments like this, he saw not only Paris but himself in it, as if he had a God's-eye view.

He would have liked to try to capture the golden glow that fell like a spotlight on the island from the slanting sun behind him, but paints were still beyond his means. His savings were dwindling fast; all he could afford was a pencil.

Some of the passersby had their collars turned up against the chill wind, but Tomas wore only a thin jacket, vest and tie. He was not cold. Back in the East, the winter winds blew more bitingly than they ever did here. Compared with Lithuania and Poland, Paris had no weather to speak of, just shifting light. The island in front of him retained its brightness, but clouds were sweeping in from both directions, so the banks on either side of the Pont Neuf before him fell into darkness. He had to hurry.

Tomas's hands were as restless as ever, but his fingers were callused and strong from the years in the Warsaw church factory, where even the journeymen hefted rough boards and carried blocks of stone. His jacket could now only be buttoned across his broad chest with some risk to the fabric. His hair, darker now than when he was a boy, still fell in a thick shock across his forehead unless he pomaded it, and he had neither the money nor the inclination to do that.

Though he had learned a great deal about being an artisan in the Spetkowski Church Factory, he wanted to be a real artist. He felt himself very old at twenty-four, and he was eager to make up for lost time. But getting a formal education in fine art was turning out to be more of a problem than he had expected. Where the Pont des Arts ended on the Quai Malaquais on his right stood the École des Beaux-Arts, where he had hoped to train. But the Beaux-Arts operated on an annual basis and would not look at new applicants for another six months. Even then, he would need to pass a competition to gain admittance and find the money to pay his tuition. He had never been so acutely aware of money as over the past few months. He barely had enough to meet the next month's rent, to say nothing of feeding himself.

To Tomas's left hulked the massive stone pile of the Louvre, a place that filled him with simultaneous rapture and despair. The art museum was bigger than any he had ever seen, so big that it could have contained the mansions of many grand dukes, *grafs*, princes and even kings of Eastern Europe. He had explored the different galleries for days, overwhelmed by their contents. He knew something of Greek and Roman sculpture because it was copied so widely, but he had never seen works from other cultures, such as the coolly formal Egyptian *Lady Touy*. In his wanderings, he overheard snatches of conversation that made casual references to artists, some of whom, like da Vinci and Giotto, he had read about in books or whose works he had seen copies of in the church factory back in Warsaw. But there were many, many others who were new to him. To improve both his French and his knowledge of art, he lingered on the fringes of tour groups to listen to what the guide had to say.

At the various masterpieces inside the Louvre stood students who had received permission to copy the works, and each seemed adept, controlling pencils and brushes far better than he ever could. Still, he remained confident that he could handle clay, wood and stone as well as anyone—or he would be able to, once he had a little more education, which he would get as soon as he had some money, which depended on finding work.

Paris was confusing to an outsider. He'd heard Russian, Polish, Yiddish, German, Romanian and many other languages among the porters, labourers and cab drivers in the city. Easterners flooded into Paris by train and on foot, all looking for work and a bright new future. He'd also seen many English and Americans, usually laughing, always rich and often drunk, who arrived in the City of Light with wallets full of money. Waves were washing over Paris from all ends of the world, then churning into a froth in which even a talented person could drown.

He felt a presence behind his left shoulder.

"Hurry, young man. The light is fading."

As if on cue, the clear sky closed up. Beside him stood a middle-aged man in a hat and raincoat, with a pipe clenched between his teeth and an art portfolio in one hand. The man peered at the pad upon which Tomas had been working.

"If you take a few lessons, you'll find your grasp of perspective will improve."

The pipe smoker walked on before Tomas could respond, crossing the road and heading into the École des Beaux-Arts. In a foul humour, Tomas spat into the Seine and closed his sketchbook. He might as well go home. He went the way the man had done, toward the Beaux-Arts and past it, up the Rue Bonaparte on the long walk that would take him to the studio he shared with two friends off the Rue du Commerce in the fifteenth district, far away from the fashionable neighbourhoods.

He could not spare the money for tram fare, and he didn't mind walking: he loved the vastness of the city, the density of it and the speed of automobile traffic along the streets. But he was hungry, and the smell of coffee from a series of cafés cut short his pleasure. To avoid temptation, he rushed by without looking inside. The entire street seemed to conspire against his empty stomach: he passed a bakery, where the aroma of bread almost made him faint, a *charcuterie* where cabbage and sausages were being cooked for dinner and a *crèmerie* whose cheeses were as appealing as the arms of a woman. Even the smell coming off the sidewalk in front of the fish store made him think of herring with sour cream and onions. He quickened his pace.

Warsaw had been a village compared with Paris, and the perpetual labour at the Spetkowski workshops had offered him very little time to explore it. In the beginning, he had been fascinated by the massive workshop, its relentless production of picture frames, religious paintings of indifferent quality and whole warehouses of plaster saints. And he loved the company of the artisans, with whom he could admire the fine grain of a piece of wood or a particularly well-made tool.

The other apprentices admired him and feared him because of his protector, Marshal Jozef Pilsudski. Tomas himself waited expectantly for the marshal's next gesture, but it never came, and over the years, Tomas almost forgot him and simply made a life for himself. In his spare time he continued his studies of French and English out of grammars he bought from the book peddler, the *bukinista,* who wheeled his bicycle-load of wares to the factory once every two weeks. He carved walking sticks and sold them for extra money at the market. He convinced himself that the training he was getting at the church factory would help him in his intention of being a sculptor, and made the best of his life in Warsaw. He even began to visit the family of a journeyman picture-frame maker, and to take tea with his daughter. Tomas might have fallen into a simple life and become a journeyman himself if the marshal had not capriciously summoned him, years after Tomas had given up hope.

A soldier came on horseback to the church works, bringing an extra saddled horse with him. Tomas was no longer a raw apprentice, but he still lived in a sort of barracks for workers who did not have families. The soldier called for Tomas without dismounting, and then addressed him where he stood in the mud of the courtyard.

"Marshal Pilsudski requires your presence immediately," he said.

The summons made his heart beat hard in his chest.

"Let me go in and change my clothes," he said.

"There is no time. The marshal wants to see you now."

"I have waited years for him. He can wait five minutes while I change my shirt and wash my hands."

They rode into Warsaw past the Belvedere Palace, where the marshal no longer had any business since he had resigned from government. He had given the Poles a country, and they thanked him very much for it, but they had decided to run the country without him. The marshal now sat out of the limelight, brooding.

Tomas and his guard rode up the leafy Aleja Roz to a house heavy with balustrades and ornamental statues. Four cars and half a dozen horses stood in the drive and a knot of soldiers fell silent as they approached and Tomas dismounted. Something was going on. This was not the residence of a man in retirement. The inside of the house was abuzz with activity, and an orderly took Tomas into a room where the marshal was looking intently at a map on a table as two generals peered over his shoulders. The marshal looked up at him uncomprehendingly for a moment, and then broke into a smile and reached for a fresh cigarette.

"So here you are at last, my Lithuanian *stumbras*. You look very well. I do not have a great deal of time. But something very important has happened and I need to inform you."

Tomas's head whirled with conflicting thoughts. He wanted to tell the marshal what his life had been like, and he wanted him to know he felt abandoned. But he was in the presence of a great man, and great men had little time.

"You are no longer alone in this country, *Pan Zubr*." Tomas looked at him, confused. "After a long and difficult negotiation, we received a pair of breeding wood bison from the Berlin zoo. I was not sure they would succeed, but the mother has given birth, and so the spirit of the nation has returned to the Augustav forest and to Poland."

The two generals bore the marshal's words with an air of long suffering, as if this was a theme that he spoke of often.

"The weight of Poland was on your shoulders, young Stumbras, and now it can be lifted off."

"So I was your good-luck charm?" Tomas asked.

"Yes."

"Then I wish luck had been better for both of us."

An air of stillness descended on the room.

"Do you feel hard done by?" Pilsudski asked. Great men were not accustomed to insolence, but the marshal chose to laugh at this point.

"I had no word from you for all those years."

"But you weren't a prisoner. You could have left at any time. Let it be a lesson to you to make your own way. Never mind, luck is going to change for me, young man. But let's concern ourselves with you. I did not forget you. I was merely biding my time. I remember that you wanted to study art, and now the time is right. I'm offering you a place at the art school in Krakow."

Tomas had dreamed of the very fine school in Krakow often enough, but now he was not to be so easily satisfied. He had done a great deal of reading and he knew better.

"I want to go to Paris," he said.

"Paris? That hole? Do you remember what Adam Mickiewicz said of Paris? 'How can I use my tired mind, here on Parisian streets, when my heart is full of curses, lies, regrets and quarrels?'"

The marshal wore an air of satisfaction, as if he were an attorney who had just made a watertight argument. But Tomas was unmoved.

"Still, I would like to try Paris."

One of the men standing beside the marshal tapped him on the shoulder, as if to remind him that more pressing matters needed to be dealt with. The marshal ignored him. He leaned forward and spoke gently.

"You are a Lithuanian bison, young man. You can't be completely civilized or you'll lose everything good about you. I have made you a very good offer in Krakow. This country needs its artists to stay where they are."

"My heart is set on Paris."

"Out of the question," said the marshal. He stubbed his cigarette, looked down at the map and began to talk with the men beside him. The audience was over.

Back at the church works, Tomas packed up his belongings and counted his meagre savings. A package came for him with a one-way ticket to Krakow, notification of money that would be paid to him quarterly and many documents from the university. Only a few months ago, these would have filled him with excitement, but now they were not good enough. Tomas wanted to go to the very centre of the solar system instead of contenting himself with the orbit of an outlying planet.

When he arrived in Krakow, he stayed only long enough to withdraw his first quarterly stipend, most of which he spent on a third-class ticket to Paris.

—

Having fought off the temptation to buy food on the street, Tomas finally reached the Rue du Commerce and turned off it into the narrow Impasse Diablotin. The entrance to his building was through heavy double doors and past the dozing concierge, Mme Martini, who slept under her knotted kerchief in her wooden chair as serenely as if she were in her own bed. Tomas passed through the dark, cobbled cavern of the passageway, tall enough to take a man on horseback, and into the courtyard of the old house. His studio was built on the cobbles themselves and along the entire length of the wall facing the entrance. The day-time illumination was very good; light poured through a leaky skylight as well as a whole wall of frosted glass. Inside, the long room was crude and undivided and had only two beds, which he and his new friends used in relay. There were two benches and two tables, as well as a cookstove, giving them all the space they needed both to work and live.

When he got home his roommates were drawing at opposite ends of a table, but the afternoon was getting on, and the light was bad, despite the large windows and the single electric bulb that hung from a long wire.

Alphonse was a Lithuanian from Šiauliai whom Tomas had met under a bridge during his first days in Paris. He had recognized the hard, white cheese that Alphonse chewed, and they struck up a friendship. Alphonse came from a family of clerks, and was by nature reserved and quiet, as if his ancestors had left their fastid-iousness like a stamp upon him. He was as tall and thin as a crane whenever he stood up straight, though most of the time he was bent myopically over his work, since he could not afford eye-glasses. His back arched like a bow whose string had been pulled back as far as possible, to the point where either the bow or the string might snap.

Tomas had met his other roommate, Sorrel, at the reception desk of the École des Beaux-Arts, where Sorrel had been arguing with the porter. Sorrel was slim, with a stringy goatee and a moustache and round eyeglasses that he liked to think made him look like Trotsky.

"I tell you there is nothing I can do for you," the porter had said. "You cannot just walk in here and gain admittance to the school. There are procedures. You must submit a portfolio in June. Then you must await the disposition of the jury. The school year begins in October."

"But it's not even Easter," Sorrel said. "What am I supposed to do until October?"

"That is your business."

"I am an extremely talented artist who walked all the way here from Romania. This very morning I passed through the Porte d'Orléans and I came here without stopping for so much as a cup of tea. That must count for something."

"This institution is supported by the French state and its people. It is paid for by the sweat of workers throughout the country. Who are you to barge in here and demand an exception to the rules?"

It had never occurred to Tomas that he might not get into the Beaux-Arts.

"Talent knows no rules," said Sorrel. "Talent must find a way to express itself."

"You can use your talent to walk right out these doors. And if I see you again before June, it will be trouble for you," said the porter.

Tomas followed Sorrel out onto the courtyard, where the Romanian stood fuming on the flagstones.

"Are you really as good as you say?" Tomas asked in French as heavily accented as Sorrel's.

"Better. Look at this." He squatted on the flagstones, drew a piece of vine charcoal from his pocket and quickly sketched a fat, jowled man in a very bad suit, with a bald head fringed by straggly hair. The porter.

"What's your name?" Sorrel asked.

"Tomas."

"Are you an artist, too?"

"Yes."

"Prove it." He passed the charcoal to Tomas.

Tomas used a few deft lines to depict a thin, bearded man raging, with his fists waving above him in the air. Sorrel recognized the caricature of himself and laughed.

Sorrel was a Romanian from high in the Carpathians. He'd never become accustomed to the thick air in the lowlands, and was always a little drunk on the oxygen of Paris. Life had been hard back home. Most of his brothers and sisters died before they were old enough to talk. But he survived, he said, because he was the toughest man who had ever lived. When food was short, he insisted he could live on pebbles. The only problem was passing them.

Sorrel and Alphonse looked up from their work as Tomas came through the door of the studio. They were such a study in contrasts that they might have been a music-hall act, Sorrel light on his feet, edgy and bearded, and Alphonse like an adolescent who had never grown out of his awkwardness.

Alphonse unbent the arc of his back and straightened himself to look at Tomas.

"What's the matter with you?" he asked.

"Does it show?"

"You know you wear your emotions on your face."

Tomas told them about what the art teacher had said to him on the Pont des Arts. "If I could afford lessons, I'd take them," he said, flopping onto the bed.

"And that's what has you distressed?" Sorrel asked. "Who cares about perspective, anyway? Toughen your heart, or you'll never get by in this city."

"Sorrel's right," said Alphonse. "You need to be patient and keep practising."

"Who said anything about patience?" Sorrel asked. "You need to work boldly, with originality, but above all you need to disdain fools, or their stupidity will infect you."

Tomas held up his hands and laughed. "One of you says to go fast and the other says to go slow. If I add up your advice, I'll go the middle way."

"Moderation." Sorrel spat the word out. "The provinces are full of moderation. If you wanted moderation, you should have stayed in Warsaw. I could have been an art teacher in Bucharest. Those who long for the middle way shouldn't bother to come to this city."

Sorrel looked down to the sketchbook Tomas had set on the table. He flipped it open to Tomas's drawing and studied it.

"Well?" Tomas asked from his bed.

"It's promising."

Tomas sighed.

"Don't be distressed. If I say it's promising, I mean it. I have a very good eye and I don't lie." He flipped Tomas's book shut. "Did you bring back anything to eat?" Sorrel asked.

"I looked for food on the way home," said Tomas, "but no one was giving it away."

They both looked at Alphonse, who was sitting back on his stool with his arms crossed.

"What? Am I supposed to feed you?" Sorrel and Tomas kept looking at him. "Ha! One of you is angry and the other is depressed. What a pair of companions you two will be this evening. Come on, I'll stand each of you to a glass of wine and a sandwich. But I get to choose the place."

He led his friends on a long, winding walk that took them toward the east side of the Place des Invalides, until Tomas was almost back where he had been sketching. Just when his companions were beginning to complain loudly about their hunger, Alphonse found the place he was looking for.

Le Chancelier stood on a street corner. Ten of its small side-walk tables were filled by men and women reading newspapers, smoking cigarettes or having an aperitif. The chairs were wobbly, the tables sticky and the prices low. The waiter looked them up and down with the supercilious air perfected by waiters in Paris, but took their order for three glasses of *vin ordinaire* and three ham sandwiches readily enough. When the waiter returned with their meals, he demanded immediate payment, another in a series of petty indignities that Paris offered to poor foreigners.

Alphonse grimaced as he sipped. "Back home, I used to dream of wine. I thought it would be sweet as nectar, but the stuff is sour."

"When you have the money for something better, you'll like it well enough," Sorrel said.

"I'm not so sure. A glass or two of vodka would be more to my taste, but to find it, we'd need to go to a Russian café."

The sandwich in front of Tomas was luxury enough. The small portions served in Paris often left him hungry. But the bread was very fresh, the crust so crisp he needed to bite carefully to avoid cutting the top of his mouth. The sharp mustard filled his mouth with a tang that lingered after he had swallowed the food, and gave him the illusion that he was eating more than he actually did. He consumed the sandwich carefully, saving an inch of wine in the glass to prevent the embarrassment of the waiter asking if there was anything else they wanted.

Sorrel nudged Tomas. "That young woman over there is look-ing at you."

"What?" Tomas glanced across the terrace in the direction Sorrel indicated. "No, she's not."

The woman in question was wearing a cloche hat below which a ring of light brown curls like lace framed her face. She had thin, painted eyebrows, long lashes and sable eyes that seemed curiously bright and deep. If Tomas had had to choose a single word to describe her, it would have been *lithe*. Her fingers were long and slim but the nails unpainted, and she had a thin body, though her legs were well formed. Her camel-hair coat was open and beneath it he could see a simple white blouse and a jacket and a short skirt that matched her coat. While her eyes seemed intelligent, her slim body was fashionable. She immediately aroused Tomas's curiosity.

As he rolled a cigarette between his fingers, Sorrel elbowed Tomas in the side. "Oh, she is definitely looking at you," he said.

"What about it?"

"Smile at her and see if she smiles back."

"Leave her alone," said Alphonse.

"I just said he should smile at her, not carry her off over his shoulder."

"Immigrants must be invisible here," said Alphonse. "They're always looking for an excuse to deport foreigners."

The two of them carried on bickering, but Tomas stopped paying attention to what they said. He waited until the young woman looked up again. He caught her eye and smiled, and the shadow of a smile passed over her lips as well. Tomas took his glass of wine in his hand, rose and walked to her table. She did not protest when he pulled out a chair and seated himself beside her.

In halting French he said, "My name is Tomas Stumbras. What's yours?"

"Jenny Smith."

She put the accent on the last syllable of her first name, in the French manner, but she pronounced her last name in the English way.

"You're English?"

"My father is, but not my mother. I'm French—Geneviève, if you like."

Tomas realized he had no idea what he should say next. He had been without the warmth of women's company for a very long time. Living in the workshop barracks back in Warsaw had been like military service, all gruff fellowship in the good times, and drunken fist fights in the bad. The woman he had courted in Warsaw was not that different from Maria, a country girl easy to understand and easy to talk to. This girl seemed so worldly—half French, half English, and sitting in a café alone. Jenny was looking at him expectantly, aware that the gap in speech was a little too long. "Are you an artist?" she finally asked.

Tomas was pleased that he looked like an artist instead of a peasant or a working man.

"I'm an artist, yes, but still a student."

"What a shame."

"What do you mean?" he sputtered.

"Students don't have any money, but they at least have the prospect of a career. An art student has no money and no prospects."

As the silence stretched again, Jenny spoke: "Have I hurt your feelings? Don't feel bad. I thought you were very handsome there, between your funny friends. Does that make you feel better?" And she put her hand on Tomas's arm and left it there.

"And how do I look up close?"

She studied him for a while.

"You're all right," she said. "Your French is not very good, but you're passable as far as looks go."

"Just passable?" he asked with a laugh.

"Isn't that enough?"

"I was hoping for better," he said.

"And what about me?" Jenny asked.

"If I didn't think you were passable as well, I wouldn't be here."

"Good," she said, and she sipped from her coffee cup. He mustered his wit to show her that he could play as well.

"Maybe I can make you think better of me if I show you what I can do."

"Are you going to paint my portrait?"

"I don't have my oils with me."

"Sketch me?"

"Better than that."

Tomas called over the waiter and asked for a flask of water as well as a whole loaf of bread, a *bâtard*, which he asked not to be cut into slices. The waiter took some convincing, but he finally did as Tomas asked.

"You must be very hungry," Jenny said with a smile.

"I am, but I intend to sacrifice this loaf of bread on the altar of art."

Tomas thanked the waiter and paid him.

"Now let me get a good look at you," Tomas said, and moved his chair so he was sitting directly across from Jenny Smith.

He took the *bâtard* and ripped it in half. Then he scooped out its soft inside, wet his fingers with some water from the flask and began to knead the bread until it was soft and pliable. He ripped a piece from this kneaded mass and flattened it down, and then formed it in the palm of his left hand until it looked like a mushroom cap. This cap he set upon the table. He dug out the remaining soft part from the other end of the loaf and kneaded it as well, and then he began to shape the dough into a ball and added a neck to it. Using the end of Jenny's coffee spoon, he began to sculpt the dough, forming ears, a mouth and a snub nose. Once he was done, he placed the cap on top of the sculpture like a cloche. As he handed the sculpture to Jenny, the man at the next table applauded.

"Well?" he asked.

"Very good."

"Better than passable?"

"Much better."

Pleased with his success, Tomas abandoned all thought of economy and ordered two glasses of wine. "I could make you another one," he offered. "I could do your bust in clay or plaster of Paris. It would be more permanent."

"Just my bust?" Jenny whispered playfully. "Are you familiar with the whole female body? As an artist, I mean."

No woman had ever spoken to him so suggestively, and he was filled with renewed pleasure at being in Paris. If nothing else came of his life here, this moment would have made it all worthwhile. "I am familiar with the female body," said Tomas, "but I am a little out of practice. I would need a refresher course."

"You could travel to the seaside in the summer and look at the ladies in their swimsuits."

"But summer is so far away."

"Alas."

She looked at her watch, and dropped the playful tone. "I have to go. I'm late for work." She began to drink down her wine.

"Where do you work?"

"I'm a dancer at the Folies Bergère."

"What's that?"

She smiled at him as she stood and did up her jacket and coat. "A special kind of music hall."

"I would love to see you dance," said Tomas.

Jenny paused and thought for a moment. "I think that could be arranged," she said. "Come on, we'll have to hurry."

TWO

TWO HOURS LATER, TOMAS WAS HIGH IN THE RAFTERS OF the Folies Bergère, lying upon a girder that bridged the wings of the stage. It had no railing, and with one wrong move he would crash onto the set below. Tomas was in a forest of ropes, knotted, hanging or looped, running through pulleys and holding up curtains, backdrops and props. One level below him were perpendicular working balconies hidden by the wings, and upon these balconies half a dozen men were knotting and unknotting ropes, pulling on rope ends or turning handles on strange machines.

Hooks hung from crossbeams around Tomas to support curtains and backdrops, and pulleys and winches that the men controlled with ropes one level below. There were higher reaches still, where backdrops were lifted up to nestle against one another like cards, hidden away from the audience. A giant, metal tulip with a lid and mirrored insides was suspended by three metal cables that ran up into the darkness above.

Jenny had sweet-talked the doorman into allowing Tomas in, but warned him to stay utterly inconspicuous or he would get them all into trouble with the manager, M. Derval, who raged if the rules were broken.

"You're taking such a big risk," Tomas had said as Jenny took his hand and led him up through the wings.

"It's fun to take chances sometimes."

"Why would you do that for me?"

"Why not? I like the way you look."

"I thought you said I was just passable."

"You've grown on me in the last hour. You can pay me back after the show is over. We'll go to a *bal musette* and dance and have some fun." Tomas was silent at this, and she seemed to read his mind. "Don't worry, it's very cheap, and we can use my money if you've left yours at home." She gave him a kiss on the cheek and motioned for him to climb up into the rafters.

Tomas had never heard of a music hall, and he had never been to a theatre. He was pleasantly warm from the intense lights, and had the advantage of a bird's-eye view upon the stage below, where a remarkable show was taking place. There were dog acts and comedians who spoke too quickly for him to understand, magicians and singers. The performers below him changed with bewildering speed. No act was permitted to last long enough to bore the audience.

His favourite scenes were the tableaux. Just then stage peasants were performing a spectacle based on a harvest scene. The men wore puffy-sleeved shirts and carried wooden-bladed scythes, and to the music of the pit orchestra, they made broad sweeps across the mechanical grass that lay down obediently in waves at each stylized swing. Then maidens arrived with rakes across their shoulders, but they never bothered to work at all, and joined in a dance with the men. The maidens' faces were rouged so thickly that their cheeks looked like marzipan apples in the pastry-shop window at Easter.

The lights came down for a few seconds, and Tomas felt something falling upon him. At first he thought it was a swarm of insects, and tried to brush them away frantically, but the soft things did not move. When the lights came back up, he saw that snow was falling on a winter landscape, and the flakes were bits of cotton. Around a frozen pond stood a series of snowmen, and off in the distance, smoke billowed from the chimney of a painted farmhouse. The snow stopped, and Jenny's dancing troupe, the Tiller Girls, swirled out on mock ice skates.

After the skating scene ended, the stage went dark again. The scenery moved around on the bewildering machinery about him. Through the darkness, a theatre twilight began to illuminate the stage, revealing a jungle scene. Black men sang quietly as a white explorer lay asleep at the foot of a tree, down which a black woman climbed. Tomas recognized the star of the show, Josephine Baker, the American whose posters covered all the kiosks of the city. Thick gold bands encircled her wrists and arms and three shell necklaces hung around her neck. Her breasts were bare. There were gold slippers on her feet, and around her waist she wore a strange skirt made of what seemed to be bananas. That skirt made Tomas want to laugh out loud, especially when the bananas began to bounce like bobbing penises as she danced. The skirt was already famous, and had become both her signature and the highlight of the show.

Josephine Baker's limbs were smooth and slim, muscular without being overtly athletic. The hair on her head was plastered down with brilliant pomade and a kiss-curl graced her forehead. She was the dream of the sleeping white explorer. Her quick movements gave way in a moment to sensual ones, then she dropped into a half crouch and flung her legs into an American dance. This Charleston was a joke, a kind of good-humoured pose, a punchline in motion that he had heard of back in Warsaw but never had the chance to see.

After the entr'acte, the show resumed with a midsummer night's bonfire, and in the darkness between scenes, Tomas became engrossed in the sight of a fireman in a shiny chrome helmet, who sat in a weak pool of light in the wings with a chorus girl on his lap. Tomas was trying to determine if this was part of the show when he felt an unusual rhythm in the girder he was lying upon, and he sensed that someone was climbing up the ladder to the place where he was perched. He had no time to move or hide himself.

It was Josephine Baker herself, her brown skin shining slightly even in the dim light above the stage lamps. The banana skirt was gone and she wore only her slippers and a skirt of silk fringes. Either she did not see him or was ignoring him in her concentration. She scrambled into the big metal tulip and crouched down inside. One of the attached cables moved silently, closing the lid over her.

A new backdrop with a spring-garden scene lit up below. Large papier-mâché flowers formed a crescent before the audience. A fanfare sounded from the orchestra pit, and the tulip began to descend from the ceiling on three pairs of cables, two each for the sides of the flower and another for the lid. Down it went on well-oiled pulleys, and when it had almost touched the floor, the lid and front opened and Josephine was revealed to the audience on the mirrored interior, a spring flower opening to the sun. The papier-mâché flowers opened behind her, and each of them was a dancer, Jenny among them. Josephine Baker rose up and began her own dance, an intense, jerky series of movements almost like an epileptic fit. This particular spring dance had no humour to it. It was ecstasy and abandon, convulsions and ironic poses without any pattern. But the audience adored it, and bellowed its approval. When the dance ended, Josephine stepped back into the tulip, and it closed above her. The pulleys began to turn silently, bringing her up again.

Suddenly a grinding noise came from one of the motors above Tomas and one side of the flower stopped rising altogether, and the tulip began to tilt precariously. A muffled shriek came from inside the flower. In a moment, the whole tulip would be on its side and Josephine Baker would be hurled out onto the stage almost thirty feet below. Already the lid was hanging open and

Tomas could see her hands grasping frantically for something to hold on to.

"Stop the cables before you kill her!" someone shouted from the wings, and the orchestra stopped playing. Josephine Baker reached out from inside and grasped one of the cables with her hand.

"I've got nothing to hold on to in here!" she shouted in heavily accented French, and indeed the mirror inside was slippery. Tomas looked above him. A motor that pulled the cables on one side of the tulip had malfunctioned. Men ran out from the wings onto the stage below, holding up their arms to catch the dancer if she fell. Shrieks came from some of the women in the audience, and a hundred men who each thought he knew the best thing to do called their instructions from the audience, the wings and the orchestra pit.

M. Derval was on the stage beside his men. He shouted orders that could not be heard above the commotion in the theatre. Up on his girder, Tomas's eyes locked on Josephine's. She was too far for him to reach.

He looked around him and spotted a coil of rope hooked on a massive cleat. Quickly, he unlooped a long length, returned to the place above the dancer and lowered the end to her. He tucked one arm around a nearby beam in order to brace himself.

"You hold," he called out in the best English he could muster. She looked him in the eye for a moment. It was risky to give up her perch on the tulip, but he tried to look calm and sure and she did as he asked. The sudden weight upon the rope pulled him forward, and he leaned back to compensate.

Slowly, slowly, he passed the rope hand under hand. She was surprisingly heavy. The rope was burning his palms, but he would not let her slip, and eventually she came down to the point where Derval and a half-dozen stagehands reached up to support her in their arms.

Ever the performer, Josephine blew a kiss up to him, allowed herself to be perched on the shoulders of a workman and was carried out to the applause of the delighted audience. Only Derval paused a moment to point up at Tomas, and to beckon him down with a crooked finger. The scene would make the papers the next day, but in Derval's retelling, he would be the man up on the girder.

The curtains were closed and the stagehands and dance girls were in a flurry of activity by the time Tomas made it down to the wings. Derval was waiting, a fleshy man in striped trousers, waistcoat and cravat. He had a receding hairline and what hair remained was brilliantined smoothly back behind his ears. He touched his hair several times to make sure it was still in place.

"You don't work here. Who are you?" His tone was aggressive.

"I slipped in to see the show," said Tomas awkwardly. Derval looked seriously annoyed, but Jenny appeared out of nowhere in a radiant costume of reflective sequins that sparkled even in the poor light of the wings.

"It's my fault, M. Derval. He's my fiancé, but he's never seen the show."

Derval turned on her abruptly. "I should fire you for this. You know the rules."

"But M. Derval, this man saved Josephine Baker's life! You should be thanking him. His name is Tomas Stumbras, and he's here looking for a job."

Derval wavered for a moment, remembered his good luck, then laughed and offered Tomas his hand. Tomas shook it, feeling the sticky brilliantine on Derval's fingertips.

"Very well, M. Stumbras, you have made a favourable impression. Josephine Baker is irreplaceable, so I'm grateful. Now that you are working for me, tell me, what exactly is it that you do?"

"He's a sculptor," Jenny said.

"What good is a sculptor to me?"

"I'm also an excellent carpenter."

"Not an ordinary carpenter, but an excellent one, eh? Just what I need, a carpenter who knows how to handle a rope. Well, you can report to the workshop on Tuesday. Now, let me see if I can find you some decent clothes and a better place to watch the rest of the show."

For a few minutes in the back rooms of the Folies Bergère, Tomas was treated as if he were as great a star as Josephine Baker. At every turn, he received pats on the back and hand-shakes; women in feather headpieces, with naked breasts, kissed him as they passed. He was carried on a wave of well-wishers into a room where two women gave him the finest suit he had ever worn. One of the women wiped his face with a damp cloth and the other brilliantined his hair and combed it back. Then he was out of the door and into the producer's box at the front left side of the stage, where a bottle of champagne awaited. Derval poked his head in.

"Here you are, young man. Enjoy the show. I'm afraid I'm too busy to sit with you, but I want you to know I am grateful."

He leaned in close and whispered conspiratorially, "Josephine Baker is grateful, too. She asks that you meet her at the stage door after the show. Young man, you have been very lucky today."

The illusions of the theatre seen from the front of the stage were far more effective than they had seemed from above. No ropes and pulleys, stagehands or managers distracted from the deception. The bright lights of the music hall—the primary colours and glitter—appealed to him and hurt his eyes. The finale of the show was called "Under a Golden Bridge." The scene was all sprinkling fountains and naked women in three tiers against a backdrop of gold mountains beneath a bridge. No church had ever used gold as extravagantly.

When he arrived in Paris, Tomas had spent a few nights under a bridge himself. The spectacle made no sense at all, but the absurdity of the image seemed to cause no one any trouble. As Sorrel had predicted, the champagne tasted better than *vin ordinaire*, and it made him feel euphoric. This was far more than he had ever expected from Paris.

He remained seated after the show ended and waited until the hall had emptied. He could barely bring himself to leave. Men with brooms began sweeping the main aisles, and the ushers were looking under the seats for any money or wallets that might have fallen. Tomas finally made his way backstage. Pieces of painted scenery leaned against the walls, scenes from castles, forests, dining halls, expensive restaurants and more. A mountain of coloured ostrich feathers lay stacked in a recess, the red ones on the bottom, and then layers of orange, yellow, green and blue, as if a rainbow of birds had left behind their plumage.

He stood just inside the open stage door, which was guarded by a short, determined doorman who faced the street with his arms crossed and a cap pulled low over his eyes. Outside, the narrow Rue Saulnier was filled with stage door Johnnies, a collection of both rich and poor who were smitten by what they had seen on the stage. Jenny Smith appeared beside Tomas. She threw her arms around him and kissed him on the lips.

"I knew you wouldn't disappoint me as soon as I saw you on the terrace. And look at you now."

Tomas wished he could make a dramatic gesture, reach into a pocket and offer her a cigarette from a silver case, but his miserable pouch of tobacco and papers was still in the jacket of his old clothes back in the dressing room.

"You're a regular Cinderella," Jenny said. "But it's after midnight. We'd better get you home before you turn into a pumpkin."

"It's the carriage that turns into a pumpkin."

Jenny shrugged. She was wearing the clothes that she had come in, her eyes glowing with pleasure.

"I hope you know something about carpentry," she said. Other performers in street clothes were passing them on their way out the stage door.

"I do," said Tomas. "Thank you for getting me in here. This place is . . ." He reached for a suitable French adjective, but could not find it.

"Fantastic?"

"Yes."

"This music hall is one of the oldest and the best. Maurice Chevalier got into a fist fight just out there on the street one night, over his lover, Mistinguett. Manet painted a girl at the bar here forty years ago, and prostitutes used to stroll the standing-room area, but Derval drove them out. He's raising the tone, insisting on good taste. Colette comes to see the show sometimes."

Tomas knew none of the names she mentioned, but he gathered that they must be important.

"What about Josephine Baker?"

"She's our latest star. Some say she came here because the Americans do not like Negroes, and in Paris, men love women of any colour. Everybody is in love with Americans and jazz since the war, and she represents all that." Jenny paused at his rapt attention to her words. "Let me guess. You're in love with her, too?"

"I don't even know her. But M. Derval said I was to wait for her here. She wants to thank me."

"I'll bet she does, and she should thank me as well."

Tomas heard a noise behind them, and turned to see Josephine Baker coming toward him with two other young women.

She looked fresh, as if she had just rested and now wanted to have some fun. Her eyes were bright and mischievous. She wore a long white winter coat and a white cloche below which her signature curl was visible on her forehead, and she carried a ukulele in her hand. The baby guitar made him laugh, and as soon as he did her eyes found his and she smiled at him, an act so magnetic that it hurt when she turned away to speak to the others.

"This is the man who saved your life," one of her friends said, and Miss Baker took him in her arms and embraced him, planting light kisses on either cheek. She was so radiant up close that she blinded him. He stood silently in front of her when she drew back from him. She must have been used to the effect she had, because she did not seem surprised that he was dumbstruck, but took his hands in hers and looked again into his eyes.

"What's your name?"

"Tomas."

"I told M. Derval that he was to take care of you. Did he do that?"

"Yes. He gave me a job."

She laughed as if nothing could delight her more.

"Now it's my turn. Let's step outside."

"I have a friend with me," said Tomas weakly, but Josephine did not even look at Jenny.

"It's crowded enough as it is," said Josephine, and she took his arm, put it through hers and led him outside.

Out on the Rue Saulnier, the men sighed collectively, and then let out a cacophony of calls. The group of stage door Johnnies had grown. Twenty wanted Josephine Baker, and a dozen more waited for other girls. Each of Josephine's admirers was shouting for her attention. One threw a bouquet of flowers over the top of the other bouquets being offered, and it fell right under her feet, where she stepped on it without taking notice.

"Who's got a car?" she asked, and a dozen voices offered. She picked a young man with pomaded hair. She linked arms with him on one side, and with Tomas on the other, and ran the gauntlet of admirers, who groaned as she passed.

The young man had his parents' car and their chauffeur.

"Le Grand Duc," Josephine said, and the chauffeur nodded and the three of them got into the back of the car.

The young man had smiled when Josephine picked him, but he was not at all pleased about Tomas's presence. He said a few words to her in fluent English, and then leaned forward and spoke over Josephine to Tomas.

Tomas could not understand the words, but the tone was clear enough.

"Now be nice, boys," Josephine said in French, "we're just out to have a good time."

The car drove along boulevards until it came to negotiate the smaller streets on the way up to Pigalle. Le Grand Duc was a tiny bar, and its star and manager, the black American singer Bricktop, was waiting for them outside.

"Where have you been?" Bricktop asked. The woman was older than Josephine, and she asked the question the way an older sister or a mother might. Bricktop had red hair and a bar that was attracting all the émigrés and many of the French themselves. Josephine had added to the draw by coming to the bar every night and singing and dancing just for the fun of it. "The crowd is waiting for you," said Bricktop, "and I have a cheese omelette on your table getting cold."

"You'd better make me another one real fast. I'm hungry enough to eat a horse," said Josephine, "and make the next one sweet—I need my dessert!"

The place had no more than a dozen tables and room for half a dozen people at the bar, but into this tiny space almost a hundred people were squeezed. The band was playing and the room was blue with cigarette smoke. Four couples were dancing, pressed up close to one another on the dance floor. There was no place at Josephine's table for Tomas and the other man to sit, and once they got inside, Josephine seemed oblivious to them. She ate with appetite, but did not wait for the second omelette. She pushed aside her plate and was up on the floor, dancing to the cheers of the others. A man jumped in to be her partner and the two of them broke into the Charleston, the dance that had taken Europe by storm.

The young swell leaned so close to Tomas he could smell his cologne—a whiff of dead flowers. "You're out of your league," he said.

"Who picked out the car, your mother or your father?"

Josephine descended on them. "Boys, boys. Don't be such children. Tomas saved my life," she said. "If it wasn't for him, I'd have been taken out by a hearse tonight."

Then she was eating again. A vanilla omelette had arrived. Tomas was amazed how much she could eat. She looked up at them and wagged her finger like a schoolteacher, and his rival seemed to decide that he had to let his noblesse oblige.

The Frenchman found a space for himself and Tomas at the corner of the bar and introduced himself as Antoine Gauthier. He was studying law, and he hated it, but less than working for his father, who had made his fortune in the largest glassworks of Paris.

Josephine was all over the small bar, talking, laughing and kissing men and women alike. Occasionally, she would swing by to give Antoine or Tomas a kiss. Once, she even took Antoine out on the floor for a dance, but he was awkward and she soon left him for another partner. Tomas and Antoine drank and ate, and Antoine paid for it all. In return, Tomas listened to him complain about problems that did not seem like problems at all. And all the time Tomas listened to the strange American music, he watched Josephine dance. She was pure energy. She had already worked for hours earlier that night, but she danced for hour after hour until suddenly her eyes drooped, and he could see she wanted to sleep. She came over to where the two men were still standing at the bar.

"Antoine," she said. "I need to pay for something. Do you have any money?"

"Of course." He reached into his wallet, removed a thousand-franc note and held it between his fingers. "Whom should I pay?"

"Me."

She snatched the bill from between his fingers and kissed him lightly on the cheek. She took Tomas by the arm, asked Antoine to wait and walked out of the bar onto the street. It was already light and the street sweepers had begun their work, clearing away the empty cigarette packages and dog turds that had appeared on the sidewalk overnight.

"I want you to take this money," Josephine said.

Tomas's back stiffened and he shook his head slowly. A man did not take money from a woman. A look of irritation flitted across her face, and she stuck the money in his breast pocket anyway.

"Tomas, that's all I have to give you." Antoine was waiting for her in the doorway and she left Tomas to go to him.

"Come on, honey, let's go home. I'm tired," she said as she went inside to get her coat.

Tomas could have run after her then and insisted she take back the money. Or he could have returned it to Antoine, who was watching him with a smug look on his face. Tomas considered. The money meant nothing to Antoine. Tomas had his pride, but on the other hand, he thought of the art lessons he could now buy. He shrugged and walked away down the street.

He had never been to Pigalle before, but the way back to familiar territory was easy enough to find. He just had to keep on walking downhill until he came to the river. The morning was still very young, but the fruiterers and grocers were already putting out their wares. Last night's rain had given way to one of those rare Parisian mornings when the sun shone with promise and the streets still glistened, like newly shined shoes. And yet the streets did not seem half as vivid to Tomas as the scenes in the theatre the night before.

He found Sorrel and Alphonse lying in the two beds of their studio. Tomas sat down on the edge of Alphonse's cot with every intention of waking him and telling him of his good fortune, but then decided against it. Feeling slightly guilty, he removed his clothes, took a spare blanket, wrapped it around himself and lay down on one of workbenches to sleep. The light was already coming in brightly through the frosted glass, and it kept him awake for a long time.

THREE

WITH HIS NEW-FOUND WEALTH AND THE PROSPECT OF A JOB,
Tomas began to look in earnest for a private art school. The
Académie Colarossi had a good reputation, as did the Académie
Julian, and a dozen other schools clustered in the Montparnasse
quarter of Paris. But the Académie Carrel, which was not far
from Tomas's home in the fifteenth district, had the advantage of
charging the lowest fees—a thousand francs would not last
forever. Tomas had somehow neglected to tell his friends about
the windfall, and the wealth became a guilty secret.

Carrel had made a modest name for himself especially among
the English with his portraits of gypsies back at the turn of the
century, and he had opened his school to capitalize on his name.
His career stalled at about the time of the appearance of the
Demoiselles d'Avignon, and it never really recovered, but he was
said to be very good at training artists from the ground up, giving
them a solid base from which they could go out into the world and
make careers of their own.

When he was in a good mood, Carrel would regale his students
with stories of the bohemians of the turn of the century, when the
Swedes and the Germans filled the cafés. Most often, though, he
was severe and exacting, and today he was using his sternest eyes
as he flipped through the pages of Tomas's sketchbook. Tomas
said nothing as the white-haired, white-bearded old artist turned

the pages. Carrel wore a white stocking cap, as well as a clean smock, and the picture he created was that of Saint Peter examining Tomas's artistic soul. He snapped the book shut.

"You have a grain of talent," said Carrel, "but you have not been trained in any serious way. You have taken on bad habits, and left to your own devices, you would surely come to nothing better than commercial art. I take it that is not what you have in mind."

"No. I want to be a sculptor."

"Very well. Are you serious?"

"Yes."

"Then you must begin at the beginning, with still lifes and some small clay models. I will review your work once a week and make corrections."

An indeterminate sentence in purgatory. For the next three weeks, Tomas worked in the studio with two other beginners, neither of whom could have been over twenty. Tomas longed for the camaraderie of his friends, but felt he could not reveal that he had entered Carrel's school.

The big, drafty room of the academy had the requisite high ceiling and north light. The walls had once been painted a deep red, but they now were stained black with years of grime and woodsmoke. Students had been scratching graffiti onto them for decades, and the surface was covered with portraits, torsos, sayings whose meaning was long lost, as well as a particularly fine drawing of a beautiful woman's foot that someone had appreciated so much that he set glass over it. The dust from the stone carving and polishing in the other room floated into this one and hung in the air.

Tomas looked for Jenny on his first day of work at the Folies, and he found her at the foot of the staircase that led up to the dressing rooms. She was wearing slippers, a skirt and a tight shirt for rehearsal, and her hair was wrapped in a scarf. When he called out her name, she looked at him, but did not take her hand from the rail.

"Well, well, if it isn't Cinderella in her everyday attire. What happened to your nice suit?"

"I gave it back."

"What a shame." She began to go up the steps.

"Jenny," he said.

"What?" She did not even turn around.

"I had a fantastic adventure last night."

"Spare me the details. I couldn't find a cab and had to walk home." And she continued up the stairs before Tomas could say anything else. Every time he ran into her after that, she looked away, and whatever words she spared for him were brusque.

Even so, he loved the job at the Folies. He worked early some days, building new sets or maintaining the building itself, and late others, when carpenters needed to be on hand in case a fast repair was required during a show. The work was very similar to what he had done back in Warsaw in the church factory, except it was secular. He made large picture frames that were set into a backdrop. A figure such as a knight in armour would stand in the frame and, from a distance, he would look like any other decorative painting. Then, at a critical moment in the spectacle, the man would reach out for a goblet of wine—this magical coming to life never failed to please the audience. Tomas's multiple skills were quickly noticed by the production manager, and soon he was making plaster busts and painting the backdrops as well.

He worked with both French and foreign men, including a large number of Italians. They were nonchalant, even a little cynical about the spectacles and the half-clad women, and Tomas learned to take on their manner without ever losing his wonder.

Josephine Baker did not spend much time at the Folies aside from her performances, and even then she occasionally arrived while the overture was playing and dressed—undressed—right in the wings. The first time Tomas saw her after the night he had saved her, he was pleased when she gave him a wide smile and a few words. But over time, he saw that she smiled at everyone. He wished he could hold her attention a little longer than all of the rest, but he did not find a way to do so.

The theatre was full of odd little rooms and nooks and crannies; there was a large, dark pit under the stage with a hydraulic lift that could raise a heavy swimming pool if necessary, and trap doors that led up to the roof in case a star needed to be lowered right above the audience.

The five hundred employees were a community with its own hierarchy, and one of the means of its expression lay in the dressing rooms. These occupied five floors, arranged in a U around a courtyard that was roofed over with glass. Fire escapes ran outside the windows. The performers used the fire escapes as an alternative means of getting up and down from the stage, for the interior staircase was narrow and they were often in a hurry. They also visited one another using the fire escapes. Open shutters indicated that guests were welcome, and closed ones meant privacy was required.

The lower one's status as a performer, the higher up one dressed. The showgirls, whose job was to do nothing more than look beautiful, stayed on the top floor. Chorus-line dancers such as Jenny stayed on the fourth, and so on down, with the biggest stars on the second floor. Mistinguett had a tiny room right in the wings, which no one else was permitted to use, even though she had not worked the Folies in some time.

One evening, passing through the arch into his own courtyard home, Tomas found Alphonse and Sorrel sitting at a table with a half-empty bottle of vodka between them.

"Come in," Alphonse said, more loudly than necessary. He rose and ushered Tomas to the table as if he were a guest. He was flushed and his eyes glowed. Sorrel was less animated. He sat at the table with his chin in his hand, a pipe between his lips and an amused look in his eyes.

"You are a lucky man, Tomas," said Alphonse. "Another hour and you would have missed your chance to celebrate with us."

"Celebrate what?"

"We are both joining you as members of the working class. It has been a lucky, lucky day."

Carrel had been hard on him at the studio earlier that afternoon, so Tomas was not in a particularly good frame of mind, but he tried to be happy for their sakes. Alphonse took a jam jar and filled it halfway to the top with vodka for him. Tomas took it in one swallow in order to catch up to them and enjoyed the afterburn in his throat.

"Well, what kind of work have you found?" Tomas asked.

"I have the glorious honour," said Sorrel, "of putting sacks of potatoes onto trains at the Montparnasse station."

"You don't sound happy about it."

"You are mistaken. I am extremely happy. Some of the others will unload sacks of coal from the trains. Potatoes have the advantage of being cleaner than coal, and I can slip a few into my pockets for our dinner."

"And you?" Tomas asked Alphonse.

"Let's just say that my job pays well."

"What's that supposed to mean?"

Sorrel answered for him. "He won't tell us where he works. It's a secret. I've been trying to get him to tell me all night."

"Oh, come on," said Tomas. "We're your friends. What job could be so terrible that you can't tell us about it?"

Alphonse smiled with the glow of alcohol, but he would not speak on the subject.

"Now that we all have jobs, we have the money to begin our studies in earnest," said Alphonse. "We'll investigate the art schools, and start producing our work."

Tomas said nothing. He looked at the bottom of his empty jam jar, and when Alphonse saw this, he filled the glass again. The gesture was full of so much goodwill that Tomas could not keep silent.

"I have a confession to make," he said.

"Very well," Sorrel said, taking on an officious tone, "we will be your priests, but you need to confess in the church of art. Do you have a string?" He was drunk and playing a game, but he insisted the rules be followed.

"What?"

"Pull the strings from your boots. We can't give absolution unless we do this right."

"You're drunk," said Tomas, but he pulled the strings from his boots and passed them to Sorrel, who tied them together.

"Alphonse splurged on a new burin today," said Sorrel. "Give it to me."

The burin looked like a bent screwdriver with a tip bevelled to a very sharp point. Alphonse was proud of this first piece of art equipment, and he had already carved his initials into the handle. Sorrel took Tomas's joined boot strings and tied the burin to one end. On the other end he tied one of his paintbrushes. He put the string over his neck so the burin and the paintbrush hung on either side of his chest.

Alphonse and even Tomas began to laugh.

"I am the priest of the church of art. This is my stole, and I am now ready to hear your confession. Speak, my son."

Smiling, Tomas beat his breast.

"Father, I have sinned."

"Of course you have. You're an artist. What else is possible? How long since your last confession?"

"I have never confessed in the church of art before."

"Ah, a new convert. Very good. Go on."

"I have been guilty of lust."

"In Paris, this is not a sin. What else?"

"At the Folies, I have offended a woman for whom I have a certain affection."

"That is beyond my power to forgive. You must throw yourself on the mercy of the woman."

Tomas stopped smiling.

"I am already taking art lessons."

Alphonse looked at him sharply. "What? Where?"

Tomas told them about the Académie Carrel.

"How could you afford it?" Alphonse asked.

Tomas explained about the thousand-franc note Josephine Baker had given him.

"Why did you find it necessary to keep it a secret?" Alphonse asked.

"I was embarrassed."

"Did you think I would want some of your money?" Alphonse asked. "I don't care about money beyond what it takes to live. Why would you hide the art school from us? It's what we want more than anything else."

"Stop your moralizing," said Sorrel. "I am the priest here, and I offer Tomas full absolution for his sins."

"I don't think this is funny any more," said Alphonse.

Sorrel turned on him.

"Who said it was funny? I am offering Tomas forgiveness because he did the right thing. What did you think, that the three of us would march side by side into glory? It never works that way. Each of us is going to succeed or fail on his own merits."

"We are a mutual self-help society at this table," Alphonse said earnestly. "When one has good fortune, he should spread it around."

Sorrel snorted.

Alphonse turned to Tomas. "At least tell us about the place." Tomas described the school and Carrel, and in the spirit of confession, told them Carrel had not been very encouraging to him yet.

"What's the matter with you?" Sorrel asked when Tomas had finished. "Why do you wilt every time you are criticized?"

"Because it stings."

"Let it sting, and remember the feeling. Let it burn on your back to spur you on. If someone points out a mistake, never make the same one again. First we need to learn a little to put some polish on our native ability. Then we need to succeed dramatically, so we reach the point where our name sells the work instead of our work selling our name."

Sorrel threw off his stole and drank down the last of his vodka.

"I didn't come here for glory," said Alphonse. "I just came here to make art. I'll be happy enough if I earn enough to live from it."

"Even if it's teaching art to children in some provincial school?" asked Sorrel.

"There is no dishonour in teaching."

"But not much glory, either."

"Glory is overrated."

"So is modesty."

Whenever Tomas worked a late shift, he tried to see at least a little of each act. After he had been working at the Folies for three months, he made his way to a spot in the wings where he was nearly invisible, and watched a spectacle he had not seen before. The set had involved a complicated web of ropes that Derval had taken special pleasure in having Tomas work on, as he considered him now to be the house rope specialist. The curtain opened and a low blue light came up on the web, in which bare-breasted men and women were sleeping, a dozen of them in stylized loincloths designed to reveal as much as they covered. As the stage lights grew stronger, these men and women seemed to be waking to another day of captivity. The orchestra struck up Beethoven's "Slave Chorus," and the trapped bodies on stage became aware of their own confinement and started to undulate in a slow mime of agony.

A slight movement in the periphery of his vision caught Tomas's attention. He looked up to the bridge that spanned the stage and saw Jenny watching the same scene. Her face was white, illuminated like a jewel in the darkness. He wondered how she got up there, for the stage manager did not permit any but the required personnel to be in their necessary places. Everyone else had to be stowed away, like a stage flat waiting for its tableau.

It was delicious to look up at her while she was unaware that she was being watched. She stood with complete unselfconsciousness, her arms crossed on the railing, studying the scene with great intensity. To guess by her expression, she was thinking the same thoughts as he had. He felt an invisible line of emotion extend toward her, and when it reached its goal, she must have sensed its touch, because she looked down at him directly, although he was partially hidden by the curtain. He gave her a small wave, but she did not return his greeting. He could not tell if she had not seen him or was ignoring him, and after a moment, she walked off the bridge to the opposite wing.

Tomas told himself that her indifference did not matter. Jenny was one of twenty Tiller Girls, and there were at least twice as many showgirls, to say nothing of some lovely ushers and the young woman who took tickets in the front booth. But to his mind none of them had Jenny's wit or intelligence. Even as he was saying these things to himself, he went back toward the steps that led up to the dressing rooms in hope of catching sight of her again, but she was gone.

Over the following days, Tomas became more determined in his search for Jenny. She could not avoid taking her place on stage, but she never seemed to be in the wings when he went looking for her. If he waited at the stage door on the Rue Saulnier, she arrived before he did or managed to come so late that he had given up hope. Her friends were impossibly vague about where she was. He scoured the nooks and crannies of the Folies in the hope that he might stumble upon her.

When he hadn't caught a glimpse of her for two days running, he decided to watch on stage. She seemed lighter on her feet than the others, as if she hovered in the air at each leap. There was no such lightness in the place he had come from, where stolidity was prized above all else. But if she was going to continue to avoid him, there was nothing he could do.

He went down to the workshop below the stage after Jenny's act ended, and picked up a paintbrush to start work on a bust for one of the shows. It was a fanciful piece of work, a Marie Antoinette that needed to be whitewashed to make it pick up the light better. It seemed to take him a great deal of time to prepare. He could not find the tin of whitewash, and then he could not find a nail to open it up with. When he finally did open the tin, he could not find the right brush. As he was looking through the workshop for it, he realized that he did not care about the job. He wanted Jenny, and he intended to find her.

The show had ended and the stairs were full of artistes going up and down, some already in their street clothes. He passed the dog trainer, who had a schnauzer in his hands, then a couple of acrobats and finally one of the other Tiller Girls.

"Is Jenny still up in the dressing room?" Tomas asked.

"The last I looked."

He made his way up and knocked on the door. One of the other dancers answered.

"Is Jenny in?"

"I'll see."

The dressing room was not so very large that she needed to look far, but the woman shut the door. Tomas waited outside, thinking it was taking her a very long time. Finally, the door opened again.

"No."

"She's gone?"

"I don't know, but she's not in."

"You're sure?"

She gave him a look and closed the door again. He waited at the steps as the various artistes left, first in a stream, and then in smaller groups. Finally, only the odd person came down the stairs, one of them a showgirl.

"Do you know Jenny, the Tiller Girl?" Tomas asked.

"Sure."

"Is she still up there?"

"I think so. She was talking to some friends."

Tomas climbed up to the second floor and stepped out onto the fire escape in the enclosed courtyard. He made his way up to the fourth floor and tried to count the shuttered windows to determine which of them belonged to the Tiller Girls. When he found the one he thought was correct, he knocked upon it.

"Who's there?" a voice asked, but he could not tell who it was through the shutters.

"Tomas."

"Jenny's gone."

"Who is speaking?"

"Teresa."

He had never met a Tiller Girl named Teresa. The voice was a little too familiar.

"Then maybe you can take a message to Jenny for me."

"What is it?"

He hesitated, not wanting to say the words through a closed shutter.

"Tell her I need to see her."

"Tell her yourself."

"But I don't know where she is."

"Wait until tomorrow."

Tomas sighed. "That's a very long time away."

"Don't be an idiot. It's only a few hours."

"It's eternity for a man in love," said Tomas.

The words startled him, coming out of his mouth on their own. He waited, but nothing else came through the shutter, and so he made his way down the steps again. As he reached the second floor, he heard the shutters open up above him. He stood as far back as he could, but he could still barely see Jenny, who leaned out over the windowsill.

"What business do you have speaking of love through a closed shutter?" she asked.

"How else was I to get through to you?"

"I've walked past you dozens of times in the past few weeks, and your love managed to keep itself mute."

She drew her head back, but she did not pull the shutters closed, nor did he hear her shut the window behind them. Tomas could see a few other heads sticking out of various dressing-room windows, watching him.

"Hey, you." Tomas looked to see a corpulent man standing at a window directly in front of him. "You can't just tell her you love her and expect her to fall into your arms."

"Why not?"

"What's in it for her?"

"Me."

The man looked him over, and his expression showed he was not impressed. He was in his fifties, and jowled, a comedian whose act Tomas had never followed, although he'd seen him around the theatre often enough. He was tying his cravat.

"You can't just win a woman with a declaration of your love," said the comedian. "You have to woo her. Tell her she's the sun."

"The what?"

"The sun."

"But she's not the sun."

"Are you an idiot? Do you want her or not?"

"Of course I do."

"Then tell her she's the sun."

"You want me to repeat your words?"

"That's right. First, get her attention. Call out to her."

Tomas did as the man said, not really sure why he was allowing himself to follow his instructions. He called out Jenny's name several times, but the only heads that showed came from other windows.

"She's not coming out," said Tomas.

"Of course not. But she's listening. Now tell her she is the sun."

Tomas looked at the man strangely, but unfamiliar with the language as he was, he permitted himself to be guided and did as he was told.

"Jenny, you are the sun."

"Idiot! Not stupidly, like that. You need to deliver your lines as if they sprang straight from your heart."

"Jenny," Tomas called, but she did not show. "I look to the East, and Jenny is the sun."

A basin's worth of soapy water came flying out of Jenny's window and fell upon Tomas's upturned face before he could move aside. He sputtered and wiped his face as Jenny appeared up above him.

"What do you think I am, a character in a comedy?"

The man in the cravat sputtered himself, and put down his glass. "*Romeo and Juliet* is not a comedy," he called up to Jenny. "It is a tragedy."

When Tomas looked up at Jenny, both she and the comedian laughed at him.

"Well, am I still the sun to you? Or am I a storm cloud?" Jenny shouted.

"The Paris sky is variable. I'm still hoping you'll become the sun."

"Not exactly Edmond Rostand," said the comedian, "but at least you have some wit."

"Don't try to be a poet with me, Tomas. Your French isn't good enough and you don't have a poetic turn of mind."

"So what should I be?"

"Be yourself, and if that pleases me, we can see what happens next."

"I still owe you something."

"I'll say. You'd never have this job if it weren't for me."

"More than that."

"Go on."

"On the day we met, I promised to make a bust of you in something more permanent than bread. I'd still like to do that, now that I can afford the clay."

"You want me to sit for you?"

"Yes."

"I don't know. You were rude to me."

"I meant no rudeness."

"You offended me, whether you intended it or not."

"Shame on you, Jenny!" a woman shouted from one of the windows. "You have a lover beseeching you from beneath your window. Have a heart."

"And what if he breaks it?"

"Every heart gets broken," a showgirl called from another window. "His heart might get broken, too."

She considered for a while. "How can you say you love me when you don't even know me?"

"I love what I know, and I long to know more." There was some scattered applause from the windows. "Come out with me, Jenny. I loved you when I first saw you on that café terrace, and now I've remembered it."

"How do I know you won't forget again?"

"I only know I'll do the best I can."

It seemed to be, at last, enough. Jenny called down: "Meet me at the stage door."

Tomas waited for her by the exit to the Rue Saulnier, impervious to the stares of the doorman from his stool. She came down the last of the steps and walked toward him warily. As soon as she was close to him, he took her in his arms, kissed her on both cheeks and held her tightly.

"Thank you for giving me a second chance."

"You're lucky to get it. Come on, let's get away from this place."

Jenny took him to a café around the corner, directly across from the front door of the Folies. It was a wedge-shaped room in a wedge-shaped building made by two streets that met at a tight angle. The prostitutes had been driven out of the Folies eight years before, and now they waited in the café across the way for those whose appetites had been whetted by the show. Most had already gone off to their hotel rooms with men in tow. All that remained was a very drunk, middle-aged man, whom an old prostitute was trying to rouse from his alcoholic stupor.

"This is a terrible place," said Jenny, "but it's late and nothing else is open nearby."

"I don't care about the place. Let's just sit down."

They found seats right at the window and Tomas took her hand as soon as she laid it on the table. Her hand under his was warm.

"You're dressed the same way you were when we first met," said Tomas.

"Dancers don't make enough to buy an extensive wardrobe."

"That's not what I meant. I feel as if we're in the same café, but you don't need to go to work this time. When I first saw you, you smiled at me."

"Yes."

"Why did you do that?"

"I have the right to smile or frown as I please."

"I looked at you because you were very attractive. Why did you look at me?"

"Are you after compliments?"

"No."

"I told you that day that you were handsome enough from a distance. But I could see you were very serious, too, with your brow all knotted with deep thoughts."

"You were laughing at me?"

"I was. I thought you were one of those dour Germans who wanted to talk philosophy. But the bread sculpture was fun, and then I thought there was some hope for you."

"I want to tell you something."

"What?"

He leaned in toward her ear as if to whisper to her, and kissed her earlobe gently. He would have liked to go on kissing it around the ridge, but it was covered by her hat. She did not pull away.

"I came to Paris to be an artist," he said, still close to her ear, "and I thought it was more than enough to fill my life. But now I can't take my eyes off you."

He leaned back in his chair to find the waiter at his side.

"Two coffees, two brandies," Jenny said, and the waiter went away. Her cheeks were flushed and she seemed less confident and ironic. After a moment she asked, "Why did you want to be an artist?"

He laughed and she laughed with him. There was no answer to such a question. "I didn't want to become an artist. I just am one. It's necessary to me." He took her face in his hands. She did not resist. He was about to kiss her when the waiter arrived at his side.

"Go ahead," said the waiter. "I can wait."

Tomas touched his lips to hers tentatively and then more strongly, and the pressure was delightful, but he could not forget the man beside him and he began to pull back.

"You call that a kiss?" the waiter asked. He set down the coffee and brandy and went back to his place behind the counter.

They kissed again. Their tongues touched and the warmth and wetness of the brief contact made him breathless.

"I think we might both be in danger of drowning," said Jenny.

They smoked and they talked and drank, touching each other, lighting cigarettes for each other, occasionally kissing. The words came easily and fast, as if they needed to make up for lost time. Time did run out for them, as even this particular café had to close sometime, and when they were out on the street, he was not ready to give her up. They stood on the sidewalk, and her embrace was now as strong as his.

"Do you have any money?" Jenny asked.

"Three or four francs."

"I don't have much more. We can't take a cab back to my place. We'll need to walk."

"I'll take you in my arms and we'll fly."

Side by side, holding on to each other tightly, they made their way down through the silent streets to the river and walked along the quay and up the Boulevard Saint-Michel to Jenny's hotel on the Rue de l'École de Médecine.

M. Perès manned the front desk of the Hotel Saint-Pierre where Jenny lived. He was bent over the desk, reading a text by the light of a single small lamp. He looked up over his eyeglasses as the two came in.

"Could I have my key?"

"Of course, but may I speak to you for a moment?"

He took her aside and Tomas stepped back toward the front door to give them some space.

"Is everything all right?" Tomas asked when she returned.

"Nothing I can't take care of in a moment," she said. "Come on."

Tomas followed her up the curving staircase to her room on the sixth floor. When they finally arrived at the small landing, they found a man already there, leaning against Jenny's door and smoking a cigarette. He was tall, fresh-faced and curly-haired, and he wore a priest's collar.

"Tomas," said Jenny, "this is Father Fred, the chaplain of the Tiller Girls Dancing Corps."

Tomas found himself shaking the man's hand. He wore a long black coat open at the front to reveal his priest's collar. His eyes were troubled.

"Who's this?" Fred asked.

"A friend from the Folies. What are you doing here, Fred? It's almost three in the morning."

"One of the girls is in trouble and I wanted to talk to you about her."

"I can't talk now. M. Perès shouldn't have let you up."

"It's the collar."

"You used it unfairly, you naughty boy. I have to ask you to leave."

"Can I come for a lesson tomorrow?"

"Tomorrow is not a good day for me."

"When can I come?"

"We'll talk. Go to bed now, Fred. Whatever the problem is, it'll wait until I see you again."

He nodded, shook hands and walked hurriedly down the steps. Jenny fitted her key into the door.

"What kind of lessons do you give him?" Tomas asked.

"English lessons."

"But he is an Anglican priest. Why would he need English lessons from you?"

Jenny opened the door and brought him inside. Her room was very small and it had only one chair, which she offered to

Tomas. Jenny sat on the bed. She took a bottle of marc from her side table, but she had only one glass so she shared hers with Tomas, who tried to put himself at ease, but whose discomfort at the sight of another man on Jenny's landing made him grim.

"How much do you charge for these English lessons?"

"To my very own chaplain, I charge nothing, of course."

"I wouldn't mind a few English lessons of my own," Tomas said.

"I wouldn't charge you, either."

"You're very generous."

"I detect a note of sarcasm. Now come over here and sit down beside me. This is hardly a conversation we need to have now."

Near dawn, Tomas lay beside Jenny, too restless to sleep. He watched her as she slept, and if he had not been afraid of waking her, he would have gathered her in his arms for the pleasure of holding her body close to his. She seemed to wear the tiniest of smiles, and he kissed the tip of his index finger, and then touched it to each side of her mouth.

Tomas rose and went to the window to smoke. As he rolled his cigarette, he looked back at her on the bed. She lay on her side, her head a mass of curls. He had been without a lover for a very long time, too long, and now that he had found her he would take very good care of her.

Having rolled the cigarette, he opened the twin windows and leaned out to light his match. Down below was the old courtyard and operating theatre of the medical school, now converted into a studio for the École des Arts Décoratifs. Above and beyond the school lay the Luxembourg Gardens, where he walked some-times past the children who sailed their miniature sailboats in the fountain.

Soon it would be dawn. Tomas finished his cigarette and threw the glowing butt onto the street below.

The panes of each of the two windows he had opened into the room were covered with dew. He looked back at Jenny, and with his finger, he traced a line depicting her in repose. It amused him to draw Jenny this way, and he filled all six panes with her, but by the time she awoke much later, the sun had dried the dew and nothing of the finger paintings remained, except for the ghost of an outline in the dust.

FOUR

As the months passed, the studio on the Impasse Diablotin began to fill with the tools and the creations of the artists' trades. Alphonse's single burin was joined by two dozen others of various thicknesses, as well as a stack of copper plates for etching and engraving. Brushes multiplied throughout the room, many dry and upright in coffee tins, and others submerged in turpentine, which stank so strongly that Jenny avoided the place as much as she could. Tubes of paint were stacked at one end of a table, often with their caps missing or put on so loosely that the colours oozed out onto the palettes and onto the table itself. Paper, pencils, charcoal in lumps and sticks lay among the jam jars, tobacco tins and biscuit boxes. Sorrel bought canvases stretched on wooden frames, and Tomas needed large amounts of clay and plaster of Paris, as well as modelling stands and wires and pipes out of which to make armatures. He did no woodcarving, but there were blocks of stone that he chipped at, out in the courtyard when the others complained of the noise and the dust.

Alphonse might push aside the tubes of paint to make himself room to eat a bowl of soup at the table, and so cover a chisel. Tomas would move aside reams of newsprint in the search for his chisel and cover up Sorrel's new palettes. The endless clutter led to clay busts in the washbasin, jam upon a pallet because the jar had been needed and socks missing altogether because they happened to be handy when a palette knife required cleaning.

But Tomas was not as blissful as he had thought he would be. He was more at ease when he was working on the set of the Folies. Out on the street, he saw carpenters and stonemasons whistle as they went about their jobs, and some of the Italian stagehands at the Folies sang a great deal. But none of the art students he knew were whistlers or singers, at least not while they were engaged in their work. The occupation brought with it a certain restlessness, as if the artist was always searching for something that he never quite found. Tomas felt this himself, and he could see it in Sorrel, who occasionally worked a canvas until the surface was thick with paint, only to wipe it all off and begin again. Alphonse was the calmest and surest of the three, because lines scratched into a copper plate were difficult to correct, although he made mistakes too and sometimes had to burnish sections of plates to correct errors.

Tomas was troubled by his lack of confidence in his abilities. Here in Paris, there were so many skilled draftsmen, so many determined artists, that they diminished his sense of destiny; back in Lithuania his skill was unchallenged in the whole parish. He did not talk about his misgivings very much, but he did hint at them once to Sorrel, who was painting a village scene on a canvas across the room.

"Did the priests train you well back home?" Sorrel asked without turning to face Tomas.

"Well enough."

"Then remember this. Many are called, but few are chosen. You're in Paris with all the others who have been called. Now you have to find a way to be among the chosen."

"But how?"

Sorrel turned to face him. "That's the hard part. We'll figure it out eventually. In the meantime, learn whatever you can."

The three artists worked systematically through the rigorous fundamentals that Carrel laid out for them in his school, drawing, painting, mastering and remastering techniques of perspective, and practising all the branches of work from printmaking, to sculpting, to mosaic. Although Tomas, Sorrel and Alphonse were the oldest students at the school and felt at first like dunces who had been held back, they had lived more than the others, and soon established themselves as the seniors. None of them thought to go to the École des Beaux-Arts any more.

Carrel held back on introducing life drawing much longer than the other schools because he claimed that drawing from life was the pinnacle of study. Besides, he did not like to pay for models, who cost more than apples and oranges in a bowl, and he waited six months before he had a full class of students to cover the costs. On the first day of life drawing, Carrel's big studio bustled with two dozen artists jockeying for the best-lighted positions around the dais and setting up their easels. Tomas was late, and Alphonse and Sorrel stood side by side. Alphonse was sharpening pencil after pencil with a penknife.

"How many pencils do you think you'll need?" Sorrel asked irritably.

"I don't know. I just want to be ready."

"You fuss like a woman."

"Shut your mouth."

"Go somewhere else if you're going to make all that noise," said Sorrel. "You sound like a mouse gnawing at a baseboard."

"If you don't like it, you move."

Sorrel swept up his paper, chalks and pencils. "I'm going to the other side of the dais, but next time you'll be the one to move!"

Camaraderie was easy over meals and drinks, but once they started to work, Sorrel and Alphonse chafed against each other, the tiniest habits of one driving the other to irritation.

Tomas took the place Sorrel had vacated.

"What's with you?" Tomas asked quietly in Lithuanian, as Alphonse continued to fuss with his pencil.

"I've never seen a naked woman before. Anytime I happened to see one accidentally, I looked away."

He broke the lead of his latest pencil and started sharpening again.

"You won't be able to look away now," said Tomas gently.

"I know."

Maître Carrel came into the room, his face framed by his white cap and white beard, leading the model by the hand. She was wearing slippers and a robe knotted at the waist. He stopped at the steps to the dais, patted the model's hand affectionately and turned to face the students.

"You will begin by drawing a few lines to place the model in the centre of your page. Consider these an armature upon which you will drape her body. We begin with very short poses, no more than thirty seconds. Use charcoals and work quickly. Capture the essentials. Then we will move on to slightly longer poses, and finally to a half-hour sustained pose. You may use pencils for the last pose and overpaint with gouache later. So far, I have taught you to be precise and careful. Some of you have painted still lifes until the fruit rotted in the baskets. No more. Now it is time to move up to the next level. In modern times you need to learn how to move quickly. I will come back to make comments when you are done."

The model was a woman in her middle twenties with her dark hair twisted into a braid and knotted up at the top of her head to keep the hair off her shoulders. She dropped her robe on a chair at the bottom of the dais, stepped out of her slippers and climbed the three steps to the top of the platform. Her movements were fluid, but once she struck a pose, she might have been a statue herself for her alabaster skin. The students had almost no time to reflect on her beauty or lack of it. Tomas was still gathering his wits when she dropped what had been her first pose and put her hands on her hips. The other students flipped away their first sheets of newsprint and started on their next drawings.

Tomas's charcoal flew across the page. She shifted again. No time to rework a single line. Flip the page and do another pose. The model crossed her arms, or looked away, or shifted into a new pose before he had even completed the outline of the one before. Thankfully, the poses began to slow, but there was still precious little time.

He had long ago learned how to look really hard at things, to get the essentials of the subject clearly through his eye to his mind and into his hand. He had to eliminate the intermediate step of conscious thought. He needed to erase his mind. He had to allow the eye and the hand to have a direct connection. Only when she slowed to the five-minute poses did he have a moment to glance at Alphonse beside him. The man was drawing as madly as the rest of them, but he was not looking up at the model.

When the model turned over an hourglass for the sustained pose, Tomas felt as if he had a richness of time, as if all the rushing before had burned off his anxiety and now allowed him to work well. The model sat down and put one elbow behind her on the back of the chair. Tomas attacked the pose with his pencil.

When the sustained pose was over, the model stepped off the dais, put on her robe and slippers and walked into the next room to change.

Tomas felt happy with what he'd caught in the last pose. He feverishly added some detail to the face as Carrel came in and began to walk around the students. Carrel seemed to be very critical of everything Tomas did, but now that Tomas was working on the human form, the real subject for any sculptor, he felt hopeful that his strengths would stand out.

"Too stiff," Carrel said.

The two words were like a blow. "What do you mean?"

"Too academic. You draw her as if she were a fish on ice. The problem is here, at the shoulders." Carrel took Tomas's pencil from his hands and drew over the careful lines Tomas had laid down. Carrel was quick and sure. The sketch softened as he worked, and Tomas could feel the heat on his cheeks as Carrel corrected him.

"You see?" Carrel asked.

"Yes."

Carrel moved on to Alphonse.

"What's this?" Carrel asked.

Much as Alphonse had not looked up at the model, now he looked away from Carrel.

"My sketches."

"I know they are your sketches. Are they all like this? Why have you left off the breasts and the pudendum?"

"I was just concentrating on the outline."

"But you've put in the nose and the eyes."

"I'm having trouble working at this speed."

"The breasts take no time at all, young man. Look here."

Carrel took the pencil and rendered the breasts in a single line with two curves. "If she doesn't have breasts and pudendum, she's not a woman," said Carrel, and he pushed Alphonse's shoulder affectionately. Some of the other students laughed. Carrel moved on. When he came to Sorrel, he looked over the sustained pose and then flipped back through the papers to look at the shorter poses. He grunted.

"Keep this up," he said, and half a dozen students pursed their lips in envy. If Alphonse suffered the amusement of the other students, Sorrel was beginning to enjoy their admiration, and every time Carrel praised him, his reputation in the studio rose a notch.

Carrel was done with his instruction for the day. The students could stay and work in his studio awhile longer if they chose, but that was entirely up to them. If he was in a good mood, he might ask one of them to bring him a cup of coffee from the café. A particularly honoured student might be allowed to stretch canvases or sift plaster for him.

Sorrel sauntered over to Tomas and Alphonse, clearly pleased.

"Congratulations," Tomas said, using all the effort he could muster.

"Do you want to see my sketches?"

"Bring them over."

Tomas tried to beat down the unattractive emotion that was filling his chest. Sorrel brought his sheets over and set them up on the easel. He began to flip through them, one by one, looking at Tomas and Alphonse to measure their responses. Much as Tomas hated to admit it, they were good. Not that they rendered the model any more realistically than he had. But there was a sureness to Sorrel's work, a kind of confidence that took you by the throat and said: "I know what I am doing." Some of the drawings had been made without lifting the pencil off the page, and this fluid line was further proof of his talent. Sorrel had infernal confidence, and Tomas felt he could use a measure of brimstone himself.

"Now show me your work," said Sorrel, and Tomas did. Sorrel did not say much, but from time to time he grunted. He had stepped out of the herd, and flaunting his new status, he was already acting like Carrel. "Your turn," said Sorrel to Alphonse.

"Another time."

"Shy?"

"Maybe."

"Fool. You'll make someone a good wife."

Tomas winced on Alphonse's behalf as Sorrel gathered up his portfolio and left.

"You never looked at the model at all, did you?" Tomas asked in Lithuanian.

"How could I look at her? I tried again and again, but my neck would not lift my head and my eyes would not rise when I told them to."

Alphonse looked up at Tomas.

"You're just shy," Tomas said. "You'll get over it."

"I was a good painter back home, and I could draw likenesses that made my subjects weep."

"All of us were good where we came from, but this is Paris."

"Who says one needs to paint nudes, anyway? People don't walk around without their clothes on in public. Everyone wears something. Even Adam learned to be ashamed of his nakedness."

Tomas laughed.

"Don't laugh at me. Modesty is supposed to be a virtue."

"Listen, a nude is not the same as a naked woman. If you come across a woman bathing, you see her naked. It's private. A nude is simply an expression of womanhood, the idea of woman. When she slips off her robe and steps up on the dais, you approach her as an object to be rendered."

"You mean as if she were a bowl of fruit?" Alphonse asked.

"Not exactly. She does carry erotic charge, and you need to get some of that into your work."

"Fine. I see," Alphonse said. He had packed away his chalks and pencils. He was trying to appear calm, but he still had an aggrieved look around his eyes.

"So you take my point?" Tomas asked.

"No. What's special about a nude is that she's a naked woman. That's the thing that distinguishes her from a bowl of fruit, and it's indecent."

Was it possible to look at an undressed woman, ever, and think of her merely as a series of planes, as a problem to be rendered? Even though he had been working fast today, something had stirred when the model took off her clothes. Something stirred whenever he was at work at the Folies, too. An undressed woman still brought out an unbearable longing, and here in Paris that longing could be articulated. Why else did so many people come to Paris, if not to act on their desires?

"Couldn't you at least paint in the breasts and the pudendum, as Carrel calls it, from your imagination?" Tomas asked. "Then you wouldn't have been embarrassed."

"There are no breasts or pudenda in my imagination." Alphonse closed up his case and looked at Tomas defiantly, then turned and loped out of Carrel's academy.

The priests had done their job with Alphonse. His shame was greater than his longing.

Tomas lingered in the workshop, but there was not much to see that day. The master and the others had all gone out, and only the model was still there, dressed now, sieving a bucket of dry plaster through her fingers. The plaster needed to be a fine powder, or the lumps were next to impossible to remove after water was added. In the days when Tomas worked in the church factory, one could always distinguish the lazy apprentices from the careful ones. When the statues of the lazy ones came out of the moulds, noses, admonishing fingers and even whole arms came right off the statues of the saints if the plaster had had lumps that were not worked out by hand. But models did not usually get involved in the preparation of materials. Her long, dark braid was covered in a scarf, and her blue work smock was dusted grey with the dry plaster.

"Where have they all gone?" Tomas asked.

"To lunch."

"Aren't you going to eat as well?"

"I don't eat lunch."

"Why not?"

"Because I am trying to lose weight. Modern women need to be thin, or no one wants them."

She might have got away with this if he had not already seen her undressed. She had been thin enough. Maybe too thin.

"No money?" he asked.

"Enough for one good meal a day. I save my money for supper because if I go to bed hungry at night, I can't sleep."

Tomas had been hungry himself.

"You should eat a big lunch instead. It's better to be hungry at night," he said. "When you finally do fall asleep, you forget about your hunger. But if you're hungry during the day, there's no forgetting it."

Tomas dug into his pocket and examined what he brought out.

"It's a shame I have only four francs. If I had more, I would take you out to eat."

"Four francs! That's enough for both of us."

"Where could we eat for that?"

"I'll show you the place if you supply the money. Just give me a second to finish working the plaster and I'll be right with you."

Tomas went outside the academy to smoke a cigarette and wait for her.

Maître Carrel's workshop was off the beaten path, in a courtyard on the Rue de Javel. Tomas stood in the sun by the open gate to the street. It was quiet, during the lunch hour, and the sparrows chirped as they flitted from window ledge to fence post. The Rue de Javel was not a pretty street, nor was it usually a quiet one. Trucks and handcarts poured in and out of the coal dealer's three gates down, where black dust always hung in the air. Next door was a garage, and then a whole series of small repair shops, some specializing in gas engines and others in industrial machinery. Motors roared to life and died throughout the day. Far down the way, a perpetual cloud of steam issued from a laundry. The street smelled of coal, oil, gasoline and mould encouraged by the perpetual damp.

When the model came out, she was wearing a short blue dress and carrying an artist's portfolio. Tomas threw away the butt of his cigarette. "We're going to lunch and I don't even know your name."

"Estelle Stokes," she said, and he told her his name as well. "If you don't mind going a little out of your way, I'll show you something you haven't seen before. You'll be in my debt."

"I'm the one who's taking you out for lunch, yet I'm the one in debt to you?"

"That's right. I'm going to show you around."

"What do you intend to show me?"

"An unusual artists' studio. I wish I'd had someone to show me the ins and outs when I first came to Paris. Come on."

Tomas did not know what to make of this woman. She was slightly hard, like someone who had lived alone too long, yet she had a spark inside her. She took him up the Rue de Dantzig, where the street was full of butchers from the slaughterhouses, lunching in the cafés in their blood-spattered aprons. She led him farther to where the tiny Passage de Dantzig branched off at an island in the street. There stood an unusual round building, three storeys high, behind an iron gate. A pair of caryatids flanked the entranceway, and the garden was littered with sculptures. A man and a woman were sitting on a bench outside, drinking coffee.

"This is La Ruche," said Estelle.

"A beehive?"

"Yes. Because it is round and filled with the buzzing of many artists. I used to live and work here in one period of my life."

"Why did you leave?"

"At first it was better than the street, but the bedbugs were terrible. The worst anywhere. I kept the feet of my bed in tins of water, but the little vampires scrambled up to the ceiling and then dropped onto me from above."

"Was it a good place to work?"

"Very cheap, but the cows being slaughtered across the way moaned all morning. And all night, the building was full of the sobs of broken-hearted models, or guitar music, or endless discussions among the Jews."

"Jews?"

"Most of the people who live here are Jews. They come out of Russia and Poland knowing only two words, 'Passage Dantzig.'"

"I knew a Jew back home in Lithuania. He told me to look him up if I ever came to Paris."

"What's his name?"

"Jokub Lipchitz. Do you know him?"

"Of course I've heard of him, but he calls himself 'Jacques' here. He was gone from here by the time I arrived. He's too established to live in a place like this."

"What do you mean, *established?*"

"He lives well from his art."

The traveller through the Merdine tavern all those years ago, a short, unremarkable person, had succeeded in Paris. If one man could, why not another? But then Tomas remembered Carrel's corrections of an hour before and the excitement died.

"Have you spoken to Lipchitz?" Estelle asked.

"Not yet." Tomas studied the building. Since it was round, he assumed the studios were shaped like wedges, and there must have been over a hundred of them.

"This building has been around for over twenty years," said Estelle. "Probably a couple of thousand artists have worked here at one time or another, and only a few of them made anything of themselves."

"Lipchitz was one. Who were the others?"

"Modigliani. But he's dead now. So that makes about one in a thousand, by my calculations."

"Are you trying to depress me? If you are, you're doing a good job."

"The place is a lesson. The trick is to stand out from all the others and be noticed."

"Have you found a way?"

"If I had, I wouldn't be standing here with you. One of the

artists I knew here said one leaves La Ruche either famous or dead."

"But you're neither."

"Not yet. But I'll die if I don't get something to eat." She laughed.

Spurred by hunger, they walked quickly across Paris to the Rue Campagne-Première, just off the Boulevard Montparnasse, to a small restaurant called Chez Rosalie. The owner had once been a model for the sentimental painter, Bouguereau, but twenty years earlier, after she grew too old to model any longer, Rosalie opened a *crèmerie* to feed artists whom she had grown fond of. The place had only four marble-topped tables that seated six each on cane stools, and luckily there were two free places in the smoke-filled restaurant.

Rosalie looked into the tiny dining room from her kitchen when she heard them enter. She was an ugly old woman with a hook nose and a black scarf tied around her hair to keep it out of the food.

"Have you come to eat?" she asked.

"Yes," Estelle said, and she gave Rosalie a sad and famished look. But Rosalie was used to hungry artists.

"Not until you pay something against your account."

"I have only two francs."

"That will do. Give them here."

Tomas passed Estelle the money, and Rosalie slipped it into her apron pocket and went back to the kitchen.

"Now we have only two francs to split," Tomas whispered.

"She just likes to bark from time to time. Watch, we'll sit down to eat, and she'll be pleased if you give her another two francs when we're done. Now let's see what's left on the board."

A small table stood by the door with apples and oranges as well as carrots, two cucumbers and an assortment of Italian cheeses. Beside it was a chalkboard, listing vegetable soup, which Tomas knew well enough, and Italian foods he had never heard of. There were osso bucco, which was crossed out, lasagne *al forno* and ravioli bolognese, as well as a choice of two wines, a Frascati and a Chianti. As Estelle had predicted, Rosalie brought them each a bowl of soup as well as a basket of bread and two quarter-litre carafes of Frascati. Estelle suggested the ravioli, and Tomas agreed, having no opinion on the unfamiliar foods.

The vegetable soup was more of a brown purée than a soup because it was put through a food mill. Yet it was full of flavour and it took the edge off Tomas's hunger. The other patrons ate with the concentration of the poor, for whom filling the belly was serious business. Most of them stayed absorbed with their plates. Some of the men and a few of the women had telltale spatters of paint on their hands, fingernails and clothes. The walls were largely covered by drawings and paintings on paper, only one or two of them framed. Estelle saw him studying the walls.

"Look at the small landscape up in the corner to your right." Tomas did as she asked. "That's one of mine. I was too far back on my accounts and she accepted it as partial payment."

"You're a painter?"

"Yes. Surprised?"

"I thought you were a model."

"That's just the way I make my living."

"Oh, so art is your hobby?"

Estelle set down her spoon and looked him over with hard eyes. "I am no hobbyist. Remember that."

Tomas apologized. He had seen women in some of the schools and certain studios were devoted to them alone. But he had never heard of many female artists. They just never seemed to amount to much.

"I know what you're thinking," said Estelle, "and if you say it, I'll put my fork through your hand."

Though Tomas knew she was joking, he removed his hand from the table and kept it on his lap.

Rosalie came in with their dishes of ravioli.

"Tell me more about trading art for food," Tomas said.

"Rosalie accepts artwork for food only if she knows you well. If she accepted everything that was offered to her, she wouldn't make any money at all. The butcher and the baker don't accept art when she buys provisions."

"You seem to know this place pretty well. How long have you been in Paris?"

"Five years."

Tomas considered her situation. She had been in Paris all that time and she did not make enough money to pay for two meals each day. He shuddered, and Estelle read him correctly again.

"At least I'm free to paint here," she said.

"Weren't you free to paint at home?"

"Nobody painted where I came from. It was impossible to imagine such a thing. Where I lived, in backwoods Canada, the only paint available was house paint, and even that was hard to come by. There wasn't even a school. Just a room at the back of the mill store where some of the children sat with mothers who took turns teaching for pocket change."

One of their fellow diners, sitting alone against the wall, finished his glass of wine and called for another. He had a moustache and greying hair that receded a little at the temples. His shirt collar was too big. Rosalie shook her head ruefully when she went to him, but she served him more wine although he was clearly drunk already.

"That man there is a successful artist. His name is Maurice Utrillo," Estelle whispered. "And his mother is famous, too."

"If he's so successful, what's he doing in a place like this?"

"He spends all of his money on drink."

The man looked like an illiterate labourer down on his luck.

"Tell me about the place you came from," Tomas said to Estelle. "When I think of Canada, I think only of snow."

"It was no place. Nothing."

"Then I know something about it already, because I came from a place like that, too."

"I come from a town in northern Ontario. There is no road to the place where I grew up. People came in by boat. Everything from canoes to big laker ships that took away lumber from the mill. It was called Muskoka Mills, where the Musquash River runs into Georgian Bay, on the Great Lakes, if that means anything to you."

Tomas shook his head.

"There was no town, just a mill and some houses and a company store. Behind the mill there were miles and miles of forest, so deep that when I was a little girl, I thought there would be enough trees to last a lifetime. I lived on this narrow sliver of land between the forest and a lake as big as the sea."

She had finished her ravioli and was now smoking. She rested her cigarette in the ashtray and sipped some wine.

"When I was seventeen, a strange man came by the mill town in a canoe. I'd seen a few backwoods eccentrics by that time, and men who had gone crazy through sitting too long in their trappers' cabins, or been driven mad by the black flies. But this was no backwoodsman. One day I found him sitting on a collapsible stool in my father's yard, easel all set up, painting a picture of the laundry I'd hung out on the line that morning.

"I didn't know what to say. I'd never seen a painter before, and I didn't much like his painting my underwear on the line. It seemed indecent. But he was very persuasive." She smiled at the memory. "He stayed in the town a couple of weeks, and I watched him all the time. At first, I kept pointing out the details he got wrong, and he put up with me. But I was fascinated by what he was doing, and he was very patient with me."

"He made me see things differently, ordinary things, like the laundry on the line. Other things, too. Out in the lake, just a little way offshore, there was a jumble of boards that had fallen off a steamship just before the ice came in one year. The boards froze into the lake and then in the spring they sank to the bottom. They weren't worth the trouble of picking up. To all of us at the mill town, they were just part of the trash amid which we lived. But he was fascinated by the colour there, where the deep amber of the wood underlay the clear blue of the water. I wanted to see the way he did. I wanted him to teach me to paint."

"Did he?"

"A little. He asked me to look him up if I ever came to Toronto, but he wasn't all that friendly when I got there. I didn't know what to do with myself, and I wanted to paint. There was an art school, but it was expensive, and I didn't know anything or anyone."

"Why did you come to Paris?"

"He didn't want to teach me any more and he didn't want to let me go. He was a man, and he said all sorts of things. He said Europe was dead, and he was damned if he was going to paint smelly canals or encourage anyone else to do it. But he'd had an education. I didn't. He made me hungry to learn things. When I'd seen all I could in Toronto, I saved for the passage money to Paris."

"What about your parents?" asked.

"What about them?"

"Did they approve?"

"Of course not, but what could they do? My mother was almost done drinking herself to death in the loneliness of that mill town, and my father wasn't far behind her."

"Do you ever want to go home?" he asked.

"Sometimes I miss the colour of the light on the water, and the smells of the forest. But all that is behind me. Paris is much, much better. I'll never go back." She finished her cigarette and butted it out. "What about you?"

"My home was another world. I can't go back."

Estelle took a piece of bread and sopped up some of the tomato sauce on her plate. Tomas thought he liked what he had eaten, but he wasn't sure. The noodle squares felt unpleasantly slippery on his tongue, but the filling was good. He wasn't sure what to make of the flavours, especially tomatoes, which he had never eaten before he came to Paris. Tomas wanted coffee, but Rosalie did not serve it at the restaurant. It made the patrons lounge about too long and it was her business to feed her customers. They could get coffee somewhere else.

The door of the restaurant opened and a boy came in and went over to Utrillo.

"Here you are," said the boy, and he handed Utrillo a small package. The artist opened up the paper and took out what looked like a red lozenge, about an inch square. He placed it in his mouth and sucked on it. Rosalie locked the door of the *crèmerie* after the boy went out, as the lunch hour was now over and she would take no more new customers.

"Carrel liked your friend's work," said Estelle.

"He didn't say all that much."

"He never does. Teaching tires him out, but I could tell."

"I thought you'd left the room by then."

"I was watching from the door. I think I would like to be introduced to him."

Tomas felt a slight dip of disappointment. Even though he was happy with Jenny, it was unpleasant to be paying for the meal of a woman who was interested in his friend.

"He's a very tough man. He'll only make you unhappy."

Estelle tapped Tomas on the hand and pointed toward Utrillo. The man had spat the lozenge and a great deal of saliva into his glass, and he put his finger into the bottom and stirred it around.

"That's disgusting," Tomas said.

"Don't be so fast to judge."

Utrillo took his red finger and began to paint on the wall beside him. The lozenge had been a piece of dried aquarelle, a water paint. With the point of his finger he painted a crude tree, a lake and a nude woman beside the water. Rosalie watched him until he was done.

"It's not bad," she said, "but I hope you don't expect to pay for your wine with that."

"No, I have money for the wine," said Utrillo. "This is for the tip."

The door handle of the restaurant rattled. Rosalie opened the door and was about to say that the *crèmerie* was closed for the afternoon, but as soon as she saw who it was, she ushered him inside.

The man who entered filled the place in a manner disproportionate to his size. He wore an open raincoat and a suit and tie and a cigarette hung from his lips. His thick moustache needed trimming, and his eyes were those of a man who stayed up late too often and changed his clothes too rarely. He must have been in his early fifties and he showed every year of it. By the stir he created in the place, Tomas deduced that this was a man of some importance, but Estelle made a sour face and looked away. Still, the man smiled wryly when he recognized Estelle, and touched her shoulder in greeting as he passed. He made his way directly to Utrillo.

"Your mother and father are looking for you."

"They can go to hell."

"Come now, what kind of way is that to speak about your parents?"

"My father is dead."

"Your stepfather, then. They have all of my policemen scouring the cafés for you."

"I'll just have one more glass of wine," Utrillo said sullenly.

"You'll have no such thing. Rosalie, how much has he drunk already?"

"I didn't count the glasses."

"What a shame. Now, Maurice, get up and go home directly. I'll check on you in half an hour, and if you are not sleeping on your cot, you'll sleep behind bars tonight. Up you go now."

The artist rose and did as he was told. Most of the patrons followed him out. Estelle started to rise, but the man gestured to her to stay where she was.

"Can I get you a glass of wine?" Rosalie asked the man.

"A cognac and a coffee."

"I have no coffee."

"Just a cognac, then."

He returned to Estelle and Tomas and stood over them. When Estelle made no move to greet him, he bent down of his own accord and kissed her on each cheek.

"*Chérie*," he said.

"Tomas, I'd like you to meet Police Commissioner Zamaron."

Tomas rose and shook his hand, and Zamaron looked at him for a moment before sitting down beside Estelle.

"Well, my dear," he said, "have you been keeping on the straight and narrow?"

"Don't embarrass me the way you did Utrillo."

"I wouldn't dream of it. And as for Utrillo, the whole quarter knows his story, doesn't it?" He looked to Tomas, but Tomas did not know what he was talking about. "The man's mother married his best friend," Zamaron explained, "so his stepfather is his own age. It seems to bother him."

Zamaron turned to Estelle.

"And how is the art going?"

She brightened. "I have some new pieces on paper in my portfolio. Would you like to see them?"

"By all means."

Rosalie swept away the crumbs from the table and Estelle opened her portfolio. Zamaron flipped through the watercolours, all landscapes that were very strong. Tomas looked at Estelle with new-found admiration as Zamaron studied the pieces with a critical eye.

"If you wanted to help me out, you could buy something," she said.

Zamaron looked at one piece particularly hard and long, and then he sighed.

"I'm afraid you're too late. Payday was yesterday, but I have spent a bad night at the card table. I'm as broke this morning as I was before I received my pay packet. What a pity I don't have any money."

"I didn't know that policemen collected art," said Tomas.

"I'm one of the few who does, my friend, and that is why I have been given the job of policing the artists in Montparnasse. They are a valuable commodity to the state, but they need to be treated like children, with a firm hand."

"You could have it for only fifty francs," said Estelle.

"My dear, it would make no difference if the price was only five francs. I was completely cleaned out last night and I'll need to buy cigarettes on credit all this month."

Zamaron sat back in his chair and looked at Tomas. "Now, it's Tomas, right? I assume you are an artist too, or you wouldn't be here. Tell me a little about yourself."

Tomas explained that it was his first year in Paris, that he was studying with Carrel and working at the Folies.

"All very respectable. I won't even ask you for your residency papers. And has Estelle told you all about herself?" Zamaron asked.

"Yes."

"What did she say?"

"That she was from Canada."

"True enough, but what about the last five years or so? She wasn't modelling all that time."

"I want to put the past behind me," Estelle said, standing up.

"And so you shall. She was a little distracted by opiates for a while, but a certain policeman took her in and helped her regain her artistic ambition. This policeman did not think she was quite ready to go out on her own, but she is determined to strike out nevertheless. The jury is still out on her success."

"I have to go now," said Estelle. "Tomas, thank you for lunch. I'll see you sometime at Carrel's." She turned to Zamaron. "May I go now?"

"By all means," said Zamaron. "I'm not holding you back."

She packed up her portfolio and walked out, leaving Tomas stranded in the restaurant with the policeman, who sipped at his cognac thoughtfully. He leaned in close to Tomas, as if they had been friends for a very long time. "Do I look like a normal man to you?" he asked.

"Yes."

"Nothing that might disgust a woman?"

"I don't see with a woman's eyes, but you look all right to me."

"Then why won't Estelle let me get close to her?"

Tomas had no answer, and left the policeman to brood over his drink.

The following Monday, a day off for Folies employees, Tomas made his way across the city toward the Boulevard Saint-Michel and Jenny's hotel, passing through Montparnasse. Every quarter of Paris had its particular atmosphere, and although the Boulevard Saint-Michel was just around the corner from Montparnasse, it shared none of its glitter. Montparnasse had English pubs and fashionable artists who had moved there when Montmartre became too full of tourists after the war.

Tomas had no objection to fashionable cafés, but he had neither the money nor, he believed, the right to enter such places. He wanted to drink whisky at the Select as much as anyone one else, but when it came time to do so, he would be known as *maître* in his own right. For the time being, he was more comfortable around the Boulevard Saint-Michel, both because Jenny lived there and because the street was filled with people like him: foreign students, immigrants from Korea, Japan, North Africa or Eastern Europe.

France took its civilizing mission seriously. It opened its arms to capable men from around the world, and these flocked to Saint-Michel and the Sorbonne nearby. The invitation was not extended to women, so most of those in the cafés on the boulevard were local. They opened their arms to the foreign students as well.

The young women of the quarter often spent the whole afternoon with a cup of coffee, hoping for an offer from a man before the sun set. They did not consider themselves prostitutes, but researchers in the art of love. When they worked, they did so more as a hobby than a full-time occupation. They would accept meals or stockings, or they might ask for the loan of the week's rent. Sometimes the police would harass them to register as full-time prostitutes—a terrible fate, as they were often passed on to pimps by the gendarmes for a cut of the profits.

Tomas turned the corner at the Rue de l'École de Médecine, and immediately felt the shift in atmosphere. The small street was as quiet as a provincial lane with a long blank wall on the left, behind which stood the school of applied arts, and the modest Hotel Saint-Pierre on the right. M. Perès was at the desk, his nose in a book.

"What are you reading?" Tomas asked.

"Today I am looking over the essay of a young man, a lycée student who has trouble with Descartes. I have little hope for this one. Descartes is to philosophy what Mozart is to music. If you have difficulty with them, you will likely not rise much further."

Tomas had never even heard of Descartes, but he liked being in the neighbourhood where such names were bandied about as if they were part of the syllabus of his new life. Back home and in Warsaw, the intelligentsia consisted of learned people who saw themselves as members of a vanguard, upholders not only of learning but also of morals and manners. A member of the intelligentsia would never get drunk publicly, nor go to taverns, nor be seen with the town whore. But the delight of Paris lay in the mixture of higher learning and low pleasures. For all that M. Perès was an intellectual, half the residents of his hotel were café girls from the Boulevard Saint-Michel. M. Perès could be counted on not only to have read philosophy, but to be familiar with the more pliable local policemen, the reliable backstreet abortionists, reasonable drug dealers for any of his residents who needed just one last dose before quitting for good and sympathetic toughs who might teach an unfaithful boyfriend the error of his ways.

Tomas made his way up to Jenny's room on the top floor, where all the cheapest rooms in Paris lay. If he had been asked about the greatest difference between Paris and his old life on the farm, Tomas would have said that the life in Paris was vertical, whereas on the farm it had been horizontal. As a child he'd ranged far across the fields. Even in Warsaw all the workshops were in one-storey buildings. But in Paris, everything was up and down in spirals. Up one went in a gyre to see if a friend was in, and down one went again if the knock on the door wasn't answered. And even if it was, one might settle in for a talk, only to find no one had matches for cigarettes. Down again and up. Then it might be another trip to buy something to eat, only to find someone had forgotten the bread and down and up one went again. Even the best of legs and the strongest of lungs did not make it to the top without strain.

When Tomas knocked on the door, Jenny called for him to come in. She was sitting on her bed in a red paisley housecoat, the bolster upended behind her to provide a backrest as she read a book. Her hair was wet, but her curls were insistent, and already beginning to rise up from her scalp. Tomas could see from the pages that she was reading poetry, and he meant to ask her what it was, but the sight of her bare feet distracted him. He set down his portfolio on the floor and sat on the bed. As he did so, Jenny threw a sheet over her feet.

"Why did you do that?" Tomas asked.

"A dancer makes her living with her feet, and they're no prettier than the hands of a working man."

"Keep them hidden, then," said Tomas, and he slid his hand under the sheet to rub one of her feet along the instep. She did not protest.

Tomas glanced at the small table and saw another book there, an open English grammar.

"How is it that you know English so well?"

"It's all my father ever spoke to me. He was a philologist."

"Have you been giving Father Fred English lessons again?"

"Why such interest in our chaplain?"

"I'm still bothered by Father Fred. It doesn't make sense to have a chaplain attached to your troupe. Why can't the girls just go out to a priest if they need to see one?"

"It's good for publicity. The Folies are still a little scandalous to some, and the presence of a priest makes the girls seem more virtuous."

"But why would they care?"

"Listen, many men have fantasies about virtuous girls. There are prostitutes who dress like schoolgirls or nuns."

"But that still doesn't explain why the Tiller Girls need a priest of their own."

"He adds a frisson to our reputation, a shiver of delight, you understand? If you mix the virtuous with the scandalous, the result is far more interesting than either of the ingredients alone.

A virtuous schoolgirl is boring, and so is a street prostitute. But if you take a schoolgirl in uniform who wears no bloomers beneath her skirt, you have the makings of exquisite pornography."

"What's in it for the priest?"

"He wants a frisson too. He's a man, after all."

"I might get jealous."

"Then you're in the wrong city. Go back to the provinces."

"What a cruel thing to say. You were jealous of me once, too."

"Not jealous. Angry. There's a difference."

Tomas looked out the open window at the slate sky of Paris. "I had lunch a few days ago with a very charming Canadian woman, a model. She had an excellent figure," he said.

"Provocative beast."

"We ate at a place called Rosalie's, and a heartsick policeman tried to woo her, but she had eyes for someone else."

"You?"

"Much as I hate to admit it, no. She asked me to introduce her to Sorrel."

Jenny laughed. "If you like this woman at all, you won't do it."

"Why are you so hard on him?"

"He is a monomaniac. He thinks of only one thing."

"His art?"

"No. Himself."

"It's very hard to be an artist, Jenny. You have to put yourself before others in order to keep driving forward to succeed."

"You have to work hard to succeed in any profession."

"But some more than others. Sorrel has something I wish I had more of."

"He has something you need less of. Keep thinking that way and you'll become grim and bitter. You need to have a little fun, too."

Jenny shifted her other foot closer to Tomas's hand, and he began to caress it.

"If you want to introduce them, bring them along to a dance hall one night. There's a new one up the street and the dances are very cheap."

"I don't even know if they can dance."

"They can listen to the music. There's a new Argentine band."

"All right."

Tomas looked again at the grammar book. "I have a little English as well, you know. I wish I had more, and you promised me lessons once."

Jenny finally set down her poetry book and looked at him. "Say something in English."

"'To be, or not to be,'" said Tomas.

"How very predictable. Six one-syllable words. Do you know the next line?"

Tomas said it, and Jenny began to laugh. "You sound silly."

"Then it's up to you to teach me better."

He began to massage her calf and then his hand strayed to her thigh.

"I thought you were going to sketch me for the bust today. Keep that up and we won't get anything done."

"Your hair's still wet. I need to wait a little until it dries."

On their next night off, Jenny took the three young men and Estelle high up the Boulevard Saint-Michel to a new dance hall, which was really an old dance hall taken over by a new owner. The high-ceilinged room felt barnlike, for all the attempts at decoration. A bar ran along one wall, with red imitation-leather banquettes and tables nailed to the floor to keep them from being thrown in a fight. One of the walls was covered in mirrors, and paper streamers ran from the four corners of the room to a lamp with a Venetian glass globe at the centre. The room smelled of stale cigarette smoke. At the far end was an elevated balcony whose only access was by ladder from the dance floor, and up this ladder four men were climbing one after another, dressed in billowing shirts with puffy sleeves.

"What's the ladder for?" asked Alphonse.

"The owner makes money on every dance, so he doesn't want the band to take breaks. Once they climb up, he takes away the ladder and they stay up there all night."

Sorrel looked over the room. As his success in the Académie Carrel continued, he had become more critical in his assessment of most things, from food to drink to music. If he liked a place, he could animate the party. If he did not, he sulked and left early, casting a pall over those with him. Jenny acted as if Sorrel's reactions were insignificant to her pleasure, and Tomas tried to do the same, but he hoped that Sorrel would like the place for Estelle's sake.

They ordered a round of beer.

The room was filling, and already the air was dense with cigarette smoke. The patrons were mostly of the working class, the men in jackets and flat caps tilted at a jaunty angle so they looked like street apaches, and the women in short skirts and suspenders with mended stockings, some with flowers in their hair or on their breasts. Almost every female brow seemed to have a spit curl. One or two slumming French gentlemen were in the place as well. Foreigners were not drawn to the *bals musettes*.

"Why is this called a *musette*?" Alphonse asked.

"A *musette* is a bagpipe," said Jenny. "The Auvergne immigrants used to play them back around the turn of the century at their community parties. Then the Italians brought their accordions and the bagpipes disappeared, but the name stayed."

Tomas looked over at Estelle, who was dressed in the same blue dress she had worn when they went out to lunch the week before. Her hair was loose and her face seemed very pale indeed against the dark tresses and her red lips. When she had joined them in the tiny lobby of Jenny's hotel, Sorrel looked her up and down as if she were still the model up on the dais. Then he did not look at her again. Estelle said very little, except when Jenny made conversation with her. The atmosphere at the table was strained, but Alphonse seemed oblivious to it as he looked around at the band and the patrons. He stared unselfconsciously, and once a sour boyfriend shook his fist at him from across the room for gazing too long at his girlfriend.

Jenny took out a small purse and spilled out a pile of ten-centime pieces on the table.

"When you want to dance, take two of these each to pay the collector, and Estelle, if a man offers you a drink at the bar, turn him down. There are certain rules here. It means you have agreed to sleep with him, and if you refuse, he will start a fight."

"I know my way around all right," said Estelle.

Jenny turned to Tomas. "You must not get jealous if I dance with other men. A woman has no right to refuse an offer to dance in a *bal musette*, but only the man has to pay."

The four-piece band, an accordion, clarinet, guitar and double bass, struck up a polka. Immediately a man tapped Estelle on the shoulder, and she rose to dance with him. An attendant with a basket swooped down on them and the man dropped in two ten-centime pieces. The polka had been popular for a decade, and Tomas knew it from back home, so he took Jenny in his arms and they danced as well, in a fast one-two-three step that brought them repeatedly into contact with other boisterous dancers on the floor. Jenny and Tomas stayed for three dances, and Estelle did not have a chance to sit down, either, as three successive men chose her for their partner.

"You're quite a success," said Jenny to Estelle, who was sipping her beer with one hand and fanning herself with the other.

"I know all the dances, and that helps," she said.

"Will you dance with me?" Jenny asked Alphonse.

"I don't dance. My body was not built for it. But don't worry, I enjoy the music and the spectacle. Besides, I have to work tonight and I don't want to tire myself out."

"I could dance until my feet fall off," said Jenny. "It makes me feel alive. What about you?" she asked Sorrel, trying to bring him out of his funk.

"I dance sometimes, but I need to wait for my proper music."

Jenny and Tomas sat out two dances, but men were insistently tapping Estelle on the shoulder and she spent almost a full hour on the floor. By then the cigarette smoke was impossibly thick and the heat in the room made the dancers slick with sweat. Patches formed under the arms of the women, who pulled the material away from their breasts at the breaks to let the air cool them off a little.

Through all of this, Alphonse sat smiling and content, gawking to left and right, while Sorrel stared at his beer glass, glancing up rarely. Tomas watched Estelle's face to see if she was disappointed, but she was unfailingly good-humoured in the arms of various men, and she maintained this gay demeanour even when she was resting between spells on the dance floor.

By eleven o'clock, the dancers had spun their way through foxtrots, waltzes and javas and the inevitable Charleston, when the accordionist opened with an impossibly long wailing chord that heralded a tango.

"Come on," said Sorrel to Estelle, and he took her hand and led her out onto the floor. Tomas did not dare do the tango, which was the domain of the really good dancers and extroverts, and he watched the two of them uneasily. Sorrel was not a tall man, and on the dance floor his resemblance to Trotsky was startling and potentially ludicrous. Estelle was slightly taller than Sorrel, but she had worn flat shoes to minimize the difference. When the coin collector showed up at their elbows, Sorrel gestured toward his table, and Jenny dropped twenty centimes into the collection plate from the much-diminished pile in front of her.

Sorrel clutched Estelle to his chest, embraced her and then pushed her roughly away as if she had said something disgusting.

"What's he doing?" Tomas asked.

"An apache dance," said Jenny. "I'm surprised he knows it. You have to be really good to do it."

Estelle approached Sorrel, put one hand on his shoulder, then pushed him away with the other.

"It looks like some kind of fight," said Alphonse.

"That's the idea. A lovers' quarrel on the dance floor, played out with tango music. Sometimes it gets rough."

Estelle and Sorrel alternately embraced and struck out at each other. Some of the other dancers stood back to watch.

"He can really dance," said Tomas.

"He doesn't know the steps at all," said Jenny, "but he improvises well. Do you want to give it a try?"

"I don't think I can."

"Come on, we won't do the apache variation. We'll just try a simple tango. I'll help you."

Tomas did not exactly trip over himself on the floor, but he was not as sure-footed as Sorrel. Some of the others danced with full drama, the women being thrown to the tips of their partners' fingers, and then reeled back in, or bent low until their backs were almost parallel to the floor. One dance was enough for Tomas, but Estelle and Sorrel stayed out for a foxtrot and another tango before they returned to the table. From what Tomas had seen, neither had spoken a word to the other, but Sorrel was holding Estelle's hand when he brought her back.

"Well done," said Jenny.

Sorrel ignored her and addressed himself to Tomas.

"Stay at Jenny's tonight," he said, and he turned and led Estelle away. She said nothing at all, but turned back to give them a merry little wave over her shoulder as she went out the door.

"Presumptuous son of a bitch," said Tomas.

"Don't be upset," said Jenny. "This *is* what you were planning, isn't it? Besides, the mattress is better at my place."

FIVE

As the weeks and months passed, the studio continued to fill up with work. A dozen of Tomas's clay models of various sizes stood on the tables or on stands and even in the corners of the floor. He had done some very difficult pieces with varying success, scale copies of full-size sculptures he had seen at the Louvre. He had a passably good *Marsyas Awaiting Torture*, a *Winged Victory of Samothrace* whose wings had fallen off, and *Milo of Croton*, which he did not have the heart to finish after it had met the indifference of Carrel. More and more, Tomas looked at the studio with a sense of futility, and found himself taking on extra work at the Folies to avoid facing his sculpture.

Alphonse had quit Carrel's school after it became clear he would never be able to look at the models. Even after he became acquainted with Estelle, he could not bear to look at her when she had her clothes off and he could barely manage it with her clothes on. Estelle tried to put him at ease by being lighthearted and affectionate, and she succeeded to a certain extent. But Alphonse could not be fully comfortable with her until he left Carrel's studio altogether and moved to a school for printmakers, where he felt untroubled among the lithographers, etchers, woodblock carvers and engravers, who to some extent shared his sensibility.

When Estelle was thrown out of her own room in a building slated for demolition, Sorrel permitted her to move in with them. A woman among the men was a complication that changed the easy camaraderie of their early days. Estelle paid for her share of the room, which was good because it reduced their costs, but she also took up a quarter of the room, and so reduced their work space. She was a painter, and her easels and canvases joined the jumble. She tried to be discreet, but Sorrel did not care much for discretion and they were new lovers. Sometimes the noises from the far corner of the room prevented Tomas from falling asleep. Luckily, Alphonse worked nights, or he would have been mortified. As it was, Tomas sometimes felt as though he was a spectator in his own house. He wanted to move in with Jenny, but she insisted on keeping her independence.

The uneasiness caused by proximity of the pair was made all the worse by the success Sorrel was having in Carrel's studio. Tomas had never thought of himself as an envious person, but he had never had anything to envy before. And Sorrel had a keen sense of his own success. Whenever Carrel said something positive about his work, Sorrel's eyes would find Tomas, who practised looking enthusiastic and supportive until the muscles around his smiling lips were sore with the effort. Sorrel would continue to look at him, waiting to see if Tomas's expression would change. It became a kind of staring game, and lately, Tomas was declining to engage in it.

When Tomas first met Sorrel, the Romanian painted thickly, almost grotesquely, in a manner that was ugly but powerful. Tomas admired this style and found it a natural expression of Sorrel's character. But the style underwent a transformation in Carrel's school. The background of his paintings was broken into geometric planes, which contrasted sharply with the expressionistic subjects in the foreground. Thus the background of the paintings became still and portentous, like a stage set for a dramatic scene, but the foreground was twisted and full of energy. This contrast set up a kind of tension that attracted everyone who looked at it, including Tomas.

Carrel invited Sorrel to work with him in his private studio one day a week. The other students at the school began to accord Sorrel a level of admiration, the richer among them inviting him for drinks and asking Sorrel to bring Estelle along, too. She was lively and enjoyed a party and soon the two of them were in demand. Carrel's studio seemed brighter when the pair were there, and if they were not, other students would ask Tomas when they were expected to arrive.

The synthesis in Sorrel's work, the combination of his temperament and what he had learned at Carrel's and inhaled on the streets of Paris, had not occurred for Tomas. He had learned much about sculpture, and modelled a great deal in clay, but nothing came of it. When he did a bust of Jenny, Carrel said she was too Greek. He suggested that Tomas study the works of Rodin and Maillol, but the former was too tempestuous for Tomas, and the latter's nudes too still. He was restlessly looking for a manner in which to do his work, but the more restless he became, the less focused his search was, and the two impulses fed off each other to produce a deepening melancholy.

He was too ashamed to talk of these feelings to anyone but Jenny. Sometimes, after they had made love in her room and were lying side by side in her bed, he would look out of the open window and the despondency would descend on him as if it was carried on the air itself. Jenny would idly caress his hair and tell him that everything would come in time. He needed to study and absorb technique until it became second nature. He needed to be calm.

One day, when he was feeling particularly despondent, Jenny pointed out that the best artists had a certain elusive quality that attracted others to them. Josephine Baker had this quality; she filled the entire stage and excited the imagination of Paris. Jenny reluctantly realized that she herself could never hope to do that. Tomas might study and work hard, yet never have this quality either.

It stunned him to realize that what she said was true. He sat up in bed and turned on her.

"Then why do you bother staying with me?" he said, "if I don't have this magic you speak of?"

"Oh Tomas, I'm sorry," Jenny said, raising herself on her elbow. "But I love you for yourself. There are other things in you besides your need to make art, just as there are other things in me besides my need to dance. I don't love you for what you do, but for who you are. There are other ways of being successful. Some people shoot to the top quickly, and others gain renown more slowly. You might develop a way of seeing the world that is appealing to others. Or a mentor might take you up. You could have an exceptional piece of good luck."

Tomas was not consoled. He got out of bed and sat in the hard chair across from her bed. "But don't you chafe sometimes when you see Josephine Baker at centre stage?" Tomas asked. "Don't you wish you were in her place?"

"Of course I do, but what good is desire unless it can find some sort of expression? If you live with unfulfilled desire for too long, you become bitter."

"You think I'm bitter?"

"Of course not. But there is so much in life that is pleasant, it would be a shame to miss it while you are young."

"From the time I was a child," said Tomas suddenly, "I was forced to keep my head down, to practice my art secretly, but I managed to escape from that. Then in Warsaw, I began to forget about being an artist, and the world colluded. As long as I worked in the shop every day and ate and smoked with the other apprentices and journeymen, they treated me as an equal. But even these artisans smiled at me if I spent too much time carving. If I'd stayed there, I would have frittered my life away. Now you're telling me the same thing. To be content with my lot. To work with my head down. To remember to have a little fun. And what if nothing comes of that? What will I have then?"

"Shush, my darling. You're torturing yourself." She stepped out of the bed as well, naked, and knelt in front of him, and reached up to take his face in her hands. She looked into his eyes. "Even if everything you say comes to pass, you'll still have my love. Doesn't that count for something?"

He shook off her hands and stood to look out the window over the rooftops of Paris, but eventually he allowed himself to be coaxed back into bed.

Tomas was sitting in the studio, smoking, when Alphonse snorted once, coughed and sat up in his cot. He looked at Tomas and he looked at his watch, and he raised himself out of bed to go to the privy in the courtyard. When he returned, he washed his face in the basin and combed his hair.

"What are you doing up so early?" Tomas asked.

"I'm going over to the printing studio."

"You can't have slept more than a couple of hours."

"I'll sleep a little before I go in to work tonight."

Alphonse looked piercingly at Tomas. "You look bad this morning. Is anything wrong?"

Tomas hated himself for being so transparent. "I'm all right."

"Listen, why don't you come with me?"

"Thanks, but no. I'm not much of a printer."

"You look like you could use some company."

"Jenny's meeting me for breakfast at the café. Then we're spending the day together."

"Bring her along to my studio. She's never even seen what I do."

Tomas warmed to Alphonse's friendly gesture, and Jenny agreed to the change in plans when she met them at the café across the way.

The collective of printmakers that Alphonse belonged to was housed on the second-highest floor of a building on the Quai de Grenelle, not far from their own studio and Carrel's. The room was as big as a dance hall, with a bank of windows that over-looked the Seine, large presses at one end of the room and sinks of various sizes as well as acid baths for the etchers and benches and tables upon which to work. When they walked in, Alphonse was greeted by half a dozen men, and he introduced Tomas and Jenny to some and waved to others. Tomas could see why his countryman enjoyed the atmosphere here. He was among equals, and respected as such, whereas at the Académie Carrel he was considered slightly comical.

"Would you give me a lesson in engraving?" Jenny asked, and Alphonse beamed.

He took from his bag a copperplate four times the size of a book, and he laid this plate on a thick piece of glass on the work-bench. Then he opened up a rolled cloth in which he kept his var-ious burins, scrapers and burnishers, the tools that he used to gouge the plate. Each of the round wooden handles had an ornate *A* carved into it so it would not get mixed up with those of other printmakers.

"Now observe," said Alphonse. "I fit the burin in the palm of my right hand and I hold the copperplate with my left. Then I push only in one direction with the burin, and I turn the plate itself. The energy I impart to the burin is carried into the line on the plate, so I express my strength on the metal. It is a technique that carries something of me right into the plate, and it is the thing that I love best about engraving. It shares the action of cutting with sculpture, and therefore it is more honest than the deceptive line made by a pencil or a brush."

"How do you correct mistakes?" Jenny asked.

"It's best not to make them in the first place. But if I do, I cut off any burr that is too big with a scraper."

Alphonse was making a portrait of one of the men he worked with, a Spaniard with a fat, drooping moustache and black hair hanging over his forehead beneath a cap.

"You work without drawing the image first?" Jenny asked.

"He's very good," a passing colleague said. "He attacks the plate directly."

In spite of his lack of initial interest, Tomas became fascinated by the work that Alphonse was doing. The skills required were very different from the ones he used himself, and he admired his friend's mastery. He realized that he had unconsciously taken on some of the mocking attitude that Sorrel directed at Alphonse, and he felt ashamed of his lack of appreciation for the man's abilities.

"The plate was almost ready," said Alphonse. "I just wanted to add a few lines to it to give you an idea of how I work."

Alphonse took the plate and rubbed it with ink, and then wiped off the excess. The ink was now held in the thin lines he had cut out of the plate with his burin. He had wet his paper the day before to make sure it was evenly damp. He put his plate beside the paper and prepared the press.

The etching press consisted of a steel bed that ran between two rollers. Alphonse first put down a sheet of newsprint, then set his inked plate, face up, upon this sheet and finally laid the dampened paper on top of it. Then he placed three felts upon the paper and checked the pressure setting on the press.

"Come on, Jenny. You can turn the handle for me to pull the first print."

Jenny did as she was told. She turned a large handle and the plate, felt and paper moved between the rollers.

"Now come over to this side," said Alphonse, "and lift off the felts and the paper." He passed Jenny a pair of folded card-boards. When she lifted the paper from the plate and turned it over on the table beside the press, she had a moment's shock. Alphonse saw the look on her face and laughed.

"Yes, you see, here's the magic of it. The image comes out all at once."

"And it's backwards," said Jenny.

"Oh yes, you get used to that when you are a printer. When I work on my plate, I have to remember that I am making a mirror image."

Tomas looked closely at the image. He could see that Alphonse varied the thickness of lines as well as the distance between them. The hair of the moustache consisted of many fine lines close to one another, almost as fine as hair itself. The high cheekbones of the thin face were achieved with similar lines cut in short lengths to give a sense of concavity to the cheeks.

"Alphonse, this is nothing short of exquisite," said Tomas, and he patted his friend on the back. Alphonse glowed with satisfaction.

"I think you'd make a good teacher," said Jenny.

"Maybe he doesn't want to be one," said Tomas, thinking that his friend would be insulted. But Alphonse did not seem to mind the suggestion, and he gave Jenny a small, awkward hug.

By the time he had pulled his whole edition of six, it was already early afternoon and the others had gone for lunch. As it was close to the end of the month, none of them could afford to eat out for the second time in one day, and so, after Alphonse placed blotting paper between his engravings and wrapped them up, they made their way back to the studio, buying supplies for a late lunch after the stores reopened for the afternoon at three.

When Tomas, Jenny and Alphonse arrived with their bread, butter, cheese, wine and slices of ham wrapped in paper, they found Estelle and Sorrel had already come in from the art school. They had a chicken stewing with vegetables in a pot on the stove, which filled the air with the rich aroma of leeks, carrots, bay leaf, wine and the chicken itself. Estelle had tied her long hair back with a blue scarf and was standing over the pot, looking very much like an efficient bourgeois housewife.

"Well," said Sorrel when he saw them come in, "the smell of food attracts all the freeloaders."

"Sit down and have a glass of wine," said Estelle. "There's enough chicken here for all of us if you can stand to wait. This chicken is so old, it probably laid eggs for Charlemagne. I've had it on the stove for two hours and it's still tough."

"We bought food, too," said Alphonse.

"A real celebration, then," said Sorrel. "We have a first course and a second course. All we're missing is a dessert."

"I have a jar of raspberry jam," said Estelle. "We can have bread and jam for dessert."

"A real banquet," said Sorrel, and it was true that when they laid all their food on the table, it looked like a small feast.

"We have something to celebrate," said Jenny. "Come on, Alphonse, show them your new print."

"Put one out and we'll sprinkle it," said Tomas.

"Sprinkle it?" Estelle asked.

"It's a tradition we have back home. Whenever you get something new, it's good luck to baptize it with alcohol."

"Doesn't that damage the goods?"

"The term is purely metaphorical. We sprinkle the liquids down our throats. The only problem is, the ceremony is generally carried out with stronger spirits than wine, but when in France . . ."

"Wait a moment," said Alphonse. "I might have something that will help." He reached into a sack under his bed and pulled out a bottle of vodka.

"I bought this with my first pay packet and I've been saving it for a celebration. This looks like it might be a good opportunity to open it." He pulled out the cork and began to pour the vodka into jam jars.

"Not for me," said Estelle. "I can't drink like that."

"I can," said Jenny, "but show them the new print before we drink."

"You're sure you want to see it?"

Alphonse needed to be cajoled, but he looked happy enough to undo his portfolio, sweep the table clean and then lay down one of his prints of the Spaniard. Sorrel and Estelle stood over the piece and examined it carefully.

"It's lovely," said Estelle.

"Let's drink to it," said Sorrel, and he tipped back his glass and drank half the vodka. Tomas turned to Alphonse to see if he was irritated, for normally the owner of the bottle was the one who invited the others to drink. But Sorrel was a Romanian, and maybe they did things differently where he came from. Alphonse nodded to Tomas and Jenny, and they did the same as Sorrel had done.

Tomas sensed the tension and was going to say something to fill the silence, but Jenny spoke first.

"Look at the fine lines," she said, trying to encourage Sorrel to add his praise to Estelle's. "You see how expressive they are?"

"Wonderful technical skill."

"That's damning it with faint praise," said Estelle.

"Let's eat something," said Sorrel. "Cut some bread. It's good to drink on an empty stomach at first because the alcohol hits you directly, but eventually you have to put some food down there to join it."

He sat down at the table and began to make himself a sandwich.

"Listen, my friend," said Alphonse, "you're making the others uncomfortable. Why don't you say what you think of my piece?"

"If you ask me to speak, I'll tell the truth," said Sorrel through a mouthful of bread.

"I wouldn't expect anything else."

Sorrel swallowed what he had in his mouth and drank a little wine. "Then here it is. Your print shows very fine technique.

Congratulations. As to the portrait, it is good in an old-fashioned way. Congratulations again. But what I can't understand is why you would bother in the first place. Engraving is a job for jewellers. Prints should be made by technicians, not artists. Have you ever heard of a famous printmaker?"

"Albrecht Dürer for one. Rembrandt was another."

"Hundreds of years ago, yes. But who does prints now?"

"Picasso and Matisse are two," Alphonse replied immediately.

"As a sideline. It's an antiquated technology. You'll never make a name for yourself like this." Sorrel looked at his empty vodka glass and drank more wine instead. He seemed to think he had won the argument.

"It never occurred to me to make a name for myself. I just wanted to pull a good print. I like the smoothness of ink on paper better than oil on canvas. I'll make a name for myself in the print shop, where it counts."

"Oh, Alphonse, the salons and galleries are where it counts. And among the dealers, on the streets, in the newspapers. You have to think like a buyer. Each one wants to add to his prestige by buying a unique image, a one-of-a-kind piece. Buyers don't think deeply. To them, painters are artists and printers are craftsmen."

"That's a stupid prejudice."

"But you have to live in the world as it is, not as it should be."

"Sorrel," said Estelle, "you're being unkind."

"Maybe, but at least I'll be as known as an artist in this city. Would it be better to die unknown? Look, I'm having some success now. In a little while, I'll have enough canvases for a show. I'm already Carrel's protégé."

"Because you cultivate him," said Tomas under his breath.

Sorrel spun to face him. "And what if I do? He cultivates me too, and we both win something in the bargain. He will help me to show and I'll begin to sell. Then, watch out! I pay attention to the world and the times we live in. But you, Alphonse, you choose to go off into an eddy of art, a backwater, and you, Tomas, you wallow in some kind of melancholy."

Tomas felt as if Sorrel had just kicked him in the stomach. Sorrel drained his wineglass and helped himself to the vodka.

"Now you're going to accuse me of spoiling your mood," he said. "But you asked for it. Don't blame me."

"Estelle," said Alphonse, "do you agree?"

She sighed. "I wouldn't put it as cruelly as he does, but I'm afraid he may be right."

"I don't believe it," said Alphonse. "I believe the work is more important than the artist. Nobody knows who carved the patriarchs on the front of Notre Dame, but the works themselves speak for the artist. Tomas, what do you think?" Alphonse seemed close to tears.

"I used to think like you, but I'm afraid I'm beginning to think like Sorrel."

"You said you admired my Spaniard!"

"I do. He's very good, but I'm not sure he'll make your reputation."

"And what if I said I didn't give a damn about a reputation?"

"I'd admire you," said Tomas.

"Ultimately, the measure of an artist is how well his work sells," said Sorrel.

"So why not do commercial art?" asked Alphonse. "Look at Paul Colin. He makes posters of Josephine Baker and his work is all over town. He must live well from it."

"Real success is to do what you please and to get paid for it in your lifetime. This will happen to me faster than it will to either of you, because I am more driven."

"You're driven, all right," said Tomas, "but it doesn't mean you'll do better."

"I'll prove it to you."

Alphonse laughed. "What, and we'll meet again at fifty to see who has done well?"

"No, we won't wait that long. I'll make you a bet. I say the first one of us who sells a piece throws a party. A real party, with people and music and drink. And I mean a serious piece, not some sketch the size of a postcard. What do you say, are you for it?"

"There's not that much to lose," said Tomas. "Either I sell the first piece and feel good because of it, or one of you does and I get to eat and drink your profit."

"All right," said Sorrel. "The first one among us three who sells, throws a party for the other two." The men shook on it.

"What about me?" Estelle asked.

"You're a woman," said Sorrel.

"She can join us, Sorrel. You're in," said Tomas.

By then they had finished the ham, cheese and bread, and the chicken was as tender as it would ever be. They spoke of other things, but the rest of the meal was coloured by their conversation, and all but Sorrel ate gloomily. Alphonse put his print of the Spaniard back in his portfolio, where he would not have to look at it any more.

When the dinner ended, Tomas and Jenny stood up to go to work. Alphonse followed them into the courtyard and took Tomas aside.

"I wanted to talk to you about something."

"We just spent the whole day together."

"But Jenny was with us and this is private. I was hoping you could meet me at my lunch break tonight after the show. We eat at a café on the Rue des Lions Saint-Paul at around two-thirty."

"Can't it wait until tomorrow?"

"It can, but Sorrel or Estelle might be around, and I don't want to talk in front of them, either."

Tomas promised to meet Alphonse later that night.

—

Walking to the Folies, Tomas was slightly drunk, but the alcohol did not pick him up, and he listened to Jenny's animated speech without paying attention to what she said. He felt restless and sleepy all at once as they joined the rush of performers coming in through the stage door on the Rue Saulnier. Jenny gave him a quick kiss before making her way upstairs to the dressing room. From the orchestra pit, he could hear two violinists and a saxophonist fooling around with "Bye Bye Blackbird," but they could not get the American idiom quite right.

He lingered by the entranceway and his spirits lifted for a moment when Josephine Baker came in. She had a circle of radiance around her wherever she went. She was trailing her new manager, Count Pepito Abatino, who used a cigarette holder and wore a monocle and a tightly waxed moustache. He was dressed in evening clothes, so they must have been planning to go out after the show. Josephine herself referred to Pepito as her No-Account-Count, and word was that he had been a gigolo before he met her. Now he was managing her career, although it was unclear if he was saving her from her profligate ways or scooping up money for himself.

Tomas went down to the workshop, but there was no pressing work that needed to be done. He took out an oilstone and laid out the chisels to be sharpened. The regular, circular movement of the chisel blades on the oilstone brought on the first moment of peace he had felt the entire day. He drew the tools back and forth across the stone much longer than he needed to. Then he reached into his jacket pocket and removed the folding knife he had brought with him from Lithuania. He sharpened this blade as well, and the feel of the handle was good, too.

Without putting down the knife, he began to root around in the work room among the odds and ends of lumber used in set building. He found a block of pine about a foot square that felt right in his hands. He took this piece of wood to the workbench and began to rough out a shape with a rubber mallet and a gouge. Then he used both his knife and a chisel to cut at the thing.

His hands had not forgotten what to do. He barely thought of the shape of the object that he was making and was only vaguely conscious of the music of the various acts up on the stage. Searching for the shape inside the mood, he surprised himself, producing a traditional "worrying Christ" figure of the sort that had filled the countryside back in Lithuania. But he left off the crown of thorns and so the figure seemed altogether secular, more like a man deeply worried about meeting the month's rent, or paying for his son's education. By the time the foreman came by with work for him, Tomas had the whole thing almost completed in the rough. He was embarrassed to have been caught wasting time on a piece of such old-fashioned peasant art, and shoved it into a sack at the back of the shop.

The Café des Lions Saint-Paul was at the corner of the residential street of the same name in the Marais. Part of an old neighbourhood in the Jewish district, it was an unlikely place for a late-night café. That section of town had been unfashionable for a very long time, and so the old houses mouldered quietly, the flagstones on the narrow sidewalks broken and unmended. Deliverymen and washerwomen and many unsuccessful merchants inhabited the fine old houses that had been divided into warrens for the working class and the poor, just the kind of people who would be unlikely to complain effectively against a café that stayed open all night in their neighbourhood.

The door to the café was warped and scraped against the floor as Tomas swung it open. The room was very large and simple, with two dozen cheap tables and chairs and a scuffed and chipped wooden bar at which six policemen were standing on their evening break. They fell silent as he walked in, as if they had been speaking about something they did not want overheard. Among them stood Police Commissioner Zamaron, whom Tomas had met at Rosalie's. Zamaron held a cigarette between his yellow fingers and he looked just as tired as he had the first time Tomas met him. His flesh was pallid and the bags under his eyes dark. His hair had not been combed in some time.

"I know you," said Zamaron, and he pointed a yellow finger at Tomas.

"Yes, I met you once with Estelle, the Canadian."

Zamaron wavered for a moment, as if he was considering an alibi. "Estelle. Yes, I remember all too well. She has taken up with the Romanian, Sorrel."

"How do you know that?"

"I'm a policeman. It's my business to know."

"This isn't the right quarter for you, is it?"

"And why not? You're an artist, aren't you? I am found wherever the artists are to be found. Tell me, is Estelle happy?"

"They seem happy enough."

"How lovely," said Zamaron bitterly. "What are you doing here?"

"I was supposed to meet a friend on his lunch break, but I don't see him here."

"What does he do?"

"I don't know."

Zamaron looked to the bartender to solve the mystery.

"I think I know where you'll find him. His crew is working on the Rue de Jarente, just a few blocks up from here, on the other side of the Rue Saint-Antoine."

"But how can you know that?" Tomas asked.

"Go on up where I told you. He's sure to be there."

"Where on the street should I look?"

"Just go," said the barman, smiling.

Zamaron barely said goodbye.

Tomas went out the heavy door, and followed the directions he'd been given. The streets were quiet. Pimps, prostitutes and apaches were nowhere to be seen in this unpromising neighbour-hood, unlike the ones near the more popular night spots around Les Halles or Montmartre. There was a little traffic on the Rue Saint-Antoine, but then it was quiet again until he turned onto the Rue de Jarente. He heard a rhythmic wheeze and thump, and then his senses were assailed.

Several strong arc lamps were burning, and one of them was pointed down the street, blinding Tomas, so he had to hold his hand in front of his eyes. He could just make out men and horses standing about. There was a whine and belch of a great machine, a sucking and a hiss of steam. Worst of all, though, was the smell. The whole street reeked of ammonia and shit, both rotted and fresh, and Tomas had to put a handkerchief over his mouth to keep from gagging. Farm boys were used to the smell of shit, but this odour was exceptionally vile. As he approached, there came a sudden whine, a creak and then a stoppage of the pumps, followed by a hissing sound.

"*Merde,*" said the foreman, "the damn seals are giving out. Take your lunch break, men. We'll have to get Thèos to rip her apart while we eat." The machine looked like half a locomotive set upright on the back of a wagon drawn by two horses. Out of this machine came a large rubber hose, six inches wide, and the hose ran into an open manhole in the street. As with all work crews, there were far more men than seemed necessary, perhaps a dozen in all, aiming the lights, or holding the pipe, or standing about, smoking.

"Alphonse," the foreman shouted down the hole, "are you almost finished down there?"

A hollow voice rang out. "About another three inches."

"Close enough. Leave it and come up for lunch. We'll do the next street after we eat if Thèos gets the machine working."

Two workmen pulled up the hose, and Tomas went to look down the hole. With the bright arc lights above him, he could see

Alphonse in an oilskin, rubber boots and gloves, sloshing his way slowly through scum and water to the ladder to climb out of the hole. The smell was most intense where Tomas stood, a blast of putrid stench that blew up against his face.

"Alphonse!" he called, and his friend looked up. "What are you doing here?"

"This is my work. You're early. I was hoping you wouldn't see me until I had washed up. Never mind. Stand back and I'll be out in a moment."

Alphonse came up the ladder and stepped out onto the street. Tomas followed him over to the wagon, where Alphonse removed his oilskin, gloves and thigh boots.

"You'll excuse me if I don't shake your hand?"

"You're excused."

"Good! Some of the men who have worked here a long time don't even bother to wash their hands when they eat."

"Is this the only job you could find?" Tomas asked.

"It's good money. At first I hated it. That's why I didn't tell anyone. But now, my friend, nothing could dismay me. Come on and I'll buy you a drink."

They walked in a ragged group back on down to the café. Alphonse went to wash up first, while Tomas ordered two glasses of beer.

"Couldn't you work above-ground with the others?" Tomas asked when Alphonse returned.

"I used to, but I asked to be sent into the cesspits. The money is twice as good."

"Because it stinks so bad?"

"No. You get used to that, but sometimes the gases are so strong, you faint down there from lack of air. There's a risk of methane explosion, too. That's why the pay is excellent."

"I didn't know there were any cesspits here. I thought Paris had sewers."

"And so it does, but sewers are like champagne, something not everyone can afford. Most of the city still uses cesspits. The worst are the government buildings. There's no cooking or bathing there, you know, so there's less water in the system. As a result, the shit is compacted, and it's very hard to pump."

"You barely sound like the man I know. Give this up, Alphonse. I'll pay your rent until you find something better."

"You thought me too fastidious. Am I right?"

"Yes."

"Well, this is dirty work. I'll admit that. My father would die if he saw what I've come to. Our ancestors abandoned farm fields for clerking desks to get away from the manure. But no job is too low if it pays to help me do my art. And now, I have to save money for courting."

"Courting?"

"Yes. I've wanted to tell you for a while, because you are my only friend here, my countryman. I was going to do it today, but I couldn't tell you in front of Jenny."

Alphonse set his sandwich down on the paper, and leaned forward across the small table to put his hand on Tomas's arm.

"I'm entrusting you with a secret, so please don't breathe a word to anyone, not even Jenny." Tomas promised, and Alphonse continued. "I'm in love. And I'm so happy, I can't bear it. I've heard it said that lovers are giddy, but I feel nothing like that at all. My heart is beating faster, like it's never done before, and I can hardly catch my breath. Oh glory, if this is love, then how can all you lovers stand it?"

"Well, congratulations!" said Tomas. "Let's drink to love."

They drank to love, and Tomas ordered another two glasses of beer. "How did you manage to keep all of this a secret?" Tomas asked. "Why haven't you brought her around to meet us?"

"I haven't spoken to her yet."

"What?"

"I'm admiring her at a distance."

"Oh, Alphonse, you never take the easy route," Tomas said, letting himself fall back in his chair.

"That's why I wanted to tell you. I wanted advice on how to approach her."

"The direct method is the best. Go and speak to her and see if you can have a conversation. Just begin to talk. Who is she, anyway?"

"A music-hall performer."

"At the Folies?"

"No, at a smaller place called Le Chat Gris."

"Since when did you start going to music halls?"

"I thought I could accustom myself to naked women from a distance."

"You haven't told me who this woman is."

"She's an acrobat in a show. She has lips as red as strawberries and her hair is all golden curls. She is far more graceful than anyone I've ever seen before."

"You fell in love at first sight?"

"Not quite in love the first time. I was fascinated. The next time, I paid good money for a better ticket, and sat closer. And I kept on going back until I realized I'd go broke seeing her, and I rationed myself to once every two weeks. It's been three months now, and I live in fear that she will move on to some other theatre and I'll lose track of her."

"Why don't you go see her after the show?"

"I can't stay that long. I have to go to work."

"What's her name?"

"Barbette. She's an American."

"With a French name?"

Alphonse shrugged. "Don't ask me."

"But it's an odd name. Why 'little beard'?"

"I think it might have something to do with, you know, down there."

"Down there?"

"Where else would a woman have a beard, for God's sake? Do I need to be specific?"

Tomas laughed.

"Laugh all you want. Sometimes I think I was put in this world as some kind of joke for you all. But I'm in love! Is that so funny?"

"Men in love are always funny. Look at yourself, you haven't taken a bite of your sandwich. Eat something."

Alphonse ignored him and leaned forward over the table.

"My working in a cesspit will disgust her. I wash very carefully before I go home, but I probably still smell a little, right?"

"Of ammonia, sometimes."

"You see what I mean. My idea is to save as much money as possible and then quit my job before I begin my courting. Then I will have the time and the money to treat her properly."

"Listen, Alphonse. You are making far too many plans based on nothing. What if you find you don't like her when you get up close? What if she doesn't like you? Try to talk to her, at least, and see what happens."

Alphonse's happiness instantly shifted to irritation. "I can't be easy with women like you and Sorrel! I admire them from a distance, but as soon as I get close, my tongue seizes up and I feel like a fool. I still feel awkward around Estelle! I can't even look at her half the time! But I must get over this somehow. I take my life very seriously, and I take my love more seriously still. This is the woman for me. There can be no other!"

All of the shit-pumpers began to rise, and Tomas could smell them again, as if their movement had started eddies of stink in the café. Alphonse needed to get back to work. Tomas walked out of the café with the group of men and watched Alphonse, standing half a head taller than the others, go back up the street to his job. He bounced slightly as he walked, his step made light by love.

It was very late, and Tomas was tired, but the trolleys were not running yet and he could not afford a taxi. He walked down to the Seine and ambled slowly along the quays of the Right Bank. At this hour of the morning, Paris was as calm as a village. He passed the closed boxes of the quayside booksellers, under the leaves of the plane trees. A barge slid silently toward him against the current. At the upstream tip of the Île de la Cité, he could see a couple of fishermen sitting calmly in the moonlight.

Tomas hardly ever thought of his past, but the Seine and speaking in Lithuanian with Alphonse made him think of his childhood river, with its marshy banks and deep currents. As a child, he had caught frogs there, and fish. Those had been happy times, but the memories were darkened by the recollection of old Graf Momburg and the two other men he had helped stuff under the ice. He shuddered and tried to banish Merdine from his mind, but the thoughts of his home kept coming. Somewhere on the other side of Europe, his mother and father, brothers and sisters were rousing themselves for the early work on the farm. He wondered what had become of each of them. It was not so hard to send a letter, but he never did.

The young man who had existed there was now lost in a fold of time and geography that could never be found again. He had crossed some kind of line back in Warsaw, and all those people he was thinking of belonged to the past. Paris was a kind of mould into which he had been poured, and it made him into a new man, a different man from the one he had been back then.

Against his will, he remembered Maria, now dead these seven years. What would their lives have been like if they had ever made it to Vilnius together? It would have been very hard for them, especially if they had come with the child. Maybe some traces of the Lithuanian peasant were still in him after all, because the thought of her filled him with melancholy, the dominant emotion of the land he had come from. The Christ figure he had made that night was filled with it, too.

He fought back the sadness. He needed to forget the past if he was ever going to make anything of himself.

The way back to his bed was very long, and he walked more quickly to help banish the uncomfortable thoughts.

SIX

JENNY WAS SITTING ON THE BED IN HER HOTEL ROOM, WEARING a cardigan buttoned over a plain white blouse. Her hair was covered by a scarf and she had a grammar book on her pillow.

Tomas could never get quite enough of Jenny. They searched each other out at the Folies, speaking intensely and earnestly, as if every word exchanged was essential. The carpenters, painters and set designers with whom he worked under the Folies stage all accepted the presence of Jenny in the workshops at any time of day or night, and herein Tomas found the greatest difference between his work in Warsaw and Paris. Back in Poland, a man was expected to work hard all day and to leave his concern for women for his off-hours, when he could choose among women, drinking, card playing—whatever other recreations he preferred. But in Paris, it was understood that no occupation was more important than the pursuit of love. If Tomas's foreman saw Jenny at the door to the workshop, he would nod at her and send Tomas off for a cigarette so they could have a few moments together. Occasionally, he sent Tomas out to buy them coffee from the café across the way, and if Tomas went with Jenny and took a little longer than expected, well, that was entirely understood.

With a sweeping, theatrical gesture, Tomas drew out from his bag a carved wooden figure, covered with a tea towel.

Once he started carving again, he could not stop. The carvings bore a resemblance to the saints he had done back in Lithuania, but only faintly. Virgins and Saint Francises did not feel quite right any more, and he did unpremeditated variations: Mme Martini, his concierge, as a witchlike crone, Alphonse leaning on a fence, Sorrel with horns on his head and some of the shopkeepers in the neighbourhood in various poses. But the pieces he carved still embarrassed him, and he kept them in a sack, out of sight of the others.

Now Tomas held a particular wood carving covered by a tea towel, and he looked at Jenny to prolong the suspense.

"I promised this when we first met," said Tomas. And he whipped off the tea towel.

It was a bust of Jenny, her curls carved in fine detail in polished maple, and the face a remarkable likeness. She had her eyes cast down demurely and her hands were crossed over her breasts in an otherworldly pose whose inspiration was clearly devotional.

Her reaction was all that he had hoped for. She ran her fingers over the polished wood. She lifted the figure and turned it around in her hands, and carried it over to the window where the light was better. He'd refined the hair and face, but left the rest of the carving rough, like the weathered pieces he remembered from his childhood. He watched her intently to see if she would notice this and to find out what she would make of it. Finally, Jenny set the figure on the table behind him, pushed Tomas down on the chair and sat on his knees. She kissed him deeply.

"I'm glad you finally did it. Thank you," she said.

"Did you ever doubt I would?"

"At Carrel's, you spend the whole day looking at other women."

"That's professional work. I am an artist, after all."

"So you've told me a thousand times. But think what it must be like for a woman to have her lover employed in studying other women."

"And think what it must be like for a man to have his lover's breasts exposed to the audience night after night."

"That's not the same."

"Why not?"

"Because I am not tempted by the men, but you might be tempted by the model."

She looked over his shoulder at the carved bust and she laughed a little.

"I'm touched, really I am," she said. "I have no objection to being adored. But a virgin? You have a sense of humour."

She kissed him once more, stood up from his lap and straightened her scarf. "Now it is time to get back to our lesson," she said.

Tomas nodded, and opened his scribbler to look over his notes.

English proved to be the most difficult of the languages that Tomas had tried to master. Lithuanian, Polish, Russian and German were all phonetic, and although their grammars were complicated, they shared a certain kind of orderliness. Even French, which was not really phonetic, had a kind of regularity to it. But in English, the same letters often produced different sounds, and although the verb conjugations were easy and the nouns were not declined, word order was so strict that Tomas felt as if the language were a prison.

Jenny endlessly surprised him with unexpected knowledge. She knew all about diphthongs and tripthongs, the phonetic alphabet and the origins of language, as well as the means of motivating her students.

Jenny was a strict mistress who demanded to see the pages of written vocabulary that he had been assigned to learn. Every day, he copied out ten words for her, wrote each one out twenty-five times and memorized the list for the following afternoon. Then he had to pronounce the words correctly to her. She worked on the principle of the thesaurus, categorizing her vocabulary by theme. When the words corresponded to things in the room, either she or he pointed to them as he recited the vocabulary in English.

Tomas pointed to something in her room that was not on the list.

"That is called a bidet," Jenny said.

"But what is its name in English?"

"There is no name for it in English. It exists only in French. Go on with your vocabulary."

"Head," he said, touching his forehead. Then, "Chin, mouth, lip."

"Not *one* lip. You've forgotten the voiceless alveolar fricative," she said, and leaned forward to run her finger over both his upper lip and his lower one. The ancient grey sheer curtain on the window was being sucked outside, as if the air was disappearing from the room.

"Lips."

"Correct. That is a regular plural. But there are irregular ones as well. Name one."

"I can't think of one."

"You disappoint me. Say the word in English—now—what is it that man loves?"

"Woman."

"You keep forgetting we are in Paris."

"Women."

"That's better," said Jenny.

Tomas said the word *lips* again and stressed the final *s*. Then he ran his finger over Jenny's lips.

"That's all the vocabulary for the time being. It's time to turn our attention to grammar. Tell me what you've learned of the English article."

"The English article has only three variants," he said. "They are *a, an* and *the,* but their usage is very difficult to master."

"What is the difference in their use?"

"If my beloved tells me I am *the* man she loves, I prefer it to being *a* man she loves. Which am I?"

"You were once *a*, but now you are *the*. Now tell me the rules for the use of the definite article."

"In English, the definite article is used for rivers, but it is not used for lakes. The English say *the* Seine, and *the* Thames, but they say *Lake* Windermere, and *Lake* Geneva."

"Tell me about magazines and newspapers," said Jenny.

"I can't think when I'm this far away from you."

"Then come lie down beside me on the bed."

He did as he was told. She had her head on the bolster and he was up on one elbow. He leaned over to kiss her and she let him for a while, but then stopped him.

"Go on with your lesson."

"The English insist that the definite article be used with newspapers. Thus we have *The Times*, and *The Tribune*. But the tyrants who invented the language insist that magazines must have no articles. As a result, we have *Harper's*, and *Punch*."

His hand was stroking her neck.

"Exceptions?" Jenny asked.

"*The Idler*. I'm not sure I can go on without a little break."

"You must. Tell me about the use of the definite article with mountains."

"I need an *aide-memoire*."

Tomas unbuttoned her cardigan and then her blouse. Beneath it, she wore an undershirt, and she raised herself a little so he could expose her breasts.

"A single mountain takes no article." He dropped his lips to her breast and kissed gently up to the nipple.

"Examples?"

"*Mount* Everest and *Mount* Ararat." His lips barely rose from her skin to say the words.

"What about mountain ranges?" she asked.

Tomas took both of her breasts in his hands. "Mountain ranges do take articles. We say *the* Alps, *the* Andes and *the* breasts."

"I've never heard of the last ones."

"They have attracted many more climbers than any other mountains."

"Give me an exception to the rule."

"I can't. I want something."

"Say it in English."

"I must to fornicate you."

"You won't get far with language like that. Give me a polite synonym for *fornicate*, please."

"Make love."

"Much better. What is the exception to the use of definite articles before the names of mountains?"

"I don't know. Help me," he said hoarsely. She ran a fingertip along the bulge in his pants.

"The Matterhorn!" he said.

"Very good. Now let me explain how *mount* can also be used as a verb."

Later Tomas and Jenny made their way to the studio on the Impasse Diablotin. Mme Martini was sitting in her chair in the dark passageway wearing a ragged scarf over her hair as he and Jenny came by. Jenny nudged him. Tomas had a carving of her in the bag, and he felt like a schoolboy who had just closed his book on a caricature of the schoolteacher.

"It's a lovely day, Madame," said Jenny. "You should take your chair and sit in the sun."

"When my husband was alive, we used to take a small table out front and eat lunch on the sidewalk."

"Don't you want to do it any more?"

"I would only think of him. I'm old now, and I prefer to sit here, in the shadows."

They wished her good-day and went on.

Alphonse was sitting at the far end of the studio, right under the skylight, carefully engraving a large copperplate.

"I thought you'd be sleeping," said Tomas.

Alphonse barely turned around. "Who can sleep with that?" he asked, and he gestured behind him with his burin, to the mattress on the pallet in the corner.

Tomas had heard the noise when he came in, but its meaning hadn't registered. When he looked over, he could see Estelle was lying in bed with her back to them, weeping. Sorrel lay in the bed as well, staring at the ceiling and paying them no mind.

"Maybe we should go out to a café and come back later," said Jenny.

"Go nowhere," said Alphonse tersely. "They were roaring at each other when I came in from work. I tried to reason with them, but they turned on me and told me to get out. But I live here and I have the right to come in when I want, and the right to a little peace. Let *them* go out and box in the streets if they want."

"I like the portrait you're working on," Jenny said to distract him.

Alphonse brightened a little. The piece was a woman in profile, from the shoulders up. Tomas studied it as well, turning his head to avoid the glare off the metal plate.

"You like this one?" Alphonse asked.

He opened his portfolio on the table, and leafed through a series of copperplates separated by newsprint. They were all of the same woman in different poses, some full portraits. None were nudes.

"Who's the model?" Jenny asked.

Alphonse blushed furiously, but did not answer. Tomas guessed that she was the woman Alphonse had told him of.

"They're really good," said Jenny, and Alphonse beamed.

"But not as good as mine," said Sorrel. He was sitting on the edge of his bed, urinating into a chamber pot. He smiled as he held his penis down into the tin vessel, which magnified the sound of the long, heavy stream.

"Pig," Estelle muttered without turning from the wall.

"Sorrel, for God's sake, Jenny's here," said Tomas.

"Tell her to look away so she won't be jealous."

Sorrel shook the last drops off the end of his penis and began to get into his pants, talking at them all the while.

"Why do you insist on being old-fashioned? Look around the city, for God's sake. What did you come here for, if not to see what's new? Meanwhile, you sit there scratching your plates."

"You make it sound like art is going someplace," said Alphonse. "But I tell you, some things never change."

"Like what?"

"Like beauty."

"You know that's not true. Men loved women of different shapes before. Look at the ass and back of an Ingres bather. You see she has a back as wide and strong as a peasant woman's. Four more pounds and she'd have a roll of fat. He's been dead fifty years. Now take a look at Estelle's back and ass." He looked over to Estelle, still reclining in her bed. "Don't you hear me?" he shouted.

"What?" she stammered.

"Get out of bed and show them your ass and back."

"Sorrel, I haven't even had a chance to wash yet."

"I don't give a damn. Get out here."

"You're being cruel," said Tomas.

"Shut up. I have a point to make."

Estelle groaned, but she stood up and put her hands on her hips, hair tousled and sleep still in her eyes. She turned her head to one side to hide a swollen cheek.

"What happened to you?" Jenny asked.

"Don't worry for my sake. I gave as good as I got."

She crossed her arms over her breasts and looked away.

"Look at the narrow hips and small breasts. Neither is good for child-bearing, but who gives a damn about children anyway?"

Estelle wiped away a few drops of semen that had dribbled down her leg.

"Now turn around. I intend to talk about your ass."

"This is too much," said Jenny.

Sullenly, Estelle did as she was told. Tomas and Jenny were flushed with embarrassment and Alphonse had yet to look.

"She's one woman among many," said Tomas. "I could have found you a fat woman out on the street."

"Maybe, but no one would take her as a model. Estelle could only be successful as a model now, in these times. She's flat chested and thin, an expression of the present. If she'd lived a hundred years ago, there'd be some fat on her hips."

"Feed me better," said Estelle, "and there'd be some fat on my hips now."

Jenny went to a nail on the wall by their bed and removed a robe, which she helped Estelle to put on. Once she was covered, she went to the privy in the courtyard and Jenny followed her outside.

"Now look at these," said Sorrel, and he opened his own portfolio on the table. Tomas was appalled by all that had happened, but he felt powerless when Sorrel began one of his rants. "These pictures are the new language of this century."

"Wait a moment," said Tomas.

"What?"

"You didn't create these compositions. I've seen some of those pieces before."

Sorrel bristled. "Of course these aren't originals. These are my studies. I tell you, we're in the shadows of giants here. I'm trying to find some way to stand up on their shoulders."

"You're profoundly disgusting," said Alphonse, "like an adolescent girl at her first party, wondering how she looks and who will admire her. I never should have come to Paris. People get confused here and forget themselves. If you are what the future of art is, then I want nothing to do with it."

"You could learn from what I tell you," Sorrel said. "We're part of a grand game, so play it."

"We're growing tired of you," said Tomas.

"I feel exactly the same way about you two. Once I make a little money, I'll be out of this studio in a moment while you two scratch away for the rest of your lives, pining for success."

Jenny came in from the courtyard, and Sorrel turned to her.

"You have some rudimentary intelligence. You decide which one of us is right."

"Aren't you asking a bit much from a mere dancer at the Folies Bergère?"

"I want an opinion from the common woman."

Jenny laughed. "That's me, all right. What if I choose Alphonse instead of you?" she asked.

"I'm sure you won't."

"What about Tomas? Maybe I'll choose him."

"Oh, him," said Sorrel with a dismissive wave, "he's given up."

With unerring aim, the words hit Tomas at the heart of his fears. Abruptly, he swung his open hand and caught Sorrel hard on the cheek. Sorrel's head flew sideways and he fell onto the cobbled floor. He sat there stunned, and then shook his head twice and felt his jaw.

Tomas braced himself for a fight, but Sorrel could be counted on never to react as another man would. He laughed.

"Bravo! But don't be offended, Tomas. I love you just as much as I love Alphonse. But I love art even more. You two just need to be shaken up once in a while, so you don't fall into bourgeois smugness. Jenny, you see what happens to men who speak the awkward truth?"

"You're a loudmouth careerist who can draw," said Tomas, breathing heavily. "You'll impress people at first, and then they'll come to hate you."

"Do you hate me?" Sorrel asked.

"I can't be bothered to hate you," Tomas said.

"Then you must still be impressed."

Sorrel rose from the floor, put on a jacket and went out. Estelle came back in and went to the washstand, washed her face, then dried it on a towel and began to comb out her hair.

"I'm sorry you saw what you did," she said.

"Sorrel is a hard man to live with," Jenny said quietly, "and there's no law that says you have to keep doing it."

"You don't know the half of it. I'm painting better than I ever have before. He's taught me I need to do anything it takes to succeed. But now my life's a pigsty."

SEVEN

THE MODEL IN CARREL'S STUDIO SAT ON A CHAIR ON A LOW dais. She was fully dressed, with her hair pulled back in a short ponytail. She wore a blouse without a collar to reveal her upper chest so the sculpture class could model the base of her neck. Tomas stood at a modelling stand with the top turntable raised high enough that the mass of clay on the metal armature was at the same level as the model's head.

There were many ways to model a bust, but Carrel encouraged the profile method because Rodin had used it religiously. First the student captured one side of the head as a mass in outline. Then the model turned her chair one quarter, the artist turned the clay on his turntable, and so worked through the four profiles, and then systematically through the angles between the four to finish with a strong likeness of the model's head.

The clay was living as long as it was damp, and changing all the time, and both the challenge and the pleasure in the work came from the dynamic nature of the material. Once Tomas had applied the ears, nose and lips with pellets of clay, he raked the surface to smooth it, and then worked it with a kidney tool to make it flat. Finally, he applied water with a brush for a smooth surface.

From this model he would make first a negative plaster cast and then a positive. The original clay model was destroyed to redeem the clay, but on occasion the piece was hollowed out and fired in order to make a finished clay bust. Tomas smiled when he remembered how his pieces in Lithuania had exploded in the fire, both because the clay was impure and because they were too thick.

He had considered casting his plasters in bronze, but the cost was prohibitive. And he did not want to make permanent pieces because he was not good enough, not yet. He often abandoned his works before they were finished and when he did finish them, the pieces never looked right. They were competent enough, and sometimes the other students and even Carrel congratulated him on his execution. He had managed to learn a great deal about anatomy, as well as the techniques of modelling clay to make sculpture, but something was still missing, some breath of life failed to enter the work. In his calmer moments, Tomas reminded himself he was still a student, but his calmer moments were becoming rare.

Maybe this time, as he worked on the bust of the young woman up on the dais, he would find what he was looking for.

Sorrel and Estelle were painting in the next room, along with the other students. Estelle had begun to work on a series of landscapes based on her childhood home while Sorrel's work always contained people. Through the open door, Tomas could hear Sorrel explaining something about one of Estelle's canvases to a pair of young men.

"She insists on painting postcards," he said. "These pretty pictures will be bought up by the tourist boards of her country, if she is lucky."

"I paint what I want," she said sullenly.

"And nobody's stopping you. You could paint biscuit tins for all I care."

"I think this landscape is pretty good," one of the students said.

"I admit that. It is an excellent postcard, a lovely postcard, the best postcard I have ever seen."

Estelle was standing with her brush and palette in hand.

"You think I should paint people?" she asked.

"Are you deaf? That's what I've been saying since the beginning, but you are too stubborn to listen."

Her hand shot out and she slashed across his cheek with the brush, leaving a trail of ochre from his mouth to his ear. Just as quickly, he reached for the brush, took it between both hands and broke it. For a moment it looked as though they would fly at each other, but instead Sorrel started to laugh and Estelle followed. They were joined by the students, who would likely tell the anecdote to their friends over dinner that night, and so another page would be added to the reputation of the tempestuous Sorrel and Estelle.

Sorrel looked through the door and saw Tomas staring at him. Every glance was a challenge now. The Romanian's face was opaque beneath his round eyeglasses and goatee.

Tomas heard the street door open in the room where the others were painting, and he saw Alphonse come into the studio with a portfolio in his hand. Alphonse had not been to Carrel's for some time, and Tomas abandoned his clay to go and see what brought him there. He was laying out a series of four engravings of the same woman on a work table.

"Alphonse!" said Tomas. "What brings you here?"

"I have come here to make an announcement," said Alphonse. He held his back very straight, and he kept fighting back a smile.

"Well?"

"I've made a sale."

"Congratulations!" Tomas embraced Alphonse. "How did this happen?" he asked.

"It's a dealer I'd never heard of, a little man from a Right Bank gallery who told me he'd heard of my work. I laid out my prints and he made a purchase on the spot."

"How much?" Sorrel asked.

"Thirty francs."

"Not bad, but you're not going to be able to throw much of a party with that amount of money."

"Each," said Alphonse.

"How many did he buy?" Tomas asked.

"Four whole editions of fifteen," said Alphonse. "That's sixty times thirty. Tell me, Sorrel, what's that work out to?"

"I'm not good with numbers."

"One thousand, eight hundred francs."

One of the students whistled.

It was a remarkable sale for an artist at his stage. Tomas was troubled that he did not feel as happy about it as he would have liked to.

As for Sorrel, he was wearing a grin. "So I suppose you win the bet," he said. "But you'll pay dearly for it. I plan to eat and drink more than at a country wedding."

The other students in the school wanted to go out and drink to Alphonse's success immediately, but Alphonse had to meet with the dealer again and so he departed.

Estelle boiled some water and added a handful of coffee, and the three stood about, waiting for the grounds to settle.

"I never thought he'd be the first to sell," said Sorrel.

"Envious?" Estelle asked.

"Of course I am. And so are you both. I wonder how he did it."

"He's in love with the subject," said Tomas.

"In love?" Estelle asked.

"Tell us more," said Sorrel, and Tomas related all he knew as the coffee grounds steeped in the water and the clay of his forgotten bust hardened in the other room.

The announcement of the sale meant that word of the party flew among the students at the Académie Carrel, and from there tendrils snaked out into the city, passing by word of mouth from one café to another. The news leaped from the student cafés into the better ones in Montparnasse, a neighbourhood unfrequented by Alphonse. And there the rumour of the party began to grow until it caught the attention of those who ranked considerably higher in the art world than the lowly students at Carrel's.

At first, all of the attention amused Tomas. Those who had so recently found Alphonse a fool now wanted to celebrate his success. But after a time, the sustained interest in Alphonse's party began to irritate him. Sorrel became almost unbearable and Estelle was taking the brunt of it, but she covered her bruises well. Once, when no one was there but Tomas, Sorrel turned on Estelle when she taunted him. Sorrel lit a cigarette and looked at the burning end.

"I should grind this into your face," he said.

"Then you'd have the scar to look at for the rest of your life."

Tomas did not bother to defend her. Estelle had told him more than once that she could take care of herself.

On the day of the party, Estelle banished Alphonse from the studio so that he could bask in the glory of his celebration without having to bother himself with its preparations. The wine delivery man had taken six trips to bring in all the bottles, and Estelle stood over pot after pot of boiling water to make a mass of Valencian rice.

"What am I going to do all day?" Alphonse asked Tomas out in the courtyard, where Mme Martini was sweeping in preparation for the party. She had moved the garbage bins away and was wearing a fresh rag around her head.

"Buy some newspapers and sit in a café," said Tomas. "Enjoy yourself. This is going to be your evening of glory."

"I have to leave at eleven to get to work," said Alphonse.

"You can't be serious. Take the night off."

"Do you think I should?"

"Chance might come knocking on your door tonight, and how would it look if you were at work? Listen, go buy yourself a new cap. The one you have looks like hell."

"I don't have all that much money left. This party is costing me a thousand francs."

"Money well spent."

In an abrupt and awkward movement, Alphonse threw his arms around Tomas.

"You're a good friend, Tomas."

Tomas extricated himself from Alphonse's arms.

"Save your thanks for your speech tonight. Now get out, and take your sketchbook with you. It'll give you something to do to take your mind off the party."

With a mixture of affection and exasperation, Tomas watched Alphonse lope out of the courtyard. Mme Martini leaned on her broom and looked at him, too.

"Thank you for sweeping up, Madame," said Tomas.

"We have to look sharp tonight. The place is going to be full."

"Don't worry. We invited only forty guests."

"More than that will come, believe me. There are men in this neighbourhood who have noses trained to sniff out free wine. Every freeloader will try to snatch your petits fours. The music will bring them in from all the streets around."

"Music?"

"Your friend says there will be an accordionist."

Tomas shook his head in amazement. In the studio, Sorrel and Estelle had pushed one of the long workbenches against one wall and she was adjusting the bunting around a framed copy of the print of Barbette hung high on the wall.

"What do you think?" she asked.

"It looks wonderful."

"I still need to hang the Chinese lanterns, and we're going to put a chair up on the table so Alphonse can have a throne."

"We might be getting a little carried away here," said Tomas. "Chinese lanterns? And now Mme Martini tells me you'll have music, too."

"I want the place to look festive. Sorrel arranged the music."

Sorrel was whistling as he carried boxes of iron rods and cans of brushes into a corner to get them out of the way. He hefted a big sack and groaned as he lifted it.

"What's this?" he asked.

"Just some wood carvings."

"Should I put them out to decorate the place?"

"No. Leave them in the bag. You can stuff them under a table. Now, what's this about music?"

"Moïse Kisling is coming."

He said the words with such care that Tomas could tell they were somehow significant. "Who?"

"You would know him if you got to know the scene a little better. You and Jenny need to get out and be seen more often."

"Kisling is a Polish Jew," said Estelle. "He came here before the war. He's a musician and painter and a bon vivant and he hangs around with Jules Pascin. Kisling was in a duel once. He got a sabre gash across his nose and he called it the fourth partition of Poland."

"What's that supposed to mean?"

"It was a joke."

"Oh." Suddenly, Tomas felt ill-prepared for this party.

"The music is only the first of my surprises," said Sorrel. "I've been to see Alphonse's dealer and I have some explosive information. It's not the execution of the pieces that charmed the dealer so much. It's the subject matter. Barbette is a real celebrity, you know. The prints are no more than publicity pieces. They're not serious."

"I should never have told you about her."

"Too late for regrets now. But there's more."

"What else?"

"It'll be a surprise." And Sorrel would say no more.

Tomas went out for a few hours, and by the time he returned with a sack of bread at five o'clock, the glasses and food were set out on one table, and another was left bare with the chair upon it, decorated in coloured paper as if it were a throne. Chinese lanterns were strung from the ceiling, and Tomas's wooden carvings were hanging high up in the corners of the room and along the walls just below the ceiling. Estelle and Sorrel were nibbling food and sharing a glass of wine.

Tomas threw the bread onto the table. "Who said you could put up those carvings?" he demanded. "I told you to leave them in the sack."

"They look like gargoyles up there. A nice touch, don't you think?" asked Sorrel.

Tomas shook his fist under Sorrel's nose. Estelle was beside him in a moment.

"What's wrong with putting them up? They're charming," said Estelle.

"They're unfinished pieces," said Tomas hotly. "Would you put your sketches on the wall if artists were coming?"

"You need to calm down," said Sorrel.

"You've only done this to embarrass me."

"I'm doing nothing of the kind. Why do you always suspect me of the worst motives? They look just fine. Sit down and drink a glass of wine. People will be arriving at any moment. Look, here comes Jenny."

Jenny had come in through the door and studied the room with unveiled admiration.

"Wonderful! You found someplace to put your woodcarvings," she said.

"You see," said Estelle, "she agrees. Tomas wanted to take them down."

"Don't be silly. You should be proud of them."

"I thought you couldn't get the night off," Estelle said.

"I can't. I have to go. But I'll try to come after the show. I just came in to speak with my love. Tomas, can we talk outside?"

They walked to the café around the corner, where she ordered a large coffee.

"It's funny, but I can't bear the pressure of the hat on my head," said Jenny, taking her hat off and putting it on a seat beside her.

Tomas, still annoyed about the carvings, did not pay much attention to what she said.

"It feels like it's grown too small. Just my imagination, I expect."

Tomas heard Jenny's spoon clinking repeatedly against the side of her coffee cup as she stirred in the sugar. He looked at her. She was flushed and it seemed to him as if she was breathing a little fast. She was dressed very simply, yet elegantly, in a grey, V-neck dress with a white silk collar that revealed her long neck. The hat she complained of was a new cloche that matched her dress, with an upturned white brim. Her bright red lips stood out against her face. She was paler than usual, and so the contrast was great.

"Tell me what you're thinking," said Tomas.

"I'm not sure I should."

"You can tell me everything," he said, more lightheartedly than he felt.

"You're a man and your nature is on my mind."

"How can that be?"

"I wonder how steady you are."

Tomas laughed. "I am a determined man. I have thought about hardly anything but sculpture for most of my adult life."

"That's the thing."

"What is?"

"Your career comes first and I know that." She fell silent again. "It makes me wonder if you're ready to be a father."

It took a moment for the meaning of the words to sink in. She went on before he could reflect.

"There's no need to take this too seriously. I can get it taken care of quite easily."

"Jenny, I love you."

"How many lies begin with that phrase? I can't tell you how often I've heard it before."

He took her hands in his and forced her to look in his eyes. There was an unaccustomed aura of neediness about her, covered by a thin veil of banter. She could not stop talking.

"I seem to have waited much longer than I should have, and as a result, the risk is greater than it would be ordinarily. That makes me want to go to someone good, a real doctor, but then that would cost a lot of money and I'm a little short at present. I could use some help on that score."

"What are you talking about?"

"I can take care of this pregnancy in a moment. Well, not exactly a moment, but in an afternoon."

The words filled him with fear. He would not repeat old mistakes.

"If you're ready to give up dancing, I'm ready to be a father," he said.

"Give up dancing? Are you out of your mind? I have no intention of giving up dancing. More than one of the women at the Folies has a child. I would need to take a little time off because, let's face it, no one wants to look at a pregnant dancer, but as soon as I got back my shape, I'd be on the boards again. And what did you think I had in mind—some quiet home where you sat by the fire as I brought you your supper?"

"You want to get married, though, don't you?"

"Get married? What for? You could simply recognize the child as yours to give it a good name. If you wanted to keep it."

"I said I wanted to keep it, didn't I?"

"But do you understand what that means? You'd have to give me money for a nurse. You won't be able to buy the things you want. I'll be ugly and fat for a while. It's going to be hard."

"Why are you being so complicated?"

"Because I can't bear fantasies. I'm only interested in the truth and I am telling you how it will be."

"Don't you want this child?"

"I want a child sometime, and I suppose there's no reason why it can't be now. I want it if you do. If you go into this open-eyed."

"I do want the child, and my eyes are wide open."

She studied his face.

"So they are." She pulled him into a relieved embrace.

By nine o'clock that evening, the crush of revellers was so great in the studio that Tomas, Estelle and Sorrel gave up all hope of turning away people they did not know. They would have had to stand guard at the door and even at the arch into the courtyard. Alphonse was not there yet, as they had instructed him to come late, in triumph. The room already had almost seventy people crowded into it, two cases of wine had been drunk and no interdiction about touching the food until Alphonse arrived would hold back the fingers of men and women who were already half drunk. There were faces from Carrel's studio, both art students and a large number of models, two of whom had arrived in togas because they thought it was a costume ball. There were a number of middle-aged men whom Tomas and Sorrel were afraid to question because they might be someone important. The air in the room was thick with cigarette smoke and sweat and laughter, and conversation made the place as noisy as a market.

By nine-thirty, the party had spilled into the courtyard, where Moïse Kisling arrived, accepted shy greetings from the hosts with a wave of his hand and set himself on a stool in the corner. He was a thick, middle-aged man with dark hair swept back, and he smoked while playing tangos and polkas on his accordion. The three young women who came with him danced in their bare feet. Mme Martini had been drinking wine as well, and she clapped her

hands to the music while standing on her chair at one end of the
courtyard, the better to see the young people around her.

A roar came from the entranceway where some of the students
from Carrel's recognized the arrival of Alphonse, and they hoist-
ed him upon their shoulders. Kisling played a fanfare as the artist
was borne into the courtyard.

Alphonse was as ungainly as a stork on horseback. He wore his
new cap, black with a shiny patent-leather bill, and he was carrying a half-empty bottle of cognac in his hand. He wore a serene
smile as he was carried to the door, no longer the shy and retiring
man they knew, but an entirely new creature created in equal part
by the liquor he had drunk and the sale of his four editions. Sorrel
raised his hands for silence, and Estelle, a cigarette between her
lips, banged a frying pan with a hammer to get the attention of the
throng. The guests fell silent, and Sorrel spoke.

"Welcome to you, Alphonse, whose day this is. You have
scaled the height of Mount Parnassus, and we are here to celebrate your victory. You are the one who has revived the arcane art
of engraving and given it the prominence it deserves."

A series of boos came from some of Alphonse's colleagues
from the printing studio.

"Quiet, you jealous dogs!" Sorrel shouted. "It's true that
Alphonse is not the only engraver among us, but it was his genius
to choose Barbette as his model. It was his genius to marry the art
of the music hall and the art of the printed image in a way unseen
since Toulouse-Lautrec. And the public has recognized this, and
so we bow in homage before the talent of a new wave. Now bear
him up to his throne and let's hear from some of the others."

Kisling punctuated the brief speech with a dissonant chord,
and Alphonse was lowered. As soon as his feet touched the ground,
one of the models in a toga kissed him on one cheek, and then the
second pushed her way forward through the crowd to kiss him on
the other. Alphonse bore it all with a patient, if slightly unfocused

smile. He drank from the bottle of cognac, and ascended the throne on the table.

The plan had been for several men, from Carrel to the new dealer, to speak to the crowd, and then Alphonse was to have the final word. But it was clear that Alphonse was very drunk and would not wait. Therefore, Sorrel called upon him to speak first. Some of the people in the room were more interested in food, drink and conversation than any speeches. Sorrel roared to silence the talkers, and they did stop speaking, but their fingers kept shovelling food into their mouths and their hands kept raising glasses of wine to their lips.

Alphonse's face was not easy to see because the Chinese lanterns cast a dim light, except in one corner where half the paper covering had burned off several of them. The candles inside the lanterns were cheap and dripped furiously, and some of the listeners below Alphonse slapped their hands on their necks in shock at the hot wax falling on them.

"My friends," Alphonse began, slightly slurring his words, "I did not know that there were so many of you. The life of the artist is spent working quietly on his pieces, in communion with his materials. Art is a calling. It chooses us." He stopped to belch, and a few people applauded, but he held his hand up for silence. "The flame of art warms us in the coldness of our everyday lives and illuminates the darkness with its mild glow. We give up our homes and our families and we come to this city, this temple of art, to be attendants to the holy flame. Many of us work in obscurity here, and I myself was prepared to live my quiet life and to die unheralded. But it is sweet to see you all here, even the ones I do not know. Especially the ones I do not know."

Tomas could feel the restlessness of the crowd around him. They were just there for the party, and if Alphonse went on too long, they would begin to sing and dance whether he was done or not.

"Above all," Alphonse said, "I want to thank my four closest friends, Estelle, Tomas, Sorrel and Jenny. Without you, I would have fled this wonderful, this terrible city."

Thankfully, words began to fail Alphonse. He sputtered on incoherently for a time and then sank to his chair and lowered his chin onto his chest, and he did not raise it even when Estelle banged her frying pan to indicate that the speech was over and another round of applause was due.

Carrel spoke next as Alphonse slept and the restless partiers joked and whispered. He stressed how unlikely Alphonse's success was, and emphasized the dangers of so much success in so young a man, while also claiming there was no need to exaggerate Alphonse's acclaim.

The dealer spoke next, but nobody was listening any more, and as soon as he was done the party again broke into song and dance. Soon more bottles were flying around the room and glasses were being refilled. Tomas could not stand the heat inside any longer. He would have gone to Alphonse and brought him down from his throne, but the man was asleep, oblivious to all the noise, and as there was no better place to put him, Tomas left him where he was, with a Chinese lantern above him dripping wax onto the bill of his new cap.

Outside, Sorrel was rolling a cigarette.

"Well, my friend?" he asked. "Will this be the party of the season?"

"It's a good party," Tomas agreed, "but I couldn't hear a word that his dealer said."

"No?" Sorrel chuckled.

"You did?"

"Oh, yes. Everything will become clear."

Tomas surveyed the courtyard before him, a mass of dancing men and women and several drunkards already passed out against the wall. Kisling sat on his stool and played, and beside him stood a short, dark man who seemed familiar. Tomas suffered a moment of panic. Jacques Lipchitz was standing in his courtyard, somehow much smaller and less impressive than the man in Tomas's memory. Tomas had intended to go to Lipchitz for help once he had established himself in the city, but he had never summoned the courage to do so. He wanted to bring something with him to show the sculptor, something worthy, but in all this time he had not yet produced anything he could show. He wanted to flee, but he knew he could not. It would seem too odd not to speak to the man. He made his way to Lipchitz, and the artist looked for a moment at Tomas's extended hand before he shook it.

"We met once, long ago," said Tomas in Lithuanian. "My name is Tomas Stumbras. Do you remember me?"

Lipchitz stared hard at his face. "Perhaps. My Lithuanian has become poor. Speak to me in French."

Tomas reminded him of the circumstances of their meeting at the tavern in Merdine, and Lipchitz gave a small nod.

"So you're the Lithuanian," he said.

"Yes."

"I could tell by the wood sculpture inside."

Tomas cringed.

"I want to take a closer look at one of your carvings." He led Tomas in through the crush. Together, the two men squeezed through the revellers. One of the models had taken off her toga in the heat, but hardly anyone paid her much attention. Lipchitz led Tomas close to the table where Alphonse was sleeping on his throne, and he pointed up to one of the carvings. The particular piece was of Alphonse, leaning back against a picket fence with his arms outstretched behind him.

"That's what caught my eye," said Lipchitz loudly above the roar. "It's a depiction of your friend here, isn't it?"

"Yes."

"The outstretched arms take their inspiration from a crucifixion. You have filled a secular subject with religious intensity. I can sense it from here. And the technique is very good, very rough, like one of the old gods I used to see in the forests and at the wayside shrines. The light is very bad in here, but I can see, over there in the other corner, that you have taken the subject of the worrying Christ and secularized it as well," he said, pointing. "The noise here is hopeless and the cigarette smoke is stinging my eyes. Do you want to step out into the street for a moment?"

Tomas did, and they fought their way through the mass of people in the room and out into the courtyard again, which was hardly less crammed. As Lipchitz was a small man, Tomas led the way through the crowd that filled even the entranceway under the arch. Out on the street, he could finally breathe. Some of the other partiers were taking a break on the sidewalk, and groups of adolescents stood about as well, eyeing the crowd from afar and listening to the music.

"I should not even have been here," said Lipchitz, fanning himself. "But I came as a favour to Kisling. I no longer go to parties and I only come to Paris when I need to."

"You have left the city?"

"All the excitement is good when you are young, my boy, but after a while, it begins to wear thin. Drinking doesn't appeal to me and I have seen more nights like this than I care to remember. Now I live out in Boulogne-sur-Seine."

"I'm still new here, and I'm trying to find my way," said Tomas.

They began to walk along the sidewalk.

"That's never easy. It wasn't easy for me, either. Back when I first arrived, I was inept, I was hopeless, but others were even worse."

"What happened to the others?

"Most of them could not take the pressure of Paris, and they went away. I almost did, as well. I felt as if every other man was a genius and I was a fool. And the new art seemed awful to me too. I thought that cubism was terrible, just some kind of joke that people would catch on to eventually. I said that to Picasso himself, and we got into an argument.

"I studied hard and long. I learned anatomy so well I could have been a surgeon. One needs to be very patient. My life was miserable for over ten years. Even three years ago, my wife and I were hungry every day, and selling off my books to buy food. Then everything changed. So my advice to you is to keep at it and to work very hard. There is much to learn. And you have one advantage I didn't have at your age."

"What's that?"

"You've already found your way. Believe me, I can tell."

"But those pieces are nothing. I could do them in my sleep."

"If there is one thing we have learned this century, it is that there is powerful expression all over the world, in places we are unaccustomed to looking. Why not Lithuania? Why not the old wayside gods? I wish I had thought of it myself, but I am a Jew and I never paid much attention to Catholic shrines. I finally became a cubist sculptor because I was looking for a new language of expression; we all were. You have found it, too, right under your nose. There is raw power in those old wooden sculptures, and if you can transfer it somehow, you may have found a new language as well.

"But it's late. I have to go now," said Lipchitz. "I am accustomed to going to bed much earlier than this, and soon the trains will stop running. Listen, young man, believe me, you are doing well. Keep this up and show me your work sometime."

He shook hands with Tomas and walked away. Jenny found Tomas still standing there several minutes later, radiant with pleasure on the dark street.

"Who was that funny little man I saw you with?" she asked. Tomas took Jenny in his arms and kissed her.

"That funny little man is one of the best sculptors in Paris, and he just praised my work."

When Jenny looked into Tomas's eyes she saw a brightness that had been absent for some time, and so she embraced him, and Tomas was glad she did because he felt as if he needed an anchor to keep from flying away into the sky.

Jenny let him go on, and then reminded him that she had come for the end of the party, and arm-in-arm they returned to the Impasse Diablotin, where their courtyard was as full as ever, though the mood had changed. Kisling was now playing slow tangos and a pair of Swedish dancers was showing off for a tight circle of onlookers. Tomas and Jenny shoved their way into the studio where a few drunks lay on the floor and one man had a black eye, though how he had got it was a mystery. Some of the candles had burned out and the room was dimmer than before, and Alphonse was still asleep on the throne with a cone of dried wax on the bill of his cap. No food of any kind remained in the room, but Estelle saw them come in and she approached them with a full bottle of wine and two glasses, beating off guests who wanted more to drink. Some were singing, others laughing and everyone else was talking, so Estelle put her head close to theirs and shouted.

"I saved a bottle of wine for you!"

"Are we out already?" Tomas asked.

"Sorrel hid half a dozen bottles for our friends. Once we put out the word that there is no more wine, you'll see the freeloaders start to drift away."

They drank down a glass of wine each, and as Estelle refilled their glasses, brushing away hands held out with other empty glasses, another fanfare sounded in the courtyard. Soon there were cheers and Sorrel appeared at the door, leading a woman dressed in a long gown. She had a head of intensely golden curls and her lips were painted in vibrant red. Her eyes were heavily made up, and drawn out with paint at the sides to make them look almond shaped. Tomas immediately recognized the makeup of a performer, one who needed to be seen at a distance. From the courtyard, a chant began and it was taken up in the room.

"Bar-bette, Bar-bette, Bar-bette."

So this was the woman whom Alphonse loved. He could hardly have imagined anyone less Alphonse's type. Tomas turned to look at his friend, roused from his sleep by the name of his beloved.

For a man who'd just awakened from a drunken stupor, Alphonse seemed remarkably alert. He looked like a caged bird awaiting a cracker.

Barbette glanced at her portrait behind Alphonse, and she smiled at it, and then at him. As for Alphonse, the appearance of Barbette seemed like the natural culmination of his night of glory. When she approached the table, Alphonse reached out his hand and guided her up to his throne. She was a performer, and she took to the tabletop stage as if it were her right. In a friendly gesture, she reached up to Alphonse's cap and broke off the wax cone, threw it aside and then straightened the cap on his head. Gently, Barbette pushed Alphonse back in his seat and turned to face the people. Even amid the mass of people, Tomas felt a sudden chill. Something was not right.

She lowered her eyes demurely, with her hands at her sides. Then she raised her head slowly to look into the audience, and began a throaty version of "Sous les ponts de Paris." Her voice was not good, but she had stage presence, and when she was done, the applause was long and loud. Someone began the chant and it was taken up by the others.

"Bar-bette, Bar-bette, Bar-bette."

She turned to look at Alphonse, and then draped herself across his lap. She wrapped one arm around his neck, kissed him lightly on the cheek and looked coquettishly at the audience as if she was posing for a photograph.

Then she reached up with her free hand and pulled off her curly blond wig. Below this wig, her hair was cut very short, like that of a convict.

Like the rest of the crowd, Tomas stared at her for a few moments as the picture slowly began to sink in.

Barbette was a man.

Tomas felt sick amid the laughter. *Barbe* was "beard" in French, and the physique of the gymnast was clearly male. Most of the others seemed to have known of the joke, but not all.

Slowly Alphonse's expression changed. His adoring look became one of rage and disgust. He threw Barbette off his lap onto the table. The audience did not like this at all, and booed him. Alphonse looked up in horror. This was the real Paris, which had mocked him from the beginning. He started to kick Barbette where she lay at his feet. She tried to raise herself and crawl toward the end of the table, but Alphonse's foot knocked her arm out from under her and then kicked her in the side again.

The room came alive with outrage, as some leaped to pull Barbette off the table and others reached for Alphonse. Tomas caught Sorrel's eye, and the two rushed forward, took Alphonse under the arms and dragged him out of the studio. But the drunken onlookers were furious, and some followed, striking Alphonse. Tomas fought them off, but they continued to follow them into the courtyard and right onto the street. Finally, Tomas knocked down the biggest of them and then joined Sorrel again to take Alphonse under the other arm and lead him to a bench around the corner.

"What's the matter with you?" Sorrel asked, breathing hard. "I present you with your dream, and you start to kick the woman. Have you no sense of humour?"

"It was a man."

"Of course it was a man. Half the city knows Barbette is a man. Who do you think bought all those prints, eh?"

"You knew all along?"

"When Tomas told me you were in love with her, I made it my business to find out. Your dealer told me. He thought you knew."

Alphonse looked at Tomas, and then put his face in his hands. "I've been such a fool," he said.

"You made a mistake," said Tomas. "You never saw her up close, only at a distance on stage, so you were duped."

"Tomas," said Alphonse, "did you know she was a man?"

"I guessed something when she walked in tonight. Who cares? You've made a scene, but it's not the end of the world. Everyone knows you were drunk," said Tomas. "Now you can go back and apologize, or wait until tomorrow."

Alphonse was unconsoled. "I can still see that monster tearing off his wig."

"Oh, don't be so hard on yourself," said Sorrel. "Maybe you are not such a fool, after all." He had lit a cigarette and he was wearing an ironic grin.

"What do you mean?" Alphonse asked.

Sorrel looked at the end of his cigarette. "This is the age of psychology, my friend. The Surrealists look into their dreams in order to find the truth. You have had a waking dream, and the truth lies in it, too. Let's face it, anyone but a blind man could tell Barbette was a man right from the beginning. If you were attracted to him, it's obvious that in your heart, you love men, not women."

"What are you talking about?"

"Sorrel, that's enough," said Tomas, but Sorrel was not to be deflected.

"The truth is painful, but you will get over it. I understand that the homosexuals have their own world here. They have dances and bars and even marriages."

"Shut up," Alphonse wailed.

"Yes, it takes time to get used to the idea. But isn't it thrilling, really, now that you know the truth? Aren't you freer now? Of course, there will be some difficulties. You'll need to be discreet around the police. And when you write home to say you have found a new beloved, you'll have to hope they don't ask for a photograph."

"I told you to shut up!" said Alphonse. "I have been misled. Confused."

"If you are confused, then it means you are not sure. Do you want to find out the truth? Let me help you. Want me to wiggle my ass a little?" Sorrel giggled. "I sacrifice myself on the altar of your sexuality. Come back to our studio and try me out in bed."

"What's wrong with you?" Tomas asked. "Why are you torturing him?"

"I'm not torturing him. He's torturing himself." Sorrel laughed. "All right then, forget it. Come on, let's go back. There might still be some wine."

"I can't go back there," said Alphonse.

"Go on yourself, Sorrel," said Tomas. "Get out of here. You're only making matters worse."

Sorrel shrugged and began to walk down the street, but he called out to them before he turned the corner. "Oh, boys!" he shouted, and when they looked at him, he bent over and wiggled his ass.

Tomas charged after him, but Sorrel was nimble and slipped away. When Tomas went back to the bench, he found Alphonse had gone.

When Tomas returned to the studio, the place had been abandoned by all but those too drunk to move. The courtyard was empty of people except for a half-dressed model sleeping on the flagstones. Broken glasses, hats, empty bottles and the remains of Mme Martini's chair were scattered about. A dog was lapping at some spilled wine. Inside the studio itself, the electric light was turned on and Estelle and Jenny were standing in the ruins of the room.

"Where's Alphonse?" Jenny asked.

"Sorrel humiliated him, and he ran off," said Tomas.

"Don't worry about that now," said Estelle. "We have the makings of a *succès de scandale*."

"What?"

"Any news is good news. And nothing works better than a scandal. We had a hundred people as witnesses, and the story will be flying around Paris. Half the inverts in town will be lined up to buy from Alphonse now."

"And you think he would like that? You're getting as bad as Sorrel."

"Isn't their money as good as anyone else's? His dealer is an invert and so are most of his clients."

"Alphonse didn't know."

Tomas had to sit down.

"You shouldn't have let him go off alone," Jenny said.

"He ran off. What did you expect me to do?"

"Alphonse is too sensitive to be left alone at a time like this. Do you know where he might have gone?"

"I don't know. Maybe to work. I could find out if I asked at the café where he eats his lunch."

"Yes," said Estelle. "Go to him. You have to convince him that everything is going to be just fine. Better than fine."

"I'm not sure I could convince him of that," said Tomas. "But I'll see what I can do."

Tomas made his way to the Marais, hoping that Alphonse still worked in that part of town. He found the sewer-workers' café and the men were there on their lunch break, eating enormous sandwiches of salami and drinking beer and the *vin ordinaire* the café owner sold by the litre. Alphonse was not among them. Tomas recognized the Spaniard with the drooping moustache, of whom Alphonse had made a portrait, and asked after his friend.

"He showed up late," the man said, his mouth full of food.

"But where is he?"

"Said he wasn't hungry. I don't blame him. We're going to work on one of the biggest cisterns in the neighbourhood after lunch. Worse than most, a big government building. Very much shit and very little water. It's a dangerous job. He went out to find cigarettes."

Tomas asked for directions, and he finally found the street he was looking for.

"Alphonse!" he called out, and when no one answered, he called again. A pair of shutters opened on a window above him. Tomas could not see the man, but he could hear his voice.

"What's the matter with you? It's nighttime. Go to sleep."

"I thought Paris never slept."

"Thanks to people like you it never can."

The shutters closed.

Tomas's eyes were accustomed now to the weak light on the street, and he saw a figure standing with an iron bar over the cistern cover. The horse and the pump were farther down the way, as were the unlit carbide lamps.

"Alphonse!" Tomas called when he recognized him. Alphonse whirled around.

"What are you doing here?" Alphonse shouted from the distance.

"I need to talk to you."

"Stand back."

Startled, Tomas stopped where he was.

"It's only me," said Tomas. "You need to be with friends. You mustn't let this thing prey on your mind alone."

"Get away from here," said Alphonse. "Haven't I suffered enough tonight? I don't want you to see my face." It was too dark to see him in any case, but Tomas could hear the tears in his voice.

"I want to talk to you," Tomas persisted. "What happened was very hard, but it's not the end of the world. For God's sake, think of your career. You are going to be in demand now. People will be fighting to buy your work. You can do anything you choose."

"Tomas, listen to yourself. I have been humiliated. I am the laughingstock of the entire quarter, and all you talk about is my career. There's more to life than a career. First I am a man, and after that I am an artist. The man has been humiliated."

"Please, Alphonse, come with me. We'll get drunk together and talk about home and then all of this will seem like a bad dream."

There was a long silence.

"This is our home now, such as it is. Lithuania is the dream. But all right. I'll do it. Listen, I have to open up this cover to let it breathe before the others come to work. Otherwise, the fumes are too strong. Go down the street and hold on to the horse, will you? The poor old nag hates the smell of shit, and it's very powerful when the lid comes off. Go down there and hold on to her. I'll join you in a moment. You can't be close by. People who are unaccustomed to the smell sometimes faint."

Tomas did as he asked, passing by Alphonse, who kept his back to him. The horse was a good thirty yards down the street. As Tomas took the bridle in his hands, he heard Alphonse lift the lid.

"Perfect," Alphonse whispered.

"Tomas," he said loudly from the distance, "there is nothing you can do for me. Now please look away."

"Why should I?"

"Tomas, if you love me, turn away."

Tomas could hear the snick of a match being struck. There was a second's pause and then the methane gas ignited. The explosion shot a column of fire up through the manhole and as high as the top floors of the seven-storey buildings on either side of the street. Alphonse did not shrink back from the blaze. Instead, he leaped right into it and down through the column of fire into the filth below.

EIGHT

TOMAS SMELLED THE CIGARETTE SMOKE BEFORE HE HEARD the footsteps.

He was down in the workshop at the Folies, working with his knife on a piece of wood, carving Alphonse into the figure of the traditional seated Christ, elbow on one knee and head supported in one hand. The other hand did not rest on the opposite knee, though, as it did in traditional sculptures. It hung at Alphonse's side and it held a burin. The figure's avian features were exaggerated so that the nose was almost a beak, and the feet that protruded from the pant legs were those of a waterfowl. The back was arched as if it supported the sins of the world.

It was still too early for the steps to belong to any of the Folies workers, for it was their day off and the doorman did not smoke.

"Here you are."

Zamaron stood at the bottom of the stairs, still wearing his raincoat and the soiled shirt and tie he seemed to live in. He smelled of ammonia.

"What are you doing here?" Tomas asked, rising to his feet. "How did you find me?"

"I'm a policeman. You were not at your home and you were not at the hotel of Jenny Smith. Aren't you going to offer me a chair?"

Tomas gestured with his chin at a stool by the workbench, but Zamaron did not sit down.

"Why did you run away from the scene of a crime?"

"It was no crime. There was an explosion."

"I know that. But Alphonse was your friend. Why did you run away?"

Because the train of events that was unfolding in Paris was nothing like what he had expected. Because he felt he had helped to kill Alphonse, and could not bear the weight of it upon his shoulders. Tomas sighed and put his face in his hands.

"It was horrible," he said. "I saw him fall onto the fire and knew that there was nothing I could do. I couldn't bear to look. I started to run. Did you find the body?"

"There was no body, just a few bones and teeth. What happened?"

"He was smoking."

"You'd think he'd have known better. Was he drunk?"

"Maybe a little." He did not want to tell the story of Barbette. Alphonse's ghost would have been embarrassed in the afterlife to have a story such as this one make the rounds. "I heard him strike a match," said Tomas.

"Were you smoking too?"

"I wasn't smoking."

"Was he dismayed about something?"

"No, of course not," said Tomas without thinking.

Mimicking Tomas's gesture, Zamaron rubbed his face with both his hands as he pondered Tomas's words. "His foreman told me he wasn't stupid," he said. "If he wasn't drunk and he wasn't stupid and you say he was not distraught, what am I to think?"

Zamaron reached into his pocket and took out a folded newspaper. It was the *Mercure,* one of the many Paris newspapers that specialized in gossip.

Tomas read:

An Open Hand or a Closed Fist?
When and how is one permitted to strike a woman? Gentlemen say never, and to them the second question becomes academic. Those less saintly agree that instruction is permitted as long as one slaps and does not punch.

One of our foreign artists put this proposition to the test last night at a party to celebrate his success . . .

Tomas read through the account, which put the number of guests at over two hundred and peopled the crowd with celebrities such as Jules Pascin, Kiki, Picasso, Foujita and Paul Desnos, members of the Montparnasse bohemian coterie. As far as Tomas knew, none of those persons had been there. The article did not mention Lipchitz or Kisling. It did give a highly fictionalized account of the events, and had Alphonse beating Barbette senseless.

He read on:

But will the police be charging our pugilistic artist? The police were about to arrest him when it was discovered that Barbette is really a female impersonator, and so a man!

Thus an amorous reconciliation was ruled out, and the artist saved himself a night in jail!

If Alphonse had not killed himself the night before, he would have done it that morning on seeing the paper.

"So now I will be hounded by journalists who will want to know how he died," said Zamaron.

"You could say it was an accident."

"Was it?"

"What else could it have been?"

"I can think of only three possibilities. First, that it was an accident, as you say. Second, that he killed himself, but you claim he was not upset. There is a third possibility as well."

"What's that?"

"That you killed him."

"Why would I do that?" Tomas asked.

"I don't know. Envy, maybe. He was successful and you are not. You wouldn't be the first to kill a successful friend. Or the last. Believe me, in your milieu I see it all the time."

"I was happy for him."

"Liar. I have never yet seen an artist happy at the success of another. Let's leave that aside for a moment. You were seen at his workplace. What were you doing there?"

"He was a little upset by the scene with Barbette. I went to talk to him."

"So you lied earlier?" Zamaron lit another cigarette without offering one to Tomas. He looked disgusted. "I am going to write you up as uncooperative. Do not leave the quarter without my permission, and stay out of trouble."

Jenny was sitting in Tomas's bed with her back against the headboard as Sorrel and Estelle packed Alphonse's belongings into a box. These did not amount to much, as they had decided not to send his tools home to save on shipping. Tomas was composing the letter to Alphonse's parents back in Lithuania.

Rain beat against the large frosted windows and came right through the joints in the frames where the putty was old and cracked and ran down the inside wall. The wind also sought out the cracks and found its way into the studio. The lamp that hung from the ceiling swayed in the whisper of a breeze.

Tomas worded the letter to Alphonse's parents as best he could.

You will have heard much about the dissipation of life in Paris, but I want you to know that your son was not one of those artists who sits in cafés and whiles away the hours. He was the most serious person I have ever known.

He was just beginning to have some success with his portraits. He made an important sale shortly before he died in the terrible industrial accident that took his life. I am forwarding what money is left from that sale, as well as some of his sketches.

You have my sympathy for the great loss you have suffered. I want you to know that there are many in the community of artists in Paris who will be saddened by his passing. I count myself among them. Our prayers and sympathy are extended to you in this terrible time.

"Very good," said Sorrel after Tomas translated his words back to the others. "You've struck just the right note." He was standing at the table in front of Alphonse's open portfolio. "Should we give his dealer the rest of the engravings?"

"The story is in all the newspapers and there will be a run on Alphonse's work now," said Estelle. "We can raise the price and send the money to his parents."

Jenny laughed sadly. "Oh, he's made his mark. Now he'll be a real sensation."

The rain kept running down the glass wall of the studio. They would have to do something about it soon or the puddle would spread across the floor.

"It's funny, Sorrel," said Jenny from her place on the bed. "No harm ever comes to you, just the ones around you. Did Alphonse's sale bother you so much?"

Sorrel shot a glance at her from the pieces he had been studying. "What are you saying?"

"You knew he was sensitive. You were amused by his weaknesses and you played on them."

"I'm willing to take a little rudeness from you today because
you are distressed," said Sorrel. "But maybe it would be better for
you to be quiet now."

Jenny would not be quiet. "You'd sweep Tomas away in a second if he got in your way! Didn't you always say you would do
anything to succeed? One way to do it is to climb madly to the top
of the heap. The other way is to get rid of everyone better than
you. To eliminate the heap."

"You are a stupid woman and Alphonse was a stupid man.
Tomas, I'm going out, and I want her gone before I get back.
Listen," he went on, pointing at Jenny. "Alphonse stumbled into
the best luck of his pitiful career. Barbette could have been a gold
mine for him, but he threw it all away. Someone that stupid did
not deserve his victory." He put on his jacket and a hat and
turned down the brim to keep the rain off, then he left with a slam
of the door.

Estelle sat down on the bench and lit a cigarette.

"Don't be so hard on Sorrel," she said to Jenny. "He's suffering as much as you are. Alphonse was his friend, too. He just
doesn't know how to show his feelings. He has them, believe me."

"He's a bully, and you let him get away with it."

"He's just honest about what he wants. He doesn't deceive
himself. Let's face it, for all his good qualities, Alphonse did
deceive himself. He claimed he never cared about success, but you
saw how happy he was up on his throne. He wanted it as much as
anyone else."

"You shouldn't speak ill of the dead," said Jenny.

"I loved Alphonse and I will miss him, and Sorrel was terrible to him. But Sorrel didn't kill him. He killed himself. Social

Darwinism is operating in the art world. Only the fittest will survive."

"And you think Sorrel is the fittest?"

Estelle's eyes glowed. "If he encounters an obstacle, he shoves it aside. If Sorrel had made the same mistake as Alphonse, he would have gloried in it. The scandal would have made his career."

"That's terrible," said Jenny.

"It's terrible, all right, but I didn't make the rules. Jenny, at heart you are just an idealist. You simply have to recognize the ways of the world."

Estelle put on a shawl and went outside. The door blew open behind her and a draft of wind and rain came in. Tomas closed the door properly and slipped a chair under the knob to keep it from rattling against the jamb. Then he went over to Jenny on the bed, and bent forward to kiss her forehead.

"I'm upset, too," he said.

"Yes, I know you're sorry Alphonse is dead, but you can't see beyond that. Listen to what Estelle said. You're living in a jungle here and those two creeping vines will strangle the life out of you."

Tomas took her in his arms and rocked her on the bed.

"Even if what you say is true, I'm a sculptor, not a painter. I am no threat to them."

"Aren't you trying to make a name for yourself, too?"

"Yes, I am, and there's some truth in what they say. But I'm different from them."

"How?"

"For one thing, I have you, and every night when I see you dance, it fills me with delight and makes me more human."

"Soon my dancing days will be over for a while," she said.

Tomas caressed her cheeks, which felt hot below his fingers.

"What will we do with you then?" he asked.

"I can probably get a job as a dresser at the Folies. The pay is not so good, but at least I'll have some income."

"Will you move in with me?"

"Not here. I can't stand Sorrel, and after what Estelle said, I'm not sure I could bear to be around her either. Let's just leave things as they are for now. We'll have to look for a new place eventually. I can't have a baby in the hotel."

NINE

PARIS WAS A MAW THAT NEEDED TO BE FED WITH NOVELTY, and Josephine Baker was in danger of losing some of her delectability. Outside the city, her appeal continued to grow, and Vienna and Berlin hungered for her, but within the city itself the frenzy for the dancer was difficult to maintain. There were already Josephine Baker dolls, figurines in a banana skirt, and Josephine Baker pomade, guaranteed to hold down even the curliest hair and to give it the brightest shine. But demand had waned and Parisian interest needed to be whetted again and again, and Count Pepito knew how to do it.

For excitement, there needed to be a story, and Josephine inadvertently created one during an interview with a Paris reporter. She told him that she had many lovers, as was expected of a Parisian star. But when the reporter asked her if there were any war veterans among her lovers, she said that she did not sleep with amputees as she preferred her lovers to be young and whole. Paris was full of men who had lost limbs in the war, and these men took offence that she would refuse them her bed, a priori. Amputees were given special seating on buses and the Métro, and all decent shops permitted them to go to the front of the line. What kind of a woman would refuse her bed to a patriot? The *mutilés de guerre* should have not only equal rights to her bed, but priority, as they had elsewhere. Had it been possible to legislate the right of access to the bed of Josephine Baker, the government could have been pressured to do just that.

The amputees called for direct action. They gathered before the Folies to demonstrate, a thousand men missing arms, legs, eyes, ears, noses and many combinations of the above. Tomas watched them from his vantage point in the triangular café across the street. They carried placards demanding democracy and justice for amputees, and there was real danger that the police would have to fire on these veterans of the Great War. But then Josephine came out of the front door to give an impromptu news conference. She had been mistaken, she said—even ignorant— but she had set the matter right. She had slept with a man missing both hands, and had found him to be an excellent lover. She went on to praise amputees in general as superior lovers, which made perfect sense. If a blind man had his other senses sharpened by the loss of his sight, then the same could be said of a man who had lost a part of himself to a bomb, a bullet or gangrene. His remaining appendages became more sensitive to a woman's needs. The crowd outside the Folies cheered, and those who could took off their hats and threw them into the air.

Count Pepito stood at Josephine's side through all this. As well as being her manager, he was her lover and fiancé—how must he have felt, standing there at Josephine's side while she extolled the virtues of her handless lover? It did not matter. Her success was his success, and he smiled as she blew kisses to the crowd.

Tomas was running late by the time he made it around the corner to the stage door on the Rue Saulnier. He went down the steps to the cellar to the studio, where the set designer had pinned up some sketches for the new season. In the Folies, there was almost no idle time, since the design of a new show had to begin as soon as the previous one was up and running.

The centrepiece was a design for a new effigy of Josephine— another variation on the theme of the white explorer. This time the explorer would stumble upon a vine-covered ruin. The vines would pull aside like curtains to reveal Baker as a great, prehistoric goddess.

The set designer was talking with the costume maker, who wanted Josephine to wear something different around her waist this time. The bananas were too well known. Perhaps pineapples? As well, there was the problem of the effigy itself. The set designer would have preferred a giant three-dimensional figure, or a bas-relief, but the Folies stage was shallow, and a painted flat was cheaper to make.

Tomas began to work on a replacement Marie Antoinette bust. All the Antoinettes kept losing their heads to the pranksters who slipped in backstage. Tomas set about the task of mixing plaster again and was stirring the water in with the dry material when the idea came to him, so obvious that he did not know why he had not thought of it before. He needed a subject for a masterpiece, and it was right under his nose. He had sketched Josephine Baker many times. Why not take the next step? She had just remade herself in the street outside, and he could remake her, too. If poor Alphonse had been able to draw attention to his work by using a minor celebrity like Barbette, he could do the same, but on a far greater scale.

When he returned home, Tomas looked at some of the sketches he had done of the dancer, and picked out ones that might be suitable designs for sculpture. As he studied them, he began to reflect on how he would portray her. Lithuanian gods were about stillness, but he wanted to portray movement, noise, the nervous drama and humour of all things American, so that style would not do. He would need to do more sketches and work up many models in clay.

He threw himself into the project, creating a series of clay figures based on his sketches. He mimicked the breasts-forward figures of Aristide Maillol, but the stance was wrong for Baker, whose movement centred in the hips. He tried to work in the manner of Brancusi, but could not capture the idiom without being derivative. Yet none of these failures troubled him as he used to be troubled before. He knew he was on to something.

It was easy to keep his new obsession from Estelle and Sorrel. They were wrapped up in their own work and cool to him since Alphonse's suicide. He didn't want to tell Jenny about his idea until he was a little more certain of how he would pull it off. But after a few days he couldn't keep it to himself, and he went looking for Jenny in the Folies to tell her about his plans. She was doing a costume inventory, making her way along the racks of clothes with a notebook in her hand, recording the type and size of each costume and the repairs that it required. She was showing a great deal now, her face splotchy with pregnancy.

"Here you are!" said Tomas.

"Yes, here I am. Just a moment, let me sit down. My feet are swollen." She took a stool from in front of a mirror and turned to face Tomas, who remained standing.

"Is the job getting you down?" Tomas asked.

Jenny ruffled her curls, but they stayed limp and clung close to her scalp. Her eyebrows used to be very thin painted lines as required of the dancers, but she was permitting them to grow back in now, and Tomas liked the way they made her face seem more natural. He did not dare mention this because she was sensitive about her looks, and even compliments could go awry.

"This is the first time I haven't danced in years. If I weren't this far along, I'd ask M. Perès to recommend a good doctor to get rid of this child."

Tomas crouched down in front of her and touched her face. "Hush. You mustn't say that. You need to fill the child in your womb with confidence."

She shrugged. "I need to have some of my own before I can pass it on. Sometimes I wonder what I've got myself into.

Sometimes I see no reason to get out of bed. I wonder if I'll ever really go back to dancing. What kind of mother will a dancer be?"

"You once said that plenty of dancers have children."

"I know, but I never told you how they lived. This city will be difficult for a child."

"This isn't the Jenny I know. Next you'll be yearning for a little farm in the Loire, where you can grow your own vegetables and shear your own sheep."

"You've almost read my mind."

"Only city people dream of farms like that. I come from a farm and farms are all about living with animal shit. You wade through the stuff, the apples have worms and the gooseberries are bitter. You sell anything of value to the city and eat worse than a *clochard*."

"You know, Tomas, dreams change as life moves on. There's no virtue in sticking to a dream that has no meaning any more. Can't I have new dreams?"

"Of course you can. I have one, too. That's what I wanted to tell you about."

Tomas told Jenny of his idea for a life-size bronze of Josephine Baker. Jenny was not impressed.

"Josephine Baker again. I thought you were over her."

"What are you talking about?"

"Now that I'm getting fat and my feet are beginning to swell, you're looking around again, aren't you?"

"I'm not looking around at all," Tomas said sharply. "I have an idea that is going to make my career. Finding a buyer for a bronze of Josephine Baker will be no trouble at all. The piece will sell itself."

"Yes, but you'll be studying the figure of another woman as mine gets worse and worse. How do you think that will make me feel?"

"I am a sculptor. It's my job to study the human form."

She looked at him sullenly. "I have an idea," she said. "Let's go somewhere, just the two of us."

"What? Where?"

"Canada."

"What has got into you? This can't all be about the baby."

"Why is that so funny?" she asked.

"No one visits Canada, except the rich, maybe. English explorers. You go there to live."

"Would you go there with me?"

"Now? You're pregnant! It's too far and too expensive. Besides, what do you want with polar bears and Indians?"

"I want to get away from here."

Tomas had never seen Jenny like this, and he could not quite believe that she was serious.

"I don't want to go anywhere," he said.

"Do it for my sake."

"Listen to me, Jenny," he said. "I will do anything you want after I get established, but not before then. All my life I have been working toward this point, and nothing will keep me from doing this piece. Can't you understand that?"

She would not look him in the face. Her head was bowed and she seemed to be crying, and he was so angry that he barely cared. He left her behind in the wardrobe room and stomped out of the Folies.

For the next few days, Tomas avoided Jenny and tried not to think of her. He worked on his sketches obsessively, and when he reached the point where he thought he was ready, he waited for a day when Josephine arrived at the Folies uncharacteristically early. He did not want Jenny to see him knocking on Miss Baker's door, so he went up to the second floor and stepped out the hall window that gave onto the courtyard and the fire escapes. A couple of the artistes saw him, but people were always going onto the fire escapes for air or to visit one another, so no one remarked on him. He counted the closed shutters until he found the right ones. He opened up his portfolio, took out his coloured sketches and rapped smartly on the shutter. He heard a muffled voice inside, waited and rapped again. The heavy iron bolts creaked inside and the shutters swung open to reveal Pepito Abatino, in full regalia—monocle, cigarette holder and silk puff in the breast pocket of his jacket.

"What do you want?" Abatino asked.

"I'd like to speak to Miss Baker."

"What? She needs her rest. Get out of here now, or I'll have you fired."

"I want to show her my sketches. I think she will be pleased."

"She'll be incensed. The editor at *Le Figaro* is attacking her again and she is upset."

"These paintings will brighten her mood." Tomas took a handful of crumpled bills out of his pocket and proffered them. "Please, can't you find some way to let me see her?"

Abatino ignored the money and sighed. "Listen, my friend, you must not think only of yourself. You must think of what you can offer her."

"I offer to make her the subject of a bronze sculpture. She will be made immortal."

Abatino skeptically eyed the young man out on the balcony.

"And you will have your reputation made."

"Of course."

"I thought you were just a set builder."

"I am an art student preparing to make his masterpiece."

"It would be better if you already had a reputation." Abatino sighed once more. "But all right. Come in."

Although both Abatino and Josephine professed great admiration for Tomas's sketches, it was not an easy job to convince them that his project was worth their time. Tomas did not exactly lie, but he made no mention of costs. Had they known that he did not have the money for the casting process, they would never have agreed to it. While Josephine smoked and looked at the ceiling, Abatino calculated the odds: if Tomas's sketches cost Josephine nothing; if the sketches led to a bronze; if a star-struck patron paid for it; if the bronze became a monument that the city of Paris might be persuaded to install in some prominent square; if all these things occurred, it would not be so bad to permit Tomas to cast a bronze of Josephine Baker.

Tomas could sense them wavering, and he reminded Josephine that he was the one who had saved her life. She did not seem to remember the incident all that well, but the balance was tipped. And so it was that Pepito Abatino promised Tomas seven twenty-minute sessions with Josephine Baker in her dressing room until the preliminary sketches were all done.

Getting her to sit still long enough for him to do the preliminary sketches proved harder than Tomas had imagined. She was fond enough of the idea, but she was fond of many ideas. And while it was true that Tomas had saved her life, one could not be expected to be grateful forever. Josephine was always hungry after the Folies show and wanted to get out quickly to the new club she was promoting up in Montmartre. She might promise to come into the dressing room early, but she often forgot and did not like to be reminded. When she did find the time to let Tomas sketch her, it was never for the agreed twenty minutes.

After sitting for three days in a row, she refused to sit for him for the next ten. Tomas was desperate to do just a few more sketches, but she did not seem to care. If she'd cared about all the forlorn men who could not live without her, she would have been crushed under the sheer mass of them.

Tomas finally cornered her outside her dressing-room door after a show, as she swept along the hall, in a skirt of swishing, vivid yellow and red satin, her breasts bare and glistening with a sheen of sweat. She stopped as soon as she saw him.

"You still at it?"

"I need a few more sketches before I have enough to get started on the clay."

"What kind of an artist are you, anyway?" she asked. "Why can't you just use one of my photographs instead? What do I have to stand around starving for?"

She was speaking English and she was speaking fast.

"I want to make a monument to you, and that takes time. The newspaper photographs of you will curl and crumble, but my bronze of you will stand forever."

"As if I cared about forever," she said. "All I care about is now." She opened her dressing-room door and went in, but she did not close it behind her. Tomas followed her inside.

Josephine was fumbling with the clasp of her skirt. "Oh damn, I can't reach the thing. Unhitch me, will you?"

Tomas was unfamiliar with the term, but it was clear enough what she meant. He pulled the metal hook from the loop of thread, and Josephine let the skirt drop to the floor and stepped right out of it. Then she slipped out of her undergarment as well. But she did not turn, fixing on the sandwich on her dressing-room table as if seeing food for the first time. Ever since she had said that her favourite food was a pork-chop sandwich, Derval had sent one up to her dressing room nightly.

She took a bite, put the sandwich back down and turned around to face him.

Her mouth was full and her hands were on her hips, as if she were daring him to find her ugly. Tomas had to work quickly. Her willingness would not last and it was hopeless to ask her to hold a pose for any length of time. But even when she was in a bad humour, her body still exerted a powerful attraction and Tomas was not immune to it. He could never look at a woman's breasts, her ankles, her shoulders, her waist where the curve went out dramatically to the hips, without feeling an intense joy and almost religious belief in the rightness of at least some things.

Quickly, quickly, he looked at her and down to his sheet of paper. He wanted to catch the energy in her, the strength that showed in her body even when she was like this, impatient and restless.

"Are you and Jenny still an item?" she asked suddenly. Tomas was surprised she had even noticed, and he did not like to talk as he sketched, but Josephine was no ordinary model.

"She's giving me English lessons," he said. He did not want to talk about Jenny in the presence of Josephine Baker. He wanted to keep the two of them separate, if he could. Josephine's body was the real truth to her, the part of her that did not change whether she was happy or sad. The thing was to catch her vitality, the reality of her physical presence.

"One of the Tiller Girls is trying to do me harm," Josephine said.

"Oh?"

"Yesterday there was a thumbtack in my shoe."

"That could have been an accident."

"That's what I thought, but I don't have any thumbtacks in here, so how could one have gotten into my shoe?"

"What else?"

"Somebody greased the boards tonight. I was doing a slide and I thought I'd fly right into a post and break my jaw."

"Maybe something spilled on the stage."

"Are you taking me seriously or not?" He looked up to see her wagging a finger. There she stood, naked in front of him, yet he was the one who felt exposed. "It has to be one of the Tiller Girls. Singers and clowns don't care about dancers, but showgirls and chorus girls do. Somebody's jealous enough to try to do me in and I want to know who it is. You ask Jenny who it is. Do you hear?"

But he was concentrating so hard that he was not truly listening, and Josephine could tell.

"Let me see what you've done."

"I've hardly even begun. I want to get your body right this time."

"You and everybody else."

She came over to him and looked at the four fast sketches he had done. They were pretty good. He had caught something this time.

"Are you trying to make me fat?"

"You're not fat."

"Your pictures make me look like a hippo!"

"I think you look lovely."

"It's not a matter of what you think. I can see what I look like. Are you trying to make fun of me?"

"I intend to make a monument to you."

"That's what you say. I think you're a fraud. Tear up those drawings."

"I can't do that."

"Tear them up right now." She reached for the paper, and Tomas put his arm up to defend his work.

"You can't have them. They're mine," he said.

"They are not yours. Those are pictures of me and I own them. What right do you have making me look like that?"

"You're beautiful!"

"Are you blind? You call yourself an artist? Give me those pictures."

He began to close up his portfolio.

"Maybe they will look better to you tomorrow. Let me show them to you then. You're tired today."

"Tired? The hell I am. Give me those now or I'll see you lose your job. Derval will toss you out on your ass."

She bent over the half-sheets of paper, pulled them out of the cardboard portfolio on his lap and crumpled each sheet into a ball.

He had been using good paper, and it did not crumple easily. She threw the four balls into her metal wastebasket and looked at him defiantly, panting after the exertion.

"You think you're smart, don't you?" Josephine asked. "You'll sneak in after I'm gone and then you'll save the pictures. Give me a match."

It was hopeless to try to stop her. Josephine took a match, lit it and pulled the top ball of crumpled paper from the trash. The paper caught easily, and she dropped it back into the wastebasket before it could singe her hands. She watched it burn with some satisfaction, and when it looked as if the flames had gone too high, she poured half her pitcher of water on them. The room was full of smoke. Pepito came running in then, but when he saw there was no emergency, he merely shrugged his shoulders and smiled at Tomas.

Tomas went down one flight of steps to the hall, where he met Jenny. He told her what had happened.

"She's treating you like a fool," said Jenny.

"She was tired. I need to get her when she is in a good mood."

"She's turning sulky. She's never in a good mood any more, unless it's on the stage where someone's paying her to smile. Why can't you just use me as your model?"

"For heaven's sake, Jenny, I have used you. I've done two busts of you as well as the wood carving."

"But you have no intention of casting them in bronze. I don't know what you see in her."

"Half the city is in love with her. We all see the same thing."

"So you admit it?"

"What?"

"That you're in love with her."

"It was only a figure of speech."

"Well, try on this figure of speech. Go to hell."

After Jenny had stomped off, Tomas waited in the workshop and then went back upstairs to Josephine's dressing room. He tried the door, which Josephine had left unlocked, and went in. The trash can was filled with the cotton balls Josephine had used to take off her makeup, and below those were the ashes of his sketches. But at the bottom were two more crumpled balls, black around the edges and damp. He flattened them on the floor—one of them was the best he'd done.

Back at his studio, he refined the sketches, doing variations again and again until he thought he had what he wanted, a highly simplified Josephine, just the lips and her signature curl to define her head, her hands aimed with extended forefingers, like six-shooters pointing toward the stars. She was recognizably Josephine, very American and very dynamic. He began his clays and worked them until he had something that looked right, and then he began to enlarge the piece, first to quarter size, then to one-third. Over the protests of Estelle and Sorrel that he was hogging all the space, he cleared away their things and attacked a half-size enlargement. He had to destroy it twice due to errors, but was successful on the third try and then sat to study it for days.

The execution was good, yet something was missing. The tone was right, and the humour was there, but he needed something more to offset the mass somehow, to provide a counterbalance to the extreme unity of the piece. He began to play with using a spiral, and this spiral turned into a snake that twisted around her right leg to her knee.

When Tomas had completed the addition, Sorrel finally came up to him after days of silence, pulled up a stool and rolled cigarettes for the two of them. He lit both and passed one to Tomas. "Now you've got it," he said. "And all the time, I didn't think you had it in you."

"I need to make a better plaster," said Tomas. "And then I need to have the foundry make it life-size and cast it in bronze. I don't know how I'll find the money."

"Technical details," said Sorrel, picking a piece of tobacco off his lips. "Have I told you Estelle and I have had some luck, too?"

"Maybe. I don't remember."

"No. You haven't been listening to anything for days. One of Carrel's friends is interested in our work."

"Whose?"

"Mine and Estelle's. I think he is going to offer us a show."

Tomas laid his arm across Sorrel's shoulder and gave him a squeeze. Sorrel returned the favour and the two of them sat staring at the plaster of Josephine Baker as if it were going to break into movement at any moment.

For weeks, Tomas had begged Jenny to come and look at the statue, but she was always unwell or busy and he could not very well haul the piece to her. He had been making the rounds of the various art foundries, but he could find no one who would enlarge the piece and cast it for him on credit. The better foundries all had enlarging machines, but if their price was too high he could always do that himself. On the other hand, he could not do the bronze casting alone. Two of the foundrymen had even come to look at the piece, and they agreed that what he wanted was not all that difficult to do, as long as he came up with the money. They did not work on credit because even a simpleton knew that giving credit to artists was not good business.

This new setback perplexed Tomas. He had always imagined that becoming successful was like leaping over a very tall fence, with glory on the other side for those muscular and nimble enough to make it over. Now he saw that making a masterpiece was only the first in a series of hurdles. He could have waited and saved the money for the bronze casting, accumulating the funds franc by franc, but that might take a couple of years and by then he would be a father and heaven only knew what his expenses would be. He invited Josephine to come and see the

plaster, but she sent Abatino instead, and although he was enthusiastic about the piece, he would not lend Tomas one sou to help
make it happen.

"Hold on to the piece and make more," Estelle had said. "Once
you have a larger body of work, the foundrymen will believe in
you."

"I'm in a hurry," said Tomas.

"Rodin took twenty years to make his doors."

"But he was already famous, and he could afford to tinker over
a lifetime. Besides, I'm going to be a father in a few months."

When Jenny finally did agree to come, Tomas watched her
with keen interest, both because he wanted her opinion and
because he had a favour to ask. He sat on his cot and observed her
as she circled the piece. She did not look well. The curl had gone
out of her hair and her face was puffy and pale. Her eyes were
swollen. She wore two sweaters because she was perpetually cold,
and something was wrong with her feet; she hobbled slightly as
she walked around the statue, which he had set up on the table.

"Well, what do you think?" asked Tomas.

"I can't say I like the piece," said Jenny, "because divas are fun-
damentally boring to me, but I have to admit that the addition of
the snake might be a stroke of genius. It's amusing to think of
Josephine like this in the Garden of Eden."

"I didn't intend any metaphor. The snake is just the embodi-
ment of a spiral, a shape that suits the piece."

"Yes, yes, yes. And the curl on her forehead has nothing to do
with Josephine Baker, either. Please, you can talk your art talk all
you like, but I know you are looking for a buyer, and the buyer is
going to be attracted by the snake. Very clever."

She came over and sat beside him on the bed.

"You look tired," Tomas said, picking up one of her hands in his.

"All the time, but I can't sleep properly. I feel that I'm walking
around in a dream."

"How much time is left?"

"A couple of months I guess, maybe less."

Tomas stroked her forehead. She felt slightly warm, and he shifted onto the bed so his back was against the wall and Jenny sat between his knees, the two of them facing Josephine.

"I can't get a foundry to cast the piece on credit," said Tomas.

"I know."

"Do you really think my piece is good?"

"Oh, Tomas, you're like my aunt Monique. Every time she bakes a cake, she wants us to tell her twenty times how good it is."

"My Josephine is of a different scale than your aunt's cake, I hope."

"Yes, a bit bigger and softer."

"I don't think you should joke about it."

"Why not?"

"Because I need to get it cast in bronze quickly. Then I'll sell it and we'll have some money for the baby."

He waited for her response to this, but she said nothing, and he could not see her face. He had been hoping that she would have some sort of suggestion, but when she did not, he finally brought up the matter that had been on his mind.

"Do you have any money put away?" Tomas asked.

"Not as much as I'd like. Do you?"

"Nothing. I've spent everything on art supplies, but I have an idea," said Tomas, finding it surprisingly easy to ignore the small protest within him that came from his pride. "If you lend me the money you've put aside, I could cast the piece in bronze and have it done quickly. One of the foundrymen said he would do it on credit if I put some of the money down myself. It wouldn't be all that much, a few thousand francs."

She laughed.

"What's so funny?"

"You must be really desperate. I'm not going to be able to work after I give birth. Someone will have to pay for the midwife, and I wonder if you have put anything aside for her."

He did not answer.

"Just as I expected. Do you think I'm going to give you my money at a time like this?"

"I didn't say give."

"I know you didn't. But the risk is too high. If the bronze didn't sell quickly, I'd be in terrible shape."

"We could move in together to save money."

"We'll have to do that very soon, anyway. M. Perès is dropping hints."

"There you are."

"There you are, nothing. Even if I had no cares in the world, what makes you think I'd want to help you cast a bronze of Josephine Baker?"

"We've been through this before."

"Yes, and you never listen. You expect me to be fascinated by your artistic project as you work on another woman. Have you no understanding of women at all?"

"I thought I understood you well enough."

"You don't seem to understand me one bit."

Tomas pushed her forward and extricated himself from behind her. He put on his shoes and laced them and put on his jacket.

"Where are you going?" Jenny asked.

"Out for a walk."

"Don't sulk," said Jenny. "You know I can't risk my savings."

"You should go back to your hotel. I might be some time," said Tomas, and he resisted the urge to slam the door behind him.

Tomas tried to walk off his problems, but he carried them with him, and he experienced no lightening of the load no matter how far he went. When he found himself in Montparnasse, he remembered Rosalie's. The restaurant where he had lunched with Estelle would remind him of the early days in Paris, when everything had been much simpler. But when he arrived there, he found Chez Rosalie closed and shuttered. A man was standing in the street, smoking a cigarette.

"Where's Rosalie?" Tomas asked.

"Dead."

"What?"

"What did you expect? She was old when she opened the place, and she ran it for twenty years."

Tomas bought himself a sausage from a street vendor, ate it and walked some more. The passage of the hours helped him erase some of the frustration. He made his way back to the studio, and when he arrived, he found Sorrel outside, smoking a cigarette in the courtyard.

"Since when do you bother to smoke outside?" Tomas asked.

"The midwife is inside," said Sorrel. "Jenny's in labour."

TEN

A FULL-THROATED SCREAM SOUNDED FROM INSIDE AS TOMAS swung open the studio door to see the midwife on her knees between Jenny's legs. Jenny's waist was covered by a twisted sheet and she still wore the sweaters she'd had on when he left, however many hours ago. Tomas tried to kneel beside her to comfort her, but the midwife would not permit it and Jenny only stopped screaming to gather breath for more of the same. The midwife was a stout woman with her hair tied back and she wore a smock that already had some blood on it.

"Men are no good in these situations. Get out," she said.

"I just want to speak to her and hold her hand."

"She'll neither hear your voice nor feel your hand at the moment. The baby is badly turned. If you want to make yourself useful, go and get a doctor. No matter how things turn out now, this is going to cost money."

"Will she be all right?"

"She won't be if you keep standing here."

Tomas did not want to leave. He turned to Sorrel. "Why didn't you get a doctor?" Sorrel shrugged.

"Go two blocks down the street and turn right. Get Dr. Cresson. You'll see his sign," the midwife said.

After a hundred yards, Tomas realized he was going the wrong way and turned around. He had difficulty locating the sign, even though he passed by it several times, and when he finally rang the bell, the ancient maid who answered the door in her apron did not want to let him in because the doctor was eating his dinner.

"This is an emergency," said Tomas. "My wife is giving birth."

"Is there a midwife?"

"Yes, but she said to get Dr. Cresson."

The maid was unperturbed. "And how long has labour been going on?"

"I don't know."

"Longer than a day?"

"No. A few hours."

"And it's her first child?"

"Yes."

"Then there is no rush."

"But the midwife told me to get him."

"She probably just wants to get home to her own supper. You wait where you are, young man, and I will have the doctor come down as soon as he finishes eating. It won't be more than half an hour."

"I'll leave the address."

"No, no. Wait here. Believe me, first births always take a long time. There is no rush. If you are impatient, go across the street to the café."

"Can't I wait inside?"

"Not in the state you are in. The next thing I know, you'll be rushing the doctor and he will get indigestion."

She closed the door.

It was not possible to be patient. He tried to remember what happened back in Lithuania when women gave birth. He was a child when his mother gave birth to Paul, but she had been hidden away in a room of her own. Maria had not died in childbirth, but the memory filled him with unease.

The door opened thirty-five minutes later, and Dr. Cresson stepped out. He was a middle-aged man in a black coat, fleshy all the way down to the pudgy fingers that held his medical bag.

"Lead the way," said the doctor. Tomas could not move as quickly as he wished because Dr. Cresson was not to be rushed. When they arrived, he made Tomas stand outside with Sorrel.

"Calm yourself," said Sorrel. "Estelle is there now too and they'll do everything they can. There is nothing you can do but pay the bills, so there is no use getting yourself excited. Come on. I'll buy you a drink."

"I can't leave."

"Then I'll get us something." He returned five minutes later with a bottle of wine and two glasses. Mme Martini appeared in the shadows under the arch but she did not speak. She twisted the end of her apron tightly with both hands.

"I can't drink now," said Tomas. Jenny's screams carried into the courtyard.

"If you don't drink, you'll drive yourself and the rest of us to our wits' end. Now come on."

Sorrel made him drink two glasses in quick succession, and the wine did help a little, dulling the anxiety. Then the midwife opened the door and beckoned Tomas to come in.

Dr. Cresson was standing in the middle of the room. He reached into his jacket pocket for cigarettes, and then thought better of it.

"Are you the father?"

"Yes."

"The child is badly breeched, but it is still alive. I have tried everything I could, but we need to get her to a clinic where I can have her anesthetized and operate on her properly. Will you cover the cost?"

"Of course."

"Good. I'll call an ambulance."

Finally Tomas was permitted to kneel beside Jenny and take her hand. The curls of hair around her face were flattened with sweat. "Hold on as well as you can," he whispered. "You'll be at the clinic very fast, and then they'll operate."

"Is the baby still alive?"

"The doctor said it is."

"A boy or a girl?"

"No one can tell yet."

"I hope it lives. I wouldn't want to go through all this for nothing."

"I love you very much."

A new contraction began, and Jenny howled in pain.

"Can't you give her something?" Tomas asked the midwife.

"The howling itself helps the pain, and they'll give her something at the hospital." Jenny's eyes were closed and she was grinding her teeth.

When the ambulance arrived, there was no room for anyone but the midwife, Jenny and the doctor.

Tomas was about to follow by taxi, but Sorrel told him to come inside for a moment. Estelle had appeared from somewhere, and she made him a sandwich and Sorrel insisted he down two shots of vodka, and kept up a patter of words: "She was already in labour when I got here. We looked for you at the Folies and Carrel's, but you were nowhere to be found."

"Estelle, isn't the baby coming too soon?" Tomas asked. But Estelle would not look at him.

The clinic on the Boulevard Arago was light and roomy and looked as if it cost a great deal; it would eat up Jenny's savings in a few days, but he would find a way to pay for it somehow. He was not permitted to be with her. A nun made him wait in the hall for six hours before he was allowed inside.

Jenny had been moved into a ward with twelve other women,

and she no longer seemed to be in labour. She lay on the bed with her eyes closed. The doctor was writing something in a notepad as he stood beside the bed, and he looked up as Tomas came in.

"The child was a boy, but he did not survive," he said. "The cord was wrapped round his neck and he was born far too soon. There was nothing that could be done. I'm sorry. Your wife is still bleeding and she needs an operation."

"Will she survive?"

"Perhaps."

"Can I speak to her?"

"She is not conscious and we will need to operate soon. You can sit here if you want, or come back later, as you choose."

Tomas sat in a chair by Jenny's bed. No one had bothered to wash her face or comb her hair, so he did the best he could with his fingers until one of the women in another bed motioned him over and lent him a comb. Tomas combed out Jenny's hair as carefully as he could, trying to be gentle where there were knots, but her face showed no reaction even when he tugged on the tougher spots. He returned the comb and wiped her face with the end of the sheet. Then he sat down to watch her, but she was very still and he could not see her breathing, and this stillness made him uneasy. He put his hand on her forehead and found it hot. For a time he paced by her bed, but felt the eyes of the other women on him, so he went out to the hallway until they took her away for the operation.

He spent the night on a chair in the hall before she was brought back from her operation just after dawn. Jenny was awake. A nun had combed her hair again and washed her face, but she was pale except for two red circles on her cheeks. The first thing Tomas did was touch her forehead, and he felt the heat there. Jenny reached up to put her hand on his.

"I lost the baby."

"I know."

"I tried not to."

"It couldn't be helped."

He sat down on the hospital bed and gently took her in his arms. She winced at his touch. "I suppose it's for the best, after all," she said. "We weren't ready for a baby, were we?" said Jenny.

Tomas said nothing.

"You need to make a name for yourself. But then we'll try again, won't we?"

"Yes."

He did not want to cry in front of her, but the effort of holding back was very hard.

"I didn't even know for sure that I wanted the baby until I felt this one trying to get out, trying to come to life. Now I do know."

Her eyes closed and she fell away from him into sleep. He took a face cloth and dipped it in a basin of water that now sat on a table beside her bed, then wrung it out and wiped her forehead with it. She did not react.

The doctor came once and took her temperature. When Tomas asked him how she was doing, he said she had developed puerperal fever and was going through a crisis and no one could tell how it would end. Sometime during the day Estelle came with something for him to eat and drink, and she sat with him for an hour before leaving.

By the early evening, Tomas was exhausted from lack of sleep. He went to the bathroom to wash his face, and when he returned, a nun was waiting for him at the bedside.

"Where were you?" she asked. Tomas explained, and she told him not to leave the bedside for a moment. He was afraid to ask why.

Through that night, and all the following day, Tomas watched her laboured breathing, a panting that filled him with fear, especially when it stopped suddenly and he had to wait for it to resume. Exhausted, yet unable to look away, he sat beside her, clutching one of her hands in his, until in the evening one of the pauses was not followed by a renewed breath.

When he left the clinic, night had fallen and the last of the shoppers were out buying provisions. The fruit looked very bright under the shop lights, the apples more golden than usual, the oranges more orange.

As he walked, he stared dazedly at the passersby. They could be doctors, thieves, actors, politicians or labourers. He might be walking past geniuses without knowing it. And none of those passing by him knew of his heart, of his desire to be a sculptor, of his shock at the death of Jenny. What right did he have to expect them to think about him? The crowds on the street thinned as the hours passed, and Tomas kept walking. The shops closed, and soon there was only traffic between the cafés and the restaurants. He could not bear to look inside and see the animated conversations, the lovers and the jokers, the hustlers and the hustled. He made his way to Jenny's hotel, where M. Perès shook his hand gravely and permitted him to enter Jenny's room.

Once inside, he stood for a minute in the dark, then felt his way to her dresser. Digging through a drawer he at last found one of her fine woollen sweaters. He balled it up and held it in front of his face as he lay on her bed so he could inhale the last remnants of her scent.

Estelle volunteered to make all the necessary arrangements, and Tomas spent the next two days in the company of Sorrel, who fed him enough drinks to put him in a daze, but not so many that he was ever properly drunk. On the morning of the third day, he awoke nauseated, but washed himself and put on his best clothes, and with Sorrel and Estelle made his way to the crematorium.

The rites inside the crematorium took only a few minutes. Derval had sent a large bouquet of flowers and there were many other, smaller bouquets from the dancers and performers and even from some of Jenny's English students. M. Perès stood mournfully in a corner with two of the students who boarded at the Hotel Saint-Pierre. All in all, over fifty Folies colleagues crowded into the small space. Father Trethewey was there to officiate in his robes, but the man was weeping so much that he was of no use at all. No one else had prepared a speech. One of the Tiller Girls, whom Tomas knew only by sight, volunteered to speak about the woman who had died for love as the rest of them stared at the floor. Tomas could not summon even a word.

Estelle stayed with him as he watched the coffin slide into the furnace on a stone slab, while the others went off to a café for a memorial drink. After a while two workmen opened up the door to the furnace and pulled out the slab. The coffin had burned away, but Jenny's skeleton still lay on the slab, her arms still crossed on her breast. One of the workmen tapped the slab with a hammer, and the bones crumbled to dust.

ELEVEN

IN THE DAYS THAT FOLLOWED JENNY'S CREMATION, TOMAS could not bear to be alone. He was sick of being drunk, so he went in to work every day and immersed himself in the tasks of building and repairing sets. His foreman sensed his need to keep busy, and asked him to stay to do work that took extra time. As long as he could keep himself from thinking, life was bearable, but thoughts of Jenny ambushed him in unsuspecting moments— as he brought a cup of coffee to his lips, as he mixed plaster and as he went about his other daily tasks.

In the early days, dancers and singers, carpenters and even Derval himself came to Tomas to say how sorry they were about Jenny. He appreciated these words, but they made him hungry for deeper consolation. At home, he covered the statue of Josephine Baker with a sheet, but even so, nights were unbearable and sleep only came after he drank one or more bottles of wine.

A knot of anger, which he could not loosen, formed inside him. He began to cherish his own anger, to be a miser with it. He did not want to waste it by snapping at those he lived with or worked with. Instead, he saved it, affecting indifference to most things around him.

Sorrel and Estelle had been promised a joint show in seven months, and were working madly to make enough pieces to fill the gallery. Tomas did not have the energy to envy their success.

One day when he came home from a late shift at the Folies, he found Mme Martini standing in the doorway under the arch. "I've been waiting for you," she said. "You have a letter."

It was too dark under the arch to read the envelope, so he bade Mme Martini good-night and went through the courtyard to his door.

He found Sorrel drinking a glass of wine from a bottle that was still nearly full.

"Why are you up so late?" Tomas asked.

"Estelle is bringing over a buyer. This damn show of ours is costing so much in materials that we need a little extra cash."

"A buyer?"

"Yes, a policeman."

"Zamaron?"

"Yes. The lovestruck fool will likely help us out."

"Be careful, he's jealous of you, and Zamaron is a powerful man."

Tomas held his letter in the light. The stamp was from Lithuania but the handwriting was unfamiliar. He looked at the return address and saw that it came from his youngest brother, Paul. Tomas poured himself a glass of wine and sat down to read it.

Dear Tomas,

The Lord be with you!

I hope this letter reaches you. I had a very difficult time finding out where you lived. It has been almost three years since we last heard from you— why haven't you written since you left Warsaw? It's lucky that you registered with the embassy, or you would have been lost to us forever. We have thought of you often, especially Mother, who has prayed for you every night since you fled all those years ago.

I have some sad news for you. Our dear father has died. I know you two never got along well, but I hope you will light a candle for him in one of the churches of Paris. You always loved churches, and I'm sure you'll find a beautiful one in which to remember the head of our family. In his later years, Father grew very gentle. You wouldn't have known him at all. He spent all the fine days on a bench outside the church, sunning himself, smoking his pipe and talking with the other old men. He said he was happy each day just to watch the swallows swooping around the church steeple.

Our sisters and Edvard have all married. There is a new mistress in the house, a woman from three counties over whom Edvard met at the market. Mother has become very devout, and daily says the rosary before your carving of Saint Florion. Edvard is just and reasonable, a good head of the household. He is paying for my education in the high school, and his new wife doesn't begrudge me the money. Edvard says he will be able to buy a tractor soon. Andrius has become a teacher of German in Šiauliai and still advises Edvard on the newest discoveries in agricultural practice. He tells anyone who will listen that we have to look to the West, to Germany, if we want to escape the backwardness of our Russian legacy.

Edvard has asked me to write to you because something has come up that might interest you. The church in Merdine needs to be redecorated, and the priest has agreed to give you the first chance to do it because of your training in church decoration in Warsaw and your studies in Paris. There is a very good chance you could get the commission. Then, if you did well, you could redecorate other churches in Lithuania. Now that the war with Poland has settled into a stalemate, priests are spending money again.

You've been wandering among the foreigners long enough. Anyone who was born in this country is rooted in the soil, and will not find happiness unless he returns to it. Come home to us. You would not need to live here for long, just enough to get established. I have very fond memories of the toys you made for me when I was a boy. Everyone here has forgotten the past. Maria's mother has died and her brother, Feliks, sold off their little piece of land and immigrated to America to seek his fortune.

Life cannot be healthy in that big city where you are living. I'm sure you miss the sunlight and the fresh air. Storks are nesting again in the chimney of our house. We've lived in it for years now, but it would be new to you. The fields are green and the skies are thick with flocks of birds. The rivers seem to be refreshed, and boys are catching pike and carp as they have never been caught before. Even the crickets are singing louder than usual at night.

God is smiling on your home, and now it's time for you to come back and join us. Write as soon as you can.

The glory of God be with you,
Paul

Tomas could picture what the church would need in terms of new decoration. Who else knew the church as well as he did, and had the training to take on the job? No one. The church could use more light to show the gilt and paintings to better advantage. He imagined one of the walls where a window could be cut in, and although he had never trained in stained glass himself, he knew enough about it to oversee the work. He would add pews so the priest would not be distracted by the endless screech of chair legs across the stone floor. He could do a new statue of Saint Francis in bronze, one to stand outside.

What would it be like to go back now and walk up the lane? There would be new trees planted down by the road to make up for the ones they had cut when the Bermondt soldiers burned the farm. One of the old dogs might still be alive, so when the pack of them came barking down the lane toward him, it might recognize his scent. The whole family would be waiting for him on the front porch, and the garden paths would have been sprinkled with sand in honour of his return. Then they would go inside, after much slapping of backs and tears from his mother, to a long wooden table set with a linen tablecloth, with jugs of beer and honey wine and bottles of vodka. There would be bowls of soup and half a dozen bean and vegetable dishes, as well as a suckling pig and a napoleon cake. They would be fascinated with his tales of Paris, and marvel at the wonder of the place.

But then they would want to know what he had made of himself. His family would be kind, but the villagers would laugh at him behind his back. He'd be the one who had gone away and had not managed to make anything of himself, less successful than those who had gone to the coal mines in Belgium or the textile mills in America.

"Well, are you going to tell me what's in there or not?" Sorrel asked.

Tomas told him what Paul had written.

"It's a good offer," said Sorrel.

"You think I should go back?"

"A commission is a commission."

Tomas walked over to the stove. There were still traces of

warmth in it from that night's dinner. He pulled open the grate and dropped the letter inside.

"My future is here," said Tomas. "There's no going back."

"Why not?"

Tomas went to the covered sculpture and pulled off the sheet. "I have this piece to finish, for one thing."

He had not looked at the sculpture of the dancer for a long time, and for a moment wished he had not removed the sheet, and his feelings showed in his face.

"It's the right choice, I suppose," said Sorrel. "If you ever get that thing cast, you might do all right."

Tomas sat down, feeling winded.

"The piece makes me think of Jenny."

"It's time you stopped indulging in your grief. A wound that stays open too long will kill you. You need to cauterize it."

"She hated this piece, you know. She felt it was a betrayal of her."

"She's dead. What she thought doesn't matter any more."

"You don't know what she was worth to me."

Sorrel smirked. "I know how much she was worth to quite a few people."

"What do you mean?"

"Never mind. I've already said too much." Sorrel sat back and the light reflected off his eyeglasses, turning them into two circles of brightness. Tomas shifted so he could read the expression in his friend's eyes—amusement.

"Explain what you mean," said Tomas.

"Are you sure you want to know?"

"Yes."

"The truth was as plain as day to anyone who cared to look. Do you really think it was just English lessons she offered? Her clients were all men. What do you think went on in that hotel room when you weren't there?"

The anger in Tomas's belly began to roil.

"None of that matters to me."

"Good. Because the odds are excellent that the child who killed her was someone else's."

The rage rose in Tomas and he liked the feeling in his veins, the way it heated his blood and woke his heart. He looked carefully at the tools strewn around the place, passed over the scattered burins and considered the hammer—too light. An iron pry bar stood in the corner of the room but before he went over to it, he took off his jacket and placed it on the back of a chair.

"What are you doing?" Sorrel asked.

Tomas lifted the bar, and felt the heft of the cold iron in his hands.

"Don't be a fool," said Sorrel. "I was only trying to shake you out of your depression."

Tomas took two mock swings in the air in front of himself. The weight of the iron felt good.

"I loved Jenny, and I still do," he said. "What you say may be true and it may not, but that doesn't change anything. I should have done this long ago."

Lifting the bar over his head, Tomas brought it down smartly on the model of Josephine Baker. The arms shattered and pieces went flying across the room. Josephine stood now like a parody of the Venus de Milo. He lifted the bar again and swung at the neck, and her head came off in a single piece and fell onto the table. Plaster dust flew into the air. He struck at the body, but it was too thick to break with a few blows, so he hacked at the snake until it was broken into small pieces.

Sorrel shook his head. "You tell me that you intend to stay in Paris to make your sculptures, and now you've broken the best piece you've ever done. At least you still have the models."

Tomas found the two smaller models stored below the table. He flung the smallest one across the room against the wall where it exploded into dust and fragments.

Sorrel rushed forward to stop Tomas from reaching for the last one. "Don't destroy all you've worked for, Tomas. You've gone out of your mind!" Sorrel seized him, and the rage was still burning in Tomas so hotly—he was happy at last to have an enemy that fought back.

He dropped the iron bar and swung wildly, and sometimes he hit flesh and sometimes he was blocked or missed. The frustration drove Tomas to greater fury. Cloth ripped and Sorrel's teeth sank into his left hand before Tomas hit him with his right to make him loosen his grip. Suddenly Estelle was there tugging on him too, and he swung wildly at her and knocked her to the ground.

Something hard hit him on the head and then he saw sparks in the darkness.

When he came to, he was propped up against the wall. His hand was bleeding and parts of his face felt numb. Sorrel was in the same position across the room, his glasses unbroken and his face unscathed. Estelle was holding a rag to her bloody nose. Tomas made a move to stand, and a hand on his collar helped him rise to his feet, but then the hand pinned one of his arms behind him and he could not move.

"Oh, you race of artists are such a pathetic breed," said Zamaron's voice in his ear. Tomas could smell the tobacco reek on him. "Girls in a convent school could have done a better job of fighting than you two. The only one you managed to hurt was Estelle. You swagger around this city like cocks in a henhouse, but I tell you, all it would take is one fox and you'd be dinner. What's this all about, eh?" Zamaron did not let go of Tomas.

"The fool was distraught and destroying his own work. When I tried to stop him, he turned on me," said Sorrel.

"Childish spats."

"His woman has died. He is not himself," Estelle said through the rag that covered her face.

Tomas tried to twist to get out of Zamaron's grip, but the policeman jerked his arm up behind him until he thought it would break, and clubbed Tomas across the head with one fist. Then he pushed Tomas out of the door and through the courtyard into the street. He shuffled him straight into the nearest open café and slammed him against the zinc bar. He asked the owner to call for a police car. Then he bent over Tomas and spoke into his ear.

"I don't care about your broken heart. You're a menace to yourself and you're a menace to Estelle. I could have you deported in a second, but I'm going to give you one last chance. You'll spend three nights in jail to cool down, and in the meantime I'll have Estelle move your things out of that studio. If I set eyes on you again, you'll be sorry you were ever born." And he slammed him against the bar again to emphasize his point.

TWELVE

WHEN TOMAS WAS RELEASED FROM JAIL, HE BORROWED some money from his friends at the Folies and found himself a former blacksmith's shop off the Rue de Javel, close to the Seine. The place was twenty minutes' walk from Carrel's studio. The fringe neighbourhood consisted of shacks and workshops and the occasional hovel that looked as if it had been collapsing since the Franco-Prussian war. The neighbourhood had many open lots, covered with scrub grass and broken bottles, and a gypsy encampment where fires smouldered day and night but no music ever sounded.

He sent a note to Estelle with his new address, and two delivery men brought his belongings in wheelbarrows. The roof leaked and Tomas was obliged to hang a sheet of canvas over his sleeping and working area in order to keep the rain off. He wouldn't have minded his straw pallet if it hadn't been for the fleas.

He welcomed the meanness of the place.

He thought long and hard about what Sorrel had said to him about Jenny. Sorrel could have been trying to shake Tomas out of his depression the only way he knew how—brutally. But it was also possible that what he said was true. Father Fred had wept a little too long and hard at the crematorium, and when he thought of it, a few strange young men had shed tears as well. He relived various moments in his mind, gestures made by Jenny in the

Folies, looks given to her in the street. He considered the whores' café across from the Folies where Jenny had taken him the first night she agreed to speak to him again.

He searched for some kind of key that would open the door to the truth. But there was no key to be had. She had loved him, he knew that, and she had brought warmth and playfulness to his life, which he now missed sorely. She'd given him the sort of joy that he did not think he would ever find again. He wished that his last conversation with her had not been about money and the statue of Josephine Baker.

The surviving original had arrived in the wheelbarrow from Estelle. He gave it to Abatino in thanks for the time Josephine had sat for him, but he was through with the dancer now.

Tomas did not return to Carrel's. On his own, he tried to sketch but he could not concentrate. Instead he opened up his bag of carved wooden sculptures and set them around his room. They had been made to stand outside, and they could withstand whatever rain leaked on them from the holes in the roof. The pieces reminded him of Lipchitz, and he decided he needed to see the man who had sown the idea of Paris in him in the first place. He gathered up his wooden gods, put them in a canvas sack and boarded the train to the suburb of Boulogne-sur-Seine.

Tomas stood before Jacques Lipchitz's door with his hat in his hand, his collar sticky against his neck. It had rained just before he boarded the suburban train and then again when he arrived at Boulogne-sur-Seine. He had had to wait in the station café until the downpour passed and the sun broke out again since he could not afford an umbrella. The sky was unpredictable, changing from rain to brilliant sunshine in the time it took to cross the street.

Back in Paris, the poor were never very far from the rich, but here in this suburb, there were no poor, or at least none were visible, and he felt every scuff on his shoes and every stain on his jacket. The shopkeepers watched him from their doors as he walked up the sidewalk. When he finally found the address he wanted, he hesitated again. The three-storey house stood behind a wall, which had no openings except for a garage door that was locked shut. The facade was very new, stripped of ornamentation and self-consciously modern. A large window overlooked the street, but Tomas could see no other door. He had to make his way around the back, open the gate and come in through the garden. Much of the back wall of the house was made of glass, but the windows were too high to see through. He hesitated for a moment, found his courage and knocked.

The woman who opened the door to him had short hair, cut almost like a boy's, which made her look a little daring, but she wore an old-fashioned white blouse with a broad lace collar under a dark sweater. She looked him over.

"You're a sculptor," she finally announced.

"How can you tell?"

"The dust. Sculptors are never free of it. Painters always smell of turpentine. What's your name?"

"Tomas Stumbras."

"Does he expect you?"

"He told me to come and see him, but he doesn't expect me right now."

"The worst thing I could do is call him. He works in the mornings and he becomes furious if anything interferes. It's funny, isn't it?"

"What?"

"For an artist to be so regular in his hours. Lipchitz goes to bed early, arrives at dinners punctually and pays all his debts. I tell you these things before anything else because so many of you expect him to be some kind of bohemian but he's as sober as a banker and very serious about his work. You still want to talk to him?"

"Yes."

She thought for a minute.

"All right. There is a café at the end of the street. The coffee and the sandwiches are cheap, and they have free newspapers. Wait there for a few hours and come back early in the afternoon. I'll tell him you'll be here."

The café windows were covered with condensation from the steam from the coffee machine and the damp in the patrons' clothes. The place stank of black tobacco and wet leather. He tried to read the newspapers, but it was too hard to concentrate, so he nursed first a beer and then a coffee, and smoked a chain of cigarettes before he finally went back.

When the woman opened the door to him, she said, "Now Jacques is sleeping. I'm afraid you will need to come back another day."

"But I've come such a long way."

"From Paris? You call that a long way? When I was sixteen, I went from Russia to Capri, mostly on foot, because I wanted to meet Maxim Gorky. *That* was a long way. And when I saw he was not the man I had expected, I went to Paris to be the chess partner of Leon Trotsky. *That* was a long way. To come here from Paris is a pleasant stroll."

"Originally, I came here from Lithuania. That's a long way, too."

"Lithuania, eh?" In Polish she began to declaim: "'*Oh Lithuania, you are more to me than my home, you are my whole life. Only those who have lost you can find you again.*'" Then she looked at him to see if he knew the piece.

"It's the opening of *Pan Tadeusz*, by Adam Mickiewicz," said Tomas.

"He's not as good as Pushkin," she said.

"Maybe not, but he's pretty good."

"Come inside. I'll make you some coffee and we'll wait until he wakes up. My name is Berthe."

She took him into the studio workshop and left him there with instructions to look around while she went up to the kitchen to make the coffee.

The studio had been built with a very high ceiling to accommodate some of Lipchitz's largest pieces. On one workbench was a rod of metal nine feet high, the beginning of an armature for what would be a huge piece. The size of it impressed Tomas. He couldn't even dream of making sculptures on that scale while he was still poor. On a side table was a bronze deer, more realistic than Tomas had expected to see in the studio of a man known for his cubist style.

More familiar pieces stood in various states of completion, from plaster-of-Paris models to fired clays and bronzes. There were variations on Lipchitz's signature piece, the *Sailor with Guitar* from a decade before, and a similar piece executed in bas-relief. There was a "seated man with guitar," though the piece looked to Tomas more like a giant holding a propeller. It was clear that the technical language Lipchitz was trying to find was more compelling to him than the subject matter. Tomas had been in Paris long enough to know that although inspiration might come from somewhere else, a piece of art was really about itself.

The rest of the cubist pieces in the studio—a toreador, a woman with a long braid, a harlequin with an accordion, a few tall abstracts that looked like groups of skyscrapers and a bust of Berthe in bronze—did not seem newly done. None of them was being worked on at the moment, so Tomas put down his sack and moved on among the works to try to divine which Lipchitz was doing at present. He stood for a long time in front of a rough bronze of a stick-figure man with his head in his hands. The longer he looked, the better he liked it and the more it made him smile.

"What's so interesting about that piece?" a voice asked, and Tomas looked up to see Lipchitz himself standing at the door from the stairs to the living quarters above. He was dressed in a smock, open at the neck with a work shirt beneath. He held in his hand the collar of a large mixed-breed dog with frizzy, long hair.

"The lines of the legs, body, arms and hands have been made into parallel loops and they trap the figure inside," said Tomas.

"Come over here and take a look at this other piece. Tell me what you think about it."

Lipchitz gestured at an upright piece in bronze about three hands tall. There was a frame around the piece, bars inside the frame and in front of the bars two triangles, one on top of the other. A pair of arms came out from the triangles and held on to a ladder.

"It's a Star of David," he said.

"Not exactly," said Lipchitz. "The bottom point has been cut in two, so it is a seven-pointed star. Anyone can see that. But let me tell you something. This is the piece that saved my life. For a year I didn't know what to do, and now this piece has shown me the way. Can you see what there is about it that elates me so?"

"If it took you a year to make this, what makes you think I'll understand it in a few seconds?"

"Try."

Tomas looked hard at the piece. It was certainly nothing like what he had expected, nothing like what he ordinarily thought of as sculpture, all roundness and three-dimensionality. But what was the key?

"It's flat," he said hesitantly.

"Bravo!" Lipchitz applauded him as his wife, Berthe, had done at the door. But as soon as his hand was off its collar, the animal bounded forward.

"Maraud!"

But it was too late. The great creature jumped up on its hind legs and placed its giant forepaws on Tomas's chest, licking his face furiously with a tongue as big as the leaf of a book.

"Congratulations. Even the dog likes you," said Berthe from the steps, "and he's the most difficult critic of them all. Come upstairs, I have made coffee."

"I've brought some carvings," said Tomas, holding up his bag.

"He can look at them after he drinks some coffee. He'll be in a better mood then," she said.

The walls on the way up were bare. Berthe caught him looking.

"We tried to hang some paintings, but when Charles, the architect, came in and saw them, he flew into a fury. He said his walls were designed to be bare."

"But it's your house!" said Tomas.

"He's Le Corbusier. The house is his work of art," said Lipchitz. "He said he had built a machine for us to live in and anything we hung on the walls would gum up the works."

The sitting room was a cavernous room almost as big as the studio below. As Berthe served coffee and slices of pound cake, one of those awkward moments descended on them, when strangers sit together intimately, each hesitating to speak. Lipchitz drank from his cup and the silence grew too long.

"Maybe you could tell me what it was like when you came to Paris," Tomas finally said.

Lipchitz laughed and the moment's awkwardness passed. He talked about the early days, repeating some of what he had said to Tomas when they'd last met.

"That's all?" Berthe asked when he finished.

"What else should there be?"

He spoke with the special sharpness couples reserve for each other.

"A young man comes to you for help, and you tell him your life story. You're not old enough yet to speak only about the past."

"What do you want from me?" Lipchitz asked Tomas sternly, as if he were the one who had criticized him instead of Berthe.

"I just wanted to look at your sculpture and have you look at mine. I want to learn from you. Maybe you could tell me about the piece below. Why is flat sculpture so important?"

Lipchitz's irritation fell away in an instant.

"With cubism I learned that art does not need to be an imitation of nature—but I had not yet learned what would take the place of the old idea. I needed to learn a new syntax. I was looking for laws of this syntax, and I tell you, the last two years have been torture.

"Once I had some success and made some money, I realized that the difficulties were only beginning. I needed to meditate, but I was always very close to despair. Remember that old dispute between Michaelangelo and Leonardo da Vinci? Leonardo had said that painting was superior to sculpture because sculptors were more like masons than artists. Sculptors were mere *ouvriers*, and sculpture was a deficient medium. Even wise men say foolish things, I know that, and yet what Leonardo had said struck me like a blow. Especially his notion that sculpture was less than painting because sculpture could not represent transparent or luminous things.

"I turned this over in my mind, and the more I thought about it, the more I came to believe I was enslaved by my materials instead of made free by them. I felt things in my heart that my hands were incapable of expressing. Some of my friends thought I was a fool to be thinking like this."

"Not just your friends," said Berthe.

"Yes. Berthe as well. She has a poetic soul, but even she could not understand what my problem was. She told me that my success had ruined me. I suffered for months. I could not work. But one day the answer to my problems came through my hands. I made a small figure, similar to the one you saw downstairs. I made it in cardboard first, a technique I had learned from Picasso, but then I went further. I remade it in wax with no armature. It was flat, as you said. I turned my back on the history of sculpture and its language of volume. But I did more than that. I had pierced the work as well, made it transparent. I took the wax to Valsuani, the foundryman, and he laughed at me. He said the thing could not be done in bronze, not using the lost-wax process. But together we managed to cast the piece, and now we have cast others like it. I have come through a tunnel. There is light. There is much that I need to do."

"Well?" Berthe asked.

"Well, what?" Lipchitz answered.

"Do you remember the printer from Grodno?"

"What printer?"

"You've told me the story often enough, but today you only want to tell certain stories. The printer from Grodno, the one who knew your parents. He lived in Paris and he told you to come see him if you ever went to Paris. Do you remember what he told you?"

Lipchitz nodded ruefully.

"Anecdotes. I had nothing to eat, and he told me stories. Berthe, you are right as always. Tomas, let's take a look at what's in that sack of yours."

"Some of these you saw at a distance the night of the party," Tomas said. First he reached into his bag and removed the Alphonse he had done the day after he died, setting it on the table. He was about to reach in and take out another figure, but Lipchitz held up his hand. "Let's look at each one carefully." He turned the sculpture around and around, then set the piece down and looked at it, as if from a distance. Only then did he ask Tomas to take out another. In this manner, Lipchitz looked at the eight carvings, finishing with two variations on the Madonna theme with Jenny as the model. He carried one of these over to a windowsill and set it there to see how the light fell on it. Then he came back.

"Young man, I was not deceived the night I saw these up in

the corners of your room. They are well executed and there is something both old and fresh about them. Now tell me what you plan to do next."

"I don't know what to do next," said Tomas. "That's why I have come to you."

Lipchitz sat back in his chair and crossed his arms over his chest. "Sometimes young people ask me impossible questions, but you have asked me a very easy one. What you have shown me is very good. Keep doing what you are doing. Go on. You're on the right track."

"You mean wood carvings?"

"Not necessarily wood. Take what you have learned with the wood and see if it works in stone or bronze. Any one of these carvings is worthy of more work, perhaps enlargement as well. And the final two, the Madonnas, are very strong indeed. Start with this theme. Find that model again, treat her very well and have her sit for you and work the problem through."

Tomas swallowed hard. He wished that Lipchitz had not made him think of Jenny. He forced himself to breathe and in his mind groped for what he might say to them, but when he opened his mouth, nothing came out but a croak. Tomas reddened and tears began to come out of his eyes. He could not have spoken to save himself and he covered his face with his hands.

Lipchitz looked astounded, but Berthe came and sat beside him on the couch and held his head to her shoulder.

"What is it?" she asked.

"I'll be all right," Tomas finally said, but it took him a little longer than he had imagined. In fits and starts, he told them about Jenny and then he told them everything, even what had forced him to leave home in the first place—not the pursuit of his art but the death of Maria.

An unexpected kindness infused Lipchitz's words. "I never suffered your losses, young man, but it was hard enough for me to come to Paris, even so. And the suffering goes on and on. You must find a way to continue despite the pain in your heart."

"I have no intention of giving up," said Tomas.

"I'm glad to hear that. Talent and even doggedness are still not enough. You will need one other element in order to succeed. Without it, you will be nothing."

Berthe grew impatient as Lipchitz let the silence stretch. "Tell him what the thing is!" she said.

"Help. You will need help. Within a short time after my arrival in Paris, I had already made myself known to all the artists of the city, Picasso, Modigliani, Gris and others. But what good did it do me to be admired if I was starving? For almost fifteen years, I barely scraped by. There was a dealer, Paul Guillaume. We had argued. I did not like him, but one day he knocked on my door and he was standing there with an American. This man wore a coat that spoke money, as did his hat and gloves and even the smell of the cigar between his fingers. He wore tinted glasses, but even through them I could see the fiery eyes of a man who was accustomed to giving orders. Guillaume introduced him as Dr. Albert Barnes. Yes, I thought, the man has the kind of firmness that only Americans, doctors and sea captains share.

"They came into my studio. I was already ten years older than you are now and I did not know what to make of them. Barnes did not even take off his coat, or speak. He had a notebook in his hand and he walked around my sculptures. Some were very large, twice the size of a man, and I had scraped together all my money to make them. Some were bronzes on which I still owed the foundry fee, and others were just plaster models that I could not afford to cast. And Guillaume, that self-important ass, pranced about like a rug merchant trying to make a sale.

"Finally, the doctor asked me to name a price on one of my pieces. Remember, Berthe and I were on the point of starvation. What good did a huge piece of bronze do me when we needed to eat? I named him a low price because we needed the money, and I was both happy and defeated when he accepted it.

"Then he showed me another piece he wanted, and now that I knew our bellies would be fuller, I named a far higher price. He nodded and made a note. And then he went on. He indicated piece after piece and I kept raising the prices until they were perfectly outlandish. By the time he came to the eighth piece, I thought he was mad, some kind of impostor whom Guillaume had brought in to torture me. It was a fantastic moment, so I named him a fantastic price.

"Barnes did his sums. He added up all that I had asked for, and then knocked ten percent off the top. Would I accept that sum for all the work he had chosen? I agreed. Why not? It was just a game. I was half tempted to spit in his eye, but I played along with him.

"After he left me with promise of payment, I told Berthe what had happened, and the two of us sat down in shock. Was it possible that he was a real collector? We did not know whether we should celebrate. We went out for a walk in Montparnasse, unable to stop anywhere to eat or drink because we were just rich in theory. But the story was out already—Guillaume had told everyone. Our friends in the cafés fell upon us and I had to buy celebratory drinks on credit. It was the famous Dr. Barnes, they all said, the rich American who appeared like the fairy godmother out of *Cinderella*. We ate and drank and danced all that night in celebration, and thank heavens Barnes was as good as his word.

"That is how my life as an artist changed. Suddenly the dealers in Paris all wanted my work. My pieces grew so popular so fast that I wanted to shake people and tell them that it was only me, Jacques Lipchitz, not Matisse they were talking about. Overnight, I was transformed.

"The point of my story is this. Work hard. Do something big and cast it in bronze. Then call me and let me look at your work again. I will see what I can do for you. Perhaps nothing, perhaps something."

Berthe reached forward to take Tomas's hand again. "Everything he says is true, and it will help you with your work. But your heart will take its own time to heal."

Staring through the train window on his trip back to Paris, eating slices of black bread Berthe had given him for the journey, Tomas finally felt he had something to grasp on to. He looked at the ugly backs of factories and apartments, at the wattle fences and gardens of houses whose yards came down to the tracks, but he barely saw them. He felt as if he was entering Paris for the first time, but this time he had the blessing of Lipchitz to sustain him. He was keenly aware that it had only come about because of Jenny. He thanked her again for all that she had given him, and as the suburban train drew close to Paris, he remembered Maria, and he thanked her in his mind as well.

THIRTEEN

THE SCULPTURE TOMAS HAD IN MIND WAS NOT AN EXPLICIT rendering of Jenny, but it would have something of her in it. He thought far, far back to the images of his childhood, the stiff, formal *Virgin of the Dawn Gate* that he had seen in Vilnius with his uncle Longin. He thought of the Madonna in wood that stood in the wayside shrine at the entrance to Merdine. The piece was grotesque but powerful. He recalled Maria and tried to picture her precisely, adding a new dimension of pain to his thoughts, the muted throbbing of an old wound.

He could not determine a formula in his head—his hands needed to find the expression. He sketched and he worked in clay, trying to see if he could move from the medium of wood to one that would lead him to a bronze. Many of his sketches were only worthy of the wastebasket, and most of his models were good for nothing but to be smashed up for the redemption of the clay.

Slowly it came to Tomas that he would not do a Madonna as such, but a mother and child. And the child needed to be present, but lost, a being who caused the opposite of contentment in the mother. The woman would be down on one knee and the child would not be in her arms, but on her back, reaching forward over her shoulders toward her breasts. The woman's head would be craned back, as if she was both looking for this lost child and bearing its great weight even in its absence. And the child must be large, not an infant but the memory of a child and therefore much larger than a real one, for the weight of memory was far heavier than any living weight. The surfaces would be grainy, and there would not be great detail in either of the figures, no exact renderings of a face so that the figure could encompass all of the women he had known.

He sketched the figure a hundred times, and built at least twenty small models, destroying all but two of them. He continued to work at the Folies, and his foreman had to reprimand him more than once because his thoughts were elsewhere, on the figure of the woman with child waiting for him back in his canvas-draped studio. Tomas worked on her by day and by night under his single electric lamp.

He made mistakes. Again and again, he ripped off the clay and reformed the armature. He saw no one outside of the Folies, but the isolation did not bother him. He thought of nothing but the shape that was forming and reforming under his hands day after day.

And then a crisis occurred at the Folies. One of the flats collapsed onto a stage set, crushing various busts and other flats. Thankfully, no one was hurt, but all the carpenters were called in to rebuild in a hurry. As Tomas was useful in wood, paint and plaster, he needed to work longer than most, so much so that he slept for three nights at the Folies itself in the tiny dressing room in the wings that was ordinarily reserved for Mistinguett.

He felt like a father whose child was left at home alone, but there was nothing he could do until the set was ready. When he finally returned to his studio at the end of the miserable Rue de Javel, he froze when he saw the shape on his table. He turned on the electric light and circled the piece, before he pulled off the hanging tarpaulin so that the light reflected from the ceiling and illuminated his work.

He studied her for flaws and fought back the urge to refine her. He had seen other artists build up their pieces and then work them into mannerism through excessive attention to detail. Part of being a good sculptor was knowing when to stop. In order to be sure, he draped her again and again and forced himself to go out for walks so he could look at her with fresh eyes on his return. For three days, he played that game, and then he went to the closest post office and sent a telegram to Lipchitz.

Lipchitz brought Tomas a package of bread, sausage and cheese that Berthe had sent along. He looked around briefly at Tomas's tarpaulin-draped studio, and then went straight to *Woman with Child*. He walked around her slowly. When he was finished, he sat down at the table and asked Tomas for a pencil and a piece of paper.

"This is the name and address of a very good foundry," said Lipchitz. "It is run by an old man named Valsuani, the one I told you about. Tell him I sent you, and ask him to come and look at the piece. If he likes it, he will cast it for you in bronze. Let me know what happens."

Lipchitz shook his hand and left. Tomas looked at the scrap of paper in wonder.

Valsuani's massive shoulders and broad chest seemed all the more remarkable on such an old man. He had a ring of thick white hair around his bald crown, and grey stubble on his chin. His clothes were those of a working man: blue smock, jacket and cap. Although Valsuani's sons had taken over much of the work at the foundry, the old man still took an interest in what the upcoming artists were doing. Like many old men, he had come to think of the hereafter. The hand of God could be discerned everywhere, sometimes even in a form made of plaster. He liked interesting things and he occasionally worked on credit, but he was not in the habit of losing money.

Valsuani walked around the plaster *Woman with Child*, looking at her carefully. He touched the surface, and examined some of the details with the help of a large magnifying glass he pulled from his jacket pocket.

"You don't want to finish her?" Valsuani asked.

"She is finished. I'm after a rough surface."

Valsuani stooped with the magnifying glass in front of his nose, as if he were an inspector of police. Then he stepped back from the piece and walked around at a greater distance, pausing to look at her from various angles.

"It would be much cheaper to cast her this size," he said. "Enlargement costs money."

"She needs to be double the scale," said Tomas firmly. Valsuani sighed, but he did not argue.

"I've seen harder jobs, but this one has its own particular complications. Is she worth it?"

"Yes."

Valsuani nodded.

"Do you have a buyer?"

"Not exactly a buyer. I believe Jacques Lipchitz will help me."

"He's helped you once already. I would not have come if it weren't for him. I get one or two entreaties a week, all from young men convinced of their genius. Are you a genius?"

"I'm just a sculptor."

"If you cannot pay me ahead of time, I'll have to risk a good deal of my own time and money."

He let the words hang in the air like the dust in the sunlight coming through the window. The old man sat down on a stool and took his pipe out of his pocket. He lit it and puffed until the room was full of smoke. He scratched his head and looked at the plaster. He smoked his whole pipe wordlessly, which took a good ten minutes. When he was done, he rose to his feet.

"Let's go and have a drink," he said. "And you're paying for it. It's the least you can do if I'm putting up the labour and the bronze."

—

Two days later, Valsuani's crew arrived with a small truck and carefully lifted *Woman with Child* onto the flatbed. Tomas rode beside her as they took her to the grimy brick foundry at Ivry-sur-Seine, a small town immediately to the southeast of Paris. The foundry had three kilns for firing clay models and two furnaces in which to melt bronze. The place was always busy with artisans hauling buckets of hot metal on chains suspended from the ceiling.

Tomas breathed more easily after the enlargement was complete. It did not distort her—if anything, it made her more powerful. Next was a job for him. In a room off the foundry, Tomas carefully spread his plaster-of-Paris model with liquid rubber, flicking it onto the surface with his fingers and pushing the rubber deep into the crevices with a brush so that it captured every detail of the work, right down to the fingerprints he had left on the plaster. Then he and the artisans built up the layers of rubber, let them dry and covered them with another thick layer of plaster, a "mother mould" that held the rubber in place and kept it from warping. *Woman with Child* was now made of three layers—the original plaster, the rubber layer on top of it and a final covering of plaster.

After the mother mould had dried, they cut the outer two layers and pulled them away from the original plaster statue. It was a strange moment, for now Tomas also had a negative of his sculpture, an empty space where the woman had crouched with her lost child on her back. It was as if they had disappeared into open space inside the rubber mould. In this hollow, he and the artisans built up an armature of twisted iron wires and rods to support the body of the new statue, which was going to be poured in soft cement. Then they pressed the two halves of the mother mould back together and wired them tight.

The assembly was now a bird's nest of iron inside a rubber mould covered with plaster. Through holes cut in the top, the apprentice foundrymen poured liquid cement, and when it had set, they again pulled apart the mould. Before them stood a cement copy of *Woman with Child*. Tomas examined her carefully, and found that the replica was exact. Now Tomas and two other men began to scrape down the surface of this cement statue.

"Don't scrape too deeply!" Valsuani cautioned. "You are determining the thickness of the bronze now. Bronze is heavy. It is wasteful and inelegant to make your woman too thick."

Once the entire statue had been scraped down three-fifths of an inch, it was set back in the rubber negative mould, in which it was suspended by metal dowels and rods so that the scraped cement copy did not touch the rubber. Then the piece was encased in the plaster mother mould again, and melted wax was poured into the gap so that it filled the space between the scraped cement copy and the rubber. When this wax cooled, the men pulled off the rubber mould.

Now Tomas had a wax copy of *Woman with Child* with a cement core inside it.

"Apply all of your artistic skill," said Valsuani. "We will leave it to you alone to retouch the wax. This is the critical moment. Wherever there is wax now, there will be bronze later. It is far easier to retouch her now than to attempt to rework the bronze afterward."

For weeks, Tomas either came early to the foundry to work on *Woman with Child*, or begged off the Folies altogether, pleading illness. He was tired, but unable to sleep; hungry, yet too anxious to eat. He went over the wax *Woman*, cutting, pressing and shaping. When he was done, the workmen returned to help him attach a system of wax rods—the sprues and gates that would melt away as well through a hole in the bottom. Later the bronze would run through these same channels. When they were done, the wax statue with the cement centre looked like some kind of Saint Sebastian, pierced with arrows. The outside ends of these rods were pinned to more rods, which created a kind of cage to hold the statue so that the bronze would have many directions in which to run.

Next, they mixed a slurry of ceramic soup as thin as crepe batter. Smaller pieces could be dipped in slurry, but *Woman with Child* was large, and so she needed to have the slurry painted on by hand. The men sprinkled fine sand on the slurry, waited for it all to dry and then started to make another layer, building up the ceramic covering a dozen times.

Now the whole mass was moved carefully over the base of a baking oven, and she was surrounded by walls of bricks. *Woman with Child* was burned in hot fire until molten wax ran out in a puddle at the bottom of the ceramic mould.

"This is the lost wax," said Valsuani. "There she goes, your woman, melting into nothingness. We collect the wax and we use it again and again. I have seen this thing done hundreds, perhaps thousands, of times, my young artist, but I never really appreciated it until I reached my old age. Sometimes I think the woman was most real when she was wax. So mortal. What we are doing now is making her immortal."

When the wax had all been melted out and collected and the ceramic shell baked hard, Valsuani permitted the assembly to cool completely. Then the great mass needed to be moved again into the centre of the foundry, covered in a thick layer of clay to give it strength, tipped upside down ever so carefully and buried in a pit of sand.

"There are those who claim it's not necessary to bury the mould," said Valsuani, "insisting that if she is well made there is no risk of explosions or ruptures. But it is far too dangerous to do that. Read Benvenuto Cellini, and see how his entire workshop caught fire when he tried it. He was lucky he did not burn to death himself."

The sides of the pit were filled with sand and packed securely. Now the bronze was heated in a massive cauldron until it bubbled orange-red. Small flames erupted and died as tiny pockets of gas caught fire on the surface. If the bronze was too hot when they poured, it deformed in the mould, but if the bronze was too cool, it did not run properly. Gauging the temperature took all the skill the old man had accumulated over the years. The cauldron was lifted on a chain and pulled along a rail suspended from the ceiling until it stood over the buried *Woman*. The workmen then tipped the cauldron and the boiling bronze coursed through the gates. After they were done, the only thing to do was wait. Tomas went out with Valsuani to a bistro across the street, but he could not eat.

Two days later, the artisans lifted the piece from the pouring pit, and working with Tomas broke off the outer ceramic layer with small pickaxes. Yes, there she was, with all the channels that had been attached to her now turned to bronze as well, so the woman and child looked as if they were caught in a prison of bars.

Tomas cut off the protruding bars. Then she had to be cut in half so the interior scraped-cement core could be taken away, and welded back together. After that, she was dipped in an acid bath to remove traces of the process that had made her, and then Tomas used a hammer, chisel, file and scraper to remove the imperfections.

Tomas applied more acid to her, and then covered her with straw, which was then fired to give her a sheen. Valsuani himself cleaned her with a rag, and then the two of them applied wax. When they were done, she glowed golden brown in the sunlight that came in through the windows of the foundry.

Tomas was so drained he thought he could not take another breath, and he sat down on a stool a little distance away from her. Valsuani sent out an apprentice to bring them coffee, and brought out a small bottle of marc and poured each of them a drink. The old man seemed tired as well, but not as tired as Tomas. He rose after a while and walked around the statue.

"She has something, a presence," he said. "She reminds me a little of Maillol's work. His women all have a kind of timelessness to them. But permit me to remind you of something."

"What is it?"

Valsuani went away and came back with a rubber mallet. He struck the woman across her thigh and Tomas heard the dull sound of hollow metal.

"Come here and put your hand on her," said Valsuani, and Tomas did as he was told. Again, Valsuani struck *Woman with Child*, and Tomas could not only hear the dull sound but feel the vibrations in the piece itself.

"She's hollow," said Valsuani.

Lipchitz and Valsuani greeted each other warmly. Tomas could not shake loose his anxiety, and Lipchitz did nothing to allay Tomas's fears before he walked into the workshop. There was no good in calming the young man down if he was going to have to disappoint him later.

It was a Saturday afternoon and the workshop, which closed at noon that day, was free of the din of metal and the noise of shouting men. The dust had settled and good light came in through the windows. Nevertheless, Valsuani turned on the overhead lamps. Lipchitz stood at the door with the *Woman with Child* a good twenty feet away from him. He crossed his arms and simply looked for five endless minutes. Then he began to circle the piece slowly as *Woman with Child* knelt supporting her offspring. He stepped close to examine the details in the same slow, precise manner he had examined her from a distance. Tomas was so nervous he almost jumped when Valsuani laid a reassuring hand on his shoulder. When Lipchitz was done, he turned to Tomas and nodded once, then he broke into a smile.

One of Valsuani's sons brought out a bottle of wine, and the three of them sat down on stools in the workshop.

"What do you plan to do next?" Lipchitz asked.

"Next? I could do a hundred pieces, but I have no money to cast them in bronze. I can't do anything until I sell this one."

"I have received word," said Lipchitz, "that Dr. Barnes is coming to Paris on another buying trip. He asks me for advice on his purchases, and I could show him this piece."

"Do you think he would be interested?"

"Buyers are unpredictable. But the piece is good. I will show it to him and if he does buy it, word of the sale will run up the Boulevard Montparnasse faster than a rocket."

FOURTEEN

Tomas awoke on the straw pallet in his studio and looked at his watch. Eight o'clock. He didn't have to go to the Folies until after lunch that day. He boiled water on his gas ring and took the time to shave himself carefully, studying his face in the mirror. Was this an artist on the cusp of success? He was too thin, and the skin around his eyes was puffy. He needed to put on some weight, and he needed to sleep more regularly.

As it was a Sunday morning, he put on his best clothes and ambled down the street toward the nearest café, where he took a table by the window and ordered two servings of buttered bread and a pot of rhubarb preserves. The view through the window was not particularly edifying, consisting of two wooden shacks and a stretch of uncobbled road. A woman was nursing her infant outside one of these shacks, seated on a stool by her front door. The sweet-sour tang of rhubarb reminded him of his home back in Lithuania. After chives, rhubarb was the first edible fruit of spring, and it puckered the mouths of children who ate it until they could bear no more and went looking to steal sugar or honey to sweeten the fruit.

Maybe he could go back to see his family after *Woman with Child* was sold, although the word *home* sounded odd even in his mind. He could not say that Paris was home yet, or that it would ever be, yet the farm near Merdine clearly belonged to the past.

He was floating in the world, his only anchor the bronze that stood in Valsuani's foundry.

But he would like to make some photographs of the bronze and show them to his brothers, especially to Paul, who had always liked the things Tomas made with his hands. Vilnius was occupied by the Poles, and Poland and Lithuania were still technically at war, so he would have to pass through East Prussia to avoid the closed border. It might be interesting to see Königsberg, which his brother Andrius had spoken of so often.

Tomas watched the woman suckle her child. If Maria had not died, he might still be eating rhubarb in a cottage not much better than the one he saw before him. Edvard would have helped him, and he and Maria might have made some kind of life. But he would never have made *Woman with Child*. If Jenny and his son had lived—well, he still didn't want to think of that.

There was no one in Paris besides Valsuani and Lipchitz with whom to share a drink. Jenny would have celebrated with him, and she would have laughed at him at the same time for being so serious about what he made.

He suddenly realized that for all their ego and jealousies, he missed Estelle and Sorrel, too. Whatever else they were, they were his comrades-in-arms in the war of art. How could he forget those with whom he had first gone into battle?

Tomas looked at his watch. Ten o'clock. He still had four hours before he had to go to work and his new freedom did not seem as welcome as it had when he awoke. He decided that he would meander across Paris, first through the Left Bank and then through the Right. But to get there he found his feet taking him past the Académie Carrel. And there his loneliness got the better of him, and he went inside.

A new model was up on the dais, a thin young woman who looked frightened and cold. Of the dozen men sketching her, only two were familiar, and he knew neither well enough to speak to. He wandered into the next room, which was empty except for one woman painting at an easel. And of course it was Estelle, lost in concentration, her thick, dark hair twisted into a braid that was in turn pinned on the back of her head.

He studied her face in profile and saw that she, too, had changed since he had seen her last. She looked the same, but her movements were more deft and assured. The piece she was working on was a variation on her signature seascape, a view of her childhood home on Georgian Bay. The rocks in the foreground were intensely pink, with scrubby dwarf pines and oaks growing from the crevices, and the lake was like an ocean, the far shore invisible. The light was intense, a midday light, yet the nearly golden glow seemed to come out of the water, as if the landscape were illuminated from below instead of above.

As Estelle chose another brush, she glanced his way—and her face lit up. She cried out his name and threw her arms around him and kissed him on the cheeks.

"I'm glad you've come," she said.

"I wasn't sure you'd be happy to see me."

"Well, my nose is still straight, no thanks to you." She sensed his embarrassment and went on. "Take a look at my latest piece. It's the last one I can get finished before the show. Do you think I should put it in?"

"I wish I knew how you achieved that glow."

"You've seen me paint like this before."

"Maybe, but there's something uncanny about this one."

"I looked out on that glow every day of my girlhood, and I didn't think there was anything special about it. It's only here, at this distance, that I keep coming back to it."

"This painting makes me want to go there."

"Then you should. Maybe you would understand me better if you did."

"Jenny always said she'd like to visit Canada."

"Do you miss her very much?"

"I try not to think of her, but it doesn't do any good."

"Have you been able to work?"

They sat on stools and Tomas told her all about *Woman with Child*, and his luck with Valsuani and Lipchitz. She sat very close to him and held his hand as he spoke, her eyes alive with interest. And in the warmth of her attention he spoke much longer than he had intended.

Finally he asked, "How is Sorrel?"

Estelle's eyes dropped to her hands. Seeing that she was still holding his, she let go and wiped her palms on her smock. "There have been complications. First our show was delayed, and then the owner decided there should be two shows. One for each of us."

"That's wonderful."

"So it seemed. But things changed again. He went back to one show."

"Then you are no worse off than you were before."

"But Sorrel is not going to be part of it."

Tomas was stunned. He had admired Estelle's work, but he had never truly taken her seriously.

"Since then, Sorrel has been seething. He smokes one cigarette after another without any pleasure and gives me meaningful looks, but he says very little. When I ask him what the problem is, he won't speak."

"Of course not. He must be eaten up with envy."

"I thought he would be stronger than that. He doesn't even come here any more. He works in the studio and sometimes he fills the room with his paintings, and sometimes he hides what he does from me."

"Why would he do that?"

"He tells me he's worried I'll steal an idea from him."

Tomas laughed. "But what could you steal from Sorrel? His

work is completely different, Tamara de Lempicka in the foreground and decorative cubist landscapes in the background."

"You must never say that to him."

"Why not?"

"Carrel finally told him he was in danger of being too derivative."

"But he is derivative. He has always said, 'We all live in a time
and a place. Ideas are in the air and we must stand on the shoulders of great men.'"

"He doesn't like to think of his own work like that. Tomas,
he's afraid I might make a name for myself faster than he will. He
knows he has no real grounds to complain, so he says nothing, but
the anger keeps growing in him."

Tomas studied Estelle's face. "Have you been fighting? Has he
been hitting you again?"

"He wouldn't dare, not any longer. He's not the man he used to
be." She stopped, and then confessed, "I'm beginning to despise
him a little."

Estelle had changed as much as Sorrel, Tomas thought. If he
had diminished, then she had grown stronger. Sorrel would not be
able to hold on to her.

Estelle reached for his hand again.

"You have to come over to the studio. You must see Sorrel."

"What do I need him for?"

"You probably don't need him at all, but maybe he needs you."

The idea of Sorrel in need was amazing to Tomas, an indica-
tion of how far his old friend had fallen.

"I'll come tonight after I finish work at the Folies."

When Tomas arrived at the passageway into the old studio, he was
carrying a bottle of *vin mousseux*, imitation champagne that was as
much as he could afford, and a bouquet of carnations. The light was
on in Mme Martini's apartment and she opened the door a crack.

"Oh, M. Stumbras, I'm so relieved to see you."

She did not open the door any wider.

"What's the matter?"

"There has been nothing but trouble for all of you since you moved in here. First, your tall friend dies and then Jenny, and now the two in there are screeching at each other like hellions. Maybe you can do something."

"They're fighting?"

"They were."

"Maybe I shouldn't go in at all."

"You must find out if Mlle Estelle is all right."

Tomas nodded. He bid Mme Martini good-night and heard the click of the door being shut behind him, and the screech of the bolt as the door was locked. He walked across the courtyard and knocked and a voice told him to come in.

Estelle and Sorrel were sitting across from each other at the table with bread, sausage and cheese between them, as well as two bottles of wine, one empty and one just opened. Evidently, they had prepared a small party for him, but Estelle had one puffy eye that was beginning to darken and her hair was dishevelled. Sorrel looked serene. He sat eating a piece of sausage off the tip of his pocket knife. A painting, very similar to the one that Estelle had been working on earlier that day, was propped against the wall on the end of the table.

The room itself was set up differently from the way it had been when Tomas lived there. The mattress on a pallet was gone and the two cots were pushed together. Sorrel's works lined the walls, and unframed paintings hung from wires. There must have been thirty of them, some very large, all portraits of different kinds in his signature style.

"Ah, Tomas, my old friend," said Sorrel without rising to shake hands, "I see you have gifts with you. Here, let me open your wine. It has to be better than the piss we're drinking. Estelle, find a jar for the flowers."

Tomas set down his bottle to join the others and laid the flowers beside them, but no one touched either.

Sorrel's pieces on the walls were mostly nudes, and they gave Tomas the uncomfortable feeling that he was being watched. The subjects seemed acutely aware of their own dramatic setting, as if they were characters in a Pirandello play. As Sorrel finally started to open the wine, Tomas realized that one of the paintings was of Jenny in costume at the Folies Bergère.

"I didn't know you'd painted Jenny," said Tomas. "When did she have time to sit for you?"

"She never did. I painted it from memory after she died, as a kind of tribute."

Tomas looked at Sorrel skeptically.

"Don't look at me so strangely. I liked her in my own way."

"Did you ever do a painting of Alphonse?"

"Not yet, but I will. Don't just stand there. Estelle told me you were coming and I was happy to hear it. Come on, let's put the past behind us. I'm sorry you were thrown in jail, but you know, I was only trying to save you from yourself. Let's have a drink of this wine."

Sorrel stepped forward and put out his hand and Tomas took the hand and felt his own being shaken warmly. For a moment, his mood lightened, but Estelle had said nothing yet.

"Estelle?" he asked. She met his eyes, but he saw no trace of friendship or even recognition there.

"You expect me to say something?" Estelle addressed her question to her lover.

"Of course," said Sorrel.

"Then listen to this. I'm sick of you. I'm through with you."

"Very dramatic. Such exhibitionism. And I only expected you to make a toast."

"All right. I'll make a toast. To freedom." She raised her glass.

"I'd prefer to drink to love."

"To love? Please. After what you did to me?"

"Will you accept my apology?"

"No, I won't. Don't you have ears? I said I'm finished with you."

"How can you stay angry with me? We're two passionate people. That's why we love each other." Sorrel tried to take Estelle's hand, but she pulled it away.

"Most people piss away their lives in the day-to-day," said Sorrel, "and it makes them angry to see people like us. They ache with desire to do something big. Anything. But they don't love deeply enough, the way we do, which is to say they don't *want* deeply enough. The days run out, one after another, and they do nothing at all but make babies. They hate us because we stay true to our desires, because we are building something. We are not frittering away our lives. We will not wake up twenty years from now to wonder what happened to our youth. We will know where it went. It will be in these." He pointed to the portraits lining the walls.

"What about Estelle's painting?" asked Tomas. "You didn't point at hers."

"What an astute observer you are. No, I didn't point at Estelle's piece. And do you know why? Because it's not good enough."

"Liar," Estelle said.

"This is what we were arguing about. Because I love Estelle, I've told her this piece is not good. It's not bad, but not as good as the others and it should not go in her show."

"I don't see any of the others around," said Tomas.

"No matter."

"He's hidden them away because he doesn't want anyone to see them. He's frightened."

"Nonsense, Estelle. I've just put them away temporarily so I can concentrate on my own work. After all, you have a show coming up, whereas I am still struggling, aren't I?" Estelle did not answer. "I need to see which of my pieces are the strongest. But let's not talk of my work. Let's talk of yours. I have a very good eye and you know it. I can see the strengths and weaknesses in others. I'm the one who told you your seascapes were good. Isn't that true?"

Estelle refused to do so much as blink in response.

"You know it is. I'm the one who encouraged you to come this far. But listen, everyone makes mistakes and that piece is a mistake. You should not show it."

"Why don't you let her make up her own mind?" Tomas asked.

"Because she doesn't know what's right for her. I suppose she told you that I was jealous of her. Oh yes, I know you talked this afternoon and I can imagine what she said. But I'm not jealous of anyone. I know the value of my own work and it will succeed on its own merits. But Estelle is in danger of making a big mistake. This piece is weak, and you'll come to see it in time. My dearest, you must not show it." He turned to Tomas. "Let me tell you something."

"What?" Tomas asked.

"I was an art student in Romania."

"You always claimed you were a peasant."

"And so I was. I came out of the mountains, as I told you. But I had some luck and I was sent to school in Bucharest. I even did a little engraving there."

"You deigned to be a printmaker?"

"It was one of many subjects. I was a very romantic young man. I did a plate with the portrait of a woman's face, very conventional, a woman in peasant dress, but I thought it was good. Do you know what my teacher did? He asked permission to correct the plate, and he took the burin and he cut slashes across it. It was a terrible shock. He said I would thank him one day. When I went home that night, I felt like killing him. I didn't go to school for a week, but when I finally did, I searched out this teacher and I shook his hand."

"For ruining your plate?"

"He saw what I couldn't see. I was being sentimental. I was being childish."

"I'll bet you never did another engraving again."

"That's right, but the lesson was still the right one. That image was no good. And I'm a better painter than I ever would have been a print-maker. Estelle, I know you are angry with me, and you are going to be angrier still. But I love you very much and what I do, I do out of love," said Sorrel. He reached for his folding knife where it lay by the sausage, then leaned forward and calmly stuck the blade in the upper left corner of Estelle's canvas. Before either Estelle or Tomas could react he slashed it diagonally across the painting until the image was cut in two pieces from one corner to the other. The paint was still wet in places, and the blade of the knife came out stained. Sorrel wiped the blade on the edge of the table, folded the knife and put it in his pocket.

Estelle stood up slowly from her place, her hands rising to the sides of her head. "You've ruined my painting."

"But I've made you a better artist. You'll hate me for a little while, but you'll thank me in the long run."

"You egotistical monster." Estelle stopped there. Her hands fell to her sides and her shoulders slumped. "You had no right to do that."

"I did it out of love," said Sorrel.

"You call that love? I'd rather you hated me."

Estelle took her glass and raised it. "Let's drink, after all," she said. "I choose to drink to love and to demonstrate my love as well. Come on, raise your glasses."

Sorrel did so, but Tomas said, "Estelle, come with me. You can stay at my place. This room is a hothouse."

"All of Paris is a hothouse. To tell you the truth, Sorrel is right. We have to concentrate on what we want to achieve. We have to work toward our goals without permitting distractions to get in the way. But I came to this city before any of you did. And I came from much farther away. I was the one who showed you where to eat and where to buy supplies. And I've studied at least as long as either of you."

"Quite a speech," said Sorrel.

"I'm finished with you, Sorrel."

"Yes, yes, so you've said already. That's how you feel now. But you'll come around."

"Oh no. I've learned a little about painting from you, it's true. But I've learned about the game as well, and two can play it. Give me your knife."

She stretched out her hand with the palm open, but Sorrel did not move. She looked around the table and saw the pile of tools at one end. She rose and picked up a burin that had belonged to Alphonse. She began to walk around the studio, studying Sorrel's works as if she were at an opening.

"You're being childish," he said, stepping away from the table and moving toward her.

"Am I? I don't think so. Stand back. I'm going to exercise my artistic judgment, too."

"And do what, ruin one of my paintings? I assure you, I've already made my selection. Nothing unworthy is hanging on these walls."

"Hush. I'm the teacher now. I'll be the judge."

"Estelle," pleaded Tomas. "Leave him. Come away with me."

"I'm looking to see where Sorrel's weaknesses are," she said, pacing along the paintings with the burin clasped in her hands behind her.

"I won't be a part of this," Tomas said, getting to his feet. "If you won't come away, I'm leaving. The two of you can have your lovers' fight without me."

Estelle stopped before the largest painting in the room. It was a café scene, with all the landmarks of Paris crowded together and broken up as by a prism in the background: the Eiffel Tower, Notre Dame, Montmartre and the obelisk at the Place de la Concorde. Among the crowd of characters seated and standing at the café in the foreground were certain prominent figures—Jules Pascin with his bowler hat, Picasso with his pipe, the deceased Modigliani, the model Kiki and Moïse Kisling with his accordion. They were all very well dressed, very dramatic, very sure of their places in the universe of Paris.

"This," said Estelle, "is your weakest piece. It's so packed full of clichés it's worthy of a postcard."

Sorrel stepped closer.

"Stand back from me," she commanded.

Sorrel laughed, but he did not advance any farther. "Destroy one of my paintings if you like," he said, "but you cannot touch that particular piece. It's one of my best."

"I say it's one of your worst."

"Estelle, touch that piece and you'll be very sorry."

As soon as the words were out of his mouth, Estelle took the burin and punched a hole into the painting.

"That can still be repaired," said Sorrel. "Stop now."

But his words only egged her on. She fitted the burin against the palm of her hand and punched the canvas two, three, four times. Sorrel shouted and leaped forward. Estelle drove the burin in one more time, trying to draw it across the canvas to slash it, but the burin had no edge and the canvas merely puckered at the spot. Sorrel grabbed Estelle by her braided hair, pulled her head back and was about to strike her when she pulled the burin out of the painting and drove it straight into his chest.

The action did not seem to register with him. He took Estelle by the shoulders and glared into her face.

"I have talent," he said, and was about to say more when he looked down at his chest at the wooden handle of the burin with Alphonse's initials. The point was lodged in his heart and a stream of blood was running down his shirt front. A new wave of fury took him and he removed his hands from Estelle's shoulders as if to swing at her, but he had no strength to stand on his own and he crumpled onto the floor on his back. His lips moved, but only gurgling sounds came out of his mouth. Finally, he stopped making sounds and his face broke into a grin.

Tomas stepped forward and knelt over him. Sorrel's eyes were open and sightless and no breath came from his mouth or nose. The only thing Tomas could think to do was cover him, and he found a blanket and tucked it around him, leaving his face exposed. Who was he to pronounce death? Sorrel's open eyes and grin were terrible to look at, but it would have been worse to cover them and admit the man who had just been talking to them was now dead.

Estelle had not moved since she had stabbed Sorrel.

"I'm going for a doctor," Tomas said.

"No."

"He might still be alive, for God's sake."

"Look at him, Tomas. He's dead." Estelle finally collapsed on a chair. "I'm not even sorry," she said.

"Estelle, we'll be all right. We'll tell the police what happened and they'll understand."

"A stabbing is never an accident," she said. "They will take me away. And I was about to have my first solo show."

"Forget about the show. We have to do something."

Estelle nodded. "Yes, you're right. You'd better find Zamaron and bring him here. If anyone can make it right, he can. Go across to the café and phone him."

"You won't be afraid to be alone here?"

"No. Sorrel didn't mean much to me at the end, and he means even less now."

—

When Tomas returned from the café, she was sitting with her back to the body, drinking a glass of wine and smoking one of the cigarettes that Sorrel had rolled earlier that evening.

"Did you get through to him?" she asked.

"He wasn't there, but I left a message for him to come."

"It's important they don't send anyone else."

Tomas glanced over at Sorrel on the floor to see that his grin had widened. He looked away. He went over to the table and poured himself a glass of wine and sat down across from Estelle. He saw anger, dejection, worry in her face, but he did not see remorse.

"He lunged for you," he said. "And look, you have a black eye to prove that you'd been fighting. I was a witness to it all."

"It won't be so easy, Tomas. I lived with Zamaron for a while, and I know what happens when the legal machinery begins to turn. Even if I'm declared innocent in the end, I could be in jail for a year before it's all over. Maybe much, much longer."

"But you will get off eventually."

She made no sound. She butted out the cigarette and lit another, and sat looking at her hands. In silence they drank their way through the bottle of wine before Commissioner Zamaron finally presented himself at the door. His policeman's eyes took in the scene at a glance. Without a word, he went to Sorrel, and pulled back the blanket to reveal the burin in his chest. He felt his neck for a pulse and put his fingers under his nose to feel for breath. He stood up and looked at them.

"M. Stumbras, I told you to stay away from this place. Now look what you've done."

"It wasn't me."

Zamaron looked at him skeptically and turned to Estelle. "Are you all right?"

He was standing in his rumpled raincoat, not smoking for once, but smelling strongly of tobacco. Estelle went to him and he opened his arms. She began to weep, and Tomas had a moment of unease. He had never seen Estelle cry. Zamaron held her for a long time, and then he sat her back in the chair and joined them at the table.

"You'd better tell me what happened," he said, "but first pour me a glass of wine." He took a package of cigarettes from his pocket, opened the lid and placed them on the table. He drew one out and Estelle did the same.

After Estelle had explained the events of the night, Zamaron finally turned to Tomas and asked for his version. He listened carefully, but he did not write anything down. When Tomas was finished, Zamaron sat back and considered the situation.

"Estelle was only defending herself," Tomas said, breaking Zamaron's silence.

"And it never occurred to you to intervene?"

"It happened too fast."

"Estelle had already been struck, by the looks of it. Yet you did nothing to avenge her."

Tomas looked to Estelle, who was staring down at her glass, the cigarette burning between her fingers.

"Estelle is your friend," said Tomas.

"Yes," said Zamaron. The statement seemed to irritate him.

"Is there no way this thing could be hushed up? We both know she was defending herself."

"A dead body remains a dead body. What would you have me do, dump it in the Seine? I never liked that man. But dislike him as I did, I am still a policeman and I have some sense of duty. We have a dead man here, and blame must be assigned. There are procedures that need to be followed and the courts will decide who is guilty and how the penalty is to be paid. My job is to take in all the suspects. However, there is some hope of staying out of the maw of the legal system. If the guilty party fled, I could not be blamed."

"Léon," said Estelle, "where would I go? I have no money and I have no family, and sooner or later the provincial police would catch up with me."

"I did not say you were the guilty party," Zamaron said, turning to stare at Tomas. Zamaron butted one cigarette and immediately took out another from its package. He met Tomas's incredulous look coolly.

"Well, M. Stumbras, you do seem to be a likely candidate. You were present at the death of one friend under mysterious circumstances. You have already come to blows with this particular friend and spent some nights in jail because of it. Looking at things dispassionately, one might say you are the most likely candidate of all."

"Mme Martini told me they were having a fight when I came in."

"In other words, she saw you arrive."

"Estelle," said Tomas. But she was staring into her wine again.

"Of course, you could stay in Paris to defend yourself," Zamaron continued. "I imagine you might get some sympathy. There is a kind of poetic justice in killing a man with an artist's tool. I imagine the press would appreciate the story and I doubt that you would receive the maximum sentence. If you had a very good lawyer, you might get off altogether."

"Estelle," Tomas pleaded.

"Of course, if you fled, then you would be presumed guilty. In that case, it would be best to disappear. Spain is one option, but you are fair-haired and it would not be easy to go unnoticed. Germany is a possibility, but the German police are very good. Scandinavia, maybe. But I would stay away from my birthplace if I were you. Most criminals are found when they go scuttling home to their mothers."

"You can't be serious," said Tomas. "Why would I run?"

Estelle still would not meet his eye, but finally she spoke. "Tomas, I've worked very hard for too long. You don't know how much I've suffered. I have a show coming up. My first solo show."

"And I have my first bronze at Valsuani's. Dr. Albert Barnes of Philadelphia is coming to look at it. He might buy it for his museum."

"Ah yes, he might," said Zamaron. "But who's to say he will? I think it would be a shame to put a damper on Estelle's career. And if she makes herself a reputation, the value of my collection will rise. Did I ever tell you I have a pair of Modiglianis? They are appreciating nicely."

"Estelle, you have to speak up for me."

"Justice is blind," said Zamaron. "It simply holds the scales. If there is a victim on one side, there must be a criminal on the other. And if you were to become a fugitive, well, your piece would become as well known as you are. At the very least, it would arouse a great deal of curiosity. Let's face it, people have certain preconceptions about artists. You're supposed to be passionate, and if you were so passionate that you committed a murder, and if you fled, well, your reputation would be made. I can practically guarantee a lot of exposure in the press."

"I will not sit here and listen to such nonsense," said Tomas. "I will fight this. Do you think Estelle will hold up in court in front of a good lawyer?"

"My friend, you couldn't afford to hire the bootblack of a good lawyer."

"Estelle, tell him you won't do it."

Estelle said nothing.

"Very well," said Zamaron. "In a few hours it will be dawn and there isn't time for any more talk. I can delay the hunt for perhaps six hours. I might drop the papers on the wrong desk and you'd gain perhaps a day. There are barges on the Seine that make their way to Le Havre every morning. From there, you could get a job on some kind of ship. Just don't get off at any of the bigger ports. Soon everything will be forgotten, and within a couple of years, you'll be able to walk around almost any city in the world as a free man."

"But not Paris."

"No, not Paris."

"I will not do this. It's ridiculous."

"Make your own choice, as you like. But I am giving you a good chance. Turn this down and you'll spend quite some time in a cell before the case comes before a magistrate. After that, who knows?"

"I won't do it."

"Very well."

Zamaron stood and removed a pair of handcuffs from his pocket. The sight of them made Tomas step back from the table.

"Go now, Tomas," said Estelle. "It's the best chance you will have."

Mme Martini was not at her post when the studio door slammed shut behind him. Without actually breaking into a run, Tomas headed in the direction of the Seine. His heart was pounding, and he found it hard to catch his breath. When he was several blocks away from the studio, he finally paused to put his hand against the wall of a house to steady himself. On the other side of a shutter he heard the murmur of voices, a man and a woman talking, and the voices steadied him. He began to walk again, and he forced himself to light a cigarette in order to slow his pace and give himself time to think. He could not leave Paris. Not yet.

Tomas crossed the street and made his way towards the Rue de Javel, keeping his head down whenever he passed anyone. When he reached his studio, he scanned the surroundings for police, and then entered without turning on the light. He took a small handful of bills and coins hidden deep in his toolbox, pocketed them, found a sack and threw in some chisels that he recognized by feel. Then he looked carefully out the window, but saw nothing on the street. Holding his breath, he opened the door, ready to fly at the first sound of footsteps. There was no one there.

Tomas crossed the Seine to the Right Bank and hailed a taxi to the Gare de l'Est train station. On the ride he asked the sleepy driver a few questions about trains to Warsaw. At the station, he tried not to tremble when a policeman looked him up and down carefully. He walked purposefully to a train standing by a platform, entered it and went down the length of the corridor, opening and closing the doors between the cars. When he reached the end, he looked out the window, saw no policeman and went out the opposite side from the platform and onto the tracks. He cut across to the back of the station, and walked the few blocks to the Gare du Nord, where he went into the station and then came out again like a newly disembarked traveller and took another taxi to the west side of the Place d'Italie. From there he walked to Ivry, hoping that he had left enough false scents to lose the police at least for a while.

Valsuani's foundry was locked, but the long industrial shed had many windows, and Tomas broke one of them, opened it and crawled inside. He made his way to the room where *Woman with Child* was crouching on one knee with the massive weight of her lost child upon her shoulders, and dropped his sack on the floor. A little light came into the room indirectly from a street lamp outside, but he could only see her outline and the odd glint of reflection off the metal. Tomas did not dare turn on the light.

He seated himself on a stool and waited. Little by little, the early light began to shine weakly through the windows, and his woman in bronze began to come up, a black shape at first, and then dull grey as the light became slightly stronger. For as long as he dared he drank in the massive presence of her, the sheer volume of bronze in space, but he could not permit himself to stare at his creation as long as he might have liked. He had to decide what he was going to do.

He replayed the events of the day in his mind. If only he had not gone to Carrel's, or refused Estelle's invitation that morning, none of this would have happened. He could have turned away at Mme Martini's door and let the two of them cut themselves to pieces for all he cared. But now he had to deal with what was.

He could fight Zamaron. Estelle might even be moved by his determination to save himself. They had been close, after all. Could she really betray him?

But no sooner did he play this fantasy through his mind than the image of Zamaron came up, as well as the memory of Estelle's unwillingness to look him in the eye.

He stood to walk around the foundry floor. It did not seem possible that he had worked so hard for so long for all of it to come to this. He had no illusion about what would become of his bronze. Without the artist, the piece was unsalable. Buyers bought the artist as much as they bought the work, and the finest of bronzes by an unknown artist would never make it into Dr. Barnes's museum. Valsuani would melt her down and the bronze would be used for something else. His achievement would be erased, as if he had never come to Paris in the first place.

He touched her, and then rapped on her with his knuckles, as Valsuani had done, and listened to the emptiness inside her. In his battle of art, she was turning out to be a hollow victory.

Tomas thought of the only real soldier he knew, Marshal Pilsudski. Maybe he had been right all those years ago. Tomas was a bison in a china shop in this city. The old schemer had not done too badly for himself. Pilsudski had engineered a coup shortly after Tomas left Warsaw, and now he was installed as ruler of Poland. If Tomas had gone to Krakow as the marshal had wanted him to, he might now be a successful sculptor with a friend in the Belvedere Palace. Tomas briefly considered going to him again, but Pilsudski was a great man, and could not be seen harbouring a criminal.

Tomas went to the place where the workmen hung their clothes, and chose a blue smock and large cap from the half-dozen on the hooks. A working man in Paris was invisible to any but his own kind. Tomas stuffed his street clothes deep into the back of a furnace, still warm from the previous day's fire, and watched as the dying embers fed on this new fuel.

Sorrel's last words hung in his mind. "I have talent," he had said. Tomas had talent too, and he was still alive. Talent would travel with him wherever he went. It lay in his hands and his eyes and his mind. He would take it and apply it somewhere else. Long ago, Lipchitz had told him that Jews travelled well, and maybe, in the end, that would be the best lesson Lipchitz ever taught him. Tomas would need to learn to travel well. He went to the bronze for the last time and he touched his lips to it, and found the metal as cold as a corpse.

Valsuani had said that the bronze was a monument, and so it was. But he had also said that *Woman with Child* was most alive when she was a figure in wax, malleable and mortal. Tomas thought of the wax of which the woman had been made, the so-called lost wax, *cire perdue*.

The bronze was nothing more than a fossil of the place where the wax had been. And the wax could be reformed in many different ways. The wax was alive and changeable enough to suit any form the artist could imagine. Tomas would be *cire perdue* as well, wax that was never lost, just waiting to take on a new shape.

He stood back for one last look, then turned away from *Woman with Child*. He would never see her again, but that did not matter. He carried the real *Woman with Child* inside him.

EPILOGUE
CANADA, 1929

THE LOCAL PEOPLE HAD CALLED THE LAND BY MANY NAMES, knowing it was far too vast to be encompassed by a single appellation. But when the Europeans came, with their surveying chains and mapmakers, they deemed that the whole land would be called Canada, a single name for many peoples and landscapes.

Tomas beheld them, from the French of Quebec City, to the farmers of Upper Canada and the businessmen of Toronto. He thought of Estelle as he crossed the forests and pink granite and lakes of Ontario by train, looking for romance in the Native reserves he glimpsed through windows but seeing only poverty.

When the train finally made it onto the plains, he felt as if he had descended into a sea, not only of grass but of light, which shone strong and sure day after day as the train clattered west and he made his way between cars to strike private deals with the conductors to save his dwindling cash.

In Cochrane, Alberta, a town northwest of Calgary, Tomas disembarked and asked after his uncle Nikodemus, and he was lucky enough to find a cowboy at a lunch counter who told him to go out to the MacLeod ranch, where he worked as a hand. The news surprised Tomas, for he thought of his uncle as a rich man. On a sunny day, he walked out to the property, eight miles beyond town. He was in the foothills of the Rockies, and the mountains themselves, snow covered at the tops, seemed so close that he

might be able to get there in half a day. But after he'd spent two
hours on the dusty road the mountains were no closer. He walked
among fields of unfenced grass, with cattle visible in the distance,
and finally came upon the track from the road to the ranch, a big
spruce log house with similar outbuildings. The farm dogs, three
big mongrels, came charging down the road at him, but Tomas
was accustomed to farm dogs. He threw two stones at them, and
the dogs kept back. When he got close, a man came outside.

Reg MacLeod was sixty-seven, with bushy white eyebrows. He
had a two days' growth of beard and white hair that showed
beneath his cowboy hat. His face was etched with lines.

"Nick Stumbras?" MacLeod said when Tomas asked. "Sure, I
know him. He was the longest staying hand we ever had. Fifteen
years. We called him 'Buffalo Nickel.' Know why?"

"No."

"He was always asking to borrow a nickel for a glass of beer.
And he always said his last name meant *buffalo*."

"Bison."

"Same difference. Anyway, he went off on a bender two weeks
ago and hasn't shown since."

"Is he coming back?"

"Hard to know. Leave your name and address, and if he shows
up, I'll tell him where to find you."

They were standing out in the yard, the dogs circling at a distance. Tomas felt chilled by the constant wind that blew from the
snow-topped mountains.

"I'm forgetting my manners," MacLeod said. "You must be
tired. Where's your horse?"

"I walked from town."

"Then you're hungry as well. Come inside. You'll be wanting
something to eat."

Reg MacLeod liked to talk, and, as Tomas ate fried steak and
potatoes, he told various stories about Nickel. MacLeod was an

affable man, and it became clear to him that Tomas was short of money and had no place to go, and he could always use an extra hand because the men tended to drift away without notice. When Tomas agreed to stay, Reg walked him around the property, showing him the bunkhouse, the barn and other buildings before taking him into a room off the smithy, which contained a workbench with chisels and pieces of wood stacked in the corner. The room had large windows in every direction except south, and the light was so bright inside that Tomas could see every splinter of wood on the workbench. Shelves lined three walls, and upon these shelves stood wooden figurines about a foot tall. They were mostly cowboys in various stances, some with lassos of stiff, painted string. Among them were a few animals—a buffalo, a wolf and an eagle. Tomas reached for one of the larger figures, a cowboy on the back of a bucking horse, one hand thrown high in the air and the other holding the horn of the saddle.

"It's kind of a hobby of mine," Reg said shyly, as Tomas turned the piece over in his hands. There was much fine detail to the piece, so much that Tomas needed to be careful not to damage it.

"This is very well done," he said.

"You think so?"

"But you shouldn't paint the wood. It's more honest to let the wood show through."

"You sound like you know something about this."

"I do." He was going to say that he was a sculptor, but he did not want to use the word. "I used to carve a great deal."

"Gave it up?"

"I started to cast in bronze instead."

Reg MacLeod's eyes lit up. "I always kind of hoped to do something like that."

"You have a smithy right next door," said Tomas. "I think I

could set something up for you. Some clay, plaster of Paris, wax, and you could cast these."

"This is just a hobby, you know."

"That's all right."

"I'd still need you to work for me during the day. We could do this in the winter and the off hours."

Tomas looked up at the old man. For all the caution in his words, he was beaming, and some of the light from his smile reflected back on Tomas.

ACKNOWLEDGEMENTS

This is a historical novel that contains many figures who actually lived. None of the events here are intended to reflect actual events, but are depictions of what the historical personages might have done had they met Tomas Stumbras. The historical figures are the following: General Bermondt, Marshal Josef Pilsudski, Josephine Baker, Pepito Abatino, Paul Derval, Bricktop, M. Perès, Rosalie, Maurice Utrillo, Léon Zamaron, Barbette, Moïse Kisling, Valsuani, Jacques and Berthe Lipchitz and their dog, Maraud.

There is no town in Lithuania named Merdine.

This book was written with the generous help of very many individuals and institutions over a period of seven years. To all of these and many others, my sincere thanks for your assistance:

My editors: Anne Collins, who published the first piece I ever wrote over two decades ago and who has appeared miraculously again to nurture this manuscript; Kendall Anderson, who knew so well which of my darlings needed to be killed;

My agent, Anne McDermid;

My wife, Snaigė, for her critical eye, knowledge of art and continued support and patience as I took off weekends, summers, evenings and pre-dawn mornings to get this done; my brothers, Andy and Joe Šileika, who helped me piece together the anecdotes our mother and father told us about their childhoods, which went on to become the core incidents of the Rainy Land section;

The Canada Council, the Ontario Arts Council and the Toronto Arts Council for their financial assistance; the Bibliothèque Historique de la Ville de Paris; the Forum des Images in Paris, and in particular Muriel Carpentier; the École Nationale Supérieure des Beaux-Arts and Catherine Donnellier; the Canadian Cultural Centre in Paris, Service des Arts de la Scène and Bernard Meney; the management of the Folies Bergère in Paris and Virgile Ribeiro for a stunning midnight tour of the theatre and backstage;

Joe Kertes, friend and constant supporter who read through the manuscript repeatedly and made valuable suggestions on how to make it work; John Bentley Mays, whose infectious interest in Josephine Baker opened the novel up to the influence of the music hall; Rima Puniška, my indefatigable Paris fixer and dining companion; Agnès Gauthier, Parisian printmaker par excellence;

Dr. Rasa Mažeika, Director of the Lithuanian Museum-Archive of Canada; Romas Žiogarys of the Resurrection Parish Library in Toronto, who would do anything for those who love books; Algis and Genė Valiūnas, and Jonas Zimkus for details of Lithuanian life in the period; Artūras Petronis, Genius Procuta, Rūta Melkis, Violeta Kelertas, Ramūnė Jonaitis;

David Kemp, who gave me lessons in sculpture and helped me cast my own bronze imp; Stephen Rowe for the architectural plans of Lipchitz's house designed by Le Corbusier; Brian Kelly, for lending me part of his rich library on the era; Dr. Robert Gordon, Nancy Burt, Mary-Jo Morris, Wayson Choy, Richard Handler, John Metcalf, Russell Brown, Jack David, readers and supporters; Joe Aversa and Pam Hanft, my former associate dean and dean for their flexibility.

Excerpts of this novel appeared in the *Ottawa Citizen*, *Lituanus*, *Carousel*, *Rampike* and *Kultūros Barai*.

SELECTED READING LIST

Here are some of the books that were useful in researching this novel. The Lithuanian books are occasionally obscure memoirs, often published at the writer's expense. I am grateful in particular to these uncelebrated scribblers who were witnesses to their times.

ON LITHUANIA:

Kazys Ališauskas, *Kovos dėl Lietuvos nepriklausomybės, 1918–1920.* Chicago: Ramovė, 1972.

Stasys Asevičius, *Praeitin atsigręžus.* Kaunas: Spindulys, 1993.

Bernardas Brazdžionis, ed., *Lietuvių beletristikos antologija.* Chicago: Draugas, 1957.

Kristijonas Donelaitis, *Metai.* Kaunas: Spindulys, 1940.

Juozas Jurginis and Algirdas Šidlauskas, *Kraštas ir žmonės* Vilnius: Mokslas, 1984.

Petras Klimas, *Dienoraštis, 1915–1919.* Chicago: AM&M Publications, 1988.

Petras Klimas, *Iš mano atsiminimų.* Vilnius: Spindulys, 1990.

Ignas Končius, *Žemaičių šnekos.* London: Nida Press, 1961.

Vincas Krėvė, *Raštai.* Chicago: Lietuvių enciklopedijos spaustuvė, 1956.

Adam Mickiewicz, Translated by Watson Kirkonnell, *Pan Tadeusz: The Last Foray in Lithuania*. Toronto: University of Toronto Press, 1962.

Czeslaw Milosz, *The Land of Ulro*. New York: Farrar, Straus and Giroux, 1984.

Czeslaw Milosz, *Issa Valley*. New York: Farrar, Straus, Giroux, 1978.

Aleksandras Pakalniškis, *Metai praeityj*. Chicago: M. Morkūno spaustuvė, 1976.

Aleksandras Pakalniškis, *Žemaičiai*. Chicago: M. Morkūno spaustuvė, 1977.

P. Petrauskaitė and A. Berman, *Vilnius*. Kaunas: Valstybinė grožinės literatūros leidykla,1955.

J. Petrutis, *Laisvę ginant*. Stanford: Vaga, 1953.

J. Rimantas, *Petras Rimša pasakoja*. Vilnius: Valstybinė grožinės literatūros leidykla, 1964.

Simon Schama, *Landscape and Memory*. Toronto: Vintage Canada, 1996.

A. Vilainis, *Žemaičių žemėje*. Chicago: Lietuvių knygynas Nemunas, 1952.

Žemaitė, *Raštai 1*. Kaunas: Valstybinė grožinės literatūros leidykla, 1956.

Konstantinas Žukas, *Žvilgsnis į praeitį*. Vilnius: Mintis, 1992.